THE
CONVENT
GIRL

A compelling saga of love, loss and self-discovery

TANIA CROSSE

Devonshire Sagas Book 10

Joffe Books, London
www.joffebooks.com

First published in Great Britain in 2022

Cover art by Jarmila Takač

ISBN: 978-1-80405-566-3

In memory of my dear friend and 'Hospital Lady'
Christine Barron
1930–2020

And, as always, for my husband,
whose understanding knows no bounds.

PROLOGUE

Plymouth
March 1941

I have no choice.

An uncanny, deadening silence booms in my ears, and yet a high-pitched, squealing whine fills my head until I feel it will burst. I am stumbling through nothingness, detached and yet living through it, staring at the scene of destruction as if through glass, real and yet unreal. I can feel fragments of plaster in my hair as I struggle to stay standing. Thick dust chokes my throat. I can taste it, foul, on my lips. This can't be happening. And yet, it is.

The floor shudders again beneath my feet, focusing my mind, and a booming explosion breaks through my temporary deafness. Then another. And another. The broken ceiling above my head groans, and a further shower of debris rains down on me. Dear God, I must get out before the entire building collapses. Take my chances out in the street as the bombs continue to fall.

But there is something I must do first.

In my numbed state, I can't remember why I must do it. I just know I have to. Instinct tells me that I have no choice. I have no time to think. I have to act now, this instant. A second later and another vibration could bring the upper storeys crashing down and it could be too late. Whether or not it is the right thing to do. In this moment, it seems the only thing to do. My duty.

I swallow down my rebellious, heaving stomach and turn back to the sickening sight. The front of the building has gone and the red glow of fire floods in. But I thank God that it is still murky enough inside the ruins to hide the worst of the horror. Of what Hitler's bomb has done. I will not look too closely again.

Picking my way forward once more over the bricks and broken chairs, I pull free the rucksack. I don't need to check its contents. I know exactly what is in it. I myself helped pack it, making sure everything was there. The papers. My hand scrabbles in the rubble for my gas-mask box and I wedge it into the space left by the rucksack so that it is half buried in the ruins. Now I loop the rucksack straps over my shoulders. I can see that bizarrely the suitcase is still intact, next to where until a few moments ago the front door had stood.

I scoop up the precious bundle, cradling it in one arm against my chest. Stepping as carefully as I can over jagged metal and chunks of masonry, I pick up the suitcase with my free hand and stagger out into the street. I am disorientated. The gaping, burning buildings bear no resemblance to those I have known for so long. Terror is dripping down from the sky. I pray I have not survived one explosion only to be taken by another. That would be too cruel. Besides, I have a job to do. I must succeed. I must.

I need to hurry to the nearest shelter, dodge any danger. Get as safe as I can for the rest of the raid. Yes, that is what I must do. That will be the beginning.

And then we shall have to see.

CHAPTER ONE

The Convent of Mercy, Cobh, County Cork, Ireland
Summer 1926

How had it all begun? It was a question Maisie O'Sullivan had asked herself so many times, but could never answer. All she knew was that, looking back, her life seemed to have been moulded in a strange and different way.

Her first memories were of sleeping in a large room at the top of a massive building. The sloping ceiling swooped down either side of a narrow, arched window through which, on a bright morning such as this, the sun would stream in golden shafts. If Maisie strained herself up on tiptoe, her nose just reached the windowsill and she could see out. And what a wonderful, curious world there was outside.

She hadn't been the only occupant of the room, of course. There were five other beds, each one occupied by another little girl. She knew they were girls because they were constantly being chivvied, 'Come along now, girls. Hurry up, and remember, silence.' So they were all called girls, as were all the others they met in the rest of the building. But then, if you weren't a girl, what else could you be? Unless you were one of the sisters, of course.

'Wakey, wakey, sleepy heads. Time to get up. I trust you are all dry this morning?'

The room clamped down in silence as each child scrambled to the bottom of her bed, and all eyes turned on Maisie. She vaguely remembered that she'd woken up cold and wet a few times. But that was a long, long time ago. Since before that magical time of Christmas. So why they should all look at her, she didn't know. She felt her cheeks flush, not from embarrassment but from anger.

But when Sister Agnes tilted her head and beamed directly at her, Maisie's little chest swelled with pride. She liked Sister Agnes best out of all the nuns. Some of them could be so strict. But they looked after you, and told you off. They wore long black dresses that reached their ankles and black scarves that covered their heads. Maisie often wondered whether or not they actually had hair beneath. They almost seemed a different race to her, but you had to do whatever they said, no matter what.

'Right, get yourselves dressed, then.'

Sister Agnes clapped her hands, and Maisie reached for her knickers that were waiting on the little table next to her bed. She hopped about, first on one leg, then the other, as she pulled the underwear up underneath her voluminous nightgown. For woe betide any girl who showed any of her private parts! It was the same with the vest that somehow you had to put on under cover of your nightie. Maisie poked her head through the top and pushed the vest down under the yoke of the nightgown. But pulling her arms out of the nightgown sleeves and through those of the vest was a struggle that always took her longer than everyone else.

'Let me help you, dear.'

Thank goodness. Sister Agnes was being extra kind that day, and Maisie wondered why that might be. But you learned not to ask questions. So she said a polite thank you as Sister Agnes helped her wriggle into her vest. Then she raised her arms when the sister finally lifted her nightgown over her head and slid the drab, summer-uniform dress over her shoulders in its place. Just the black, knitted woollen stockings now. How Maisie hated those, especially when it was so warm, and the scuffed, hand-me-down shoes that were pinching her toes recently.

'Oh, Helen Driscoll, you're ready. Be a good girl and help Maisie with her shoes, will you, or we'll be late and there won't be time for breakfast before prayers, so there won't.'

As soon as Sister Agnes had turned her back, Helen pulled a face at Maisie. Kneeling down in front of her, the older girl roughly grasped one of her ankles, shoved her foot into the first shoe and fastened the buckle. The stocking was rucked up, making it uncomfortable, and Maisie was about to say so when Helen glanced up with a nasty glint in her eye.

'Don't see why I should touch you, smelly wet-the-bed,' she hissed under her breath before dealing just as uncaringly with Maisie's other foot.

Tears stung Maisie's eyes. That wasn't fair. But she couldn't think of anything to say. She'd just have to put up with uncomfortable feet until she had a chance to sort them out for herself. No one would be very happy with her if she made them all miss their bread and butter and milk, and they all had to go to the toilet and wash their faces and hands before they'd be allowed anywhere near the food.

Once they'd all visited the washroom, they were marched down two flights of stairs to the refectory where they met all the other girls lined up at the tables. Grace was pronounced by the Reverend Mother and they all ate in silence. Then they climbed the stairs again to clean their teeth, before descending once more to the chapel.

Maisie loved that time of the day. It was so quiet and calm, despite so many girls squeezed together. Everyone was silent apart from the murmurings that were part of the service. Maisie couldn't remember the words most of the time — they made little sense to her — but she kneeled on the hard floor and put her hands together in prayer like everyone else. She made herself screw her eyes tight shut, but slowly they seemed to open on their own. No one ever noticed. The chapel had a certain dusty smell to it, and on a sunny morning, she found the tiny flecks of dust dancing in the air fascinating to watch. She imagined each one was an angel sent by God to make her happy. Today the sunlight was so strong that as it shone through the stained-glass window, it cast red and blue shadows on the white wall opposite. It was so beautiful that Maisie could have stayed there, watching it, all day.

And then the sisters sang a short prayer or whatever it was. Maisie wasn't sure and neither did she care. Their voices were so lovely that every morning she was sure she was being shown a tiny bit of the heaven they were told they would eventually go to if they were good. She snapped her eyes shut again and promised she'd be as good as gold for the rest of her life.

The sound of shuffling all around her made her realise that prayers were over and all the girls were lining up to go to school. Maisie clasped her hands behind her back and waited. She was the only one who didn't go to school. She didn't know why. But every day she was taken either to the kitchen or the sewing room, and had to sit quietly on the floor, playing with the contents of a small wooden toybox, while the sisters completed their daily tasks.

She glanced up. Ah, Sister Agnes was coming for her today. That was good. Sometimes it was Sister Finbar, and Maisie didn't like her. She was sharp with Maisie. Her face was lined like a prune and her hands were rough. But Sister Agnes was gentle and her hands were soft.

She bent down so that her smiling face was on a level with Maisie's. 'Sure, it's a special day today, young Maisie,' she smiled. 'I have to go to the Bishop's Palace on an errand, and the Reverend Mother has given permission for you to come with me as it's your birthday. We can spend a little time in the gardens. Beautiful so they are. Would you like that, Maisie?'

Maisie gazed up at Sister Agnes. To spend some time with her best sister would be wonderful, so she nodded with a hesitant smile and slipped her little hand into the bigger one that was held out to her. How exciting! Was this going to be what the other girls called an adventure? Was she actually going beyond the gates to the big wide world she could see from the dormitory window? She'd spent ages looking out of it, at the trees on the opposite side of the road, and then beyond them, on higher ground, a terrace of narrow houses clinging sideways up a very steep hill. Each one had a pointed roof, so that they made Maisie think of a row of teeth. Behind them, resting on another hill so that it almost looked as if it was sitting on top of the houses, a huge, grey building stood above everything else, with a spire that seemed to reach up to the sky. Further in the distance on the right was something grey and flat that sometimes sparkled in the sun. Maisie wasn't sure what it was, and had never dared to ask. Sometimes big things moved about on it, and quite often smaller ones too. Each came with a pole or two standing up in the middle, with what looked like enormous handkerchiefs attached to them. It was all very confusing.

But it also looked so exciting from the window, and Maisie often dreamt of going to see it for herself. Forgetting all about her uncomfortable feet, she trotted along beside Sister Agnes. But once she was outside, she felt small and very scared. She was so glad she had Sister Agnes's hand to cling to, and felt much happier when the nun turned her head to smile down at her.

'It isn't very far,' she told her as they crossed the road and turned up to the right. They passed a long stretch of railings and Maisie was taken by surprise as they soon turned in at some gates. She wondered what was inside the large white building in front of them. It wasn't quite as big as the house where she lived. And it didn't have the pointy bits in the roof, but was all straight lines. Maisie really wasn't at all sure about it.

But she needn't have worried. The person who opened the door gave her a great big smile and Maisie instantly liked her, even if she was a bit confused. Was she a nun? She looked a bit like one, but her dress was a bright colour and only came halfway down between her knees and her ankles. And instead of a scarf thing, she actually had hair on her head!

'Sure, is this the babby I've heard so much about?'

'Not so much a babby now, Mrs Danby,' Sister Agnes grinned back. 'It's her birthday today.'

'So how old are we, then, cherub?'

Maisie blinked up at her. 'Three,' she answered hesitantly.

'No, dear,' Sister Agnes said gently. 'Sure, you're four from today.'

'Oh,' Maisie mumbled with a frown.

'Well, while Sister Agnes takes those papers into the bishop, why don't you and I go into the kitchen and see if we can find something special for the birthday girl?' Mrs Danby beamed at her, and held out her hand.

Maisie glanced anxiously at Sister Agnes, but was met with an encouraging nod. The next moment, she was being led down a corridor and into what she recognised as a kitchen. It was much smaller than the one in the house where she lived, and the smell was wonderful!

'Now then, it must be cake for a birthday, so it must. You sit here,' Mrs Danby said, lifting Maisie up on a chair at a vast table, 'and I'll get you a slice. And a glass of milk to wash it down. Bless you, doesn't your little chin just reach the table, but I'm sure you can manage. I'm Mrs Danby, by the way. The bishop's housekeeper.'

As if by magic, a slice of cake and a glass of milk appeared in front of her, and Maisie stared at it, her mouth watering. It looked so good. She'd never seen something so tasty looking before.

'What's the matter, child? Is something wrong?'

'Y-you haven't said Grace,' Maisie managed to stutter.

'Oh, goodness me,' Mrs Danby chuckled. 'Sure, I don't think the Good Lord needs us to say Grace for a little piece of cake on your birthday. But if you really want me to, Hail Mary, full of grace, will you bless this little one on her birthday, and good Catholic that she is, she wishes to thank you for this little treat. Amen. Will that do, so?'

Maisie nodded and set to eating the delicious cake under Mrs Danby's smiling gaze. When she'd finished and had drunk the milk, she licked her lips, wishing the sweetness could stay in her mouth for ever.

'Thank you very much,' she said politely, and then waited. She wanted to get down from the table and find Sister Agnes, but that would be rude. And then something struck her. 'Mrs Danby,' she said, pleased that she remembered the name, 'what's a birthday?'

Mrs Danby's eyebrows shot up towards her hairline. 'Oh, bless you, have they never told you? It means that you've lived another whole year. You know, spring, summer, autumn, winter. We celebrate because God has protected you for another year. Did they never teach you that at the convent?'

Maisie's smooth brow wrinkled again. "Convent"? Was that the name of the big house where she lived? And now she knew what a birthday was, too. Now she thought about it, she'd seen other girls get a card from "home" on their birthday. She wasn't sure what "home" was, either, but felt it wouldn't be polite to ask the kind Mrs Danby anything else.

'Ah, there you are, Maisie.' Sister Agnes appeared at the door and Maisie jumped down from the chair. 'The bishop has kindly agreed to let us spend a little time in the garden. So come along now, and thank Mrs Danby for the cake,' the nun said, giving a knowing nod at the empty plate.

'Sure, the little soul already has. Have a lovely birthday, dear.'

Maisie smiled back over her shoulder. Her birthday seemed special already, and now she was to have another treat. Sister Agnes took her outside, at the back of the building this time. Back at what Maisie now knew was the convent, there were vegetable plots, a gravelled playground and a small garden with a grotto housing a statue to Our Lady. But nothing like this.

It was so pretty. There were large areas of grass as smooth as the velvet ribbon that edged some of the altar cloths in the convent chapel. What Maisie could only describe as stone banisters stood either side of some steps leading down towards the terraces, and the lawns were edged by flower borders vibrant with of all sorts of bright colours. Further along, tall trees gave some welcome shade as Maisie skipped along beside Sister Agnes as they made a circle of the grounds. These must be the trees she could see from the window of the convent, but how much more beautiful they looked up close. She dropped her head back and gazed up at the sky through their dancing leaves. Was God really looking down on her from up there? She felt He must be on her special day.

'Mrs Danby says it's my birthday because I've lived another year,' she said, feeling quite grown up. 'So does that mean I'll be five next year?'

'It does indeed,' Sister Agnes smiled. 'And then, after the summer holidays, it means you'll be starting school.'

'Oh.' Maisie knew school was where all the other girls went every day except Saturdays and Sundays, and during the holidays when most, but not all, of the other girls went "home". 'Why does everyone else go to school, and I don't?' she queried.

'Sure, it's because you're the youngest in the whole place,' Sister Agnes explained. 'Too young to start school yet. The other girls are all older than you. Most of their mammies and daddies pay for them to be with us because they get a good education. If they're clever enough, they might even get a scholarship to go on to the pension school for free.'

Maisie dropped her gaze and concentrated on her feet padding along the gravelled path. The last part of what Sister Agnes had said had been lost in a haze. Her thoughts had latched on to the mention of mammies and daddies. Other girls had mentioned them with great excitement when they talked about going "home", but Maisie had no idea what they meant. Now, though, with Sister Agnes and the quiet calm of the beautiful gardens, she felt confident enough to ask.

'Sister,' she ventured, feeling her heart patter, 'what are mammies and daddies?'

Beside her, Sister Agnes came to an abrupt halt. Oh, no. Had Maisie said something wrong? But then she saw the gentle smile she knew so well creep across the sister's face. Didn't she look like an angel when she smiled like that.

'Everybody has a mammy and daddy, to start with, at least,' Sister Agnes began as she stepped forward again, her voice so soft Maisie felt she could sink into it. 'When you're born, you're either a boy or a girl. We're all girls at the convent. And we nuns are just grown-up girls, really. We're married to God, but sure, most girls when they grow up get married to a boy, or a man as they're called when they grow up. And then they have babbies.'

Maisie felt something inside her soar and her face lit up with joy. 'So I've got a mammy and daddy!' she cried.

Sister Agnes's expression changed. 'Well, I'm afraid not, Maisie dear. You did have. But the dear Lord called them to Him when you were very small, and sure, that's why you don't remember them. You were only two when you came to us, the youngest girl we've ever had. Normally you'd have gone to an orphanage at that age as we don't usually accept girls until they reach school age. But your mammy did a lot of work for the church where you lived, and the priest asked us as a special favour. And sure, we've loved having you, so we have! You're very special to all of us.'

Maisie's lips bunched in a deep pout. She'd had a mammy and daddy once, but now she didn't. But she was very special to the sisters, so that must make up for it. And today she felt very special indeed, so she grinned up at Sister Agnes.

'I like it here,' she said, bobbing her head. 'Can we come again? All the pretty flowers.'

'We'll have to ask. It is a special treat. But shall we look at the flowers more closely? Look, these ones are called roses. That's what the lovely smell is. Have a sniff. This one's my favourite, so.'

Maisie leaned forward to a deep pink bloom that Sister Agnes was pointing at. Indeed the scent was so strong it made her mouth stretch into a delighted smile.

'Did God make these?'

'Didn't the Lord make everything,' the nun nodded back. 'And I thought maybe we'd take a little walk for you to see more of what He made. We took a little group of you orphans to the seaside last summer, but I don't suppose you remember.'

'No.' Maisie shook her head, mystified. 'But I was only three then, wasn't I? And now I'm four.'

She felt really pleased when Sister Agnes chuckled.

'Yes, a big girl now. So we'll just walk down to the seafront. There might be a ship sailing across the harbour if we're lucky.'

Maisie didn't know what a ship was — or a seafront for that matter. She was reluctant to leave the garden, but the world had suddenly become such an exciting place. Her head twisted this way and that as they headed downhill. People nodded at them as they passed. Did they all know it was her birthday? But then she realised they were muttering 'Good morning, Sister,' and not talking to her at all, though most gave her a smile. Never mind. This was Maisie's special day and she was enjoying it immensely.

What was this now? she thought. Fine, tall houses lined one side of the road, but once they crossed it, there was a wide walkway and then . . . There were railings and, to Maisie's utter amazement, there was the large expanse of the thing she'd seen from the window. It went on as far as she could see, like a constantly moving blanket, waving up and down, with the sun twinkling on it. She stopped to stare, half curious, half afraid.

'Sure, I'll always be fascinated by the sea.' Sister Agnes had happily come to a standstill beside her. 'And how the ships float on it and don't sink, I don't know. Liners from all over the world used to call in here. So big they had to anchor out there and bring the passengers ashore in little boats. A very important place was Cobh, so it was. But that was back when it was called Queenstown. Nowadays, the big ships go up to the docks in Cork and only small boats come in here.

But sure, I like it here and I never want to leave. You might leave it one day, though, Maisie. Quite a few of our girls end up going to England and making a good life for themselves there.'

They stood there for some while, breathing in the salty air and watching the waves lapping up and down. It filled Maisie's heart with something she couldn't explain to herself. Her eyes kept being drawn to what she now understood was a ship sailing across the vast harbour in the distance. It must be so strange to rock about on the sea and end up in a different place from where you started. Did you have to go on a ship to get to this place called England she often heard mentioned, she wondered.

'Well, I'm afraid I don't have all day.' Sister Agnes broke into Maisie's thoughts. 'But we'll go back via the cathedral. Though I think we can call into that sweet shop over there on our way.'

Maisie didn't want to stop watching the sea and the ship, but her ears pricked up at the mention of a 'sweet shop'. She'd never been in a shop, but she knew very well what sweets were. They'd each been given a little tin of them at Christmas, and if you'd been very good or done a kindness to someone else, you might be given one as a reward.

Maisie was so excited as they crossed the road to get to the shop. She flicked up her gaze to a bell over the door that clanged as they went inside. The smell that met them was wonderful! It was different from the rose, so strong, and instantly made her mouth water. On the low counter behind a glass screen, stretched a stunning display of differently shaped and coloured sweeties. Maisie's eyes opened wide.

'Good morning, Sister, and what can I be doing for you?'

'I'd like a three-pence bag of mixed sweets for this one, if you please. Soft ones she won't choke on. And cheaper ones so there's enough for her to share, as well.'

Maisie watched, mesmerised, as the sweets were weighed out and then slid into a paper bag. Sister Agnes handed across

13

some flat, round things and then, taking the bag, put it into a pocket in her dress. Maisie would have loved to carry the little bag herself, but knew she'd have to wait until after tea-time before she could pop one of the sweets into her eager mouth.

'She was like Mrs Danby,' she told Sister Agnes as they set off again, this time up hill. 'She's not a sister, either?'

It was a half-question, and was met with a half-smile. 'No, that's right. She's a lady. That's probably what you'll be when you grow up. Unless you decide to become a nun, like me. But save your breath for this steep hill, and we can call into the cathedral. I'd love you to see it. When you're older, you'll go there every Sunday. And you'll make your First Communion there.'

Maisie was lost in thought as her little legs struggled to keep up with Sister Agnes's tall ones. She'd learned such a lot that day! Being four was obviously very important. She'd even seen some boys, running along that walkway near the sea. And men wearing flat caps and clothes that clung about their legs. Sister Agnes had told her they were called trousers. Maisie was so excited. What a lot she had to tell the other girls in her room that night!

It was then that she realised they were coming to the enormous grey building that from her window looked as if it was sitting on top of the houses with the pointed roofs. Now she realised why, since they'd clambered up such a steep hill that her legs were aching and she felt hot and sticky. Sister Agnes stopped by the door to catch her breath, and Maisie glanced skywards. She gasped. It felt as if the gigantic stones were about to fall down on top of her and she clasped the nun's hand even more tightly.

'Don't worry, it's perfectly safe,' Sister Agnes assured her, following her worried gaze. 'It's just our way of sending our prayers to heaven. Come inside and you'll see how amazing it is, so.'

Maisie wanted to hang back, but if Sister Agnes wanted to go inside, she supposed it must be all right. She slid in behind her and her jaw dropped in astonishment. The ceiling was just so, so high! There were tall, stained-glass windows along the side aisles, and then along the central space were two more rows of windows above them reaching up to the ceiling that went even higher! Strong, shining pillars in a pretty pink supported arches on either side, and at the far end was the altar. Maisie knew what that was from the chapel in the convent, she thought, proudly using the new word. But this one was huge! It even had its own spires, with statues of various saints, she imagined, carved into them.

Her eyes travelled around and above her in absolute wonderment, mouth dangling open as she gazed upwards. It had almost been too warm as they'd clambered up the hill, but in here, although it was bright, there was a coolness and a calm that made Maisie feel strange. It was so quiet, with a sort of silent echo. She felt hushed, happy and yet excited at the same time. Had Sister Agnes truly brought her to the house of God? Did He really live here, where Maisie could see Him from her little window?

Sister Agnes looked down at her with a smile that in later years, Maisie would remember as serene. Like an angel. In that moment, Maisie knew. When she grew up, she'd go to see England, but when she came back, she would be a nun. And when Sister Agnes walked slowly down the long aisle to the altar, then bent her knee and crossed herself, Maisie did exactly the same. She felt she'd found home.

CHAPTER TWO

'Sister Agnes took me to the Bishop's Palace today,' Maisie proudly told the other girls in her dormitory that evening. 'The gardens are so pretty.'

Before they had to get ready for bed, the girls had half an hour to play with the little treasure boxes that they kept under their beds. Maisie always struggled to open hers. The tin lid was just too tight for her small fingers, and the other girls were always already busy playing with their treasures or doing swaps before Maisie managed to prise hers open.

There wasn't much inside. A wooden peg with a face painted on it was her only doll. It was wrapped in a white handkerchief. The edges were embroidered with flowers and in one corner was a funny shape that she'd been told was "M" for Maisie. She wondered for the first time ever who'd made that handkerchief. Was it the mammy she now knew she'd once had but who'd been called to the Lord? The only other items were an unusual piece of gravel she'd picked up in the playground, and the tiny spinning top she'd been given at Christmas. It was all different bright colours which mixed together as it whirled around.

But now she had something else to add. She carefully slipped from her pocket the fading rose bloom she'd picked up from the path in the palace gardens, and placed it gently into her box.

'Where did you get that from?' asked Noreen Malone. 'A pity it's gone brown and soggy round the edges.'

Maisie jerked up her head. 'It's still pretty, so it is,' she protested. 'And it'll all dry out now it's indoors.'

'Got it in the garden on your special visit to the Bishop's Palace, did you?' Helen sneered. 'Picked it, did you? Well, that's stealing. And stealing's a sin.'

Maisie felt her face flush with anger. 'No, I didn't pick it! It was on the ground and Sister Agnes said I could have it. You can ask her yourself. She said the gardener would only throw it away.'

Helen shrugged her shoulders. 'Sure, it still seems like stealing to me. Even if it is your birthday.'

Maisie had a job not to burst into tears. Why was Helen always so horrible to her? And somehow she always managed to get away with it. Well, this time Maisie would teach her a lesson.

'I've got some sweeties to share, but you're not having any,' Maisie told her, jutting out her chin as she pulled the little bag of sweets from her other pocket.

The other girls at once crowded around her, eagerly holding out their hands. Feeling very important, Maisie carefully took one sweet at a time out of the bag and placed one each in every outstretched palm. But when it came to Helen's turn, she clutched the bag determinedly to her chest and shook her head.

'You little cow.' In an instant, Helen swiped the bag from Maisie's hand and held it aloft out of her reach.

'Give it me back!' Maisie cried. 'They're my birthday sweeties! Sister Agnes gave them to me!'

'Aw, always teacher's pet, so we are,' Helen taunted her. 'Or Sister Agnes's pet, should I say? Just because you haven't got a family or a mammy or daddy, everyone thinks you're so special. But you're really just a stupid little babby!'

Maisie's eyes blazed with fury. 'I'm not a babby, so! I'm four now. And I did have a mammy and daddy once. Sister

17

Agnes told me so. Only they've gone to heaven so they can't give me sweeties on my birthday, so she did instead. So give them back, or . . . or . . .'

'Or what?' Helen gave a mocking laugh. 'I'll just take my fair share and then you can have them back. If I leave any, that is.'

'No, they're mine! Give them back!'

Maisie felt she would explode with anger, and lunged at the arm that held the precious bag. But the older girl dodged her grasp and ran down the other end of the room. Maisie's cheeks turned red as she scuttled after her, jumping up and down as Helen held the sweets above her head again. It was more than Maisie could take, and she bit Helen's other hand. Helen squealed, lowering the arm that had held the sweets out of reach. Maisie struck, snatching back the bag. It tore, and the remaining contents rolled across the bare floorboards in every direction.

'Now look what you've done!' Helen spat.

'Your fault!' Maisie retorted, her bottom lip thrusting forward. She launched herself at the bigger girl, knocking her off balance, and the two of them landed on the floor. Maisie didn't know what to do next. Her precious sweets were all over the place and she must retrieve them, but as she went to get up, Helen yanked her back and went in pursuit of them instead.

'What on earth is going on?' Sister Agnes sailed into the room, her face sterner than Maisie had ever seen it before. 'I leave you alone for two minutes and you cannot behave. Now someone tell me what happened or you'll all be up before the Reverend Mother.'

Maisie stared as she saw Helen lift her chin. 'Maisie wouldn't share her sweets,' the girl declared innocently.

'And is that any reason for this rumpus?'

Sister Agnes raised her voice so that Maisie shrank back. The last thing in the world she wanted was to upset her best sister, especially when she'd been so kind to her that day. But then Sister Agnes jerked her head towards the smirking bigger girl.

'Helen Driscoll, you're nearly eight and old enough to know better, so you are. And if Maisie hasn't shared her sweets, why is everyone else chewing away and licking their lips?'

Maisie held her breath, her wide eyes swivelling between Sister Agnes and Helen. How would Helen wriggle out of that one?

'Well, she shared them with everyone but me,' Helen pouted.

'Is that so, now, Maisie? The truth, mind.'

Maisie felt herself wilt under Sister Agnes's gaze. 'Yes,' she mumbled, since she'd never lie to anyone, especially not Sister Agnes. 'But only because she said I'd stolen the rose we found in the garden today. And she said I was a babby.'

Maisie watched as Sister Agnes blew out her cheeks. 'Is that so, girls?' The nun glared round at all the other girls who lowered their heads in mumbling agreement. 'Well, it seems to me, Helen, that you've been most unkind. I shall have to report this to the Reverend Mother, who in turn will report it to your parents. Now you can all get ready for bed early tonight. So no more playing and put your treasure boxes away. And then go and use the washrooms.'

Everyone obeyed in awkward silence. Helen shot Maisie a look that made her little heart tremble, and she was more than pleased to dive into bed and cover her head with the bedclothes. Her special day had been absolutely ruined, and she sucked hard on her thumb to stop herself crying.

It would have been so different if she'd still had her own mammy and daddy. How grand it must be to have someone who cared so much about you. On the way back from the cathedral, she'd asked Sister Agnes what home was. The nun had explained that it was a place where you lived with your mammy and daddy, who loved you dearly. Usually the daddy went to work to earn money to pay for food and clothes. The mammy stayed at home to look after you, although sometimes she might have a little job as well. If you were lucky, you might have brothers and sisters to play with. They could be older or younger, but you all looked out for one another. You might live in a house with lots of rooms and even a garden, or home might just be a couple of rooms in a house shared with other families. It didn't matter, as long as you were together.

Maisie's eyes were already shut, but now she squeezed them even more tightly to blank out the dormitory with the other girls and the horrid Helen Driscoll. She didn't want it to spoil the picture she was building in her head. There was just a little house, but it had a pretty garden with roses in it, just like at the Bishop's Palace. There was a smiling mammy wearing a brightly coloured dress. She was sitting in the shade of a tree, rocking a babby in her arms, and watching Maisie race around the garden in a game of tag she was playing with a bigger brother and a younger sister. Then the daddy came home from work, and they all rushed over to give him a hug.

Maisie was unaware that her mouth was curving into a smile as she forgot all about the fight with Helen. She could go to sleep now, dreaming of another world and another life. As she drifted off, she began to think that perhaps she wouldn't become a nun, after all. When she grew up, she'd find a nice daddy to live with and have a lovely little house of her own. She'd be the mammy herself, of course, and have lots of babbies to look after. She'd be so, so happy, so she would, and she'd forget all about Helen and her nasty ways . . .

* * *

Maisie sat crossed legged on her bed, fingering a petal that had come adrift from the rose. Perhaps because she'd kept the bloom in the tightly closed box, it hadn't exactly dried out, but had retained its smooth silkiness. More than anything, though, it had kept its wonderful scent. When Maisie held it up to her nose, she could still smell the heady fragrance and was instantly taken back to that special day when she'd spent time alone with Sister Agnes.

She sighed, keeping her head lowered as she concentrated on the memory. The other girls were packing up their things to go home for the summer holidays. Nobody had very much — they weren't allowed to bring with them anything other than a few photographs and books, their own missal if they had one, and their own hairbrush and comb. The whole task wouldn't take very long, but Maisie wished so very much that she had to do it, too.

A clap of hands made her look up. Sister Agnes had entered the room, a beaming smile on her face.

'Now then, girls, as it's the last day of the school year, remember you have a special tea,' she announced, her gaze taking in each girl. 'Come along and wash your hands, and we'll go down.'

Maisie didn't remember a special tea the previous year. But then she'd only been three, then, hadn't she? She put the petal back in her treasure box and closed the lid, then jumped up from the bed. As she filed out of the door towards the washroom, she saw Sister Agnes catch Helen by the shoulder.

'Not you, Helen,' the nun said quietly. 'The Reverend Mother has spoken to your parents and they agree that a suitable punishment for your wickedness the other day is that you should miss the special tea. Instead, you will stay here and write out a hundred times, "I must not be nasty". Here is paper and a pencil. And I've written it at the top for you to copy.'

Helen's face blew up like one of the balloons they'd had to play with at Christmas. Maisie scuttled off to the washroom, wanting to get away from her as quickly as possible. But as she lined up with the others a few minutes later, Helen brushed past her.

'I'll get you for this, just see if I don't,' she hissed under her breath, and disappeared towards the toilets.

Well, Helen needn't think Maisie was frightened of her. Sister Agnes would see she was all right. And it served Helen right for being so horrible.

The special tea was lovely. There was fish paste and cucumber in the sandwiches, and bread with jam to follow, instead of just butter. Brightly coloured jellies glistened and wobbled in the centre of the tables, and a slice of cake each finished off the treat.

Back up in the dormitory, the other girls collected their things and went off downstairs, chatting excitedly. Helen gave Maisie a dirty look and then flounced out of the door. Maisie listened to the fading clatter of feet on the stairs as girls descended from the other dormitories as well, and then it suddenly seemed very quiet.

She padded over to the window. The familiar row of houses with the pointed roofs, and what she now knew were the cathedral and the sea, seemed extra bright in the afternoon sunshine. She could hear voices down below, and craned her neck to see. The wide courtyard immediately below was too close, but on the road outside the convent railings were several motorcars. Maisie watched as girls ran up to their mammies and daddies, hugged them, and then either climbed into a waiting car, or walked away down the street, some waving back at their friends.

'All right for some, isn't it?'

Maisie jumped. She'd thought she was alone, but Noreen appeared at her shoulder. She was all right, was Noreen.

'Aren't you going home?' Maisie asked her curiously.

Noreen shook her head. 'Sure, I don't have a home. My mammy died, too, and my daddy's in the army. I never see him. So I'm staying here for the summer. So, shall we be friends? At least we won't have to put up with Helen Driscoll!'

Noreen pulled a face, and Maisie couldn't help but laugh. She didn't know what the army was, but if it meant that she would have a friend for the long holiday, she didn't really care. Noreen was older than her, of course. But she was kind. So the summer was going to be special. And so it should be, now Maisie was four!

CHAPTER THREE

Eight years later
1934

'Come on, Nor. There's no one around, so.'

Maisie winked at her friend, eyes dancing with mischief, as they paused at the top of the main stairway. Noreen's forehead was pleated in a frown, but as her gaze swept about them, confirming that they were indeed alone, her face spread into a grin.

'All right, then,' she agreed, and with a stifled whoop of joy, wriggled her bottom onto the banister rail from where she stood on the step above the younger girl.

With a whoosh, they were off, sliding down the polished wooden handrail, fingers just steadying themselves in the groove that ran conveniently all the way from top to bottom. Round the corners they went, down two flights of stairs. When they hopped off onto the last step, cheeks pink with exhilaration, Maisie's eyes were sparkling.

'Come on,' she said, racing back up the stairs. 'One more go before someone comes.'

Noreen puffed out her cheeks. She wasn't quite sure. But Maisie could be so persuasive.

They slithered all the way down again. It was more fun than they'd had for ages. But as they rounded the last bend for the final straight, a dark figure was waiting for them at the bottom. Someone must have seen them and gone off to report it.

Both girls stopped at once and slid off the banister, their hearts thumping. A finger was beckoning them.

'What do you girls think you're doing?'

Maisie's lip trembled, but she knew it was her fault. 'I'm sorry, Reverend Mother,' she murmured. 'It was my idea, not Noreen's. I persuaded her.'

'Well, I'm surprised at you, Noreen,' the Reverend Mother scolded, lips wrinkled with severity. 'Letting Maisie lead you astray. You're the older one, so sure, you should have stopped her, not the other way round. And you wanting to become a novice, that requires obedience in all things. Not only is behaviour like this forbidden, it's highly dangerous, so it is. If you'd fallen, you could have been killed. Now, what am I to do with you?'

Oh, goodness. Maisie was overwhelmed with guilt as she heard Noreen hiccup back her sobs. It wasn't the thing to challenge the Reverend Mother, but Maisie's loyalty to her friend was stronger than her fear. She must defend Noreen, even if there were consequences.

'I'm the one to blame, Reverend Mother, really I am,' she insisted. 'Please don't punish Noreen when it was all my fault. Punish me twice instead.'

She felt sweat break out under the collar of her shirt as the Reverend Mother's eyes bore into hers and she lowered her head. The ensuing silence pounded in her ears and she waited for some terrible retribution to fall upon her. It seemed an eternity before the Reverend Mother drew in a breath.

'Well, at least you're honest,' she said sharply. 'I shall have to think about this. You will confess your sin on Sunday, of course, and see what penance Father McBride decides upon. In the meantime, I will think of something suitable to remind you never to disobey our rules again.'

There followed a swish of material as the Reverend Mother spun on her heel and moved away. With a muted sigh of relief, Maisie lifted her head to watch the ominous figure march away — only to see Helen standing at the end of corridor, smiling.

Fury bubbled up inside Maisie's chest. She might have known!

* * *

'I guess it isn't so bad, so, scrubbing the chapel floor.'

Noreen plunged the scrubbing brush back into the bucket and swirled it round in the already grey water. A few feet away, Maisie wrung out the floor cloth she was using to mop up after her friend's efforts, then sat back on her heels.

'Sure, if it weren't for me, we wouldn't be doing it at all. I'm that sorry, so I am.'

But Noreen's face broke out in a grin. 'Sure, it was fun, though, wasn't it? And what would life be without a bit of fun?'

'Well, we wouldn't be on our knees doing this.' Maisie used both hands to swipe the cloth hard over the floor, taking her anger out on it. 'If anyone else had seen us, they wouldn't have reported it. But it had to be Helen, didn't it? Always had it in for me, so she has, and I don't know why.'

'Wasn't she jealous at first because you were treated so special? And then you started playing into her hands. Hiding a spider in her nightie, pouring some water into her bed.'

Maisie chuckled. 'Oh, I enjoyed that!'

'But didn't it escalate matters, so you've only yourself to blame.'

'Sure, you'll not take her side?' Maisie scowled. 'What I did was only small. Don't you remember when your class was learning about centrifugal force, it was a few years ago now, and you older girls were washing your plimsolls in a bucket of water? You started whirling the bucket round in the air to see how it worked. Anyway, it looked such fun that I wanted a go, but everyone said I was too small. Then madam came over and told me to try it with the tin of boot blacking we little ones were using on our shoes. So I did, and it went all over the freshly painted wall. I got the cane for that, so I did. And I was locked in the coal hole all day. Sure, I'll never forget that!'

Noreen arched her eyebrows. 'If I'd seen her sneak over to you, I'd have stopped her,' she sighed. 'So I could say that was my fault, so that makes us quits. But I really don't mind doing this. I've always loved being here in the chapel. It's so peaceful.'

Her voice drifted off and as she brushed back a strand of hair, her gaze lifted reverently to the altar. Maisie watched her, softly pursing her lips.

'I used to think that, too. But not anymore. But then I don't want to become a nun, so I don't. And are you really sure you want to? You're sixteen. It's still so young. Don't you want to live a bit first?'

Noreen turned to her and laughed. 'Sure, you sound like an old lady yourself! And you just coming up to twelve, and all!'

'Exactly! I want to have a proper life. I want to have a job and the freedom to do whatever I want. And then I'll find a nice man to marry and have children and a home of my own. A proper family like I've never had. Like God meant us to be.'

'My family will be the church,' Noreen said softly.

Maisie caught her breath. There'd been a time, she remembered, when she'd been very small, that she'd planned on becoming a nun, too. But that had been before she'd been able to read about far off places she longed to visit. The convent represented an oasis of calm, somewhere she could return to visit on occasion, but the outside world now held a much stronger appeal for her. Besides, what she'd just said was true. As much as she wanted to have her own independence and see the world, she yearned more than anything to have a home and family of her very own. Fate had denied it to her as a child, so she'd jolly well make sure she made up for it in adulthood!

'Well, as long as you don't join an order of complete silence,' she told her friend now. 'Because when I come to visit you, sure, I'll want to tell you everything and I won't want to be talking to myself, so I won't.'

She waited for a moment for Noreen to realise she was teasing her, and her heart lifted as the older girl chuckled in response.

'And sure, I wouldn't want to listen to you rambling on without being able to interrupt you, so,' the older girl bantered back. 'But just now I reckon we must get on with this floor. I wouldn't want the Reverend Mother to come back and find we haven't finished.'

'You old taskmaster, you!' Maisie laughed, and twisting her floorcloth round between her hands as she held it over her bucket, squeezed it as tightly as she could.

* * *

Maisie frowned to herself as her feet crunched on the gravel. To be summoned indoors during playtime on a Saturday was usually a prelude to some sort of reprimand, but she couldn't for the life of her think of anything she'd done wrong since, well, since ages ago. Since she and Noreen had been caught sliding down the banisters, in fact. She'd been determined to be as good as gold from thereon in. She really mustn't get Noreen into trouble again and ruin her chances of joining the order as a novice. She'd never forgive herself!

Annoyance as much as anything tugged at Maisie's mouth as she made her way towards the door. And then to top it all, she realised Helen was following her, face set in its habitual sneer. And yet there was something else in her expression Maisie couldn't quite fathom. What was she up to now?

'Been telling tales again, have we?' she accused the older girl.

'Sure, I don't know what you're talking about,' Helen retorted. 'Unless you've been misbehaving again, of course.'

Maisie had to grit her teeth. What lies had Helen been telling this time? She'd soon find out. It seemed a little strange, mind, that she'd been told to go to the main hall rather than the Reverend Mother's office, and by the looks of things, so had Helen. So what was going on?

They each pushed open one of the double doors as together they entered the hall. The Reverend Mother, Sister Agnes and Miss O'Rourke, who taught them Irish dancing once a week, were standing by the piano. Mystified, Maisie marched forward in front of Helen. She knew she'd done nothing wrong and wasn't going to be cowed by any false accusations the other girl made.

Sister Agnes, though, smiled at them as they approached. 'Just sit down for a moment, girls, while we wait for the others,' she instructed.

Others? Maisie glanced at Helen, but her arch enemy, for once, looked as baffled as she was. They each dutifully took a seat among the chairs that had been pulled out and waited while a dozen or more other girls came to join them. Three were in Maisie's year, but the others were in either older or younger classes and she only knew them by sight.

'Right, well, I think we're all here.' Sister Agnes stepped forward, consulting a list. 'Now, Reverend Mother has something very exciting to tell you.'

Maisie was all ears. Something exciting sounded right up her street. At least, far better than being punished for something she hadn't done!

'Well, now, girls,' the Reverend Mother began. 'The news is that the archbishop is coming to Cobh. The entire convent will be attending the service he is conducting in the cathedral, but he is also doing us the honour of visiting us afterwards. It is my intention to display the vast range of talent we have in the school. So among many other things we have to show him, some of you will be performing some traditional Irish dances. Miss O'Rourke has selected you as the best dancers, but we only want one square set, so we'll need to whittle it down to eight, I'm afraid. So, if you'd like to put on your plimsolls, we can put you through your paces.'

Maisie was sure she was the first to spring up. How she loved to dance! The two long walls of the hall were lined with small cupboards, each one allocated to a girl with her name on the front in a brass holder. It was where they kept their plimsolls and small play items such as skipping ropes if they were lucky enough to possess one.

Maisie couldn't wait to get started and changed her shoes with lightning speed. What a pity Noreen hadn't been picked, too, but Noreen was never the most enthusiastic dancer. Maisie knew she wasn't the best herself, but she really hoped she'd be chosen. Might they even be dressed up in some special clothes? Now that would be something!

At long last, they were assembled in a line and began to dance, jigging up and down, hopping, tapping, shuffling, arms by their sides and backs as straight as ramrods. Miss O'Rourke called out the steps, while Sister Agnes accompanied them on the piano. Maisie poured all her concentration into making her legs work exactly in time to the music, pointing her toes when required and keeping the movements fluid while her body remained rigid.

Her heart was beating hard, not just with exertion but with nervousness and the longing to be chosen. They were then divided into two square sets to perform some of the formation reels Miss O'Rourke had taught them. Maisie's brain whirred as she nimbly anticipated each step. When the music stopped, Miss O'Rourke began separating off her definite choices, and Maisie's spirits sank when the teacher got to seven. Only one more to go. She glanced down the line. Surely there was a better dancer there than she was.

'I'd say it's between Maisie and Helen, would you not agree, Reverend Mother?' Miss O'Rourke declared. 'So let's see you two dancing side by side again so we can decide.'

Maisie snatched in her breath. Please let them choose her! Suddenly it seemed she needed this more than anything else in the world. She must keep a clear head, force every ounce of her energy into a perfect performance. She stretched up her neck as Miss O'Rourke counted them in.

When they got to the end, Maisie stood erect, tamping down her emotions. The Reverend Mother and the dance teacher exchanged murmurs, and then the Reverend Mother stepped forward.

'Well done, both of you,' she smiled. 'It was very close, but, Maisie, there was something, sure, I don't know, honest in your performance. So Miss O'Rourke and I agree it should be you.'

Maisie's heart soared. Thank you so much! She promised she'd never be naughty again! But as they turned away, she caught a glimpse of Helen's face. Goodness, the older girl's chin was quivering and there were tears glistening in her eyes. Did the dancing mean so much to her too?

For a moment, Maisie felt sorry for her, even a little guilty for being the one who'd been chosen. Should she apologise, tell Helen that she'd try and make it up to her in some way? But she didn't get the chance as Helen dashed from the hall, choking back a sob. Maisie gave a small sigh. The girl probably wouldn't have appreciated her sympathies anyway, and Maisie didn't want her moment of happiness to be spoiled. So, forgetting all about Helen, she changed her shoes and ran off to tell Noreen the good news.

* * *

Only two days to go. Maisie was so excited she could scarcely sleep. She'd forgotten all about the contest with Helen now. The older girl had even been nice to her on the few occasions they'd bumped into each other. So maybe the hard feelings between them were softening. Maisie was glad, really. She didn't like the sense of animosity that had been going on for years. Perhaps the dance competition had enabled them to reach some sort of understanding. Maisie sincerely hoped so.

Tentatively, she held out her bag of sweets. It had been her birthday that week, and since she had no family to send her a little gift, Sister Agnes still treated her to a few pennyworth of confectionery each year. Now, wouldn't it be grand if the offering put an end once and for all to the feud? It all seemed so stupid and immature.

She watched as surprise registered on Helen's face, and then a half-smile stretched the other girl's mouth.

'Sure, thank you,' she answered, delving her hand into the paper bag.

Maisie's heart sank. Helen had only taken Maisie's favourite, a large chocolate ball that concealed a hazelnut inside. Oh, botheration. But it was her own fault. She should have eaten the best ones herself before offering the bag to Helen, but she'd been saving the best until last. Now it might be another year before she tasted one of those delicacies again. But she mustn't let Helen see her dismay.

'I guess that makes us quits,' she said in a hopeful voice.

Helen nodded slowly, unable to answer with the chocolate filling her mouth. She made a show of relishing its flavour and swallowing before she spoke.

'You don't mind if Siobhan has one, too, do you?'

Maisie bit the inside of her lip. Yes, she did mind very much. Siobhan Feelan was Helen's partner in crime, but what could Maisie say? She didn't want to lose another of her precious sweets, but she didn't want to cause any more ructions by saying no.

'Of course not,' she managed to say, holding out the bag to Siobhan who had appeared as if on cue.

Siobhan helped herself and popped a sweet into her mouth. Then the two girls linked arms and turned away, laughing, leaving Maisie standing there, nonplussed. Her eyes dropped to the bag. Just two sweets left, one each for herself and Noreen. She just hoped it would be worth it.

Still, she had the archbishop's visit and performing in front of his Excellency to look forward to. The final rehearsal was to take place in the hall in five minutes time.

31

Maisie quickened her pace, so she could be there, ready and waiting. She'd take what remained of the sweets with her, and put the bag in her individual cupboard with her shoes. She wasn't going to risk leaving them by her bed and finding them gone when she got back.

She skipped, brimming with excitement, to the top of the stairs. She was still so chuffed to have been chosen, and couldn't wait for the big day. She stepped gaily off the top step.

Something seemed to tug at her foot in mid-air. A split second of panic was followed by a desperate effort to right herself. But oh, crikey, she was falling and she couldn't stop herself. She wasn't aware of her scream as she tumbled down the stairs, arms outstretched as she tried to break her fall. Driven by instinct, she somehow managed to grab hold of one of the thin spindles of the metal banisters, wrenching her shoulder as she brought herself to a stop.

For a moment or so the world came to a standstill. Oh, thank heavens. She'd landed only halfway down the flight of stairs. She'd gone head first, and she realised that if she'd crashed to the bottom, she might have smashed her head on the wall of the half landing, and maybe broken her neck. Swamped with relief, she offered up a quick prayer of thanks to Our Lady.

But then she tried to move.

She felt battered and bruised all over. There were horrified voices above her on the landing. As she glanced up, she saw Siobhan's gloating face disappear round the corner.

Before she had a chance to react, other girls were around her, and then she heard Sister Agnes's calm, direct tones coming up the stairs towards her.

'Holy Mother, what happened here? Are you hurt, child? Ah, Noreen, someone with a sensible head on you. Go down to the hall and tell the Reverend Mother what's happened. I think we'd better fetch the doctor to check Maisie's all right. Now let's see if we can get you up, but if it hurts, you must say and we won't move you.'

All the faces around Maisie seemed to blur, but her thoughts were crystal clear. Why had Siobhan been there at the top of the stairs? And Maisie would never forget that look on her face.

Now, though, she must concentrate on getting herself the right way up. Gingerly, with Sister Agnes supporting her, she managed to stand upright. She felt somewhat shaken and a bit sore, but nothing worse than that. Then as she tried to take a step up the stairs, pain shot through her ankle.

'What is it, child?' Concern rippled through Sister Agnes's voice as her grip tightened around Maisie's shoulders.

'My ankle,' Maisie groaned. 'I can hardly put my weight on it.'

'Well, let's try to get you to your bed. And you're sure you're not hurt anywhere else?'

'A bit, but it's mainly my ankle. Oh, no!' Maisie wailed. 'What if I can't dance for the archbishop?'

'I'd say that's the last thing you should be thinking about right now. If it's broken, you'll be having to go to hospital and have a cast put on it. Now lean on me and hop,' the sister instructed as they reached the top of the stairs again.

Maisie gritted her teeth against the pain as she hobbled along the landing to her dormitory, leaning on Sister Agnes's arm. It was a huge relief to get to her bed and have her leg raised up, but as the burning eased, her tears turned to sobs of despair. All she could think of was that it seemed unlikely that she'd be able to take part in the dance display that had filled her soul for so many weeks now. She had so little excitement in her life, and now even this relatively small thing was being taken away from her.

'Oh, my goodness, what've you been up to now, Maisie O'Sullivan?'

Maisie's heart missed a beat as the Reverend Mother swept into the room. She never came into the dormitories unless it was something really serious. Maisie began to quake. The Reverend Mother wasn't going to be best pleased with her, and she shuddered at the glaring expression on the woman's face.

'Haven't you been told before not to ride down the banisters, and on these narrow ones, as well. I told you how dangerous it could be, and now look at you! I've had to send for the doctor, so I have, and you've disrupted the rehearsal.'

Maisie had cowered under the Reverend Mother's tirade, but now her anguish turned to indignation. 'I wasn't climbing on the banisters, really I wasn't! I don't know . . . Something caught my foot, and I just fell.'

'Really.' The Reverend Mother's voice was disbelieving, but to Maisie's surprise, she asked, 'Did any of you see what happened?'

Yes, surely someone must have seen? It was to do with Siobhan, Maisie was sure. But the girls who had clustered around the bed all shook their heads. And then she heard Siobhan's voice from somewhere near the door.

'Sure, I did, Reverend Mother. She just seemed to trip over her own feet at the top of the stairs. I think she was so excited about the rehearsal, she was just going too fast. Such a pity if she won't be able to do the performance, mind. I suppose Helen will have to take her place as she was next in line. Shall I go and tell her to get ready for the rehearsal instead?'

'Good idea. Thank you, Siobhan. And tell her not to run! Sure, we're not wanting another accident on our hands.'

'And I'd better get back as I'm playing the piano,' Sister Agnes put in, 'though I don't like to leave you, Maisie.'

'No, Sister, please don't worry about me,' Maisie gulped, though to be honest, she would rather Sister Agnes had stayed. But at that moment, Noreen came into the room, leading the way for the doctor who was puffing and red in the face from having climbed several flights of stairs. He only had breath to grunt and nod at the Reverend Mother, who moved aside so that he could examine his patient.

'So, what have we been up to?' he panted. 'Took a tumble on the stairs, I hear? So, where does it hurt?'

'My ankle mainly,' Maisie winced as she moved her foot slightly.

'Hmm. Let me see.'

Maisie had to hold back hiccups of pain as he gently moved her ankle this way and that. The discomfort took her mind off the burning question in her head, but then the doctor nodded as he rested her foot back on the bed.

'Nasty sprain,' he pronounced. 'I'll strap it up, but there'll be no putting your weight on it for some weeks. I'll see if I can find you some crutches, but I want it elevated as much as possible. You're only to move about for essentials like going to the bathroom. But if you can lie back down, young lady, I want to check you've no other hidden injuries.'

Maisie did as she was instructed, tensing as the doctor felt all over her, but nothing more particularly hurt. Within ten minutes, she was sitting up in bed with a pristine cream-coloured crepe bandage enclosing from her foot right up to her knee. The Reverend Mother had shooed all the girls away apart from Noreen, who she knew to be Maisie's best friend, before accompanying the doctor back down the stairs, leaving the two girls alone together.

'How does it feel now?' Noreen asked, her face screwed up with sympathy.

'More comfortable with the bandage. But, listen, Nor.' Maisie grasped her friend's arm and gazed earnestly into her face. 'I didn't just fall. Something happened, and I swear Siobhan had something to do with it. I wasn't pushed, but it was as if something tripped my foot, so. I reckon she did something deliberately so that Helen could take my place in the dancing.'

Noreen's eyes opened wide. 'Are you really thinking so?'

'Yes, I am. Could you go along to the landing and see if there's anything there?'

'W-well, yes, sure. But . . .'

Noreen lifted her shoulders, but dutifully did as Maisie had asked. Maisie waited, her forehead creased in a frown. Noreen was back in a trice — dangling a length of string.

'Didn't I find this around the corner,' she said, shaking her head. 'But sure, it doesn't prove anything.'

Maisie's mouth twisted. No, it didn't prove anything. But she was convinced Helen and Siobhan had been involved somehow. Anger and frustration boiled up inside her, but what good would it do? Helen was taking her place in the dance display, and that was that. She could feel tears prickling her eyes, but if she gave into them, she would be letting the other girls win.

Instead, she pushed out her chin. 'Sure, I didn't want to do the stupid dance anyway. Not without you, Nor. Now those two might be as thick as thieves, but aren't you and I better friends than they'll ever be. Stick together all of our lives, won't we? No matter where we are, we'll always keep in touch.'

'Where would I be without you to get me into trouble, anyway?' Noreen chuckled back. 'Best friends always.'

She leaned forward and enclosed the invalid in a tight hug. Maisie stifled a small wince as she felt generally sore all over, but she felt herself fill up with warmth. What did she care about enemies when she'd have someone like kind, thoughtful Noreen as a surrogate sister for the rest of her days?

CHAPTER FOUR

'Maisie O'Sullivan, you're to come to the Reverend Mother at once.'

Maisie froze, the half-eaten slice of bread and butter suspended on its way to her mouth. She glanced along the row of refectory tables where her year was having breakfast. Sister Finbar had stationed herself at the far end, shoulders squared like a warship about to launch into battle. A mixture of trepidation and defiance drove through Maisie's heart and her pulse began to rattle. What now? What minor misdemeanour had Helen trumped up to accuse her of this time?

Her mind swiftly scanned the last few days. The only thing she could think of was that she'd been on the rota to do the washing up in the nuns' kitchen, a task she actually quite enjoyed. It made a pleasant change from the normal routine and she liked to imagine it was her own kitchen in her own home, and she was doing the work for her own little family — her husband and however many children they had.

Of course, there was also the chance when you were in the nuns' kitchen that there might be some leftover food to purloin. The nuns' fare always seemed superior to their own and you could usually find some way of smuggling something out. This time, it had been easy. The apples had been harvested from the trees in the garden at the back. There was a whole barrel load of them in the cold pantry and surely even the eagle-eyed Sister Finbar wouldn't notice if a couple were missing? So Maisie had stuffed two shiny green and russet fruits into her knickers — the usual method of transportation. As was the custom, she'd shared them with the other girls in her dorm. It grieved her not to be able to give one to Noreen because she was in a different dorm, but all the senior girls were on kitchen duty at some point, so Noreen's turn would come round again before too long, and there would surely be some extra she could help herself to then.

Maisie's gaze now sought out her friend as she scraped herself to her feet. Meals were eaten in silence, but at Sister Finbar's imperious command, even the clatter of plates and cutlery ceased as all eyes turned on Maisie as she stood. Noreen's class sat at a different refectory table, and across the room, Maisie caught Noreen's eye, fearful and questioning. But the older girl looked just as bewildered as she was.

Maisie turned away and clenched her jaw as she began the long walk between the tables, taking small steps so that it would delay her punishment by a few seconds more. How on earth had Helen found out about the apples? Did she have a spy? Maisie couldn't imagine any of the other girls in her dorm betraying her. They'd all relished their share of the apples, after all. So how did Helen know?

Just now, though, that was the least of Maisie's problems. She came to a halt in front of Sister Battle Axe, heart hammering yet fired up with rage against Helen who she could never forgive over the dance display back during the summer term.

'Please, Sister, won't that make me late for school?' she plucked up the courage to ask.

She blinked as Sister Finbar's brow knotted. 'You don't need to worry about that now, child, so you don't. Now hurry up and follow me.'

Not worry about school? Apart from religion and everything connected with it, they'd had it drummed into them at every opportunity that their education was of paramount importance. So if she wasn't to worry about school, this must be something very serious indeed. Maisie's heart sank even further as she scuttled along behind Sister Finbar's retreating figure that seemed to skim along with the wind in its sails. She was really in for it this time, whatever it was about.

'In here first, child.'

Maisie nearly bumped into the nun's back as she stopped abruptly in front of a door. That was odd. This wasn't the Reverend Mother's office. She'd walked down this corridor a million times, but this particular door was permanently shut. What could be behind it? It flashed across Maisie's mind that it could be a hitherto unknown punishment room. She recoiled with a shiver of terror, then winced as Sister Finbar's bony fingers dug into her shoulder and propelled her inside.

Maisie hesitated as she peered about her. A woman she didn't recognise stood up from a chair and approached her with a kindly smile. What was going on, Maisie asked herself in confused panic.

'I'll come back for you later,' Sister Finbar announced before gliding out of the room and closing the door behind her.

Maisie turned back to the woman, expecting to be reprimanded. It was only then that she noticed a long trestle table beneath the window, piled high with a jumble of clothes, and an open suitcase at one end. Her brow wrinkled into a frown. What was this all about?

'Come, child, let me look at you,' the woman beckoned, a warm smile lighting her face. 'You're on the small side for your age, so. But we can still find you things to fit, I'm sure. Take off your gymslip and shirt. And those dreadful black stockings. Sure, we can find you some nice new socks instead.'

Maisie eyed the woman suspiciously. Undress in front of this stranger? She wasn't at all sure about that! But the face that looked at her appeared honest and encouraging, so Maisie decided to go ahead. It was better than having her hands caned as she'd anticipated.

The woman took her discarded items of clothing, and dumping them on the chair she'd just vacated, went to rummage in the pile on the table.

'Hmm, these look about right,' she mumbled as if to herself, and held out a bundle of garments. 'Try those for size while I root out some more. You'll need three or four outfits, warm ones with the winter coming on.'

Maisie took the clothes from her in dazed silence. She was supposed to try them on, was she? Whatever for, and why had she been picked? Mrs X — for that was what Maisie decided to name the woman — found her two serviceable skirts in black and navy serge respectively, and a third in a soft grey that flared out towards the hem. Maisie felt the bee's knees in that one, despite the fact that it had been drummed into her all her life that vanity was a sin. 'That could be for best,' Mrs X declared, throwing Maisie into utter confusion.

It also struck her as odd that she'd been prevented from going to school. She should be at her desk, concentrating on her lessons. There was no clock in the room and she didn't own a watch, but it seemed to her the morning must be half gone by now, and still she was being instructed to try on more clothes for size.

A couple of white shirts like her uniform came next. She could see the cuffs had been turned, just like the nuns had taught them to do in their sewing lessons. So the clothes weren't brand new. Two coloured ones next, and a couple of thick jumpers. And then Mrs X held up a twin set in pale blue with a white Peter Pan collar.

'Sure, that'll go splendidly with the grey skirt. You can wear it to the Mass on Sundays. Oh, and with this coat, won't you look just the thing? It'll be on the big side, but won't you grow into it in a year or two?'

Mrs X winked as she held up the most beautiful coat Maisie had ever seen. It was navy blue with lighter piping about the edges of the collar and gold-coloured buttons that shimmered down the front. The elbows were worn, Maisie noticed, and it swamped her somewhat as she shrugged into it. But despite the wear, and it being on the big side, she could sense how smart it must look, and wished there was a mirror to see her reflection in. But perhaps it was best there wasn't. It'd make it all the harder when she had to give back the lovely clothes and don her drab school uniform again.

'Perfect!' Mrs X's delighted voice confused Maisie even more. 'Now you must put on these socks while I pack the case. I'm afraid you'll have to keep the same shoes. But look, here's a couple of nightdresses that look the right size, so,' she added, holding up some nightwear before starting to fold all the items and place them in the case.

Maisie blinked, utterly bewildered, but dutifully obeyed, pulling on brand new beige socks that were soft and luxurious around her calves compared to the scratchy, black knitted stockings she was used to. The shoes she'd been given fairly recently were relatively new and surprisingly comfortable, but she fumbled with the buckles as she fastened them. She really didn't understand what was going on, and butterflies were fluttering in her stomach.

Sister Finbar re-entering the room made her even more nervous.

'Are we ready yet?' the nun demanded sourly.

'Indeed we are,' Mrs X beamed, and Maisie heard the clicks as the woman snapped shut the latches on the suitcase. 'Here you are, Maisie. And here's the key to the case. Keep it safely in your pocket. I hope the case isn't too heavy for you, but I'm sure you'll manage. Well, good luck, my dear, and God bless.'

Maisie slipped the smart coat back on to save carrying it, and taking the case that was being held out to her, mumbled her thanks. She still didn't have a clue what it was all about, but she hurried to catch up with Sister Finbar who was holding open the door for her, impatience stamped on her face. It was just as well, mind, since Maisie was finding she needed both hands on the handle to carry the case, it was so heavy with everything that was inside. She was so busy putting all her efforts into lumbering along with it that she hardly had a chance to think as she was ushered into the Reverend Mother's office.

'Leave the case by the door,' Sister Finbar hissed, and then took up a position standing guard in front of the door as if to block Maisie's escape.

'Come forward, Maisie, child.'

Maisie turned from setting down the case against the wall. Light from the low autumn sun illuminated the square window, against which the Reverend Mother was a black, faceless shape. Maisie stepped forward slowly. She still didn't know what this was all about. Surely, she was about to meet her doom?

'Well, my dear,' the Reverend Mother continued. My dear? Where did that come from, Maisie wondered, bracing herself for the worst as the Reverend Mother went on, 'Today is a very special day for you. It's been a long time coming, so it has. A whole decade, in fact. But now I want you to meet your father, Mr Francis O'Sullivan.'

CHAPTER FIVE

Every muscle in Maisie's body froze in shock. She couldn't move, was scarcely able to breathe, let alone think. It was some seconds before any sense began to trickle back into her numbed brain. She hadn't heard right. Surely.

It was only then that she realised someone else was in the room as well. Sitting in the shadows against the wood-panelled walls was another silent figure who stood up and stepped slowly into the light. A man, not very tall, and slight of build, was looking her up and down as if inspecting her. His silvery, short-cropped hair was almost bald on top, and his lined face sported a ridiculous grey moustache. *Father?* Slightly stooped in a crumpled, worn suit, he looked nothing like the smart, strong-looking fathers she'd so often observed coming to collect their daughters at the convent gate. He looked ancient. And besides . . .

'B-but I don't have a father,' she stuttered, finally finding the courage to speak in a tiny voice. 'Or a mother for that matter.'

Oh, what on earth was happening? Was this some sort of nasty trick? A dream? But it felt real. By the way her heart was crashing against her ribs, she was sure it was.

Then she saw the Reverend Mother steeple her fingers. 'Yes, it's true that you don't have a mother,' she conceded, her words slow and calm. 'She died when you were a baby. But she left your father on his own. For a couple of years, he was able to pay a neighbour to look after you, but that all changed. He was once a master miller, but with so many mills here in Ireland closing down, he'd no work in his profession so he'd gone to work on the land. But he was older than your mother by many years and with failing health, he could no longer do physical work. So he left you with us as a charity case. We don't usually take on girls before they're five, as you know. But your mother had done such good work in the community that when your father asked, we couldn't refuse and we took you in as a two-year-old. He wanted the best for you, and that didn't include an orphanage. But now you're twelve years old, it's time for you to go and live with him. You're a bright, sensible girl, Maisie O'Sullivan, so I know you'll understand.'

Bright? Sensible? Maybe, but living with an elderly relative who was a complete stranger to her was never in Maisie's plan. Well, she wouldn't go! But she was smart enough to realise she must appear composed and level-headed, or she wouldn't stand a chance of talking her way out of it.

'But what about school?' she insisted, trying to hide her desperation. 'I can continue at the pension school, can't I? You know I won a scholarship . . .'

The Reverend Mother released a sigh. 'That would be ideal, of course it would. But it's up to your father, and he's requested that you go to live with him. You'll continue at school until you're fourteen, at least. But not here. Your father's home is in England now. That's where he went to find work. He has employment sufficient to support you both now, so you must be thankful that you can now be reunited.'

Maisie felt as if her world had been blown apart. England! She might have wanted to visit it one day. But to go and live there, leave the only life she'd ever known, all her friends? She realised in a flash just how much she loved the convent, despite all its harsh rules and regulations. She'd even wanted to become a nun herself once, after all. To have the rug whipped out from underneath her feet was unbearable.

Before a suitable reply could rush into her head, the man took another step forward and grasped her arm. Her caustic gaze swivelled to his, and she yanked herself free. She really didn't like the look of him at all!

'It's all decided. You're coming with me,' he said firmly.

Oh, no, she wasn't! Maisie felt she would burst with rage and frustration. 'No,' she glowered back at him. 'And, Reverend Mother, how do you know he's really my father? He could be anyone.'

'Oh, my dear child, you don't think I'd let anyone take you away if I wasn't a hundred per cent sure who they were? Now, I understand this is a huge shock for you and I appreciate your concerns. Your father brought you here himself, with Father Michael from Buttevant, where you lived and where your mother is buried. It was on Father Michael's recommendation that we accepted you. Mr O'Sullivan and I met when I took you in, in this very room. He's older now, of course, but there's no doubt. Besides, I have kept in contact with him on your behalf all these years. So, yes, this gentleman is most definitely your father.'

If Maisie had ever wanted to throw a tantrum it was now. But what good would it do? It had all been decided. She felt crushed. Defeated. There was no point in trying to fight it.

'So when do I have to leave?' she mumbled, her head hanging low.

'Today,' the Reverend Mother declared, relief clear in her voice. 'Sister Agnes is waiting for you in the dormitory to help you pack anything you wish to keep from there. And then you'll be on your way.'

'That's right,' her father spoke sharply again. 'The *Innisfallen* docked in Cork first thing this morning, and I came straight here to Cobh on the train. We've got to get back to Cork as quickly as possible. We sail this evening and we mustn't miss it.'

Maisie was shot through with defiance. 'What? Can't I even catch my friends up at school to say goodbye? Noreen—'

'Will be told this evening,' the Reverend Mother interrupted her. 'She is older than you and will see the reason more readily. It'll be less painful for her than a personal farewell. Instead, when you're settled, you can write to her and tell her all about your new life, which I'm sure she'll find very exciting. You can write to each other as often as you will. Now, hurry along. The ship won't wait and your passage, I understand, is booked and paid for.'

'And can you possibly find her a different coat, Reverend Mother?' Maisie's father opened his mouth once more, his tone just as terse. 'Something plain, a gaberdine, perhaps. Something suitable for wearing to school, because I won't be able to afford a new one for her, and she doesn't need a fancy one like the one she's got on.'

Maisie's jaw stiffened in resentment. Was the smart coat to be snatched from her as well? She shot a bitter glance at the Reverend Mother, but to her surprise, she saw the nun's eyebrows lift in sympathy.

'Maisie, you may take your school coat with you as well,' she said softly. 'Collect it from the cloakroom when you come back down. Look upon this one as a parting gift from the convent. We don't encourage vanity, Mr O'Sullivan. But under the circumstances, I feel Maisie should be adequately equipped for her new life. Now, God speed, my child, and may the Grace of our Lord Jesus Christ and Our Lady his mother go with you.'

She made the sign of the cross, her expression angelic, and a lump suddenly choked Maisie's throat. She realised that despite the times she had stood on this very spot being reprimanded, she truly respected the Reverend Mother. How should she react? They'd never been taught about goodbyes. So she performed a small genuflexion and, with a mumbled thanks, turned away with tears misting her vision.

Sister Finbar was already holding the door open for her, and she fled past the elderly nun and up the stairs to the dormitory. Why had this man who was apparently her father, turned up out of the blue?

In one fell swoop, he had ruined her plans. She was doing so well at school. Was top of the class. She enjoyed her studies and was so looking forward to it leading to a good job. There might even be a chance of going to college, she'd been told. It would all bring her independence, and with any luck would eventually bring her the opportunity of finding a decent husband and a happy home and family of her own. And now all her dreams had been shattered. The Reverend Mother had said she would stay at school in England until she was fourteen, but that would mean she'd be leaving with her education only half complete.

She shoved open the dormitory door, scarcely keeping her temper at bay. Sister Agnes was sitting on Maisie's bed, and Maisie frowned as she saw her own treasure box on the nun's lap, and a few other of her personal items spread out on the eiderdown. On seeing Maisie, Sister Agnes put the box to one side and rose to her feet, and Maisie marched up to her, eyes blazing.

'Why did you lie to me?' she shrieked, her jaw jutting fiercely. 'All these years—'

'Aw, my little pet, I wasn't knowing myself until last night, I swear to you. And I feel so awful about it, so I do.'

'B-but Reverend Mother kept the truth from me, and isn't that a sin?'

'Well, the Good Lord understands that sometimes a well-intentioned fib is forgivable. It was obviously thought best, and it was your father's wish apparently. But . . . Oh, Maisie, come here.'

Maisie felt tears welling in her eyes, and when she glanced at Sister Agnes's face, she saw that she was already crying. In an instant, they were holding each other close, sobbing in each other's arms.

'We'll write, so we will,' Sister Agnes murmured as she finally pulled away. 'I've a mind to go to Africa for a while. Do some missionary work. But our letters can pass through the Reverend Mother. And look. I stayed up all night making these for you.'

She gestured towards the bed where Maisie now saw a knitted hat in a pale dove grey that had been placed on top of a carefully folded matching scarf. Maisie went to open her mouth, but Sister Agnes spoke first.

'No time for thanks, I'm afraid, if you're going to be on that great big boat when it sails. And here's your treasure box, your missal, and a book from me. I was never sure it was one I should be reading, so I kept it secret, but now I want you to have it.'

Maisie was too choked to speak, so she nodded instead, her mouth pulled in an ugly grimace as she fought back more tears. She watched as Sister Agnes popped everything into Maisie's shoe bag and tightened the strings.

'Off you go now,' she gulped as she handed it over. 'Your plimsolls are in there, too. You make sure you keep them as white as the driven snow. And promise me you'll always be the stubborn, determined little girl I've always known.'

So this was it. Maisie nodded, somehow managing to force a laugh through her tears. And the last she heard of Sister Agnes was of her crying softly again as Maisie quietly shut the door behind her — for the last time.

CHAPTER SIX

'Come on, keep up,' Francis O'Sullivan growled. 'We can't miss this boat. It's booked and paid for. And there's not another one for two days. We'd have to sleep on the quayside. I don't have money for lodgings.'

Maisie was struggling along with the suitcase. She'd put her arms through the strings of the shoe bag so that it was bouncing about on her back like a rucksack, and she'd slung the school coat over her shoulder as there simply wasn't room for it in the case. But she had to keep stopping to hike the coat back up as it was in constant danger of falling off onto the ground.

Now she stood the case on the pavement and flexed her aching muscles. Her father was glaring at her, lips pressed together as he waited impatiently for her to catch up. How on earth could this be happening? A few hours ago, she was happily anticipating the school day, full of learning about interesting topics. Now she was leaving to live with some cur-mudgeonly old man in a strange country full of the English, whom they'd been told so constantly had dominated and plundered their land for hundreds of years.

'It would help if you were to carry something!' she retorted, her chin set. 'This suitcase is heavy.'

'Huh, they warned me you had some lip on you,' he snarled back. 'Well, you can't expect me to carry it. I'm not a well man, or hadn't you noticed?'

Maisie bunched her lips. She hadn't noticed anything about him that suggested he was ill, although now he mentioned it, she saw that he kept his left hand in his pocket. Was that what he meant? She didn't understand, but she certainly wasn't going to ask.

'Well, could you possibly take the coat for me? Please,' she added as an afterthought. 'It's not heavy, but it keeps slipping off my shoulder and slowing me down. That's if you really want us to catch this boat.'

She saw his eyes narrow in anger, and he threw her a look of contempt but he held out his right arm. He indicated with a jab of his head that she should sling the coat over it, then marched on. But not before grunting over his shoulder, 'Why you need two blessed coats, I'll never know.'

Maisie gave a wry grimace of satisfaction. But her shoulders protested as she picked up the suitcase and tottered on as best she could. Perhaps it would have been better if Mrs X hadn't given her quite so many new clothes. But at least it was downhill all the way. The convent and the Bishop's Palace were both behind her now. Would she ever see them again?

They finally arrived down near the waterfront and the promenade Maisie knew so well. And there was the station. And shortly there'd be a train that would take her away from her home.

'Well, you'll be pleased to know that because you took so long, we've missed the train I was aiming for,' her father barked. 'And there's not another one until after lunch.'

Oh, might that give him time to change his mind? But the scowl on his face stamped out that idea. 'Well, I'm sorry, but I walked as fast as I could with the case,' Maisie replied curtly.

'Yes, but you took long enough when you went upstairs. Lucky the boat doesn't sail until this evening. And I suppose you'll want something to eat.'

Maisie blinked in surprise. Her stomach had been tying itself in knots and food was the last thing on her mind. She hadn't expected him to take any of her feelings into consideration — but then again, he probably hadn't and was just getting hungry himself. But she didn't want him knowing that she was so upset that her appetite had vanished. He'd take it as a sign of weakness, and she wasn't having that! So she made her tone as cool as his as she answered, 'Sure, I was pulled out of breakfast before I'd finished. So, yes, I'm hungry.'

'Huh,' he grunted. 'Well, you wait here and I'll see what I can get us. And no thinking you can run off. You wouldn't get far without any money, and we'd have the Garda find you in no time.'

With a look that could kill, he dropped the school coat over the suitcase and marched off towards the shops. Maisie watched him go, her mouth an angry line. There would have been time for her to say goodbye to Noreen had she been allowed. Now her friend would think she'd abandoned her. The first thing she'd do when she arrived at her new home — home? — would be to write.

There was a bench just a few yards away, so Maisie moved the case across and sat down. Despite the autumn sun, a cold wind coming in off the sea made her shiver. What did the future hold for her? She didn't even know where in England she was headed. It would mean a new school, new friends. But would she ever find happiness? What was it Sister Agnes had said? That she must always be determined. But at that moment, all she wanted to do was run back up the hill to the convent. Her eyes instinctively lifted to the cathedral that dominated the town, and she prayed fervently to St Colman, to Our Lady or to anyone who might be listening that her father might never reappear and she could go back to the life she knew and loved.

No such luck. There he was, coming back towards her with a package in his right hand, his left hand still in his pocket. So what was wrong with it, she wondered. He sat down, his face in what seemed a habitual scowl, and put the newspaper package on the bench. The smell made Maisie's mouth drool as she realised that she really was hungry after all. Fish and chips, a treat so rare it was like hen's teeth.

'Go on, you open it, and don't you dare drop a morsel. And it's to share so don't go thinking you can scoff the lot.'

Huh! How could he speak to her like that? Maisie had to bite back a retort. She unwrapped the newspaper with the greatest care as she wasn't going to be called clumsy. Inside was a small piece of fish but plenty of chips. She drew back, waiting. He flicked his gaze at her, mouth wrinkled.

'Divide it in half,' he ordered, and she did so as evenly as she could. He seemed satisfied, and Maisie watched as he broke some fish off his portion using just his right hand. So, could he not use his left one? Well, if it was paralysed for some reason, she felt sorry for that. But it was no reason to act in such a surly manner towards her. After all, she should be the one to be furious with him, springing all this on her and turning her life upside down.

She said nothing as she slid a chip into her mouth and chewed. She could have done with a drink to wash it down, but she might be pushing her luck if she asked, and if they called into a tea room, they might miss the next train as well, and there'd be hell to pay.

They ate in silence, but that suited her just fine. She couldn't believe this was the last time she would see Cobh, and tried to imprint the memory of the place on her mind. What if she never came back? The last piece of fish stuck in her throat as misery threatened to overwhelm her.

When they'd finished eating, they started making their way along to the station. Oh, God, please make something happen to stop this. She wasn't taking His name in vain. She really meant it. But her prayer went unanswered.

They joined a few other passengers waiting in a queue at the ticket office. Her father had obviously purchased a return ticket for himself from Cork, and just bought a child's one-way ticket for her. As they went through the barrier, Maisie's heart sank further. She'd never been on a train before, and this should have been a wonderful adventure. But as it was, boarding a train was the last thing on earth she wanted just now. Even when the great gleaming engine eventually rolled in next to the platform pulling several carriages behind it, and let out a cloud of hissing steam like a fiery dragon, it couldn't arouse her interest.

Passengers banged open doors and the station echoed with noise and excitement. Maisie just wanted to block out all the clamour. Then her father gave her a shove towards an open carriage door and she had to heave the case up inside. Clambering up after it, she shuffled into the compartment her father indicated. The case was too big to fit in the luggage rack, so had to stay on the floor. Maisie dived onto the far end of the right-hand seat and turned her face to the window. They were joined by one other passenger, a man in a cloth cap who slunk into the corner by the door and pulled the peak down over his eyes as if all he wanted was to sleep. Ten minutes later, a woman puffed into the compartment, declaring that she'd just made it, but an icy stare from Maisie's father seemed to silence her and she said nothing more after that.

Only moments later, the train lurched and hissed and began to rumble forward. Maisie bit down hard on her lip. This was truly goodbye to her old life, her friends, Noreen, Sister Agnes. The guard blew his whistle and the train inched out of the station, slowly gathering speed.

* * *

By the time they arrived in Cork, grey, dank clouds had rolled in, dampening Maisie's spirits even further. They'd passed the journey in complete silence. Maisie had gazed out of the window, watching the countryside pass her in a blur of tears. She should have been enthralled since she'd only ever known the confines of Cobh and the nearby shoreline, but now her heart was truly breaking and nothing could distract her.

When she risked a furtive glance at her father seated next to her, she saw that his eyes were closed. She didn't care if he was asleep or not. At least it meant she didn't have to talk to him. Whenever they came into a station, she wondered if she should slip past him and get off. Heaven knew what would happen to her if she did. But she'd seen that you had to give up your ticket at the barrier and her father had hers, so there was no point even thinking about escaping.

They finally reached their destination, and Maisie hefted the case down from the carriage. They'd arrived right down by Penrose Quay where the *Innisfallen* was berthed, and she found herself mildly distracted for the first time all day. The broad quayside thronged with people going about their business, and the hustle and bustle at last drew her interest. What was everyone doing? A few people were well-dressed, but most were in drab, shabby clothes. One or two motorcars and creaking lorries rumbled past them, wending their way round slow, plodding horse-drawn carts. Under other circumstances, Maisie might have found it exciting, but now it made her wonder what sort of place her father was taking her to live. So far, he'd told her nothing of what her future life would be like.

The drizzle had turned to rain, making the ground shiny and releasing the acrid smell of wet paving. Maisie paused for a moment to take it all in. There was the *Innisfallen*, somehow not quite as large as she'd imagined. The boat — or was it a ship — boasted two squat funnels with a sail-less mast at either end, three open decks at different levels and one covered area. Thank goodness it had lifeboats! The idea of being tossed about on the sea and possibly shipwrecked suddenly made Maisie's pulse accelerate. And then she frowned. Bunting fluttered above the decks, bravely defying the rain. Bunting usually signified celebration, when all Maisie wanted was to scream her anguish and run away and hide.

'Come on,' her father barked. 'Let's get on board and out of the rain.'

Well, at least that was something they agreed on! Maisie lumbered forward with the suitcase, the shoe bag dangling on her back. The quay was alive with activity, men in worn suits and flat caps milling about, loading or unloading goods from lorries. Packing crates were being taken up ramps into openings in the side of the ship and Maisie prayed it would be watertight once it set sail.

She followed her father to the bottom of the passenger gangway. Two men in uniform stood there, and Maisie put down the case as Francis handed the gaberdine coat to her and fumbled inside his jacket to extract some papers. Maisie waited, her heart thundering. She should have been brimming with excitement at this adventure. Had she been able to say a proper goodbye to her friends, and had her father been a kind and loving man, one who'd always written to her or even come to visit her once in a while, it might have been different. As it was, all she felt now was a mixture of fear and resentment.

'Let me take that for you, miss. Can't have a wee colleen carrying that, so we can't.'

Maisie glanced up from trying to manoeuvre the case onto the narrow gangway. The steward threw a dark look at her father's back as he strode up the walkway, then smiled broadly at Maisie as he took the suitcase and carried it up and onto the ship. Maisie followed, her pulse flying as she crossed the gap between the quayside and the looming hull, trying not to imagine falling over the handrails and into the murky water. The ship seemed to swallow her up as she stepped onto the deck, and there was an unpleasant salty, metallic smell that seemed to cling to her lips.

'What's your cabin number, sir? I'll take your—'

'Do I look as if I have money for a cabin?' Francis snapped. 'We're in steerage. And don't expect a tip. My daughter can carry her case herself.'

'Sure, I wouldn't let the poor girl do that, little will-o-the-wisp that she is.'

The steward cast a surreptitious wink in Maisie's direction and led them along a passageway and down several flights of steep stairs. It seemed they were descending into the bowels of the ship, and Maisie's heart was racing with panic. They must be below the waterline. What if the vessel began to sink? They'd be trapped and would surely drown.

It wasn't helped by the fact that when they reached the bottom, a few other passengers were already milling in the low, cramped space that was lined with rows of narrow bunks. They were stuffing their cases or bundles in the spaces underneath, and were far poorer than anyone she'd ever seen before. Were they all hoping to find a better life in England? She knew that times were hard for many in Ireland, that there was little work and poverty was rife. Didn't the poor of Cobh come to the convent once a week to receive a shilling or two of alms? But these poor souls were dressed in little more than rags with broken shoes on their feet. She realised at once what a privileged life she'd led at the convent, so maybe her father had done the best thing for her, after all. And at least he had a job, or so she'd been told, so she wouldn't go hungry like some of their fellow passengers evidently did. Some of them were thin as rakes.

'Come along, miss.'

Maisie realised the steward was beckoning her, and squeezed along the narrow space between the berths, jostled and knocked by other people trying to get organised. She held her breath as they got further away from the stairs and her escape route, and felt little relief when the man finally stopped.

'Right, these are yours,' he said, indicating the steel number plates fixed to the bedrails. 'I'll put your case underneath. I'd keep an eye on it if I were you. Some of these people are desperate, so they are. Good luck if I don't see you again, miss.'

He turned and began shouldering his way back down the line, not bothering, Maisie noticed, to hover by her father for a tip.

'You can have the top bunk,' Francis growled at her now. 'Can't expect me to climb up there.'

Maisie glanced up. There was so little headroom on the upper berths that she'd be in danger of hitting her head on the metal beams above if she wasn't careful. To be fair, the lower bunks fared little better. How they were supposed to sleep that night anyway, she had no idea. More passengers were cramming into the crowded space, the noise growing louder and louder. She could hear more than one baby crying as whole families shuffled in, and children were shouting or complaining in equal measure. The smell of unwashed bodies and wet clothing was becoming overpowering, and Maisie felt panic rising nauseously inside her.

'I'm going back up on deck,' she announced, near to gagging.

'No, you're not,' came her father's harsh reply. 'You heard what the steward said.'

'I'll take the school coat and the shoe bag with me,' she answered back. After all, the bag contained everything that really mattered to her. The clothes were lovely and she wouldn't want them stolen, but if her father was that worried, he could jolly well guard the suitcase himself.

'I said you're staying here.'

'No, I'm not, and you'll not be stopping me. You'll not deny me saying goodbye to the home you're dragging me away from, so you won't! I should just be able to see the cathedral at Cobh once we've sailed out of the passage. I might not have been here before, but I know what it looks like on a map.'

Her father shook his head with a snorting laugh. 'You stupid child. I told you we don't sail until later so it'll be dark by the time we get out into Cork Harbour. And with this rain, you wouldn't see a thing anyway.'

Maisie felt as if she'd been doused in icy water. Not see the cathedral standing proudly against the sky at the top of the steep hill? The cathedral where she'd been taken to worship every Sunday since she could remember, and where she'd made her First Communion? And she'd hoped she might catch one last glimpse of the convent atop the opposite hill to the left, the long building with its attic windows high up in the eaves where most of the dormitories were. She'd even imagined she might see something fluttering from one of those windows as, seeing the *Innisfallen* crossing the harbour and knowing she was aboard, Noreen would be vigorously waving a pillowcase in fond farewell. They'd done that sometimes for fun, wondering what adventures the passengers were planning. Only now did it dawn on Maisie that it was only during the long, light days of summer that they'd seen the ship either arriving early in the morning or leaving in the evening.

Her heart fell with dejection, and she dropped down onto the lower bunk. It was all her father's fault. He'd stolen — yes, stolen — her life from her, and she hated him for it.

'Well, if we don't sail until later, why all the hurry to get here?' she demanded. 'I could have said a proper goodbye to my friends.'

'Because you don't know what delays we might have had getting here, you little fool. What if the train had broken down? And you can see how getting organised on board can be chaotic,' Francis snapped at her, jerking his head at the other passengers.

Huh, she'd rather not be reminded. The space was now heaving with fellow passengers, some excited, others weighed down with the cares of the world, or so it seemed. Maisie sat still, working her lower jaw. She shuddered when her father sat down beside her. Why oh, why had he come for her?

'So why haven't you got any luggage?' she demanded accusingly.

'What, for just two nights on board? And I'd only have to lug it around with me.'

Maisie supposed that made sense. But why was her father being so sharp with her? There were so many other questions she wanted to ask, but they would wait until later. Just now, it was taking all her courage not to give way to tears. And to make things worse, as her father swung his legs up onto the berth, he kicked her and then, lying down, he closed his eyes. So that was it. She was dismissed.

Gazing absently at the shoe bag on the bed beside her, Maisie suddenly remembered the book Sister Agnes had given her. Well, that might provide a distraction for a while. She carefully took it out. It was bound in red linen with the lettering, *Jane Eyre* by Charlotte Brontë, in black. As she opened it, Maisie saw that something had been written in a neat hand on the fly leaf.

To my dearest Maisie,
Always remember that I am by your side.
May God go with you.
Sister Agnes

A huge lump swelled in Maisie's throat. Dear Sister Agnes. Would she ever see her again? Brushing aside the moisture in her eyes, Maisie began to read. The light was poor and she was aware of so many people milling all around her, but by the end of the first page, she was already being drawn into the story. The sombre tone echoed her own mood. Jane Eyre was being treated like an inanimate object with no feelings of her own, just like Maisie was experiencing now.

Within minutes, she was totally absorbed in the book, and it took her by surprise when she heard the deep rumbling of the engines suddenly increase. They must be about to set sail, and all the anxiety sprang back into her. She glanced at her father. He hadn't moved. Maisie slipped the book back into the shoe bag and, slinging it over her shoulder, elbowed her way through their fellow passengers towards the stairs. She wasn't going to let her father stop her watching their departure, her last chance to say goodbye to the country that would for ever be home.

She finally reached the open deck, and gulped fresh air down into her lungs. She joined a group of passengers who, like herself, had gathered to watch. They had happy, smiling faces, not like those down in steerage, and were far better dressed. In her smart coat, Maisie felt more comfortable beside them, her unease less intense. She saw then that they were waving to others standing on the quayside by a parked motorcar. It made her wonder what their circumstances were. Off on an adventure, perhaps, or visiting friends.

Maisie sighed. She wished she felt like that, excited, eager, instead of feeling as if she was falling headlong into the unknown. Leaning on the rail, her eyes wandered over the scene below. The light was fading just as her father had said it would, the lamp posts on the quayside already lit and shining on the wet ground, and she saw the gangway — her last means of escape — being hauled away. Dockworkers on shore were lifting impossibly huge ropes from around giant bollards, letting them fall into the water with loud splashes, and then she could see that they were being drawn up into holes high up on the ship's hull.

The ship's horn gave a deafening roar, reverberating in her ears. And then the deck vibrated beneath her feet. They were moving. This was it. She tried to blink away her tears, but this time it was hopeless and in seconds, they were streaming down her cheeks. She angrily brushed them away. She didn't want her final vision of home to be blurred.

The ship edged slowly away from the quay and began to head down river. She knew they had to navigate the passage to the west of the island on which Cobh stood before they reached Cork Harbour and the open sea beyond. But she'd see nothing of it. The rain had turned to a fine mist like low cloud that was obliterating everything beyond a few yards away. A tide of loneliness washed through Maisie, despite the crush of other passengers all around her. Would she ever see Ireland again?

CHAPTER SEVEN

'There you are,' her father's voice hissed in her ear. 'I thought I told you—'

Maisie's heart landed somewhere deep in her stomach, but she wasn't going to kowtow to this stranger. 'You won't be telling me anything, so you won't,' she rounded on him. 'And I see it's all right for you to come up on deck. I thought you were worried about the suitcase.'

'Well, they're your clothes. If they're stolen, you'll be the one with nothing to wear.'

'Then let's hope they're not.' She gave him a quick, sardonic smile and went to move away, but he caught her arm and spun her round.

'Don't you backchat me or I'll—'

'Or you'll what? What more could you do to hurt me? Within a few hours you've ruined my life, taken me away from my friends and my home, and are taking me to live in a strange country against my will. I was always told you were dead. That I had no father. When all the time you were living in England. Never once did you even write.'

She ground the words out between clenched teeth, barely controlling her anger. Hot tears were burning at the back of her eyes again, but she wouldn't let them fall. If she had to go and live with this man, she wasn't going to let him humiliate her, too.

'Shut up,' he reprimanded, his fingers tightening on her arm. 'You're causing a scene. If you can hold your tongue for long enough, we'll go and find some supper and I can explain.'

'Yes, I think you've got a lot of explaining to do, so!'

Though anger bubbled inside her, she supposed she ought to listen to whatever he had to say. And he was right that people were looking, those that were still on deck. The dense cloud had made the autumn evening close in even earlier and there was literally nothing more to be seen through the darkness, so she might as well follow her father back inside.

The interior of the ship was like a maze, but Francis must have learned his way around on the trip over. He sat Maisie down on a hard chair at one of many small tables that she noted were fixed to the floor in an on board tea room, for want of a better way to describe it. Her stomach rumbled with hunger, though she felt that if she tried to eat anything, she would gag on it. She watched, her eyes hard with contempt, as her father returned from the counter carrying a cup of tea in his right hand.

'There's another cup and some sandwiches waiting up at the counter,' he told her gruffly as he put the cup on the table. 'It's easier if you go and get them.'

So, there really did appear to be something wrong with his left hand, Maisie observed as she obeyed. And it was just as well she'd done as he asked. The ship suddenly rolled, making her stagger slightly, but she reflected that it could have sent her father sprawling. The *Innisfallen* must have left the calmer waters of Cork Harbour and hit the open sea. Fortunately Maisie had kept her balance, otherwise her father would doubtless have reprimanded her for spilling the tea.

She sat back down opposite him and met his gaze steadily, her eyebrows fiercely arched. Whatever he had to say, it had better be good.

But he made her wait, sipping at his tea before he spoke and making her pulse beat harder in anticipation.

'When your mother died,' he began at last, his voice terse, 'I had nobody to turn to. No family to look after a baby. So what was I to do? I'd been a master miller, as were my father and grandfather before me. I'd managed mills for their owners in various places all my life. We'd had a good life, your mother and I. Always a nice house. We saw different parts of the country. We'd married late, and I was fifteen years older than your mother. We never thought we'd have children, and that suited me fine. I liked things the way they were, just me and your mother. And then you came along.'

He paused, his eyes narrowed as if observing her keenly. Was he telling her that he'd never wanted her in the first place, or that her mother had died giving birth to her? In the latter case, she could understand why he'd wanted nothing to do with her. For a while, at least, until his grief had run its course. But she'd been two years old when she'd been left at the convent. Surely that was long enough?

'Are you saying that . . . my mother died because of me?' she faltered, not wanting even to contemplate his alternative meaning.

'Yes,' he barked back, and she recoiled at his sharpness. 'But everything else was changing, too. So many of the mills had closed down. The one in Buttevant where we were living actually burned down shortly after you were born. As manager, I was blamed, though it wasn't my fault. So I knew I'd never get another job as a miller, even if there were any to be found. I'd been paying a neighbour to look after you, but once the mill burned down, I had no income. The British Army had left so there was no work to be done for them, even if I'd wanted it. You know all about the British, I suppose? The nuns taught you more than just how to pray, I hope.'

Maisie nodded as she swallowed a mouthful of tea. Despite herself, she was becoming interested. The Reverend Mother had touched on her past, but she'd been so shocked at the time that she hadn't taken much of it in. But now her father was telling her about who she really was, even if it was true that he had never wanted children. She'd never known anything about her past before, and it intrigued her.

'Sure, of course,' she answered, and even found herself reaching for one of the sandwiches as her appetite returned. 'We were taught how the English treated our land like their own for hundreds of years. And then there was what happened after the uprising in 1916. Don't I know the history of Ireland as well as anyone.'

She saw him raise a surprised eyebrow. 'A good thing, too, not that it'll get you far where we're going. We Irish are still looked down on by so many in England. So the sooner you lose that accent of yours, the better.'

Maisie blinked hard at him. If England was such a terrible place, why had he made it his home, and why was he dragging her there when she could have made herself a good life in Ireland? And when he didn't really want her anyway? But she was nevertheless curious about her own background.

'So what happened, then? After the mill burned down?' she prompted.

'With no work, my savings soon ran out,' her father answered, and she could detect bitterness in his voice. 'There was a massive British barracks in the town. When the devils had left, that, too, had been burnt down. All that was left was the massive perimeter wall, and outside it, a couple of rows of tiny, back-to-back houses. Married quarters for the common soldiers, so they were. Wouldn't have been at all bad when they were first built, but they'd been allowed to deteriorate. But before the British left, someone in the town had seen an opportunity and bought them from the British to rent out. With so little money, I was reduced to renting one of them. Living in a hovel with no wife and a small baby to take care of.'

Maisie lowered her eyes. It was a sad story. Her story. She could imagine how humiliated her father must have felt. She'd noticed a slip of his own tongue, mind, even if he'd pretty well lost his own accent in the ten years he'd been living in England. Would she have to be careful herself? The future felt even more unsure than ever.

'And then?' she pressed.

'I got the odd bit of work as a farm labourer so I could pay the woman who looked after you while I wasn't there. I scraped by. But only just.'

Maisie nodded thoughtfully. It was a lot to take in. No wonder he'd considered she'd be better off at the convent. 'So . . . my mother died having me?' she dared to ask.

Her father's lips tightened. 'A couple of weeks later. From the sort of infection women can sometimes get after childbirth. She seemed all right at first, but she went down with it about ten days after you were born and it took her very quickly.'

'Oh, that's dreadful, so it is.' Maisie couldn't help but reach out to squeeze his arm, for the first time, feeling some connection to him. 'I'm so sorry.'

'You can keep your sympathies,' he snorted, shaking off her hand. 'You were a millstone round my neck. A couple of years later, the stress of it all gave me a stroke, if you know what that is. I was fifty-seven years old and left with a useless left arm. I couldn't even work on the farms when there was work to be had, and I was saddled with a bawling two-year-old. So there was no choice but to leave you at the convent. You should consider yourself lucky. It was better than going to an orphanage.'

'Yes, I can see that,' she conceded grudgingly, feeling stung at his rejection of her attempt to give him sympathy. She could understand his rancour at what fate had thrown at him, but not how he seemed to blame her for it. But maybe if she could prove to him over time what a good person she was, she might be able to bring him round. 'I've always been very happy at the convent. But why did you have the Reverend Mother lie to me all those years? Sure, it wouldn't have hurt for me to know I had a father living in England, and she'll have had to do such a lot of penance.'

'Huh.' Francis gave a short laugh which irritated Maisie further. 'I'm sure the Good Lord would forgive her such a fib without her having to say too many Hail Marys when it was for your own good.'

'My own good?' How on earth could he think that, Maisie asked herself. 'I don't know how you worked that one out!'

'Do I have to spell it out? If you'd known, you might've wanted to come and live with me, and I wasn't in a position to look after a small child, so that would've upset you. And don't forget, I'd had a stroke. Once you've had one, you might easily get another one which could kill you. In case that happened, I felt it better you always believed I died when you were a baby. That way, you'd just accept it and would never have to grieve over me.'

Maisie had been listening intently, but now she glared back at him. 'Sure, that seems a mighty strange way of looking at it,' she fumed, just managing to keep the lid on her anger. 'So what's changed now that you're forcing me to come and live with you?'

'You've grown up, of course. Old enough to know the truth and to look after yourself. The Reverend Mother says you're very mature for your age, even if you have got into a few scrapes over the years. And you'll be out at work in two years' time, all the better to be familiar with your new surroundings before you start. And before you say anything, you'll stand a much better chance of a good future in England than in Ireland.'

'I hardly think so!' Maisie retorted. 'I'd have stayed at the pension school until at least sixteen. There was even talk of college—'

'Bah! Pie in the sky! Get a job at ground level and work your way up. And you'll be earning some money while you're doing it.'

So that was it! As soon as she turned fourteen, the summer after next, he'd have her go out to work and earn money to give to him. Well, when the time came, she'd jolly well find a way to forge a life for herself and wouldn't give him one penny!

'So,' she said, her mouth rigid with sarcasm, 'we're off to London to make our fortunes, are we, if the opportunities are so good?'

'No. Not London. Plymouth. It's a big town on the southwest coast. Plenty of work, but you've got the sea. I thought you'd like that. A bit like Cobh only a lot bigger. And you can catch a train up onto the moors.'

'Oh.' Well, Maisie supposed that sounded a lot better than London, but she wasn't going to say so. After all, she was sure that if her father had been living and working in the capital, he'd have dragged her off there without a second thought. She'd heard that London spread out for miles and miles with narrow back streets lined with small Victorian terraces that only had tiny back yards, and she didn't fancy that. There were public parks, of course, but they'd be crowded with other people, and it would hardly be the same as the gardens at the Bishop's Palace. Sister Agnes still sometimes managed to get permission for her to visit there with her, she loved it so much. That was something else she was going to miss dreadfully.

Francis had fixed her with eyes that radiated a mixture of scorn and self-satisfaction, but Maisie wasn't going to let him get away with that. Instead, she neatly changed the subject.

'So how come you ended up in — where did you say? It's a long way from London, I'm thinking, if it's in the South West.'

'Plymouth. And yes it is. Nearly three hundred miles, I'd say. In the county of Devon. It's where the Pilgrim Fathers sailed from, if you've done that in history.'

'Oh, well, yes, we have,' Maisie nodded, pleased that she could talk confidently about it. 'I remember about Plymouth and the Pilgrim Fathers now. Puritans, so they were. The ship they set out for America in was called the *Mayflower*. There's a famous painting about it.'

'Hmm,' Francis grunted, almost as if he was disappointed that she'd robbed him of the chance to ridicule her ignorance. 'There's a big naval base there, too,' he went on instead. 'Called Devonport. I bet you didn't know that.'

She lifted her chin. 'No, I didn't. But I'm only twelve. You can't expect me to know everything.'

She glared at him challengingly, though what she expected him to reply, she didn't know. She just wished so vehemently that she was back at the convent, doing her homework before bedtime. But she really mustn't think like that or she might give in to tears again. Then he'd consider her weak and bully her even more.

'Well, you've a lot to learn then, haven't you?' he said with a smug sneer.

'Of course. As I expect you did, too, when you first went to England.' Maisie managed to turn the tables on him. 'So you're working in a mill now, are you, in this Plymouth?'

She felt pleased with herself when, for a just a second, her father looked as if the wind had been taken out of his sails.

'Actually, no.' She noted with grim satisfaction his discomfort at answering. 'This ferry route wasn't running in those days, so I landed in Liverpool. I tried for some time, but I couldn't find suitable work in the area, and someone I got talking to suggested I tried either East Anglia or the West Country, as they call it. So I tossed a coin, and ended up in Devon. I found some mills, all right. One was even a papermill. But no one needed a manager and I can't do anything manual for obvious reasons. So I went to Plymouth and got whatever clerical work I could until I eventually ended up in the accounts office of a big department store. Dingles, it's called. I'm in charge of a small section, but I only earn enough to get by. Once I got established there, I started sending money to the convent for your upkeep and now I'll have to pay for all your needs here. But don't think I'm well off and don't expect to be spoiled.'

'Spoiled?' Maisie retorted. 'Are you thinking I was ever spoiled at the convent? I watched other girls get birthday presents from their families, or go home for the holidays and Christmas, and I so wanted to be like them. If it hadn't been for Sister Agnes in particular and my best friend, Noreen, who stays there because her dad's away in the army, I'd have had nothing. I was just like the handful of other orphans there, when all the time I had a father living across the sea! But I didn't know, and not once did he write or come to visit me!'

'No, I didn't, so there's an end to it,' Francis barked back at her. 'Now, if you've finished your tea, we'll go back down and get some sleep. We've a long day ahead of us tomorrow. And I hope for your sake that the case is still there.'

Maisie could see from the expression on his face that the conversation was indeed at an end. And it wouldn't change the past, anyway. Or the future. At least she knew a little more now about where she was going. Not that it helped or gave her any more confidence. There were so many more questions she wanted to ask, but she really didn't want to hear the answers from her father's tight-lipped mouth.

She followed him back down the flights of stairs to the steerage accommodation. The ship was rolling rhythmically from side to side, and she found it easier to keep her balance if she walked with her feet apart. The airlessness and stale odour of so many bodies crammed together hit her once again as they shuffled along the row of bunks to their allocated berths. Children were already curled up asleep, and most adults were ready to doze off. But Maisie knew that for her it was going to be a long night.

The first thing she did was to check on the suitcase and the gaberdine stowed under the lower bed. She sighed with relief as thankfully her new wardrobe of clothes was still there, the locks on the case intact. Her father jerked his head, indicating that she should get up into the top bunk. She took off her coat and threw it up, then clambered up after it.

She'd seen that pillows and blankets were provided, and tried to make herself comfortable. Her new clothes would get creased, but she wasn't going to take anything off and she was pleased she was wearing the navy skirt and a thick bottle green jumper rather than the outfit Mrs X had gleefully proclaimed would do for best. The blanket was of poor quality and scratchy, and the thin mattress seemed to dig into her bones, but she didn't want to wriggle around to find a better sleeping position as it would only give her father another cause for complaint. At least the pillowcase smelled freshly washed, though the pillow itself was lumpy. Maisie wondered how many others had lain their heads on it over the years. She hoped she wasn't going to catch lice from it.

With that disgusting thought in mind, she tried to settle down for the night, listening to the creaking of the ship as it rocked from side to side. She was surprised to find the motion quite soothing. Others obviously didn't, and a couple of times she heard someone vomiting into the bowls provided, adding to the putrid stench. She tried to ignore the sounds around her, people breathing heavily in their sleep or snoring, someone coughing or a baby crying. She could hear a few people still talking in whispering voices. She wished she could hear what they were saying as it might take her mind off her own anguish, but she couldn't distinguish their words.

Instead, the awful events of the day whirled around inside her head. What a monster her father was, to make the Reverend Mother lie to her all those years, and now she was being forced to go and live with him. She really couldn't believe what was happening.

Misery wreathed itself about her. Though a couple of dim lights glowed from the low ceiling, the darkness seemed to close in on her, crushing her young heart. She wanted to be strong, just like Sister Agnes had said. But just now, she was broken. All she could think of was Noreen, lying awake in her bed too, no doubt crying her heart out because they'd been so cruelly torn apart. And Sister Agnes, weeping in her room.

Slán, my dearest friends, Maisie whispered into the night.

CHAPTER EIGHT

Maisie trudged along behind her father, her feet placing themselves mindlessly one in front of each other like some mechanical puppet. On and on they went, and Maisie wondered if they'd ever arrive or if she was living through some endless nightmare. She was so tired, her mind felt numb and empty, and it was a struggle not to just give up and dissolve in a heap on the pavement.

She'd hardly slept a wink that night aboard the ship. She was sure the rocking motion would soothe her into welcome oblivion, but no such luck. The sounds and closeness of so many strangers all sharing the same fetid air had been suffocating. Whenever she'd felt she might drift off, her stomach started churning again, her thoughts racing. More than anything, images of the convent and her friends pierced her closed eyelids, and made tears squeeze out beneath them again. The only way she could stop herself crying in full flow was to tell herself that at least she'd never have to come up against Helen again. Huh! She felt just now that she'd rather face a hundred Helens if it meant she could be back at the convent.

She glared at her father's back as he walked ahead through Plymouth's darkened streets. He clearly felt nothing for her, so why *had* he gone to all that bother to get her back? All day, fury had blazed inside her, but now she was too worn out to feel anything but exhaustion.

Once they'd docked at Fishguard that morning Maisie had paused to gulp in the fresh air, but her father had chivvied her along. They had a train to catch — along with almost everyone else, it seemed. Unlike the train on the previous day, this one was packed. Finding a seat had been a scramble, and as she'd discovered the previous day, the case was too big for the overhead luggage racks. So, to the annoyance of at least one other of their companions in the compartment, she had to put it under her seat and prop her feet up on the bit that stuck out.

She'd hoped her father might be more pleasant today and talk to her on the journey, maybe tell her more about the place that was to be her home from now on. But no. Most of the time, he either turned his head to stare out of the window or closed his eyes as if asleep.

'Will you be going all the way to London?' a young woman sitting opposite asked her with a nervous smile.

She seemed a pleasant sort, and Maisie returned her smile. She might have a little decent company for a while at least.

'Er, no, I don't think so,' she replied. 'We're going to Plymouth.'

'Plymouth? Sure, where's that?'

'Down in the South West, so I think we have to change trains a couple of times.'

'Of course, we do,' her father snapped, suddenly opening his eyes.

Maisie glared back at him, biting her tongue. Why did he seem to want to belittle her at every turn? Fortunately, his eyelids drooped again almost at once, and Maisie turned her attention back to the older girl who pulled a face, in sympathy with Maisie at having such a belligerent travelling companion.

'What about you? Are you going to London?' she asked, determined not to let her father's presence stop her having a pleasant conversation to help pass the time.

'I am so. Me cousin's got us a job as a housemaid at the big posh house where she works. Ever since the war, posh people have had a job to get staff. Most women prefer to do other work nowadays, in offices or whatever. But sure, I don't mind hard work and I love the idea of living in a proper grand house. Me cousin says you have plenty to eat and the master and mistress treat you well. Have to, if they want you to stay,' she concluded with a wink.

Maisie nodded back. She supposed that made sense but she felt a twinge of jealousy. The girl sitting opposite had a choice in the matter, whereas Maisie had been forced to come to England.

'But aren't I guessing you're young enough to still be at school,' the stranger was saying. 'From what you said, sounds as if it's your first time in England, too.'

'It is so,' Maisie confirmed. 'And yes, I've got two more years at school. I'd have liked to stay on and go to college, but I don't suppose I'll get the chance now,' she added glumly.

'Sure, I've never been too good at the learning,' her new friend came back cheerfully. 'So this is a grand opportunity for me to travel away from home. Paying my fare, so they are.' She nodded at the window. 'Pity it's such a miserable day. You can't see much out of the windows for the rain, even if they weren't all misted up with us all squashed in here like sardines.'

Maisie nodded in agreement. Had it been a clear, sunny day, gazing out of the window might have provided a distraction. She knew from her geography lessons that the railway must skirt the bottom of the Welsh mountains. She wondered whether she would have been able to see them, or whether they were too far away? She'd never know. At least chatting to this friendly young woman helped that leg of the journey pass more quickly, and Maisie was disappointed when her father told her gruffly that they'd be changing trains at the next station.

'Good luck!' the housemaid-to-be called as Maisie struggled out of the compartment with the case.

'You, too!' she called back over her shoulder as they shuffled along the corridor and negotiated the steep step down to the platform.

Meeting the girl had been the best part of the journey. Changing trains more than once, heaving the case up and down flights of steps and along platforms and up into carriages had made her shoulders protest. It was such a relief when her father informed her they were on the final train, although it would be a good couple of hours before they reached Plymouth. They were soon steaming through countryside, but Maisie could still see little of it for a heavy mist, and now the light was fading fast.

It was fully dark and raining hard as they chugged into Plymouth. Maisie managed to drum up a spark of enthusiasm as dull street lights punctuated the blackness. From what she could see, it was nothing like Cobh, as her father had described it. The buildings seemed to go on for ever, and they'd already stopped at one station, so the place must be massive to have more than one. They hadn't reached their own stop yet, and she hadn't caught so much as a glimpse of the sea as her father had promised. So had he been lying to her about the place that was to be her home from now on? It wouldn't surprise her.

'So where's the sea, then?' she couldn't stop herself demanding as they finally got off the train at another station which seemed enormous with several tracks running through it.

'Those other lines run down to the docks,' Francis answered curtly as they emerged onto the street outside. 'And the sea's beyond those. Plymouth Sound it's called. Now stop asking questions and hurry up. We're going to get soaked as it is.'

Well, he was certainly right there. Maisie had managed to pull the gaberdine on over her new best coat, but she couldn't fasten the buttons down the front. It did give her a little extra protection, though. She'd tied the strings of the hood under her chin which at least stopped the rain running down the

74

back of her neck. But it still drove into her face and dripped from her chin. Her father, unsurprisingly, forged on ahead, collar turned up and hat rammed down on his head.

Very shortly, they crossed what seemed a fairly busy road underneath a wide railway bridge that Maisie realised they must just have gone over when still on the train. Peering through the sheeting rain, she could see that the street was dead straight, disappearing into the distance, and went on a fair way in the opposite direction, too. Tramlines ran up and down it, and the pavements were lined with shops, many of which must still have been open since there were a lot of people about. But it was mainly men, oddly all wearing white hats, Maisie noticed, who were scurrying about in the rain before disappearing inside.

'Get a move on,' her father barked over his shoulder, and Maisie hurried to catch up with him.

They continued on for what seemed an age, past where the road opened up into a town square shaped like an octagon. Why didn't they get on a tram if they were going so far? Soon afterwards, they turned down what appeared another main street, and then kept going. Maisie thought it would never end. She longed desperately for a rest, but her father was putting more and more space between them. Why wouldn't he wait? She called out to him once or twice, but either he didn't hear through the battering rain or he chose to ignore her.

At long last, he turned off into a side street, and yet again he failed to wait for her. Maisie was scared she'd get lost in a maze of back streets, and tears of despair began to spill down her cheeks, mingling with the rain. She was cold, wet, hungry and more miserable than she'd ever been in her life. She no longer cared where they were going. She just wanted to get in out of the rain, curl up in a ball and fall asleep. And she really wouldn't care if she never woke up again.

Then, thank goodness! She saw Francis had stopped in front of a door a little way along, fumbling briefly inside his pocket for a key, she assumed. From the jaundiced glow of a hazy street light, she'd seen that they were walking down a narrow back street with humble, terraced houses fronting directly onto the pavements on either side. But it hardly registered with her as her father turned the key in the lock and pushed open the door.

He must have flicked the light switch as a moment later, she saw they were standing in a narrow hallway. Her father was disrobing himself awkwardly of his sodden coat and hat. Should she go to help him? But that would probably be wrong, too, so she dumped the case on the floor and pulled off her drenched gaberdine. Both of them left a puddle on the linoleum, but Francis didn't seem too bothered, so Maisie copied him in hanging the garment on a simple hall stand at the bottom of a flight of stairs. Although protected from the worst of the deluge by the gaberdine over the top, her best coat was still damp, and she hung that up as well.

'That's the parlour,' her father suddenly grunted, jabbing his head at a door and making Maisie jump as he broke his taciturn silence of the journey. 'It's out of bounds to you. I keep it locked, so don't think of trying to get in. Your bedroom's the one at the back,' he informed her, pointing up the stairs. 'There's sheets on the bed, but you'll have to make it up yourself. Hurry up and come down when you've done. I'll make us some tea, and then it's off to bed. I've work in the morning and you've got school.'

Maisie swallowed down her anguish as he retreated through another door by the stairs. School? Couldn't she have just one day to settle in? Obviously not. She picked up the dripping shoe bag by its strings and grasping the case, heaved it up the bare wooden steps. At the top was a tiny landing, and it was clear which room was hers. Her heart jumped a beat as she opened the door. So this was to be her home until — well, she didn't know when.

Her hand found the switch and a bare light bulb gleamed from a twisted cord in the middle of the ceiling. Looking around, she supposed it wasn't too bad. The room was small but adequate, with an iron bedstead much like the ones she'd slept in at the convent, complete with sheets, two blankets and an eiderdown folded over the bottom. There was a chest of drawers but nothing else, not even curtains at the window, she realised as she felt her spirits land somewhere at her feet again.

Always be that stubborn, determined little girl I know, she heard Sister Agnes's voice in her head.

Oh, no! The book! Maisie swiftly pulled open the strings of the shoe bag and extricated her prized possession. It was wet through, the red dye on the thin leather streaked and leaching into the edges of the pages. She could have wept, but there was no point. She must pull herself together. If she could peel the pages apart as they dried, perhaps she could rescue it. But she mustn't be long. She still had the bed to make up. At least it should be more comfortable than the berth on the ship.

She took off her squelching shoes and socks. Mrs X had given her some soft, plush shoes that she'd called slippers, and Maisie was so grateful for them now. She rummaged about in the case to find them, pushed her feet into them, and padded back downstairs.

The room at the back was evidently the kitchen, not that there was much to show for it. At the far end of a scratched and battered table was a brick fireplace housing a tiny version of the huge coal range the nuns had in their kitchen. But it wasn't lit, so how could her father make them any tea? Then through a further door, she spied him standing by a small cabinet next to a sink. On top of it was a metal tray on which stood a small contraption with flames coming from a burner. A dented kettle was balanced on top, and steam was billowing from the spout.

'What took you so long?' her father growled. He must have noticed her staring, as he then said with exasperation, 'I suppose you've never seen a primus stove before. I'll have to show you how to use it without burning the place down. But not now. There's food on the table. You cut up the bread and I'll bring in the tea.'

She paused. She'd never cut bread before, but she managed to hack a couple of thick slices from the half loaf on the table. All there was to spread on it was dripping in a chipped enamel mug. She knew what dripping was. The nuns used it for cooking, but she'd never had it on bread. The girls always had creamy butter instead.

Her father made two trips over with the mugs of tea. He threw a disparaging glance at the doorsteps she'd cut, but said nothing as he pulled the dripping towards him and ladled some onto his bread. Just as well he made no remarks, as Maisie was ready to tell him he should have cut the loaf himself if he thought he could do any better with only one hand!

'Where's the lavatory?' she asked instead. He couldn't object to her asking that now. Or could he?

'Out the back,' he grumbled at her. 'There's a torch hanging on the back door. But don't be long. Batteries cost money.'

Maisie's heart dropped even further. She'd never used an outside privy — and in this rain! She'd have to be quick or she'd get soaked all over again, and she didn't want to ruin the lovely new slippers. Still, she was glad to escape her father's presence for a few minutes. She found her way by torchlight out into a yard at the back. There were two doors into a single-storey extension to the house, and mercifully, the first one was what she was looking for. It seemed clean enough but it was freezing cold. And there were probably spiders lurking in the shadows. At least there was a proper chain to pull. She let herself feel grateful for small mercies. And then she had to face her father again.

Back inside, she washed her hands under the one tap over the butler sink in the little scullery, aware out of the corner of her eye of her father sitting stiff and upright in the kitchen. As she went to sit down again, he nodded at a sheet of paper that had appeared on the table, together with a key on a string.

'Those are directions of how to get to your school,' he instructed. 'I have to leave for work earlier, so I can't take you. You have to be there for nine and it's a quarter of an hour's walk if you don't dawdle, so don't be late. I see you don't have a watch, but the clock on the mantelpiece is always right. I've had a key cut for you, and put it on a string to wear round your neck, so don't lose it. I'll expect the washing up to be done and the table laid by the time I get home at half past six. There's potatoes in the scullery. You can peel half of those ready for cooking, and you can make my bed, too. You can go into my room just for that and nothing else. Do I make myself clear?'

Oh, yes, very clear! But Maisie simply nodded her head. She was too tired to argue. She'd gone beyond her normal self, even the hunger that had been gnawing at her stomach for the last few hours of the journey. The bread was stale and dry, even with the dripping. But thankfully the tea was hot and sweet and helped her to force the bread down. She didn't want to wake up hungry in the middle of the night in this strange house.

When she'd finished the scant meal, she asked politely if she could get down from the table, said goodnight and went up to her room. She was even too tired to come back down again to clean her teeth. Especially as the scullery seemed to be the only place with running water — unless there was something behind the second door in the yard.

Up in her room, she extricated one of the nightdresses from the case, quickly changed into it and dived into bed. It struck as cold as ice and she lay there, shivering and quaking with unease, while she slowly warmed up. She heard her father come up the stairs not long afterwards, moving around in the room next door for a few minutes before thankfully all went quiet again.

So this was it. Her new life, such as it was. She supposed she must make the most of it. The moment she had the opportunity, she'd write to both Sister Agnes and Noreen and tell them how she was getting on. The thought brought her some sort of comfort. But her heart lurched when she remembered that the next morning she was to make her own way to her new school and introduce herself to the teachers and her new classmates. She was hardly looking forward to it, and her pulse began to thump again. But if she could face Helen, she was sure she could face anyone. Surely no one would be as horrible as she was.

Holding that thought in her head, Maisie snuggled down further in the bed. She'd forgotten her prayers, so she said a quick few words to Our Lady, hoping she'd be forgiven for making it so short, and tried to let her mind drift away. But exhausted though she was, it was some time before she finally slipped into a fitful, nervous sleep.

CHAPTER NINE

Maisie dragged herself from a confused, unsettled sleep. She'd been woken by loud banging, and, gazing bewilderedly around the room, remembered with an unwelcome jolt where she was. Sure, that must be her father knocking on her bedroom door, and then wasn't it his voice she heard calling.

'Wake up! If you don't get up soon, you'll be late for school!'

Oh, goodness, school! Maisie launched herself out of bed, her mind leaping into gear. She'd been so exhausted the previous evening that she hadn't unpacked and had simply collapsed into bed, even if she'd been too ill at ease to sleep properly in the end.

'I'll be down in a minute!' she called, frantically delving into the suitcase.

It must have satisfied her father as he stopped shouting and Maisie heard him going down the stairs. Well, at least he'd had the decency not to enter her bedroom, so that was something, she supposed.

School. Well, the navy skirt she'd travelled in lay crumpled on the floor, but it had already looked like a dish rag before she'd taken it off. At the convent, they'd been taught how to iron in their sewing lessons, but there was no time for that now, and heaven knew if her father possessed the necessary equipment anyway. She picked up the skirt and hung it over the bottom of the bedstead in the hope that the creases might fall out on their own. In the meantime, fingers crossed the black skirt hadn't got too squashed in the case. It would have to do anyway. She pulled on one of the white shirts and a dark blue jumper as well before hurrying downstairs.

To Maisie's relief, everywhere looked less intimidating in the daylight. The rain had stopped and there was even sunlight hovering at the windows. On the kitchen table sat the remains of the previous night's stale bread and the evil mug of dripping.

'Right, I'm off,' said her father in his usual gruff tone. 'You've got twenty minutes before you have to leave. Don't forget what I told you last night. And don't forget your key. You just pull the door behind you and it locks automatically.'

With that, he strode out of the room, and a minute or so later, Maisie heard the front door clunk behind him. He was gone.

Maisie realised she'd been holding her breath. Phew! Peace at last. She felt the tension drain out of her body and sank down on one of the chairs. Well, at least now she could investigate her new surroundings properly without him breathing down her neck. But, wait, she couldn't, could she? Just twenty minutes to have some breakfast, such as it was — upon investigation, there was tea in the pot, though it was only lukewarm — brave the lavatory again and clean her teeth before it was time to set off. If only he'd woken her earlier.

When she closed the front door behind her, she knew she was already behind schedule and would have to run. She just hoped her father's scribbled directions were easy to follow and that she didn't get lost. But if she did and she arrived late because of it, surely the school wouldn't blame her and would be appalled that she'd been left to find her own way on her very first day.

'Who be you, maid?'

The cackling voice behind her nearly made her jump out of her skin. She turned round to collide with a stooped, very old man with a grey, stubbly jaw which swung open, revealing toothless gums. She hadn't quite caught what he'd said and she certainly didn't have time to ask him to repeat it. And to be honest, she felt a bit frightened of him.

'Sorry, can't stop, so,' she mumbled, and ran away down the street.

As luck would have it, her father's directions were pretty precise. She didn't have time to take in her surroundings as she was too busy looking out for street names, and soon found herself standing outside the daunting edifice of the school. Other pupils were still walking in so she wasn't late. Oh, crikey! Some of them were boys! Was this a mixed school? Maisie had hardly ever seen boys, let alone spoken to one, and now she was going to be in a class with them. She realised then that there were two entrances, one with a carved lintel overhead that read Infants while the other read 1893. The older children were entering through the second archway, so gathering her courage, Maisie slid in behind a group of girls.

Once inside, she found herself in a corridor busy with pupils who obviously knew where they were going. While the boys were tramping up one set of stairs, all the girls were heading up another, so she followed them up to the first floor. From the sound of things, the boys had separate class-rooms on the floor above, so that was a relief! But now what? Catching sight of a woman among the students, she decided she must be a teacher.

Stubborn, determined.

Right, here goes. She marched straight up to her.

'Sure, good morning to you,' she blurted out in a rush before she lost her nerve. 'I'm Maisie O'Sullivan and my father says I'm starting here today, so please can you tell me where to go?'

'Oh.' The woman's eyebrows lifted in surprise. 'Are you on your own? Well, I'm not expecting anyone new in my class, but come with me and I'll find out for you. Class, I'll be back in a moment,' she called through the open door to a classroom. 'Come along now, cheel, and we'll get you sorted.'

Cheel? What the heck was a *cheel?* But the teacher at least seemed quite kind, and Maisie trotted along beside her. She wished she was going to be in her class, but after a few minutes of waiting in the corridor, she was ushered into a different classroom.

'Miss Mitchell, your new girl, Maisie O'Sullivan. Good luck, my dear,' the first teacher added as she turned away.

Maisie found herself standing alone in front of a class of about thirty girls seated at double desks, and cringed as she felt all eyes turn towards her. She wanted to turn and run, but the soles of her feet appeared glued to the floor. But then Miss Mitchell, a younger, thin woman with round, thick spectacles turned to her with a sharp nod of welcome.

'Maisie's come all the way from Ireland to join us,' she announced, 'so I want each one of you to make her feel at home. Now, let me see. Kitty Barron, you can look after her. Show her where to hang her coat and then come straight back. Maisie can share your desk as Irene's now left us.'

Maisie trembled slightly as she wondered what this Kitty would be like. The girl who stood up was on the chubby side, her pretty face framed by coppery brown hair cut in a fringe while two long plaits hung down around her shoulders. She gave Maisie such a beaming smile that Maisie found herself relaxing for the first time since she'd been dragged from her breakfast in the convent two days previously.

'Hello,' Kitty said, still smiling. 'It's this way.'

Chatting in a low voice as they went, she led Maisie back downstairs to where the cloakrooms were on the ground floor.

'Ireland sounds a mortal long way off,' she sympathised. 'Were you sad to leave? Only ever been as far as Saltash, me. Or up on the moor. Ah, there you go,' she said, pointing. 'That was Irene's old peg. You'd best have that one. Irene and me was best friends, but she's gone to live in America.'

'America? Sure, that really is a long way. Why has she gone there?'

'Got family in New York, I think. An uncle doing really well. Only been gone a week, but I really miss her. But you can be my best friend now, if you want. I like the way you talk. Your funny accent.'

'Well, to me, don't you talk funny!' Maisie found herself chuckling. 'But sure, thank you. I'd love to be your friend. I only arrived last night and I don't know anyone.'

'That's settled, then. I'll introduce you to everyone at playtime.'

'So tell me, what's the teacher like?' Maisie asked as they made their way back upstairs.

'Miss Mitchell? She can be a bit sharp, but she's all right if you work hard. Oh, looks like they've finished prayers, so it's straight into lessons.'

They went back into the classroom, and Maisie sat down at the desk with her new friend. It felt good to have someone on her side again. Perhaps her new school wouldn't be so bad after all.

'Now then, seeing as our first lesson is Geography,' Miss Mitchell announced, walking down one side of the room to various maps fixed on the wall, 'we'll look at our map of the British Isles. I wonder if you'd like to show us where you come from in Ireland, Maisie? And perhaps you'd like to tell us about your journey to get here. I'm sure the girls would love to hear about it, as most of them have never travelled outside Plymouth.'

Maisie felt her courage had been torn to ribbons again. Stand up in front of this class of strangers? She could feel herself trembling as she got to her feet and squeezed between the desks to stand by the map. She took a deep breath to calm herself, and then took the pointer Miss Mitchell was holding out to her.

'Well, this is Ireland, of course,' she began, her voice a small croak. 'And here's where I come from, down the south. This is Cork Harbour, where the big ships come. A bit like your Plymouth Sound.' That at least gave her some confidence. She remembered what her father had said the previous evening, so at least she didn't appear too ignorant. 'Only it wasn't Cork itself where I was brought up, but a small town on the waterfront called Cobh. You'll see the Irish spelling, C O B H, but isn't it pronounced Cove. But we had to get the train into Cork to get the boat, and we sailed overnight to Fishguard in Wales, which is . . . there,' she said, studying the map and reaching up with the pointer again. 'And then we got another train, but didn't we have to change several times to get here.'

'Very well done, Maisie,' Miss Mitchell smiled, taking the pointer from her. 'Now, has anyone any questions?'

Maisie saw Kitty's hand shoot up, and the teacher nodded her head at her.

'So why did you leave Ireland, then, if you don't mind us asking?'

Maisie froze. Surely she wasn't going to have to stand in front of this class of complete strangers and tell them all about herself? But she could tell Kitty was genuinely interested. And she supposed, after all, that her story would come out eventually. So she might as well brave it now.

'I was brought up in the convent in Cobh,' she began, her chin lifted. 'By nuns. My mammy had died when I was a babby, and my father couldn't look after me when I was so little. So he came to England and ended up living and working here in Plymouth. So now I'm old enough to take care of myself, he came and fetched me to come and live with him, and we arrived late last night. So here I am.'

She stopped, holding her breath as an awkward silence descended over the classroom. She certainly wasn't going to tell them all that she hadn't even known her father was still alive all those years, or that he'd been nothing but nasty and unkind to her ever since she met him just two days ago. She wanted them to think she was quite happy about it, excited to be starting a new life when she'd been separated from her father all that time. She didn't want them knowing that nothing could have been further from the truth.

'Well, I'm sure we'll all do our best to help you settle in, won't we, girls?' Miss Mitchell declared, her words spoken with a challenge — as if defying any one of them to disobey. 'You may sit down now, Maisie, and thank you for sharing your story. Now, then . . .'

Maisie felt as if she was clawing her way through a thick fog as she made her way back to the desk and sat down next to Kitty. The other girl gave her a warm, sympathetic smile as if she understood everything Maisie had kept hidden. Maisie acknowledged her with a nod, but was grateful to be able to turn her attention back to Miss Mitchell who was now instructing another girl to go up and point out various other places on the map.

Phew. Maisie was glad she was no longer the object of the class's attention, and settled down to join in the lesson. Mercifully, she soon felt just as if she were back in her school in Ireland, writing in one of the exercise books that had been placed in front of her. Green was for Geography at the front and History at the back, Kitty explained in a whisper, then it was blue for Arithmetic and red for English. As the morning wore on, Maisie's taut insides gradually untangled themselves and by the time the bell rang for lunchtime, she felt more relaxed. The lessons had been easy. There was nothing she didn't already know, but she kept that to herself. Sure, she didn't want to be labelled a know-it-all and make enemies before she'd even started. Hadn't she had enough problems with Helen and didn't want a repeat of that situation.

'As you don't appear to have a packed lunch, I assume your father gave you some dinner money?' Miss Mitchell asked her as they lined up by the door.

What? Maisie felt uncomfortable around her collar. Dinner money?

'Oh, sure, no he didn't,' she mumbled, somewhat taken aback and feeling deeply embarrassed. At the pension school, dinner had just appeared and she hadn't thought anything of it. But surely her father must have known what the situation was, she thought angrily. Had he deliberately not made provision for her so that she would be the object of mockery at school on her very first day?

'Well, perhaps he meant for you to go home for lunch?' Miss Mitchell suggested. 'You do have a full hour.'

Maisie's brow creased into a confused frown. 'He didn't say so. And there wasn't any food in the house. I had the last slice of bread for my breakfast.'

The only other food she'd seen were the potatoes she'd been ordered to peel when she got home. There wouldn't be time to cook them and have some for her lunch if she was to be back in time for afternoon school. Besides, she could only imagine her father scolding her for eating something that was destined for his plate.

But now she felt so stupid, standing there in front of the whole class. Miss Mitchell's expression was a mixture of surprise and sympathy, but Maisie daren't imagine what the other girls thought of her. But then her new friend, Kitty, came to the rescue.

'You can share my packed lunch,' she offered, waving a couple of packages. 'My mother always gives us far too much and expects us to eat it all. But you can help me out.'

'Well, I'm sure that's most generous of you, Kitty.' Miss Mitchell sounded genuinely impressed. 'But just this once. Maisie, please speak to your father and have something sorted out for tomorrow. If you're going to want school dinners, we collect the money on Monday mornings for the whole week, and I'm afraid you can't chop and change.'

'Yes, Miss Mitchell, of course. Sure, I expect my father just forgot. And thank you, Kitty. That's very kind. But I don't want you going hungry, so I don't.'

'Course not,' Kitty beamed. 'You'll be doing us a proper favour. Mother gets cross if I don't eat it all. Funny set ways she has. Come on. It's this way.'

The girls filed out of the classroom and down the stairs to use the cloakroom, then back upstairs to what was evidently the girls' school hall. It was already echoing noisily as other classes had already assembled and were putting up trestle tables and moving chairs. Three ladies in overalls were standing by trays of delicious-smelling hot food which tantalised Maisie's nostrils after two days of having so little appetising food to eat. But she was grateful to Kitty for offering to share her packed lunch. Otherwise, sure, what would she have done?

It turned out that only two others in the class, Beryl and Philippa, didn't have school dinners, and Maisie found herself sitting at a table with all three of them. Her stomach filled with butterflies again, driving away her appetite, because now she had to talk to these strangers and discover if they were indeed as pleasant as they appeared.

'I've got a whole round of egg sandwiches, and a pasty,' Kitty was saying as she unwrapped the two packages of greaseproof paper. 'Which would you like, or would you like half of each?'

'Sure, I can't have half,' Maisie answered awkwardly.

'Course you can. You look as if you need fattening up, and I'm not really that hungered.'

'Oh, well, in that case, half and half. But, did you say pasty?' Maisie asked, looking at the contents of the second package. 'That's not a pasty. Is it?'

Her heart shrivelled as she watched all three girls raise their eyebrows. They weren't going to laugh at her, were they?

'Ye-es,' Kitty replied hesitantly, and then her face broke into a grin. 'I suppose you don't have them in Ireland.'

'Not where I come from, no. But up in the north, they have something called a pasty. Though sure, they're more like a ball of mince and chopped onion fried in batter. Nothing like that. So what's in it?'

'Well,' Kitty said with a touch of pride, 'this sort of pasty is what the miners used to take down the mines back along. Meat and teddies — that's potatoes to you — and onion at one end, and jam at the other. Traditionally, leastways. Mine's all savoury. The miners held it by the pastry edge cuz their hands were filthy and there was no water to wash with down the mines. But nowadays we have clean hands so we eat the crimp as well. I'll just break it in half if that's all right with you.'

'Certainly is, thank you.' Maisie took the half pasty Kitty handed her. 'But I wasn't realising you have mines here. I thought the coal mines were all up north in England.'

'Most of the coal mines are, yes,' Philippa, who Maisie had gathered during the morning's lessons was top of the class, informed her. 'But there are some in Kent, as well. That's in the far south east of England. But we have other mines here. There were hundreds of mainly tin mines in Cornwall back along, and going up the River Tamar from here and onto the western edge of Dartmoor, it was mainly copper. Virtually all closed down now, but there are a few still working.'

'Well, thanks for that. I've got a lot to learn, so I have.' Maisie nodded, biting into her half of the pasty as she realised the girls were as friendly as she'd hoped. 'Mmm, this is delicious,' she mumbled through her mouthful of food.

'So it should be,' Kitty grinned. 'Mother made it and she's a brilliant cook. And she's gradually teaching me, too.'

'We were starting to learn the cookery in the convent, but just this term so I haven't learned much yet.'

'So what were it like being brought up by nuns, like?' Beryl chipped in. 'Sounds like summat out of a story book.'

'So does that mean you're Catholic and have to go to confession?' Philippa asked.

Maisie swallowed her first taste of the pasty. 'I do, so. I suppose there's a Catholic church in Plymouth somewhere?'

'Must be,' Kitty shrugged. 'So were the nuns proper strict, like?'

'Fairly,' Maisie answered, feeling her heart lurch as she thought about her home. Was it really only two days since she'd left her old life behind? 'They had to be with so many of us living together, but most of them were very kind underneath. Except for Sister Finbar. A right old crow sure she was! But my favourite was Sister Agnes. She was younger and didn't she always look out for me. I must write to her. And my best friend, Noreen.' Her last words nearly stuck in her throat and she felt tears prick her eyes. She wasn't ready to tell her new friends how she'd been dragged away from the convent without being allowed to say goodbye.

'It must be lovely to be reunited with your father, mind,' Beryl suggested.

Maisie's lips twitched. Her new friends were making her feel so much at home that she wasn't going to keep everything back from them. 'I wouldn't call it being reunited,' she admitted cautiously. 'I'd never met him before, so I hadn't.'

'What?' all three girls chorused.

'Did he never come to visit you?'

'No.' Maisie couldn't lie now, could she? Lying was a sin.

'Lordy love,' Kitty exclaimed. And for a moment, there was silence as the three girls exchanged appalled glances. But then Kitty piped up, 'So what's he like, then? Can't be that nice if he never came to visit you. And he didn't give you any dinner money.'

Maisie felt so grateful that the girls were clearly on her side. She felt she needed to tell someone or she might burst. So she decided to trust them with the truth. 'To be honest, I don't think he's very nice at all. But perhaps we just haven't had time to get to know each other properly yet. The journey was very tiring and he'd done it twice without a break. And he is quite old. A lot older than the daddies of the other girls of my age at the convent. So perhaps it was just that and I've got the wrong impression.'

'Well, I hope so.' Kitty's voice rang with sincerity. 'But you can always come round to my house. I'll ask Mother if you can come to tea tomorrow and you can have a nice meal with us. And then it's Saturday, so I can show you around Plymouth and maybe we can go to the flicks.'

Maisie felt herself glow with excitement. That would really cheer her up. Not that she knew what the flicks were, but she was willing to find out! But then doubt put a dampener on her sudden happiness. 'Oh, I should love that so much. But I don't know what plans my father has for me. So can we wait and see?'

'Course we can. But now we've all finished eating, we have to go outside. There are separate playgrounds for the infants, the boys and the girls. My little brother, Alan, is in the infants so we can't be together at playtimes. It's nice and sunny now so we won't need our coats, but I'll just fetch my skipping rope from the cloakroom as we go past.'

Maisie glanced round at the three girls as they stood up. 'You won't say anything to anyone else about my father, will you? It's just between us?'.

'Course not,' Kitty assured her, and Philippa and Beryl both nodded gravely. 'But come on. Let's have some fun while we can.'

Carefully folding the two sheets of greaseproof paper, she linked her arm through Maisie's. Together they scuttled along to the cloakroom and a few minutes later, joined Philippa and Beryl outside in the playground. Kitty organised a series of skipping games, and other girls came to play as well, several of them talking in a friendly manner to Maisie as she joined in wholeheartedly with the fun. She dreaded to think what her home life was going to be like, but she wasn't going to let that thought spoil this moment of happiness. Kitty had given her hope, and she felt in her bones that they really were going to be the best of friends. She was going to be happy at school, at least. Though what it was going to be like at home with her father remained to be seen, and she was dreading going home at the end of the day. But that was a few hours off yet, so she determined to blank it from her mind.

CHAPTER TEN

Maisie's heart plummeted to her boots as she turned the corner into the street. Sure, she hadn't expected to enjoy the day at her new school so much, and she was certain that the three girls, and Kitty in particular, were going to prove good friends. But now, in less than three hours' time, she would have to face her father again. Nevertheless, she was determined to make the best of it and would begin by getting to know her surroundings.

Last night, in the dark and with the lashing rain, she'd noted little about the street. And in the morning, she'd been in too much of a hurry and too anxious about finding her way to take much in. Now she saw that the humble terraced houses on her side of the street had flat façades with no architectural features to break the monotony. Some had window frames beginning to rot or with peeling paint, a picture of run down, faceless anonymity. The houses opposite, though, boasted small bay windows downstairs and altogether looked more inviting.

Never mind. At least her father's house and the one next door looked in relatively good repair. She stopped in front of the door, and started pulling up the string with the key on it that she'd worn around her neck, hidden beneath her jumper. As she went to put the key in the lock, from out of nowhere, a figure appeared at her shoulder, making her jump. She turned. It was the whiskery old man again, giving her a wide grin, although this time he appeared to have put in his false teeth. Maisie noticed, too, that his eyes were a pale watery blue, and that they darted about mischievously. Somehow she didn't feel so frightened of him this time.

'Hello,' she said, feeling more confident. 'I'm Maisie. Mr O'Sullivan's daughter. Come from Ireland. Sorry about this morning. I had to find my own way to my new school, so.'

'Ah.' The old fellow rubbed his stubbly jaw. 'His darter, eh? He did make mention of a darter, I do mind. When he got rid on his woman who does. Brave aud uproar it were. He said if she couldn't do the work he paid her for proper like, she could take hersel elsewhere, and he'd get his darter back from Ireland, and she'd do it fer nort. Yeard every word, I did, they arguing out yere in the street.'

Maisie clamped her lips together. That was hardly a surprise. It was already clear to her that her father hadn't wanted her back for any reasons of affection, nor because he felt she might stand a chance of a better future in England. He just wanted an unpaid skivvy! But to think the whole street knew made her blood boil.

'Really,' she murmured, struggling to hold back her anger. Well, if her father wanted a free servant, she'd jolly well make sure he'd pay in other ways!

The bitterness must have shown on her face as the next moment, the ancient fellow was shaking his head. 'I be master sorry, maid. I shouldn't have telt you that. I be yer next-door neighbour, Ezekiel Doidge. But folk just calls us Zeek.' He held out a calloused hand and Maisie took it reluctantly. His skin was dry and scaly, but as he pumped her hand up and down, she read sincerity in his watery eyes. 'If he gives you any trouble, you just come round and talk to aud Zeek. In fact, would you like fer come in fer a cuppa now? I's got the aud kettle on.'

Maisie thought of the cold, stewed tea in the pot on the table indoors. She was sorely tempted to accept Zeek's invitation since she didn't know how to light the — what had her father called it — yes, that was it, the primus stove. But she also thought of the list of chores her father had given her, and how she'd best get on with them so as not to incur his wrath when he arrived home.

'That's very kind, so it is,' she answered. 'But we only arrived late last night and I haven't even unpacked yet. I've heaps to do, but sure, I'd love to come round another time.'

'You'm always welcome, cheel.' Zeek's leathery skin wrinkled into a smile. 'Come straight in. I only locks the door at night.'

'Sure, thank you, Mr . . . er . . . Zeek. I will so.'

She turned to unlock her own front door, noticing out of the corner of her eye Zeek shuffling inside his home next door. Maisie smiled to herself as she, too, went indoors. She might have felt a bit afraid of him that morning, but now Zeek seemed a genuine, friendly chap, and she felt she'd have an ally living just through the wall.

Now then, where should she start? Her father might have forbidden her to enter the front room, but having hung up her gaberdine next to her new best coat, her hand closed around the door knob. The handle turned but then refused to open. She tried again, but it was definitely locked. Oh. So what secrets did her horrible father have hidden in there? It felt like another slap in the face. He'd dragged her all this way to be his glorified cleaner, yet she would be confined to her bedroom and sharing the kitchen with him.

Fuming, she stomped up the stairs. The first thing she'd do was unpack, and if it meant she hadn't finished everything by the time her father came home, well, just now, she didn't care.

There wasn't enough space in the tiny chest of drawers next to her bed for all her clothes, so she decided to leave in the case the items she'd need least, and pushed it under the bed which she then made neatly, as she'd been taught in the convent. The skirt she'd left hanging over the bottom of the bedstead looked a little less like a rag, but a few coat and skirt hangers would be good. There was no wardrobe to hang them in, but at least she could hook them over the iron bedstead.

The book Sister Agnes had given her, *Jane Eyre*, was lying on top of the chest of drawers, still in a sorry state. It had dried out a little, though, so she managed to peel more of the pages apart. But some of them seemed irrevocably glued together, so she'd have to read the story with missing gaps. She gave a sigh. Sure, didn't she feel as if she'd let dear Sister Agnes down.

Ah, dear Sister Agnes. Maisie felt sure that had the nun — or indeed the Reverend Mother — known how her father was going to treat her, they'd have fought tooth and nail to keep her at the convent. She wondered, if things turned out badly as she expected they might, and she wrote and told them, might they try to get her back home to Ireland?

Comforted by the thought, she placed the damaged book back on top of the chest of drawers and stepped over to the curtainless window. How could her father expect her, a girl, to get dressed and undressed, when anyone could see in? Well, sure, that was something she was going to tackle him about when he got in, that and the dinner money. She might let him get away with some things, but not those.

Lips closed in a determined line, Maisie looked down onto the back yard and the roof of the single-storey extension that housed the privy and whatever else. Strangely, it looked as if there was a small chimney in the roof further along from the privy, and Maisie wondered what was behind that second door. Beyond the extension was a coal bunker with the top and the hatch firmly padlocked, and a gate in the high, rendered wall at the bottom of the yard, also with a lock and bolts top and bottom. The ground in the yard had been roughly concreted over and was cracked in places, and a double washing line was slung from a hook on the house wall to another on the wall next to the gate.

So that was it. She'd be allowed access to two rooms in the house — as well as her father's bedroom for cleaning purposes only — and a small enclosed yard. She suddenly yearned for the view from the convent dormitories over the beautiful gardens of the Bishop's Palace and across the pretty houses to the cathedral with the glittering sea off to the right. The image filled her head, blurring her vision with unshed tears.

She shook her head, thumbing away the moisture from her eyes. Sure, Sister Agnes would expect her to show more spirit than that. She must think ahead, to the new opportunities Plymouth had to offer and that her new friend, Kitty, would surely show her. So, what was beyond that gate in the wall? Well, not the back of another row of houses, anyway. Maisie couldn't see exactly, but on the other side of what looked like an alleyway were some storage buildings or maybe they were workshops? Only one had its doors open, and the sounds of machinery were grating through the air. If only there'd been a little park or a green space of some sort instead. But as it was, Maisie felt hemmed in on all sides.

Another sigh, this time of self-pity, scraped from her lungs, and she turned away from the window in despair. But as she did so, a flash of colour caught her eye. In the adjacent yard — Zeek's back yard, as she now knew it to be — were rows of pots, some with the plants still in flower, on shelves fixed onto the wall of the outbuildings. As she looked along the terrace of little houses, Maisie realised that even if the wall between her yard and Zeek's was too high to see over, she could talk to the old man if they both happened to be outside at the same time.

Oddly, the thought brought her some comfort, enough to give her the courage to enter her father's bedroom. She didn't know what to expect, but there was nothing to give anything away about him. She'd hoped there might have been a photograph of her mother. Or even one of herself as a baby. But there was absolutely nothing on display at all. An iron bedstead, a simple dark-stained wooden chest of drawers and a wardrobe — at least he had one. The tiny grate, like the one in Maisie's room, showed no sign of having been lit recently. If it hadn't been for the tousled bed, which she set herself to making, she would have been forgiven for thinking, she told herself, that nobody had lived there for years.

Back downstairs, she went outside to investigate. The second door of the outbuilding was unlocked. Inside was a washing copper set in bricks over the cavity, where you'd light a fire to heat the water above, Maisie assumed, which explained the little chimney. So this was where she'd be expected to do the laundry. Already a basket of dirty sheets was waiting. So much for the bathroom she was hoping to find. Instead, she spied hanging from a hook on the wall, an old enamel hip bath.

Maisie cringed. Is that what she'd have to bathe in? Jesus, Mary and Joseph, she could have wept.

But she pulled herself up short. This wouldn't do. She'd just have to put up with things until she could find a way out. And she was determined that she would!

She braved the privy again. It wasn't in too bad a state, but she could make it cleaner and brush all the cobwebs away. Maybe she could persuade her father to get some plaster to fill in the cracks in the walls and ceiling to stop so many spiders coming in. It would still be freezing in the winter, but there was nothing she could do about that.

Back indoors, she had a good look around the scullery and kitchen to see what equipment there was in the drawers and cupboards. As expected, just the basics. When she opened the door to a small metal box, she discovered it had a marble base which felt icily cold to the touch, and realised it was for keeping food cold. She should have put the dripping mug in there instead of leaving it on the table all day. She hastily retrieved it and hoped it would get colder quickly so that her father didn't notice when he got home.

On the draining board in the scullery waited the mugs and plates from breakfast and the scant meal the previous night. Maisie drew aside the curtain beneath the butler sink and found a grey washing-up mop and a scourer. She didn't like the look of those, but it was all there was, so she rinsed through the crockery, found a tea towel to dry them and put them away on an empty shelf. The wooden kitchen table didn't look that clean to her, so she scrubbed it down with salt and left it to dry, then went in search of the potatoes. The only other food items she could find were a packet of gravy browning and a drum of custard powder. Well, they wouldn't get very fat on those!

By the time the clock showed her that it was just gone six, the newly scrubbed table was set for tea, the floor swept, and the dubious washing-up mop, scourer and dishcloth had been soaking in a weak solution of some bleach Maisie had rooted out from beneath the sink. The potatoes were peeled and waiting in one of two saucepans she'd discovered. She didn't know how to use the primus stove, much less how to light the range, so couldn't start cooking them. But anyway, she imagined her father would be bringing some meat or something to cook with it.

It was half an hour before the ogre reappeared. Well, she hoped he'd be impressed by what she'd achieved. She secretly admitted to herself that she'd quite enjoyed it once she'd got going, pretending it was her own home and that she was doing it for her own little family. At some point in the future, she promised herself, that was exactly what she'd be doing. Blow Francis O'Sullivan and his mean-tempered ways. She was determined to make a good life for herself and have a family of her own one day — no matter what it took!

But Maisie's insides nevertheless flipped over when she heard the front door open. But she'd had time to think and decide on her strategy. Having done all the preparation she could, she was sure there was nothing her father could find fault with. She'd be polite and friendly, not giving him any-thing to criticise her for. So when she put in what could only be seen as reasonable requests, he couldn't refuse. Or could he?

He came into the room, gave a cursory glance at the neatly laid, newly scrubbed table and grunted as he placed a loaf of bread and two small packages on it.

Maisie was determined to get in first. 'Good evening, Father,' she greeted him, jumping to her feet. 'Did you have a good day?'

'As best as can be expected at work,' he answered sourly. 'Put the butter in the cold box if you've found it, and the sausages are for dinner. And have you done as I said and peeled the potatoes?'

'Of course,' she said flatly. Sure, she wasn't going to let him upset her with his surly attitude. 'I couldn't cook them because I don't know how to light the primus stove. You were going to show me. I don't know how to light the range either. But if you show me, I can do it in the future. I would've filled the coal scuttle, but the coal bunker's locked and I didn't know where you keep the key.'

'Hmm,' her father snorted in reply. 'Well, let's get those spuds on and while they're cooking, I'll show you how to light the range. It won't get hot quickly enough to cook on, but the spuds'll stay hot while you fry the sausages on the primus.'

While *she* fried the sausages? Well, as it happened, she was only too willing to learn. But it was the assumption that she'd be doing everything that rankled — especially after what Zeek had revealed to her earlier. She managed, though, to show some enthusiasm as her father showed her how to set up the primus stove.

'Best if you do it,' he ordered. 'It's difficult for me with only one hand.'

Maisie nodded. She'd rather have the experience of doing it herself in case she needed to light it when she was alone in the house. She followed his instructions, filling the top little reservoir with methylated spirits and letting it burn right away as it heated the actual burner above, then slowly pumping up the paraffin from below and lighting that in turn. The saucepan was soon boiling away, and her father showed her how to regulate the flame using the air valve on top of the main reservoir below. Leaving the potatoes to boil, he turned her attention to the range.

'I don't normally let it go out, but obviously I had no choice,' he grumbled as he instructed her to riddle out the cinders and lay a bed of twisted newspaper and kindling. 'It isn't good for it to go from hot to cold and back again too often. It can make it crack and the landlord wouldn't be too pleased about that.'

Maisie jolted with surprise, and the words were out before she had a chance to think about them. 'Landlord? Are you not owning this house, then?'

'Of course not,' he snapped. 'Do I look as if I could afford to own a house?'

'Well, sure, I don't know,' Maisie answered, making her voice equally sharp but without sounding rude. 'Now presumably we're needing coal, so if you give me the key, I'll go and fill the scuttle.'

Her father gave her what could only be described as a glare before he went to a drawer in the dresser and handed her a bunch of keys on a ring. 'It's this one,' he said grudgingly. 'Now you make sure you lock it afterwards. I don't want any Tom, Dick or Harry climbing over the wall and helping themselves to my coal.'

'Of course not,' she agreed, still speaking in a sharp tone. She wanted to add that she wasn't stupid, but thought better of it. If her life was to be at all bearable, she needed to keep him as sweet as possible. So she instead went obediently out into the yard. It was still just about light enough to see especially with the light coming through the kitchen window, and she set to, scraping the lip of the scuttle into the coal and trying to fill it without getting herself filthy. It wasn't easy, and she wondered how her father could possibly have managed — unless it was something else he'd expected his "woman who does" to do as well. No wonder the poor woman had rowed with him, and she'd probably be much better off working for someone else! Maisie remembered what the Irish girl on the train had said. Domestic staff were in short supply nowadays, and they could pick and choose where they worked. And no one in their right mind would choose to work for her bad-tempered father, she was sure.

Back inside, the starter fuel was burning nicely in the range firebox, and Francis instructed her to use tongs to place individual lumps of coal where the flames were strongest, without snuffing out the air supply. Maisie already knew from her science lessons at the pension school that fire needed air to burn. She quickly got the hang of it, even judging which vents on the range to open and how far, and instinctively turned to glance up at her father with a grin. It was met with a scowl.

'At night, we have to bank it up so that it stays lit until the morning,' he growled. 'That's the tricky bit. And again during the day while we're out.'

'Oh, well, I'm sure if you show me, I'll manage it, so,' Maisie replied cheerily, while inside she was seething. 'But those tatties should be done now, so I'll cook the sausages and then we can eat.'

Without waiting for a reply, she went into the scullery to wash the coal dust from her hands. Then taking the saucepan from the primus, she replaced it with a small frying pan and added the two sausages. One each didn't seem much when her stomach was growling with hunger, but there were plenty of potatoes to go with it. She'd never cooked meat before, but knew that it could be dangerous if not cooked through to the middle, so it made sense to her that you needed to keep turning them. When she was satisfied all was ready, she served everything equally onto two plates and placed them on the table where her father was waiting.

'You don't think you're having a whole one, do you?' he barked. 'Little thing like you doesn't need it. Cut it and give me half.'

Oh. Had she really thought things couldn't get any worse? He was to have one and a half sausages while she had to make do with just a half? It was barely a mouthful.

But knowing she had other things to request, she decided it was best to do as she was told.

'I enjoyed my first day at school, by the way,' she said when they'd eaten their meal in tense silence and she was clearing away. 'I enjoy the learning. I'm sharing a desk with a girl called Kitty. She's very nice. Even shared her packed lunch with me, seeing as you didn't give me anything to take with me. Did you know they're not giving you dinners like they did at the pension school? You have to pay for them or take your own.'

There, she'd said it. She hoped not in a rude way, but letting him know she thought it had been his fault. She couldn't judge his reaction to her tone as all he did was narrow his eyes slightly before he replied.

'So how much are they? The dinners?'

Maisie could have kicked herself. She hadn't thought to ask.

'I'll find out tomorrow,' she murmured. 'But they collect the money for the whole week on Mondays.'

'Well, if they're not too dear, you'd best have them. But don't expect to have a proper meal in the evening as well. You can cook mine, but bread and dripping will do for you. I can't afford both. And that's what you can take to school for your lunch tomorrow, bread and dripping.'

Maisie felt as if she'd been kicked in the guts. Bread and dripping when Kitty and her friends had all had a feast by comparison? Sure, she'd feel so ashamed when she opened her own pittance of a meal.

'Sure, what would people think of that?' she blurted out. 'Can't I at least have bread and butter now that we have some?'

Francis glared back at her darkly. 'If you insist. But just a scraping of butter, mind. And the milkman will be back tomorrow. I'd cancelled an extra day in case we got delayed on our journey. If it's here before you leave for school, make sure you bring it in and put it in the cold box before someone pinches it.'

Milk. Now that'd be nice, rather than having black tea as they'd had the previous night.

'Yes, of course,' Maisie replied, hoping to keep up the pretence of obedience when her thoughts were straining with rebellion. 'Talking of which, shall I put the kettle on the range? I reckon it'll be hot enough now, and we can have a cup of tay.'

'It's *tea*, remember,' he corrected her Irish pronunciation. 'And while you're at it, put some water in the range boiler. It's not clean enough for drinking, but it's good enough for doing the dishes. There's some soda crystals under the sink. You'll need those for the pans.'

'Righty-ho.' Yes, she'd seen the packet of soda. She knew from the nuns' kitchen that you could burn your hands with it if you weren't careful. They'd only used it for badly burnt pans, but had something gentler for most of the washing up. As for the range boiler, she'd have to work that one out. She then noticed there was a tap to one side of the firebox, so that must be it. She could see where the water must go in, and picked up the oven glove to open it with as it was sure to be hot even though she hadn't been warned. Was her father hoping she might burn herself, or had he just not thought to tell her? Either way, it was all helping her pluck up courage for her next request.

'By the way, are there any curtains for my bedroom?' she asked as casually as she could. 'There are men in those workshops at the back, and sure, wouldn't it be indecent if they saw me getting changed.'

Put like that, how could he refuse? But it was a moment or so before he deigned to reply, 'No, there aren't.'

Oh, really? Well, she wasn't going to put up with that! 'Sure, I'm not exposing myself to any Tom, Dick or Harry, as you put it,' she told him with an emphatic nod. 'Is there a market somewhere I can get some cheap material and make some, then? Something I'm really good at is the sewing, so it is.'

'We-ell, I suppose so,' her father agreed with obvious reluctance.

And before he could change his mind, Maisie jumped in, 'Good. My new friend, Kitty, said she'll show me around Plymouth on Saturday, and I'm sure she'll know where there's a market. A few shillings should be enough, I think. You said you work on Saturdays, didn't you, so it'll give me something to do.'

'As long as you don't get into any mischief. But there's the washing for you to do on Saturday—'

'Yes, I saw. Well, I'll be getting that done first. So that's settled, then. And Kitty's asked me to her house next Wednesday,' she told him, expanding the truth. Wednesday was his afternoon off, wasn't it, so going to Kitty's would mean less time to spend with him. And then she added her parting shot. 'So you won't have to feed me anything at all that night, will you?' she said, trying to hide her triumph. Well, he couldn't argue with that, so he couldn't!

CHAPTER ELEVEN

On the Saturday morning, Maisie was almost dancing with
excitement as she pegged the final item of laundry on the
line in the back yard. She'd got up before it was light, thrown
on some clothes and crept downstairs so as not to wake her
father. Remembering how he'd lit the fire in the range the
other evening, she'd soon got a good blaze going beneath
the copper out in the wash house. Carrying in the water
from the scullery, it was soon heated enough to start adding the soapflakes that she had to grate from the block of
Sunlight.

She began with the sheets, then the couple of pairs of
undies and socks and a shirt of her own, and finishing with
her father's grubby clothes. She only had the block of soap
and a ridged washboard at her disposal, and the cuffs of his
shirts were particularly grey. But he'd complain, she was sure,
if they weren't washed to his satisfaction and forbid her to
go out until she'd scrubbed them again. So she rubbed away
until her fingers were raw. Next she had to drain out the dirty,
scummy water, refill the copper with fresh to rinse out all the
laundry — which she found she had to do twice before the
water ran clear — before carrying everything outside to put
through the mangle and peg on the line.

Shortly before half past eight when she was only half-way through, her father came out to check on her. His beady eyes darted over everything and he disdainfully picked up one or two items between his right forefinger and thumb as if eager to find fault. But when he could see nothing to criticise, he merely wrinkled his nose with a grunt.

'There's a ten-bob note on the table,' he grated from between tight lips. 'You can get some cheap material out of that for your blessed curtains, and any essentials you need. And our food for the weekend. No fancy cuts of meat, mind. I expect to see change out of that.'

So saying, he turned on his heel and went back inside. Maisie exhaled through whistling lips. At first, the mention of the ten-shilling note had seemed a gift from heaven — until she learned what he expected it to cover. Didn't want much, did he? Nevertheless, as she finished the laundry, her heart felt light.

When a sharp rat-a-tat sounded on the front door at the appointed hour of ten o'clock, Maisie flew to open it. Kitty was standing there with her usual merry smile, and Maisie felt her spirits instantly rise. The sun was shining down warmly from a clear autumn sky, strengthening her determination to enjoy her adventure. It was the most optimistic moment she'd experienced since she'd been told she had to leave the convent.

'Morning,' Kitty grinned, a little dimple appearing on each of her rosy cheeks. 'You ready? You look nice.'

'Does it look all right? It's the best outfit they gave me.'

'It's lovely. Now come along, I've heaps to show you. Oh, d'you want to put that in my bag?' Kitty nodded her head at Maisie's string bag as she proudly flexed her shoulder where a grown-up bag hung from a strap. 'I had this for my last birthday. Mother said it were time I had one of my own.'

Maisie felt a stab of envy. Oh, to have a proper birthday present. Sister Agnes always gave her a little gift on her birthday for which she was more than grateful, but to have something more substantial from one's parents would be bliss.

But more than that, a bag like Kitty's would be so practical. She wouldn't have to keep her front-door key on a string around her neck for starters. Double-checking it was indeed still there, she pulled the door shut behind her.

'You off somewheres?'

Maisie recognised Zeek's crackly voice. 'Yes,' she smiled back at the old man who seemed to have appeared from his house like magic. 'This is my new friend, Kitty, from school. She's going to show me around the town.'

'And I'm taking her to the flicks this afternoon,' Kitty chimed in. 'They're showing *Flying Down to Rio* with Fred Astaire and Ginger Rogers again. I thought she'd like that with all the dancing.'

Maisie's head started spinning. By the flicks, did Kitty mean a picture house where you watched what she believed were moving photographs called films? That sounded exciting, but surely you must have to pay to go in?

'I don't have that much money,' she faltered. 'My father only gave me a ten-shilling note, and I've got to get that curtain material I mentioned as well as food out of it, and he said he wants change—'

'Yere.' Zeek delved into his trouser pocket and brought out a handful of change. 'There's one and six,' he said, extracting three silver sixpences. 'Enjoy yersel, and treat yersel to fish and chips and an ice cream or summat.'

Maisie felt her cheeks redden. 'Sure, I couldn't possibly—'

'Yes, you can.' Zeek grabbed her hand and pressed the coins into her palm. 'You can pay us back by coming in arter school one day and telling us all about it. My aud legs won't take us too far nowadays, so you can be my eyes on the world. Look upon it as a little job.'

Maisie filled up with gratitude. 'That's so kind of you, so it is.'

'Well, you two had best be off. Have a proper grand day.' And before Maisie could thank him again, he turned back inside.

The two girls exchanged surprised, happy glances before setting off down the street.

'He seems mortal nice,' Kitty nodded in approval. 'Why don't you put that money and your dad's ten-bob note in my purse? It'll be safer than in your pocket, and it's got two compartments so we can keep it separate. Tell you what. I think Mother has an old handbag she were going to give to a jumble sale, so you could have it, like. And maybe we can find you a cheap purse in the market.'

Maisie frowned doubtfully as she popped the money into the purse Kitty held out to her. 'D'you think so? I've a lot to get out of that money, so.'

'We'll see. We'll go to the market first and then I'll show you around the town centre. We're meeting Philippa and Beryl outside the Gaumont at one o'clock. And on the way back, we'll call in at the butchers we use. Mother says he's master good value for money. So don't you worry about ort. We're going to have us a proper good day.'

'Sure, as I've spent the morning so far scrubbing my father's shirts and his smelly old smalls, I'm looking forward to it!'

'Oh, yuk,' Kitty grimaced. 'And what, scrubbing with just soap?'

'It's all there was, a bar of soap, a grater and a rubbing board.'

'We'll have to get you some Oxydol, then. That's what we use. Works for both laundry and washing up. Kind on the hands, too.'

'But I'm not sure I've got enough money—'

'It's about thruppence ha'penny a packet, and that'll last for ages. Maybies cheaper if we can find some in the market. And what about soap for yourself? I suppose his nibs only has carbolic?'

Maisie turned to her with an amused lift of her eyebrows. 'Sure, you've got the measure of Mr Meanie O'Sullivan. You're too polite to say, but I reckon you've smelled the carbolic from me.'

Their eyes met, and then both girls broke into fits of giggles.

'Then it'll be some Palmolive for you,' Kitty spluttered as their merriment subsided. 'Thruppence a bar. And I bet he still uses dental powder. Well, you don't want to share that with him, I'll be bound!' she exclaimed, pulling a face. 'We'll get you a tube of proper toothpaste, like. And proper shampoo. Got a funny haircut, you have. Really short, so you'll only need a tiny bit of shampoo, so it'll last for ages. But you ought to grow your hair. You've a mortal pretty face, and it'd look grand if it were framed a bit more by your hair.'

Maisie didn't know how to react to Kitty's comment. It was meant kindly, she knew, but she wasn't sure how she felt about it. By now, they'd turned the corner and were walking along the main road. Maisie vaguely remembered it from three days previously when she'd dragged herself along behind her father, lugging the heavy suitcase in the pouring rain. It seemed so different now in the sunshine and with Kitty for company.

'We had to have really short hair in the convent,' she confessed, feeling the need to explain. 'We had to brush it a hundred times a day. To make it shine, we were told. But sure, I reckon it was to stop us getting nits.'

Kitty grimaced. 'Oo, nasty little critters. Managed never to catch them myself. But seriously, like, you should grow your hair. It'd look lovely. I can see it's nice and thick, even if it is so short.'

'Is it thick?' Maisie lifted her shoulders in surprise. 'Sure, how would I know? There weren't any mirrors in the convent. Vanity's a sin, so it is.'

'What?' Kitty's eyes were trying to pop out of her head. 'Never seen yourself? Aw, well, we'll have to remedy that!' She shook her head. 'Sounds dreadful, like, this convent.'

'Sure, I was very happy there. I already miss it so much. The dormitories all had a lovely view over the gardens of the Bishop's Palace. Well, over the tops of the trees, but didn't I used to go there often with Sister Agnes. It was a sort of treat when I was little, having no family of my own. The gardens were so beautiful and peaceful. I'm going to miss the open spaces, so.'

'Well, don't despair! You wait till you see the sea front and the Hoe. And next weekend, if it's nice, we'll take the train up onto the moor. Some places up there you feel as if you can see for ever.'

'Sure, that sounds grand!'

'It is. But you can get blown to bits up there, even in summer,' Kitty laughed as they crossed over another main road. 'But that's for next week. Tell you what. Makes you feel all different about where you live, showing someone around. Going to enjoy it, I am!'

They continued on in happy silence, Maisie trying to take everything in so that she could find her own way in the future if need be. They eventually turned into the long, straight street with the trams that she remembered from that first traumatic night. Now, though, it was even busier. Among all the pedestrians were a good number of men wearing the white hats she'd seen before, but they were all dressed in smart, dark blue uniforms which she realised now they'd probably worn beneath their coats on that drenching night.

'Sure, these men in uniform, they're sailors, aren't they?'

'They are indeed. If you follow this road right along, you end up at the Royal Navy Dockyard at Devonport. This end's called Union Street. Quite famous for the sailors. It's where they come when they're on shore leave. For all the pubs and other entertainment.'

'Other entertainment?' Maisie frowned. She knew roughly what a pub was. It was where men drank something called Guinness, and if they drank enough, it could go to their heads. It was called being drunk and it was one of the worst sins. Some men turned violent, she'd heard. She wasn't at all sure about being on this Union Street, though there were plenty of respectable-looking folk around.

'Well, there's a few different cinemas and a theatre or two,' she was relieved when Kitty explained. 'But some just want to find a woman to have a drink with in a bar, or a bit of a dance, like. But it's not just sailors. You get officers and captains, too. There are some proper posh restaurants they go to, and genteel tea rooms.' Kitty paused to drink a pretend cup of tea, her little finger crooked out to the side, making Maisie giggle. 'And there are lots of shops, too,' Kitty went on. 'Clothes, hats, butchers and so on. But Union Street isn't the place for a woman on her own at night. Up this end, it'd be okay if you were going to the theatre or summat with someone else. But you wouldn't go up the other way towards Devonport alone. Union Street doesn't have a reputation among the sailors for nort.'

Maisie glanced nervously about her. She couldn't imagine her father would let her out at night on her own anyway. Not that she was likely to want to. And she'd certainly not come down here, especially after what Kitty had just told her.

But walking along Union Street with Kitty in the October sunshine, Maisie's anxiety soon subsided. Although there were indeed some sailors among the crowds, not one of them appeared threatening, and all the civilians were merely going about their business. Maisie was fascinated by the trams rattling along on their rails, clanking as they went, with passengers sometimes not waiting for them to stop before they jumped on or off. Although Maisie found the number of people around unsettling, at the same time, she was tingling with excitement.

They passed beneath the rank of railway bridges Maisie recalled from the other night, and shortly came to the end of the bustling street. She clung onto Kitty as they negotiated a busy junction, dodging the trams and the few motor vehicles on the road. Kitty led her up another main street that was alive with hustle and bustle, and then pointed to the immense façade opposite as they waited for a gap in the traffic before they could cross over.

'The main bit of that's Dingles, where Father works,' Kitty informed her proudly.

Maisie's heart gave a thump. 'Sure, that's where my father works, too. Maybe they know each other.'

'Really? What department? My dad's in charge of the men's outfitters department. What about yourn?'

'Accounts of some sort.' Maisie felt a shadow pass over her as they crossed the road and walked past the front of the huge department store. She guessed her father must work in an office either at the back or on the top floor somewhere, so it was highly unlikely he'd happen to see her. He knew she was going into the city with her new friend from school, but the thought of him being so near made her shudder and she was glad when Kitty took her down another street and they entered a covered market.

Half an hour later, they re-emerged with Maisie's small personal purchases tied up together in some newspaper so they wouldn't fall through the string bag, as well as some material, thread and a length of stretchy curtain wire with hooks at both ends. Maisie had chosen some cheap red gingham. She couldn't afford proper, heavy curtain material that would help keep out the draught in winter. So as it was just for modesty's sake, she reasoned she only need cover the bottom half of the window, so only bought a yard and a half. She already had the little sewing kit — needles, thimble and scissors — that Sister Agnes had given her last Christmas, so she was all set.

A packet of Oxydol, some cheap writing paper and envelopes and a little purse, which Kitty put in her bag for safekeeping, completed her purchases. She'd never done any shopping like this before, and was so glad she'd had Kitty by her side. Kitty had even bartered with the stall holder over the material, something Maisie knew she'd never have the nerve to do herself.

'Right, off to the Hoe, then,' Kitty said, leading the way. 'You'll love it. It's a big open space and you can see right over the Sound and out to sea, like.'

Maisie couldn't wait to see it. It would be like being home in Cobh again. When they eventually came out onto a vast expanse of short grass that seemed to reach to the horizon, she couldn't help but give a little squeal of pleasure.

Behind them were terraces of beautiful, opulent villas, but it was the green area in front of them that filled her with a sense of freedom. So many people had come to enjoy the autumn sunshine there — young couples with arms intertwined, older people strolling, a nursemaid pushing a pram, children racing about playing games — and yet the grass spread so far that it didn't feel in the least bit crowded.

Maisie turned to Kitty in delight, and saw the pride radiating from her friend's face.

'Proper grand, isn't it?' she grinned. 'Come on. I'll show you everything.'

As they wandered on, Kitty pointed out a bowling green and pavilion to the left, and beyond them, an old lighthouse that Kitty explained originally stood on dangerous Eddystone Rocks a few miles out to sea. It had been replaced with a new one but re-erected here on the Hoe as a memorial to the architect who built it, one Mr Smeaton. There was also a towering monument that had been erected to commemorate the sailors who'd lost their lives in the war.

As they reached the end of the houses, Maisie was amazed to see that the lawns opened up to the right as well, with more grand residences looking out to sea. They crossed over a broad promenade where people were resting on benches. Under her mother's watchful eye, a little girl was zooming up and down on a scooter. Sure, wasn't she a lucky girl to have such an expensive toy, Maisie couldn't help thinking.

Kitty pointed out the statue of Sir Francis Drake and the Armada Memorial, then led Maisie on towards the sea front. She showed her what was known as the Belvedere, a building like a great canopy overlooking the sea where the public could shelter while admiring the view or watching the Royal Navy ships sailing to or from Devonport. A pretty bandstand not dissimilar to the one in Cobh lay up to the left, but Kitty took her down one of the grand, curving staircases of the Belvedere to what she said was Grand Parade. Most enthralling, though, was the pier that stretched out over the sea on a skeleton of ironwork supports.

'A bit short as piers go, but I love it,' Kitty announced proudly. 'All sorts of things go on there, especially in summer. Entertainment, acrobats, concerts, afternoon tea with music. Or you can take a little boat trip. And then inside the building, you can hire roller skates, and at night they have dances. Mother says I can go when I'm older, but only with friends, and one of them'll be you. Maybe we'll find ourselves sweethearts or even husbands there. That's how my parents met.'

'Really?' Maisie tried to put some enthusiasm into her voice. She couldn't imagine her father would allow her to go to a dance in the evening even when she was older. And to be honest, though she longed to have a home and a family of her own, the thought of talking to boys filled her with dread. She'd never spoken to one in her life.

She kept those thoughts to herself as they meandered along the parade with the water below them twinkling in the sunlight. She could see steps leading down to some terraces below, with more steps leading down to the water's edge, but no one was paddling despite the warm autumn day.

A gentle breeze was wafting the familiar smell of the sea into their faces, suddenly enveloping Maisie in a pang of sadness. She'd been relishing the day out so far, but the reminder of home was unexpectedly overwhelming. She felt a lump rising in her throat, but she mustn't spoil things for Kitty. She'd been so kind and Maisie didn't want to appear ungrateful. Despite the tearful moment, she found the open grandeur of the Hoe so utterly impressive that she could envisage spending many a happy hour there. Sure, it'd be a grand place to get away from her father.

When at last they gained the far end, they had to skirt what looked like a massive, daunting castle that Kitty said was called the Citadel. It towered menacingly over them, and Maisie was relieved when they were past it and came to some protective walls guarding the entrance to a harbour. A small boat was gliding in, its sails a bright copper against the turquoise sky. The scene would have been idyllic but for the industrial backdrop opposite and the strong odour of fish.

Kitty glanced at her watch. 'This is Sutton Harbour where the fishing fleet comes in,' she said briefly. 'That's what all those boats are. Behind the fish market there's an area called the Barbican. Lots of little medieval streets and alleys, but we haven't got time to explore. Save it for another day. We'll just grab us some fish and chips, and then we'll head back to the Gaumont.'

'I don't know if I can afford fish and chips,' Maisie said doubtfully. 'I've still got to buy food for the weekend, and then there's the cinema—'

'Trust me, you can. I know the cheapest little shop. If you're worried, just get chips and you can share my fish. Come on, I'll show you.'

They ate their lunch sitting on a wall at the top of the Mayflower Steps. Maisie savoured every mouthful — unlike when she'd shared fish and chips with her father back in Cobh on the day of her enforced departure. Afterwards, Kitty hurried her through a maze of busy little roads back to Union Street where Philippa and Beryl were waiting for them outside the cinema.

Maisie was awestruck. She'd noticed the outside of the building on the way and again was struck by its architecture. It was different from anything she'd seen before. And inside, sure, it was as cavernous as Cobh Cathedral! It was decorated throughout in delicate shades of primrose, green, lilac and gold, but weren't the seats peculiar and mighty uncomfortable.

Glancing around, she noticed that she was sitting so much higher than her friends.

'Stand up,' Philippa whispered in her ear.

She did, feeling stupid and embarrassed as Philippa pushed down the folding seat for her. But as she sat down again, there was no time to feel ashamed. The lights went down, plunging them into blackness. Sure, Maisie didn't like such intense dark, but then something quite extraordinary happened. Out of the floor in front of the screen, brilliantly illuminated, rose up an enormous organ, its tones so loud her eardrums rang. It really was like being back in the cathedral, but instead of solemn hymns, the musician was playing fast, jolly tunes. Maisie began to relax. She was almost disappointed when organ and organist sank down into the bowels of the cinema again, but before she knew it, the giant screen was lit up in varying shades of grey, showing a short film about the wonders of Venice. Maisie couldn't believe her eyes. It was like magic.

All too soon, the lights came on again, making Maisie blink. Was that it? Was it over? But she didn't ask it out loud. She didn't want to look a fool again.

'Come on, I'm busting. We'll go to the ladies afore the main film starts,' Kitty instructed, getting to her feet and giving Maisie a little shove. 'Pippa, will you look after Maisie's shopping?'

Maisie found herself shuffling along the row of seats. Fortunately, there weren't too many people to disturb, and she followed Kitty out of the auditorium. And oh my, she found that the lavatories were just as sumptuous as the rest of the building. And they had mirrors. Maisie was aware of her heart bouncing around in her chest. So that was what she looked like. She stared, mesmerised by her own reflection. Cropped hair with a tinge of copper, face the shape of a heart, green-blue eyes that seemed too big, and pink lips with a pleasing bow to them. Oh. Sure, that was her, Maisie O'Sullivan. Not just a voice inside her own head, with feelings and emotions, looking out on the world around her, but a real person.

Then she noticed that Kitty was standing behind her, contemplating her in the mirror and grinning like a cat. 'Told you was pretty, didn't I, like? Actually, if I were less chubby in the face, we could be sisters, only you'd be the prettier one. So now, seeing yourself in a mirror isn't such a sin, is it?'

Maisie blinked back at herself and a strange feeling overwhelmed her, as if she was being born all over again. She had a new life, new friends — one of whom did indeed look rather like her — and, despite her horrible father, she was jolly well going to make the most of everything the future could offer her!

CHAPTER TWELVE

'So let's see what muck you're going to serve me up with, then.'

Maisie clamped down her jaw. Who did he think he was? But if she voiced the cutting retort in her head, sure, it would only make matters worse. Well, she'd show him, so she would. She could hear Sister Agnes's voice in her head. Discretion is the better part of valour was one of her sayings. Maisie hadn't understood what it meant when she was younger, but she certainly did just now.

As soon as the main film, *Flying Down to Rio*, was over and to Maisie's surprise, everyone stood for the National Anthem, she and Kitty had said a brief goodbye to Philippa and Beryl, and hurried in the direction of home. On the way, they'd called into the shops Kitty had recommended. At the butchers, under her advice, Maisie had purchased half a dozen eggs and some scrag end of mutton, and then some vegetables and a pound of Cox's apples at the greengrocers. At the end of everything, she indeed had some change left over, just as Kitty had predicted. Maisie was relieved, as she wouldn't have enjoyed explaining to her father where all the money had gone.

They parted company on the main road, each heading to her own home. Maisie's main fear was that the range would have gone out, but she saw with pride that she'd evidently banked it up correctly before she'd left that morning. By opening the vents and carefully adding a little more fuel, the coals were soon glowing red hot. Maisie swiftly set to, making a casserole from the meat, onions, carrots and the gravy browning from the cupboard. By the time it was ready to go in the oven, Kitty had returned as promised with some herbs from her mother's windowsill, which she said would give it added flavour. At four thirty on the dot, Maisie slid the dish into the range oven. It would need at least two hours to cook, so it was perfect timing.

'Thanks so much for your help,' she said, hugging her friend. 'Sure, I couldn't have done it without you.'

'Nonsense.' But Kitty blushed all the same. 'And here's that bag of Mother's I told you about. It's a bit worn, but it's got a long strap which I always think's a good idea.'

'Will you be thanking her for me.' Maisie was overwhelmed. It might be scuffed here and there, but the bag was of good quality. Real leather if she wasn't mistaken, with years of wear in it yet.

'You can thank her yourself. She says Wednesday's fine for you to come to tea. But look, Alan wants me to play football with him in the garden afore it gets dark, so I'd best be off.' She turned before spinning back round again. 'Oh, I nearly forgot. There's a piece of paper in the bag. From what you were saying about your dad, you know, that you don't think he goes to Mass, like. So I asked Father, and apparently there's a Catholic cathedral church in walking distance. Never noticed it myself. So he's drawn you a map of how to get there. Anyways, I must go. See you Monday. Hope the dinner goes down well!'

Before Maisie had a chance to thank her, Kitty had skipped along the hallway and let herself out of the front door. Maisie felt her spirits flag as the door closed. But she had plenty to do. She had to bring the washing in off the line for starters, raising some of it up on the pulley on the ceiling to air, while the rest was folded ready for ironing. Her father did have an iron, she'd discovered. Then there were the potatoes to peel, and the cabbage to chop up to go with the casserole, and finally the table to lay.

While she worked, Maisie let her mind wander over the fantastic day she'd had. Plymouth was such a huge, bustling town, and she wasn't keen on that aspect so much. But the Hoe was so open and impressive with those stunning views over the Sound and the coast in both directions. Kitty had promised her a ferry trip one day across to what she said were the quaint villages of Cawsands and Kingsands on the other side of the Tamar estuary over in Cornwall.

If she were honest, the weather had been so splendid that Maisie would have preferred that to sitting inside the cinema, marvellous experience though it had been. Both the building and the moving, flickering black and white images, especially the aeroplane scenes, had flabbergasted her. But she'd also found the film unsettling. When Kitty had mentioned dancing, she'd imagined the stiff, upright bodies and tapping feet of the Irish jigs she was used to. But it had been nothing like! Men and women had danced together in a sort of embrace, their bodies lilting and swaying. Even when there were lines of chorus girls, they were kicking their legs in the most indecent fashion, and some of the costumes were, well, ungodly! But soon Maisie had been swept up in the extravaganza, to say nothing of the rhythm of the music that seemed to fill her head.

But — had it been sinful to watch such a spectacle, she asked herself? And what about seeing herself in the mirror? It had been a heart-stopping moment. A moment of revelation. And she still didn't know how she felt about it. She tried to imagine what advice Sister Agnes would have given her, but already she was finding it hard to conjure up the nun's voice in her head.

There was still some time before her father would arrive home, and everything was already prepared, the potatoes simmering on the range and the table laid. So Maisie nipped up to her room to fetch the pencil from her treasure box and then sat back up at the kitchen table with the writing paper she'd purchased. She'd have preferred to use her father's pen from up on the mantelpiece, but felt she daren't do so without his permission.

So, who should she write to first? Sister Agnes, seeking her spiritual guidance? But part of her was still cross that the nun hadn't made any effort to stop her being spirited away. Not that it would have done any good, Maisie was sure. They'd been able to say goodbye whereas she hadn't had the chance to speak to Noreen, so she decided to write to her first. She'd tell her how she'd been so shocked herself at what had happened, and that she missed her terribly and that they'd always be friends. But she wouldn't want to make her too sad, so she'd tell her all about the exciting day she'd spent with her new friend, Kitty.

So engrossed was she in the letter that she didn't hear the front door open, and she jumped with shock when her father slunk into the kitchen. Had he deliberately tried to catch her in the act of some misdemeanour? Well, she'd done nothing wrong. But she wasn't going to attempt to engage in polite conversation only to be rebuffed again. So she rose in silence to pop the chopped cabbage into the saucepan of water she had ready simmering on the range.

'Dinner will be five minutes, as soon as the cabbage is cooked, so,' she announced flatly.

Her father gave a grunt, and headed past her out to the privy. When he came back inside to wash his hands at the scullery sink, Maisie took the casserole from the oven and placed it on a mat on the table. She ignored her father's caustic remark about her cooking as he sat down. Sure, it smelled grand to her, and she knew it would taste better than anything he could have cooked himself. She served the steaming food onto their plates together with the vegetables without a word, praying it would all taste as good as she hoped. To that end, she put her hands together and muttered a simple grace.

'Huh, I'll have none of that clap-trap,' he snapped.

Well, he couldn't stop her saying it in her head now, could he? Despite the rebellion in her chest, she held her breath as he took his first mouthful of the casserole. She saw the flicker of surprise on his face. Hadn't expected it to taste that good, had he?

'Some of the meat might be a bit gristly,' she told him archly. 'But didn't you tell me not to buy any expensive cuts.'

'So where's my change, then?'

'On the mantelpiece,' she answered, trying not to smirk with satisfaction. 'And I got the material and other odds and ends out of it as well, just like you said to. And food for tomorrow. There's enough of this for another couple of days, and I bought eggs to make sandwiches for tomorrow teatime. And I had a lovely day with Kitty. She showed me the Hoe,' Maisie went on, ignoring his silence. 'Very impressive, so it is. And I saw where you work. Dingles.'

Francis flashed her a dark look. Hmm, well, she'd keep quiet about the fact that Kitty's dad worked there, too. Might be wise. She wasn't quite sure why, but she was learning to be cautious. She certainly wouldn't tell him about the money Zeek had given her, or that fact that she'd been to the cinema.

'It looks a grand place, Dingles, so it does,' she went on, thinking that a bit of flattery might put her father in a better mood. 'Not that we went inside. Sure, it'd be too expensive. I did most of my shopping in the market.'

'So I should think,' he snapped. Oh, well, she'd tried, so she had. But he was tucking into the food well enough and wasn't complaining about it, which must be a good sign. Praying she was right, Maisie plucked up the courage to ask her next question. She needed to know where she stood on that score.

'So what time is the Mass tomorrow?' she enquired in as casual a tone as she could.

Her father looked up sharply from his plate. 'I told you, you can forget all about that mumbo jumbo. There are some people who still look down on the Irish. It can stop you getting on. I should know. It's happened to me, and I don't want you spoiling what I've achieved. So the sooner you lose your accent and stop beginning every sentence with "sure", the better. And going to Mass gives away that Irish connection as well, so get it into your thick skull that you won't be going anymore.'

Maisie felt as if she'd been punched in the stomach. All those years of learning her catechism, of praying and worshipping had become part of her being. She imagined herself back in Cobh Cathedral, drowned in its grandeur, its awe, its sense of peace. The sense of belonging. Watching her beloved Sister Agnes absorbed in her devotions. Now all of that was being snatched away from her as well. And after everything the convent had done for her over the years. Tears of anger stabbed at her eyes and she was ready to yell at her father. But she knew it would do no good. So as soon as they'd both finished eating, she simply cleared the table in silence and then placed an apple in front of her father.

'Pudding,' she said sharply, and bit hard into her own fruit. But even that brought back memories. The apples down her knickers. She remembered conveying a couple of prunes in an Oxo tin in the same place once when she was much younger. It had leaked, and she'd had to put up with sticky, congealed juice in her undies until it was time for clean ones. The memory now made her smile. Surely Sister Agnes must have known, but she'd never spoken a word about it.

Thoughts of the nun filled Maisie's head while she did the washing up. She would try to get the letter to Noreen finished that evening and then write to Sister Agnes tomorrow. She could ask her if she could be forgiven for looking in the mirror and for going to the pictures.

With the plan in her head and the chores completed, she sat down at the table and went back to writing the letter. Her father was reading the newspaper spread out before him, deeply engaged in something on the sports page and making notes on a piece of paper. Maisie inwardly sighed with relief. At least she wouldn't need to talk to him. Or so she thought.

'What's that you're writing?' he asked curtly.

'A letter to my best friend, Noreen,' she bristled back. 'The one I wasn't allowed to say goodbye to. And then I'll write to Sister Agnes as well.'

'Huh, it's not cheap to send letters abroad, you know,' he grumbled. 'I'm not made of money.'

Oh, dear. Maisie hadn't thought of that. She'd never had to write a letter before, let alone post one.

'Tell you what, mind.' Amazingly, his voice suddenly sounded lighter. 'Give them to me when you've finished, and I'll put them through the post at work. Then it won't cost me anything at all.'

Maisie lifted a surprised eyebrow. Sure — or should she say well? — that was thoughtful. She wasn't sure it was entirely honest, but as long as her letters were sent, at that moment, she didn't really care how. And it would be her father committing the sin, not her.

'Thank you,' she answered. 'Will you be posting them on Monday? I'd like them both to get my letters as soon as possible so they know I'm thinking of them. But I'm sure they'll write to me soon, if they haven't already. It's not as if they're waiting for the address, for doesn't Reverend Mother know it anyway.'

Maisie thought she heard her father take in a little, jerky breath. 'So she does,' he murmured, and Maisie frowned as she wondered quite what he was thinking.

* * *

'Where the devil have you been?' Francis roared at her.

Maisie gulped hard. Going out so early on Sunday morning, she'd expected to slip back inside before he realised she was gone. But he must be a lighter sleeper than she thought and had heard her leave. Either that, or he'd been banging on her bedroom door and gone in when she hadn't answered. Either way, she'd been caught.

But why should she feel guilty? She hadn't robbed a bank or anything. Going to the first Mass of the day when most of the world was still asleep had brought her some peace. There hadn't been many in the congregation, and the priest had given her a warm, surprised smile, welcoming her as a new member of his flock, especially with her being so young and on her own. She hadn't waited to offer any explanation, but had hurried on home before she was missed. At least, that was what she'd thought. But now she had to face the music.

'I went to the Mass,' she told her father defiantly. 'You've no right to try and stop—'

'How dare you when I forbade you to go!' he bellowed, and the next instant, Maisie felt her teeth rattle as he slammed the palm of his hand across her cheek. She staggered sideways, knocking her hip painfully against the kitchen table. 'We've things to do on a Sunday. I have my weekly bath in the morning. I'll even let you go first if you behave yourself. Then you've got the ironing to do.'

Maisie glared at him, ready to retort that Sundays were meant for prayer, doing homework — not that she'd been given any — and possibly a walk if the weather was fine. But she thought better of it. If her father was in a bad mood, it would only aggravate him. Nevertheless, she was going to stand up for herself, so she was.

'Don't you ever be hitting me again,' she snapped. 'I'll go straight to the police if you do. Sure, there's laws against hitting a child for no reason.'

'Hah!' Francis gave a sarcastic laugh. 'That's what you think. Well, do as you're told, and I won't need to again. Now go and light the fire under the copper and fill it with water. It can be heating up while you make me a cup of tea, and you can fry me one of those eggs you bought yesterday to go on my bread.'

Maisie felt like telling him to fry his own flipping egg — that was a word she'd learned from Kitty in the last few days — but instead she dutifully went out to the wash house and got the copper going. She wouldn't mind a bath, even if she eyed with suspicion the contraption hanging on the wall. She knew she couldn't get it down on her own, but between them, perhaps they could manage. She imagined the woman Zeek had told her about must have had to do this, too. It was no wonder she'd been happy to leave if Francis treated her as badly as he did his own daughter.

Half an hour later, the bath was full of hot water from the copper, and more water had been put to heat, ready to top it up for her father when it was his turn.

'Well, I said you could go first, but the water cools down quickly out here, so don't be long,' he barked.

'No, I won't,' Maisie answered truthfully. She liked the idea of getting clean, but the bath looked none too comfortable, and having to bathe out in the wash house wasn't exactly inviting. 'I'll just fetch my soap and towel. Where do you keep the shroud?'

The look on her father's face was so astounded that it was almost comical. 'Shroud?' he repeated in amazement.

'Yes. You know, so we don't see ourselves and neither does God.' Maisie frowned at his expression.

He blinked at her, and then threw back his head with a roar of jeering laughter. 'What on earth did they teach you at that convent? And you don't think God would be interested in your scrawny body, do you?' Then he poked his nose towards hers. 'Normal people,' he told her, with the emphasis decidedly on the word *normal*, 'just take all their clothes off to have a bath. Only lunatics would ever wear a shroud.'

Maisie swallowed hard. Oh, help. But she supposed there was a curtain to pull across the little window in the wash house and there'd be nobody else there to see her. So she scuttled off to get her precious Palmolive and the shampoo, and shooting the bolts across on the inside of the wash-house door, stripped down to her vest and knickers.

'Please, God, forgive me, but I have no choice,' she muttered, and pulling off her remaining clothes as quickly as she could, stepped into the bath and sat down.

She mustn't look down at herself. Sure, that would be the real sin. But sitting in the warm water, it was virtually impossible not to if she wanted to soap herself in the relevant places. It was such a strange and uncomfortable experience, feeling the air against the bare skin of her body.

She washed herself quickly with the Palmolive, rubbed a pea-sized dollop of shampoo into her short locks, and rinsed it off. The lather made the water a little murky, thank heavens, but she couldn't help notice that her chest was beginning to swell a little, just like Noreen and Sister Agnes and all the other older females she knew. And as she stood up to grab the towel to dry herself, her glance grazed on the rest of her naked body.

She hadn't meant to look. It made her feel dirty and sinful, and she was waiting for the thunderbolt to come and strike her down as she rubbed the towel over her wet skin and dived back into her clothes. But miraculously, none came.

All the while, for the rest of the day, as she reheated the casserole for dinner, ironed her father's shirts — thank goodness she'd been taught how to heat a flat iron on a stove — finished her letter to Noreen, wrote a shorter one to Sister Agnes and started work on the curtain for her bedroom, a million thoughts and twisted emotions ricocheted around inside her head. Getting to know her new surroundings and the open expanse of the Hoe, the experience of going to the cinema, looking in the mirror and later seeing her own body for the first time. More than anything, the hollow emptiness each time her mind drifted back to her life in the convent and the friends she'd left behind.

Oh, blow her father! Why hadn't he just left things as they were? Well, she supposed she'd have to put up with him for now, while she was still at school. But the moment she was able to go out to work and support herself, she'd be off like a shot. Just see if she wasn't! And see what Mr Francis Bully O'Sullivan would think of that!

CHAPTER THIRTEEN

'Had a good time, then, like?'

Maisie nodded back at the old man as he welcomed her with a beaming smile. It hadn't seemed right walking straight into Zeek's house. So she called hesitantly as she let herself in through the unlocked door when she got home from school on the Monday afternoon. His voice had answered her from the kitchen and when she'd opened the door, delight had radiated from his wrinkled face.

'You sit yersel down and I'll put that aud kettle on. If you've got time fer a cuppa, that is?'

'That'd be grand, so it would. Thank you. And thank you so much for the loan of that money. I wouldn't have been able to go to the cinema with my friends without it.'

He waved a gnarled hand. 'I telt you, you can repay us by telling us all about it.'

'That's so kind of you, so it is,' Maisie answered, nevertheless feeling somewhat embarrassed. 'Well, first of all, Kitty took me to the market,' she began, settling herself in one of the easy chairs either side of the range.

As she related the events of Saturday to Zeek, her eyes wandered from his bent back as he moved the kettle onto one of the hot plates and then collected cups and saucers from a pretty dresser. Although a mirror of her father's kitchen just through the wall, the room felt totally different. Rather than the rustic rectangular table that filled most of the space next door, Zeek had a small, drop-leaf table in polished wood standing against the wall beneath the window, with an equally small upright chair on either side, leaving room for the armchairs that sat cosily beside the range. There were a couple of fine paintings of rural scenes on the wall, and several framed photographs either side of an ornate clock on the mantelpiece. Overall, the room felt warm and welcoming, so different from the stark emptiness in the adjoining house.

'Well, cheel, sounds like you had quite an adventure.' Zeek smiled, passing her a cup of tea in a bone china cup with pink roses on it. 'Sugar? And I reckon as I might have one of they Mars bars tucked away somewheres.' He winked, delving into the bottom of the dresser. 'Ah, there they be.' He drew up a tiny, low table to put everything on, and sat down in the other armchair with his own cup of tea.

'Yes, that there Fred Astaire be a dancer and a half,' he went on, nodding appreciatively. 'And that Ginger Rogers, and all. *Flying Down to Rio* were the last film I went to see when it first came out last year. Not been since cuz of my aud legs. But they talking films with their music and all be proper grand. Back along when I were a tacker, you just had the pictures. Flickered all over the place, they did. Any words came up written on the screen so as you could read it. There'd be a live pianist watching the screen and playing summat suitable to match what were going on. And then the big, newer picture houses had organs instead of pianos. Which is why in some of them you still has a bit of organ playing. Shows my age that, mind, don't it? But maybies I should treat mesel to a taxi once in a while to go to the flicks again. I did used to enjoy it.'

Maisie listened, full of interest, as she sipped her tea and then bit into the chocolate bar. She'd never heard of a Mars bar, and she thought she'd never tasted anything so delicious. She felt so relaxed and happy in Zeek's company. He was so easy to talk to that she wondered if she shouldn't confide in him her doubts about the morality of such films as she'd seen on the Saturday. But she felt she already had her answer. Zeek evidently approved wholeheartedly, which went some way to putting her mind at rest.

'Sure, perhaps you should,' she smiled back, feeling easier.

'Yes, you'm right. Never seems quite right, mind. Not without my Ruth. Loved the flicks, she did. Yere.' He heaved his small frame from the chair, and reaching up to the mantelpiece, handed Maisie a photograph of his younger self with a handsome woman she assumed was his wife.

'What a lovely picture,' Maisie commented with a smile.

'She were a beautiful woman, my Ruth.' For just a moment, he seemed lost in sad contemplation and Maisie wondered what she should say next. But then Zeek continued, 'But she went many a year back, and it's just been me ever since. We were never blessed with chiller, so to have a sweet young maid like you move in next door is like a breath of fresh air fer me. A bit of young company once in a while is just what an aud fellow like me needs. If you've time, of course.'

Maisie's heart jerked. Zeek and his wife had obviously wanted children but none had come, while her father had told her he'd never wanted a family. He'd never wanted her. She was a millstone round his neck. She remembered his exact words, and they came back again like cruel barbs in her skin. He only wanted her now as a convenience. How different he was from Zeek whom she was already growing fond of. Well, she'd be more than happy to call in whenever she could.

'I'll need to do some shopping after school tomorrow,' she told him, frowning thoughtfully. 'And I'm going to Kitty's house on Wednesday. But I could call in again on Thursday if you like.'

'I'd really appreciate that, cheel. I hesitate to ask, but if you could pick up a couple of bits fer me while you'm at the shops, I'd be master grateful. These aud legs, you see. I'd pay you fer the trouble.'

Maisie's eyebrows lifted. 'Of course I can do some shopping for you. But I don't want paying. My father's always going on about money being tight, so you must be the same. Rent to pay—'

Zeek interrupted her with a deep belly laugh. 'Oh, I don't have rent to pay, cheel. It might be modest, but I own this house. Every brick of it.' The surprise must have shown on Maisie's face as he went on, 'Back along, my parents built up a successful tailoring business in Union Street. They made mainly cheap but good quality civilian clothes fer the sailors, and even better but reasonably priced ones fer the naval officers. Worked day and night, they did, gradually building up their reputation and the business until they employed six tailors. I could sew afore I could read, and when I grew up, I naturally trained in the same profession. You'm looking at a master tailor, cheel.'

Zeek grinned, preening himself proudly. 'Anyways, with no chiller to pass the business onto, when I retired, I sold it, what, ten year back. Could have bought somewheres a lot grander than this, but I preferred to have money in the bank so as not to go short in my aud age. So if I wants to pay some young maid I've just had the good fortune to meet to run some errands fer us, then I will. It'll boost the meagre pocket money I'll wager that aud skinflint gives you.'

'Pocket money?' She frowned. 'What's that?'

'Well, cheel, most parents give their chiller a little spending money of their own,' Zeek explained. 'If they can afford it, of course. And I bets my bottom dollar your father can. Cas'n be that badly paid, his office job at Dingles. But I'm sure a little extra from Uncle Zeek won't come amiss.'

'Sure — I mean — well, that's very good of you. Why don't you write down what you need? I can go to the shops now if you like. There'll be a limit to what I can carry, so better do it separately from my own shopping, then I can get more for you. I've only got to re-heat the last of the casserole for tonight, so I've got time.'

'Well, if you don't mind, that'd be champion, maid. Thank you.'

Maisie sat back in the chair, feeling really pleased with herself. A little job. And a step towards independence. It might only be enough for her to enjoy her Saturdays with Kitty, but at least she'd feel she'd earned it. And she had time. Kitty had told her they were rarely given homework and even if they were, she found the schoolwork so easy after the convent that she was sure it wouldn't take her long.

While she waited for Zeek to make a list, she noticed again that splash of colour out in his back yard. She went to look out of the window and was delighted to see even more ranks of pots and troughs than were visible from her bedroom.

'You likes my little pot garden?' Zeek asked, standing at her shoulder. 'Pretty well finished fer the summer now, of course. I'll be bringing in the geraniums in the next day or two. Use the spare bedroom to overwinter the tender plants. Take cuttings from some of them in the spring. And I grow annuals and vegetables from seed. I'll teach you, if you've a mind. So you can pretty up your own back yard, too.'

'Would you?' A grin blossomed on Maisie's face. 'I'd love that! I used to visit the Bishop's Palace in Cobh and the garden was just so beautiful. I'm going to miss it so much.'

'Well, I'd love to hear all about it.' Zeek's leathery face crinkled into a smile. 'Now, that should cover the shopping,' he said, handing her some money and a short list. 'And while you'm out, I'll start sorting through my Ruth's clothes. Kept them long enough, I have. I'm guessing you don't have much in that department, like. I cut things down for you. It'd be nice to use my aud skills again, and I can't think of a better use for Ruth's things. Better than mouldering away in a wardrobe. How about a nice warm pair of slacks fer the winter?' He gave a broad, wrinkled smile. 'My, given us a new lease of life, you have!'

Maisie felt her spirits leap. She might have been forced to leave her friends at the convent and live with her mean, sour-faced father. But new experiences and new people were coming into her life: bright, adventurous Kitty, and now kind and generous Zeek. Perhaps the future didn't look so bleak, after all.

* * *

'Sure, it's very kind of you to have me, Mrs Barron, so it is,' Maisie said politely as Kitty ushered her into the sitting room of her home after school on the Wednesday.

A plump woman, dressed in a tweed skirt and a pink twin set adorned with a string of pearls, glanced up from where she sat on a sofa, drinking a cup of tea. The smile froze on her face at Maisie's words and her nose twitched slightly. Maisie could hear a hint of disdain in her voice as she said, 'Kitty, you didn't tell me your new friend was Irish.'

Maisie flinched as she recalled what her father had said about people still looking down on the Irish. So perhaps he was right in that, at least. But she hadn't expected to hear it from Kitty's mother.

Kitty, though, merely shrugged as her little brother who'd walked home from school with them pushed past her and flung himself on the floor to play with a brightly coloured toy lorry. 'Didn't I?' she replied. 'Well, she is.'

Maisie was reeling from Mrs Barron's rebuff and couldn't think of a thing to say. So instead she dropped onto her knees beside little Alan. 'What's in your lorry?' she asked the child. 'Is it delivering something to somebody?'

'I don't know,' Alan answered.

'Sure, why don't you ask the driver?' Maisie suggested.

'Oh, all right.' The boy picked up the lorry and his lips moved in a brief, silent conversation. 'He says he's taking coal to the dockyard,' he announced.

'Better let him get on with it, then.'

Alan at once went back to pushing the toy along the floor, and Kitty tugged on Maisie's sleeve. 'Come into the kitchen and I'll pour us some tea. Don't know about you, but I'm gasping.'

Kitty led Maisie back out into the hallway, past another open door which Maisie could see was a separate dining room, and then into a kitchen behind it. It was smaller than the one at her father's house, but Maisie supposed if you had both a separate dining room and a sitting room, the kitchen only needed to be big enough to cook in. The house was almost new, Kitty had told her, with three bedrooms and a plumbed in bathroom and toilet upstairs. Indeed, Maisie noticed that instead of a range, a modern gas oven stood proudly on its tall legs, although there was a small coal stove in one corner which Kitty explained supplied their hot water.

'Sure, your house is lovely,' Maisie said admiringly, managing to disguise the hurt she still felt from Kitty's mother's remark.

'I know. I'm proper lucky. Mother's mortal proud of it.' Kitty's face fell slightly as she poured two cups of tea from a pot on a work surface against one of the walls. Lowering her voice she said, 'Sorry about her just now. She can be a bit of a snob at times, but she'll like you once she gets to know you. Come on.'

She handed Maisie one of the cups and took her back into the sitting room. Maisie sat down in a chair and sipped nervously at her tea.

'It's a very nice house you have, Mrs Barron, so it is,' she said, hoping that some flattery might get her into the woman's good books. 'Have you lived here long?'

She noticed Mrs Barron's expression soften. 'Four years, since soon after it were built. And what about you? Kitty tells me you're new at the school.'

'I only arrived here last week. But hasn't my father lived here for years. My mammy died when I was a babby, you see, so I was brought up in a convent back home in Ireland.'

Mrs Barron's eyebrows darted up towards her permed hair. 'A convent girl, eh? Well, you should know how to behave. Kitty tells me you're interested in cooking.'

'I am so. My father lost the use of his left arm, so it's difficult for him, and I'd only just started cookery lessons at the convent.'

'Well, they wouldn't teach you as well as me.' Mrs Barron stretched her neck out of her pearls. 'Come into the kitchen when you've finished your tea, and you can help me get dinner. I were going to bake a sponge for pudding, so you can learn how to do that, as well.'

'Thank you, Mrs Barron. I'd love to be able to surprise my father,' Maisie told her, even if that was only the half of it! She wanted to stun him, shock him into realising she was more than just a skivvy. 'We don't have a lot of money, mind,' she went on, 'so I'd only be able to use the cheapest ingredients, especially when it comes to things like meat.'

She noticed Kitty's mother stifle a sniff as she rose to her feet. 'Even cheap cuts can taste good if you know how to cook them. And I suppose none of us knows when we might need such skills. I'm already passing my knowledge on to Kitty, so why don't you come every Wednesday, and I can teach you at the same time?'

The woman's superior attitude hadn't dropped — indeed, she appeared to be basking in self-satisfaction — but it was a generous offer, and would prove jolly useful! Maisie had no one else to teach her, and if she could satisfy her father in the food department, it should make life less fraught.

'Thank you, Mrs Barron,' she beamed, genuinely excited. 'I should love that.'

'Well, hurry up and finish your tea, the pair of you,' Mrs Barron instructed as she left the room, 'and us can get started.'

Maisie had to smile to herself. In the week she'd been living in Plymouth, she was already beginning to recognise the various degrees of the Devonshire accent and dialect. Some of her classmates spoke it so strongly that she had a job trying to decipher what they were saying, while others, like Kitty, were more of a halfway house, she supposed. She guessed that Mrs Barron wanted to speak 'more proper, like,' and that using 'us' instead of 'we' was a little slip.

'There, I told you she'd get to like you,' Kitty whispered with a conspiratorial wink. 'She's not as prim and proper as she appears.'

Maisie nodded cautiously. Time would tell how she'd get on with Kitty's mother. She was beginning to learn that families weren't always what she'd imagined. She'd envied Kitty her family and the loving way she talked about them, yet her mother was obviously on the prickly side. As for Maisie's own family — if you could call it that — well, wasn't she better off before she knew her father even existed? But it made her even more determined that one day, she'd create a happy home of her own with a husband who treated her like a human being, and adorable children at their feet.

* * *

'My goodness, it's stunning!' Maisie gasped as she gazed out of the train window the following Saturday morning. 'We have mountains in Ireland, but I've never seen them.'

'They're not mountains,' Kitty chuckled. 'Mountains are much higher. These are called tors. That's a big one, mind. Sheepstor. There's a hamlet of the same name at the foot of it. We'll go there one day. You get off at Burrator Halt above the reservoir and walk all the way round. But today's so nice we'll go right up on the moor. We get off at Yelverton, then change onto the little train that'll take us right the way up. We'll get off at King Tor Halt and I'll show you the old quarries. Amazing they are.'

'Sounds wonderful, so it does!' Maisie exclaimed, almost breathless at the undulating landscape that rose to the distant horizon, dotted with craggy outbreaks of granite. 'And such a beautiful day for it. Lucky I earned that extra bit of money from Zeek for the rail fare, mind. Old meanie wouldn't have given it to me, that's for sure.'

'And that I had a spare pair of wellies for you to borrow. Couldn't come up here without some waterproof footwear. But I don't know why your dad's always pleading poverty,'

Kitty mused, her tone becoming serious. 'When I told Father, he managed to find out what sort of job your dad has. Apparently, he's in charge of a whole section in accounts, so he can't be badly paid.'

'Well, he does have the rent to pay—'

'Which won't be so much on that small house,' Kitty scoffed. 'Father says he probably doesn't earn an awful lot more, and he has the mortgage to pay and all three of us to support cuz mother won't go out to work. So when your dad says he doesn't have any money, 'tisn't rightly true, the old fraud.'

Maisie puffed out her cheeks, frustrated at her father but determined not to let it ruin her day. 'Sure, it wouldn't surprise me. But I don't want to be thinking about him today. I just want to enjoy this wonderful scenery. But how come you're knowing Dartmoor so well that your mammy and daddy let you come here on your own?'

'Not on my own. I have you,' Kitty grinned. 'Mother said you seem a sensible maid, otherwise she wouldn't have let me come. And to be honest, she thinks Beryl and Philippa were coming with us, too, so don't forget that if she says ort about it on Wednesday.'

Maisie was aghast. 'You're wanting me to lie?'

'It'd only be a teeny-weeny sin,' Kitty giggled, slowly squeezing her forefinger and thumb towards each other. 'And I know this part of the moor pretty well. Father's been bringing us up here for years. It were never summat Mother wanted to do, but Father's walked on the moor all his life and I've learned from him.'

'We-ell, if you're sure we won't get lost—'

'Don't you worry none. I'd only do walks I know really well. The main thing I've learned is that you must respect the moor. Today, we'll never be that far from the railway line. But we'll need to keep an eye on the time. There's not that many trains a day, so we must make sure we don't miss the last one back down to Yelverton.'

Maisie nodded back. Kitty seemed to know what she was talking about, so Maisie cast her misgivings aside as she sat forward to feast her eyes on the spectacular scenery. The moor seemed to stretch out for ever, vast and exposed, with not a house to be seen from the train window, although Kitty assured her there were farms and cottages dotted about all over the place. Sheep and ponies grazed wild, apparently. There were even cattle roaming free, although it was wise to keep your distance from them, and never get between a cow and its calf, Kitty explained. Maisie felt a little wary at that, but the moor was so extensive that it couldn't be that difficult to give any animals a wide berth.

The train was slowing and eventually coasted into Yelverton Station, stopping with a gentle jolt. The little engine on the Princetown line was already there, puffing softly as it waited to depart on its long, slow haul up onto the moor. Maisie waited while Kitty had a quick word with the guard, although what about, Maisie couldn't hear. Then they clambered up into a compartment in one of two carriages, and shortly afterwards, they could hear the guard slamming shut all the doors before blowing his whistle. Then with a clunk and a hissing of steam, the train gave a lurch and they were off.

Maisie felt she could burst with excitement. Within minutes, they'd left the settlement of Yelverton and were chugging along at a steady rate. Breath-taking views opened up on either side, and after the little station at Dousland, the line swung round and soon they were looking down on the shimmering waters of the reservoir Kitty had described. The climb became steeper, and they could hear the engine straining as it slowly snaked its way upwards, curling around the contours of the wild and savage landscape. Maisie found herself skipping from one side of the compartment to the other, not wanting to miss a moment of this enthralling journey.

The train finally stopped at a wooden platform in the middle of nowhere and Kitty opened the door and jumped down. Maisie was full of joy as she hopped down beside her friend. The guard waved to them, and then they watched the little train weave its way from the halt and gradually disappear into the distance until all they could see were puffs of grey smoke against the blue sky.

Silence echoed about them. Maisie thought she'd never felt so awestruck in her life, and she stood there, wanting to breathe it inside herself. But then she realised Kitty was grinning at her.

'Told you it were wonderful, didn't I? We'll walk along to Foggintor Quarry first. It's just so impressive. Then we'll cross over that way,' she said, pointing in the opposite direction, 'and I'll show you round Swell Tor. We'll see the train going past a couple of times, but we'll catch a later one over the other side of the loop. There's no halt, but the guard said he'll stop the train for us to get back on. Bit of a climb up, but we can manage. I've done it heaps of times afore.'

Maisie blinked at her in surprise. Sure, this really was an adventure! And for the first time, she felt glad that she had ended up here, after all.

CHAPTER FOURTEEN

Maisie yawned and opened her eyes, stretching her arms above her head, then she instantly drew them back and tucked them under the bed covers again. The air in her room was arctic, hardly inviting her to get out of bed. Wouldn't she love to stay there all day, huddled beneath the blankets, but she knew she couldn't. Her father would be wanting her to make him a pot of tea, get breakfast and cook him Christmas dinner.

Huh! Christmas Day. She couldn't help imagining how everyone would be celebrating it back at the convent. The previous year, she'd been allowed to go to Midnight Mass at the cathedral for the very first time. It had been magical, with the awesome interior illuminated by candlelight alone, the choir sounding even more angelic than ever. But now, a year on, Maisie was too frightened to creep out to Mass in case her father discovered her deception and hit her again. Or tried to stop her going out with Kitty, one of the few things that made her life bearable.

As she lay in bed, she tried to guess what Noreen and Sister Agnes would be doing that special morning. The great chasm of emptiness that had become so familiar opened up inside her once again. Why had neither of them written to her? She'd sent letters to them every week, her father posting them in the office for her. She'd made them both Christmas cards and had eagerly awaited the post every morning. Surely they'd remember her at Christmas? Each day she'd watched the postman coming down the street, but the only envelopes dropping through the letterbox were addressed to Francis O'Sullivan. But surely yesterday something should have arrived for her?

Her father had been at work, of course, it being Christmas Eve. Maisie had gone to Kitty's house where they'd had such fun baking mince pies and wassail biscuits under Mrs Barron's instruction. After a quick snack for lunch, she and Kitty had walked into the town centre to window shop and soak up the festive atmosphere in the market.

Wandering back home, they'd treated themselves to a pot of tea and a slice of cake each in one of the genteel tea rooms in Union Street. The place was run by a friendly, jolly lady who greeted all her customers with a welcoming smile. Tinsel hung merrily from picture frames on the walls, and each table had a little decoration of holly, with glitter twinkling around its bright red berries. Among the customers were a couple of sailors entertaining two smartly dressed young women, and a naval officer obviously home on Christmas leave, enjoying time with his wife and young family.

It was such a happy atmosphere that Maisie was reluctant to leave, knowing she'd be able to cut the air with a knife once she arrived home and her father got back from work. But home she must go, and she gave Kitty a crushing hug as they parted company. But one thought buoyed her up. She truly expected that something with an Irish postmark would have arrived with the second post. Surely it must, and she pushed open the front door with eager anticipation. But there was nothing whatsoever on the door mat.

Sure, she couldn't believe that Noreen and Sister Agnes had forgotten her, but apparently they had. Then she thought maybe they'd misjudged the time it would take for the post to arrive, and it would turn up in a day or two. The thought gave her the strength to jump out of bed and pull on her clothes. She chose that best outfit she'd been given at the convent. After all, even if she was going to hate every minute of the day closeted with her horrible father, wasn't it still Christ's birthday? So she should dress up to mark the occasion.

Downstairs, she stoked up the range and set the kettle on to boil. Her father wasn't yet up, so while the house was still free from the tension of his company, Maisie took the opportunity to open her Christmas cards from Kitty, Philippa and Beryl that she'd been saving for the day. Miss Mitchell had given each girl in the class one, too, so that made four to put on the mantelpiece. They were the only ones as her father hadn't received any at all.

They'd spent the last morning in school making Christmas cards for their families. Maisie had made one for her father, going along with it as she didn't want to reveal the dire circumstances at home. She'd made a second one for her Uncle Zeek, and with some of the money she'd earned from doing his shopping, she'd bought Zeek and her father a box of Black Magic each. She didn't know how Francis would react, but at least she'd have made the effort.

'Merry Christmas to you,' she greeted him with feigned cheeriness when he appeared, and holding her breath, handed him the envelope and the small package.

He had the decency to look surprised, and, opening them with a grunt, put both up on the mantel shelf. 'I hope that doesn't mean you're expecting something from me,' he grunted, and sat down at the table to drink his tea and munch one of the biscuits Maisie had baked at Kitty's the previous day.

Maisie felt utterly miserable. He wasn't even going to say thank you. She turned stiffly and made her way out to the back yard without a word. Slipping into the privy, she shot home the bolt and sat down on the toilet seat. She didn't think she'd ever felt so wretched. Sobs raked her throat. There was no point holding them back, so she let them come, tears streaming down her cheeks as her shoulders shook. The events of the past couple of months tumbled down on top of her, and she sank beneath their weight.

But it was bitingly cold, with the bitter air causing an icy draught through the gap underneath the door, and she couldn't stay there for long. At least it was warm in the kitchen — or the backhouse as Zeek called it. Remembering that her elderly neighbour had invited them in to listen to the king's speech on his radio cheered Maisie up a little.

'What do I want to listen to that for?' her father had scoffed when she'd passed on the invite.

She was secretly thrilled that he'd declined. It meant that she could have the dear old man to herself for an hour or so, and she couldn't wait. Thank goodness Francis hadn't tried to curb her friendship with Zeek. He didn't seem to mind her shooting off next door provided she'd completed all her chores. And it didn't even bother him that she was earning a few shillings doing Zeek's shopping. Sure, he was probably pleased that she was, as it meant he didn't need to cough up any pocket money for her himself!

Praying there were no traces of tears on her cheeks, she went back inside and placed the frying pan on one of the range hotplates. While she waited for it to heat up and melt the spoonful of dripping she'd added to it, she prepared the Christmas dinner. Francis had actually seen fit to give her some extra housekeeping money, which she'd spent on a joint of brisket. Not the best cut of beef, of course, but better than flank. It still needed slow cooking as a pot roast, but she knew how to make the most of it. Thank heavens she had Kitty and her mammy to teach her. She still wasn't quite comfortable in Mrs Barron's company, but she was learning so much about cooking from her that she was willing to put up with the woman's condescending attitude.

'There's your breakfast,' she announced, placing the fried bread with an egg on top in front of her father. She was in the habit of cutting his food up for him, but he never thanked her.

'So, what d'you normally do on Christmas Day if you won't go to the Mass?' she asked, unable to resist the little dig. 'It's cold but it's dry. So we could go for a walk if we wrap up.'

'Huh, don't you think I do enough walking going to and from work?' he grumbled back. 'But you can go as long as you're back in time to finish off dinner. I want it at one o'clock sharp.'

'Of course,' she bristled back. 'I'm going to Zeek's to listen to the king's speech at three, so I'll want to have washed up and everything by then, anyway.'

She bustled around the room, clearing away and making sure everything was ready for when she returned. She couldn't get away quickly enough, and was soon out in the crisp, fresh air away from the oppressive atmosphere indoors. Where could she go? There wasn't time to make it worthwhile going to Kitty's. Besides, she'd been invited there for Boxing Day.

She walked aimlessly down the street, her thoughts drifting back to the convent and feeling that bottomless hole in her heart again. Her feet were taking her towards the town centre, and then, as if drawn by some invisible thread, she turned up the road towards the cathedral church. Surely she could risk it? If there was a service going on, she could slide in at the back. She didn't want to be obliged to speak to the priest and have to bluff her way out of answering why she hadn't been again since that first time. He'd be bound to ask. The important thing was that her father didn't know where she'd been. If he suspected, she'd deny it this time. Wouldn't God forgive her such a sin if it was to save herself from being hit again. She'd say a few Hail Marys in secret as her penance, using her rosary that she'd managed to keep concealed in her bedroom.

As it happened, when she pushed open the side door of the cathedral church, all was silent and eerily echoing. Not a soul was in sight. It must be between services. So Maisie was able to say a few prayers and then leave again without any awkward moments.

The visit, though, had made her feel much better. When she arrived home, she hummed to herself as she got on with the dinner. Her father hadn't questioned her, but had his nose in yesterday's paper. What he always found so absorbing among the sports pages, she didn't know. But at least it kept him out of her hair for a while.

She'd decorated the table with some sprigs of holly she'd bought for a penny in the market. Remembering the decorations at the tea rooms the day before, she'd arranged them in a jug surrounded by a red paper circle from the paperchains she'd strung along one wall. It was the best she could do.

'Don't go thinking we'll be having a Christmas tree,' Francis had growled when he'd found her sticking the strips of coloured paper together.

She'd merely tossed him a glance. Humbug to you! And then she'd almost laughed as she imagined him cowering when being visited by Marley in his chains alongside the other ghosts, like Scrooge in *A Christmas Carol*. Miss Mitchell, when she'd discovered her love of reading, had suggest various titles Maisie might like, and she'd borrowed some of them from the public library, one of the few joys that had softened the blow of being dragged away from the convent.

The memory of that humbug moment made her smile to herself and helped her get through the miserable lunch. Then, as soon as she was able, she scooted round next door.

'Merry Christmas, cheel!' Zeek called from the backhouse when he heard her come in the front door. 'Come through. You'm just in time.'

Maisie stepped through to the now familiar room. The flap of the drop-leaf table was up, bearing the remains of Zeek's Christmas dinner and a glass of beer. He was seated in one of the upright chairs, tuning the wooden-cased wireless.

'Ah, there we are,' he beamed, and indicating the armchairs by the range, gestured for her to sit down in one, while he moved into the other.

Maisie sat down, the card and present she had for the old man on her lap. Zeek's radio was a complete fascination to her. She didn't know what to expect from the king's speech. It was coming from somewhere in the countryside and was apparently introduced by a local shepherd. Maisie didn't quite understand all of what George V was saying, but it sounded both grand and friendly at the same time. Afterwards, the local church choir sang some carols, adding to the festive cheer.

'What did you think of that, then, maid?' Zeek asked her when it was over.

'Well, hasn't it made me feel a lot more Christmassy,' Maisie grinned. 'More like a wake it's been next door, so.'

Zeek gave a deep-throated chuckle. 'Miserable aud bugger your da, if you'll excuse my language. Well, let's see if Zeek can cheer you up. You go into the parlour while I put the kettle on.'

'Thank you, Zeek. But first, haven't I got something for you.' And she held out the envelope and the small package to him.

'Aw, cheel, that's master kind of you.' Maisie detected a catch in his voice as he began to open them. 'Not had a proper present since my Ruth went.'

'It isn't much, I'm afraid—'

'But they'm my favourite, Black Magic! Thank you, maid. And what a lovely card! Made it yoursel, I see. Pride of place that'll have, in the middle of the mantel. The other cards are from a few neighbours, but yourn is the best. Now go and make yoursel comfy next door, and I'll be in in a jiffy.'

Glowing with pride and happiness, Maisie went back out into the hallway. She'd never been inside her father's front room as he kept it permanently locked. But neither had she been in Zeek's. She pushed open the door. And gasped.

Behind an ornate fireguard, a mound of coals gleamed a bright, orangey red in an attractive cast iron fireplace with pretty tiles either side. Next to it, a small Christmas tree dripping with lametta twinkled and sparkled with tiny electric lights and shiny scarlet baubles. Dancing garlands of silver tinsel were strung along the picture rails and a jumble of holly and ivy cascaded from the mantelpiece, with a red candle in a brass candlestick at either end. Outside, the daylight was fading, making the whole effect magical.

Maisie stepped inside, steeped in amazement as if she was entering a fairy wonderland. The mystery, the excitement, the joy she'd always experienced at Christmas in the convent came flooding back, and she felt a lump rising in her throat.

'It's . . . beautiful, so it is,' she murmured as Zeek came up behind her.

'Did it special fer you, like,' he replied. 'Always used to do it like this fer my Ruth, but since she's gone, I never had the heart to do it again. But you've given us back my life, cheel, and I cas'n tell you what it means to me. Now let me put down this yere tray, and you can open your presents.'

'Presents?'

'Under the tree, maid. Brought us such joy it has, making them. And it were as if my Ruth were sitting next to us as I worked. Brought her back to me, and all, you have.'

'Oh, Zeek,' Maisie breathed, holding back tears.

'Well, go on and open them while I pour this tea,' Zeek urged, blinking away the moisture in his own eyes.

Maisie kneeled down by the tree and pulled four soft packages towards her, all wrapped in brightly coloured Christmas paper and tied with red bows. She hardly dared open them, and did so as carefully as possible to make sure she didn't spoil the paper, so that it could be re-used. Waste not, want not, the nuns had always taught her. But it tested her patience, as she couldn't wait to see what was inside each one.

It didn't take long for all to be revealed. Zeek had fashioned her a pair of blue tartan slacks in the softest wool, another pair of trousers in a strong, serviceable material, a pretty cream silk blouse, and a floral skirt that flared at the knee.

Maisie was overcome by a mixture of joy and gratitude. 'Oh, Zeek, all this work you've done!'

'It were a pleasure. I haven't quite finished off some of them cuz you need to try them on, but I reckons I judged your size pretty well. Now we'll have this yere tea and cake, and then I'll go and wash up while you tries them on. You can call us when you'm ready, and I'll pin up the hems or whatever else needs doing.'

Maisie sprang to her feet. Sure, wasn't this old man the kindest, loveliest person in the world. She simply couldn't stop herself, and wrapped her arms about him, squeezing him tightly.

'My goodness, cheel, you'll have us fainting!' he chuckled, and meeting his teasing eyes, Maisie giggled back. Christmas Day really hadn't turned out so bad in the end.

* * *

'Maisie! Happy Boxing Day!' Kitty chirped as she opened the front door. 'I were worried old misery guts would change his mind and not let you come. But come on in. It's proper snipey weather today.'

Maisie stepped gratefully into the warm hallway and took off her best coat. 'I'm thinking he couldn't wait to see the back of me. I've left him a meal all ready to heat up in the range oven and sure, that's all he cares about.'

'Well, you're here which is all that matters. And nice and early so we can spend the whole day together! We're all in the sitting room, so you can open your presents straightaway.'

Maisie followed her into the front room where Kitty's parents and young Alan were sitting around a low table playing snakes and ladders. Just as at Zeek's the previous day, a coal fire was blazing in the grate, its happy glow reaching out to her.

'Hello, Maisie, dear. Come in and warm up,' Mr Barron greeted her.

'Thank you. Sure, it's freezing outside. But haven't you made this room look lovely! And what a pretty tree.'

'It's got presents for you underneath,' Alan declared excitedly, jumping up. 'Everyone's got you something. Mine's only small, but I bet you'll like it the best.'

Maisie couldn't help beaming. 'I'm sure I will. But it's very kind of you all. I've got some things for you, too. Not much, but I'm afraid I don't have much money.'

'Let me see!' Alan demanded.

'Alan, manners!' his mother reprimanded.

'Well, let's see now. Will you be Father Christmas for me first, Alan?' Maisie asked, delving into her string bag. 'This one's for your mammy,' she said, giving him a small package. 'And then this is for your daddy.'

The child was back in an instant, so Maisie handed him his own present from her. He tore open the paper, bursting with excitement to discover two brightly coloured Dinky Toy vans.

'To go with your lorry,' Maisie smiled at him.

'Say thank you, then,' Mrs Barron prompted.

'Thanks, Maisie! *Brrm, brrm*,' the boy said, delighted, and at once started to run the toy vans along a line in the rug in front of the hearth.

'And this is very kind of you, too, Maisie,' Kitty's father beamed as he waved the two tuppenny bars of Cadbury's Whole Nut in the air.

'And very finely stitched, these,' Mrs Barron said in her prim way, admiring the handkerchiefs Maisie had given her. 'Did you make them yourself?'

'Sure, not the handkerchiefs themselves, but I did all the embroidering and put on the lace.'

'Well, you made a lovely job, especially for one so young. Thank you.'

'We were taught the sewing from a very early age at the convent, and I always enjoyed—'

'Oh, look at this!' Kitty interrupted as she held up a knitted pink bolero. 'It's proper beautiful. Did you make it yourself, and all?'

'I did, so. That's what I was going to say. How I enjoyed the sewing and the knitting. I made it a bit on the large side so you can grow into it.'

'I won't need to wait after Mother's Christmas dinner yesterday!' Kitty laughed.

'But you will get taller,' Maisie said earnestly. 'I bought extra wool so I can knit it longer when you need it.'

'My, you're proper clever, you! And you're my best friend now. Thank you so much!' Kitty stepped forward and gave Maisie a hug. 'So now you can open our presents to you,' she added, her eyes shining.

'Yes, here's mine!' Alan leaped up and grabbing a small packet from under the tree, thrust it into Maisie's hands. 'Go on, open it.'

'Why, thank you,' Maisie answered, so amused by his enthusiasm that she opened it immediately. 'Ooh, chocolate. Cadbury's Milk Tray! I'll have one every evening and think of you each time I pop one in my mouth.'

The boy beamed at her, his ruddy cheeks aglow. 'Told you she'd like mine best.'

'Silly, how can she tell until she's opened them all?' Kitty laughed. 'This one's from Mother, and then this one is from Father.'

Maisie lowered her eyes to the brightly patterned packages, feeling embarrassed by so much attention. She hoped it didn't show in her face as she unwrapped the presents, a cookery book from Mr Barron and some utensils from his wife.

'I remembered things you said you don't have when we've been cooking on Wednesdays,' she said proudly, 'so I thought I'd get you some.'

'Sure, that's so thoughtful. Thank you both so much.'

'And now open mine,' Kitty said. 'It's definitely the best.'

Maisie took the present Kitty held out to her, a frown corrugating her forehead as she opened it. She could feel it was something soft, and when she eased it out from the wrapping paper, some sort of undergarment in a peach-coloured silky material was smooth in her hands. It was very pretty, but she wasn't sure what it was.

'Oh, it's lovely,' she murmured, red with embarrassment and really not knowing what to say.

'Come up to my room and you can try it on. Come on.'

Maisie scuttled out of the room after her friend and followed her upstairs. What a relief not to have to show her ignorance in front of Kitty's parents. It was only when they reached Kitty's bedroom and shut the door behind them that she plucked up the courage to mutter, 'Thanks so much, Kitty. It's beautiful, but . . . what is it?'

Kitty stared at her for a moment, eyes like saucers, and then burst out laughing. 'Don't you know? Oh, I suppose not having a mum to explain . . . It's a brassiere. Or bra for short. You wear it under your vest. It supports your chest as it grows. And you've got a bit now, I've noticed. Not like me. Still flat as a blooming pancake. If it's a bit loose as yet, you can stuff some cottonwool down it until you fill it out proper like. So go on, try it on. I'll wait outside if you like.'

Alone in the bedroom, Maisie felt utterly confused. Yes, she supposed her chest had grown quite a bit in the last couple of months. She hadn't thought much about it, always taking her weekly bath as swiftly as possible. She wasn't sure she wanted a . . . what did Kitty call it? A bra? But now as she reluctantly stripped off, she found she did partially fill the garment.

Dressing again, she called her friend back in. 'Thank you, Kitty. Sure, it fits quite well,' she said, trying to convince herself. 'Though I'll need to pad it out a bit like you said.'

'Well, I'm hoping I'll need one soon,' Kitty sighed enviously, 'even if it means we'll soon be getting the curse.'

Curse? What was Kitty on about? Maisie felt her life had been cursed enough recently and couldn't she do without any more bad luck. But Kitty must have seen her puzzlement.

'You know, your monthlies,' Kitty went on with a quizzical frown. 'Getting our bodies ready to have babbies.'

'Babbies!' Maisie was utterly shocked. 'Sure, you don't have babbies until after you're married, and that's a long way off!'

'You can have babbies afore you're married,' Kitty replied knowledgeably, looking mysterious, embarrassed and animated all at once. 'If you do it. You know. With a boy.'

Maisie stared at her, quite bewildered. What did she mean? Had Kitty gone mad? She was talking in riddles.

But then Kitty shook her head. 'D'you really not know? Oh, Lordy love, don't say I've got to tell you? Well, maybe we'd better sit down. I heard it from Philippa back in the summer. You know she's the oldest in the class, so I suppose she knew it first. And she wants to be a nurse when she grows up. She were very matter-o-fact about it, so I'll try to be, too.'

Maisie slowly lowered herself onto the bed beside her friend, at an utter loss. Heat rose in her neck as Kitty began to explain, her stomach churning at each word until she felt sick. Despite Kitty's stiff and starchy mammy, nowadays Maisie felt at home in the Barron household. For the first time in her life, she felt part of a family, strengthening her determination to create one of her own when the time came. But if you had to do that to have a babby, then she wasn't at all sure she wanted a husband and a family after all!

All her dreams came crashing down around her. She was trembling, felt shocked and angry and . . . and cheated. Sure, did God really want you to do that? Was that what so-called love between a man and a woman led to? She vaguely recalled that Noreen hadn't been much older than she was now when she'd announced that she was going to take holy vows. Was that because she'd learned what Maisie just had, and wanted to be a nun so that she never had to do *that*?

'Sure, that's disgusting, so it is,' she declared fiercely.

'I know it sounds like it,' Kitty tried to soothe her. 'But if you think about it, that's how everyone in the world comes about, so it can't be that bad. And Philippa says that when you grow up, you get chemicals in your body that make you want to do it, and people enjoy it. So there's no need to be scared, and it's a long way off for us yet. Only,' she faltered, catching Maisie's arm, 'Mother doesn't know that I know, so you won't let on ever, will you?'

Maisie met her friend's gaze, her pulse still hammering. How could she get through life if that was what awaited? She felt shaken to the core. Hadn't she been looking forward so much to today, and now it was as if a big black cloud was pressing down on her. As she followed Kitty back downstairs, she wondered how on earth she was going to act normally for the rest of the day and join in the fun and games she knew Kitty had planned. Oh, why had Kitty said anything? She'd ruined everything!

The celebrations continued and the company ate and laughed their way through a sumptuous Boxing Day dinner, but Maisie's mind wasn't on the festivities. She smiled and nodded politely, but all she could think of was what Kitty had revealed. She couldn't wait to go home so that she could be alone with her own thoughts and emotions. The minute the light began to fade, she left the house, though it was much earlier than she had intended to leave, giving the excuse that she needed to be home before dark.

She walked slowly, trying to absorb her new-found knowledge before she had to face her father again. She couldn't ever imagine she'd want to do what Kitty had described, even if it was way off in the future. But as Kitty had pointed out, it was how each and every member of the human race had been created. And God had created Adam and Eve, so it must be God's will for people to carry out such an act, however obscene it seemed to her.

Her heart was heavy as she turned her key in the lock. She must somehow try to put it to the back of her mind. She was only twelve years old. There was more than enough time to contemplate such matters in the years ahead. For now, she just needed to focus on putting up with her father.

She went indoors and found the atmosphere was as stony as ever. So as soon as she felt she could, she took herself off to bed with a book she'd borrowed from the library. But try as she might, she couldn't concentrate. All she could think about was Kitty's revelation — and why she hadn't received any news from Ireland. If it hadn't been for Zeek's kindness and her day at Kitty's house, she would have wept.

CHAPTER FIFTEEN

1935

'Are you sure you won't come?' Maisie said, feeling she should ask while silently praying her father hadn't changed his mind.

'Why would I want to celebrate an English king?' he snapped back.

Maisie cocked an eyebrow. 'So you do still have some loyalties to old Ireland, then?' she suggested enigmatically, before swiftly bringing the conversation to a close. 'I'll be off, then. I might be back late, so don't worry.' As if he would, she scoffed in her head, except that he might worry about losing his unpaid skivvy. 'I'll be with the others, so I'll be perfectly safe,' she concluded as, sweeping her sandwiches from the table, she skipped out of the kitchen and took her shoulder bag from the stand in the hallway.

Within moments, she was entering the neighbouring house, calling Zeek's name. The old man appeared, grinning, from the backhouse, and Maisie took in a surprised breath, he looked so smart in a jacket and tie.

'Morning, Zeek. Isn't it a grand day? Will you be warm enough like that?'

Zeek chuckled and tapped his chest. 'Well, it's a nice day fer it. And I've got a thick vest on underneath, and a jumper under my jacket. And I've that rug to put over my knees if need be. Such a good idea of yourn to get a wheelchair fer us. I wouldn't have wanted to miss today.'

'Well, this won't be the only time we take you out in it, so,' Maisie assured him, manoeuvring the said wheelchair from where it 'lived' in the front room and along the corridor to the front door. 'Especially with summer on its way.'

'I bless the day you arrived yere, cheel, I don't mind telling you. Never mind what some people say about today's youngsters. Some of you be proper grand.'

Once they were outside, Maisie put her own sandwiches with Zeek's in the bag slung from the handles of the wheelchair. Then she helped him get comfortable before wheeling him off down the street. It was lovely to be out in the fresh, early May morning, knowing they had such an exciting day ahead of them. It wasn't every day the king celebrated his Silver Jubilee, and Plymouth was going to do it in grand style.

When they reached the main road, Kitty and her family were coming towards them, as arranged. There'd be thousands of people jostling around the town that day, and Kitty's parents had declared that they wouldn't let her go alone with just Maisie. Not that the girls minded. And besides, Maisie had wanted to bring Zeek, not just to repay the old man's kindness, but because he was such good company. He'd lived in Plymouth all of his eighty odd years, and had many an amusing story to tell. Maisie knew that when he began a sentence with, 'Back along when I were a tacker,' she was in for a treat. There wouldn't be the opportunity for such reminiscences today. The crowds promised to be phenomenal, and there was going to be such a lot to see.

After swiftly introducing Zeek to Kitty's parents and young Alan, the little troop set off down the road. Not everyone wanted to join the crushing throngs that promised to jam the Hoe later on, and they saw people setting out tables for street parties instead, and stringing bunting across from lamp posts and windows. Coming into the town centre, crowds were beginning to gather. Streamers were hung from every possible point, and flags flapped noisily in the breeze, not just handkerchief-sized ones, but most were the size of sheets. When Maisie looked up, she could barely see the sky between the tall buildings for fluttering Union Jacks and other flags she didn't recognise.

'What a sight, eh?' Zeek twisted his neck to grin at her over his shoulder as she pushed him along. 'Paid fer by the town council, no doubt. And firms like Dingles and Burtons and all they assurance companies will probably have done everything outside their own places.'

'*City* council from today.' Mrs Barron bobbed her head majestically, bristling with pride as if the king's bestowing city status on Plymouth as part of the celebrations was all her doing!

Maisie met Kitty's eyes, and they both had to suppress a giggle as they shared the same thought. What difference would it make to their lives if Plymouth was a town or a city, they wondered? All Maisie knew was that today was going to be so special. But wasn't there a sadness lingering at the back of her mind. Nothing like this would be going on in Cobh and she felt a little guilty at her own happy anticipation of the celebrations. But then, why should she? She'd not had one communication from Noreen or Sister Agnes, and recently, with heavy heart, she'd given up writing to them, too.

Burying the thought deep inside, she nodded gratefully as Kitty helped her negotiate the wheelchair up a kerb. The pavements were becoming even busier, and after a while, Mr Barron insisted on taking over, leaving Maisie and Kitty free to link arms as they continued onwards.

Eventually, at the appropriate time, they made their way to the Hoe. By now, the paths and walkways were heaving with thousands of merrymakers waving flags, jostling and bumping each other as they lined the promenade, everyone wanting to have a good view.

'Let the little lad through to the front,' someone called, seeing young Alan, 'and his granddad in the wheelchair!'

Maisie was pushing Zeek again, and saw him grin at the misunderstanding, but they weren't going to say anything. It meant, though, that Maisie and Kitty were able to stand on one side of him and Alan on the other, so that they had a perfect, uninterrupted view. Stationed behind them, Kitty's parents were able to see over their heads. It couldn't have worked out better. They had positioned themselves near the massive Royal Navy Memorial where they knew the height of the ceremony was to take place.

It wasn't long before the parade began. Soldiers had been posted at short intervals to remind the multitudes of spectators to keep back, but the first of those to march into position were sailors. Hundreds and hundreds of them formed lines right the way along the promenade, so smart in their dark blue uniforms with their white hats brilliant in the sunshine. The parade was huge, and Maisie was amazed to see so many seamen amassed altogether. Sure, the British Navy was a million times bigger than she'd ever imagined.

Lost in admiration, she wasn't aware for a moment of Kitty prodding her in the ribs.

'Proper handsome, some of them, aren't they?' she whispered in Maisie's ear, her eyes shining. 'I do like a man in uniform. Happen we'll find ourselves husbands among them one day.'

Maisie gave a weak smile. She wouldn't be looking to find herself a husband anywhere, not after what Kitty had told her about how babbies were made back on Boxing Day. She'd managed to banish the very idea from her mind, and she certainly didn't want it to spoil her enjoyment of today.

At that moment, however, a dozen naval dignitaries — admirals and the like, Maisie assumed — wearing bicorn hats and uniforms adorned with heavy gold braiding, began inspecting the ranks of sailors. Despite all the spectacle, it was getting quite tiring, and Maisie felt envious of Zeek sitting in the wheelchair. In fact, Alan was complaining and so

Zeek had invited the boy to sit on his lap. But at long last, the naval inspection was completed, and Maisie ducked at the roar of a small plane flying low overhead. The next thing she knew, teams of sailors were pulling up huge gun carriages and stopped almost in front of them.

'Look, cannons!' Alan cried.

'Usually call them big guns,' Zeek told him. 'Put your hands over your ears. Mortal big bang they'll make.'

Maisie watched, fascinated, as the guns were loaded. She was ready to cover her ears, and was glad she did. The explosions were deafening even so, the ground vibrating beneath her feet. She saw the gigantic guns bounce with the recoil, but the next instant, they were enveloped in a pall of thick, white smoke. Maisie found it quite unsettling and held her breath while the blinding veil slowly dissipated.

Already there was movement and the spectacular parade started to move off. Next came a contingent of marines in their distinctive uniforms, followed by hundreds of infantry, marching along with rifles over their shoulders. It was all very impressive and there were so many of them that it took some time for them all to march past. The whole exercise was so enormous that it must have been another hour or so before it was all over and the crowds began to break ranks.

'Well, that were summat to behold,' Zeek declared, nodding vigorously. 'I be master grateful to you all fer bringing me. Wouldn't have missed it fer the world. And so good to see us've got such a proper grand army and navy to defend our shores, should it come to it.'

'You don't think it ever would, do you?' Mr Barron asked.

Zeek wiggled his head pensively. 'Well, I hopes not. But I don't like the way Germany's brought in conscription again. And as fer that Hitler chap declaring hissel chancellor and Führer, well, I don't trust him one iota. But enough of that. What'll us do next?'

Maisie had half listened to their conversation, sensing the unease between the two men. She didn't understand what

Zeek had said, but nevertheless felt relieved when he changed the subject. Some people were heading back towards the city centre, perhaps to join in street parties back home. Others evidently plumped for staying on the Hoe, enjoying the warm weather and celebratory atmosphere. The little group decided to do the same, although they all agreed it would be too tiring to stay on until dark when the towering bonfire was to be lit and the bandstand illuminated by its strings of electric lights.

'Well, if you've all had enough,' Zeek suggested some time later, 'why don't us head back home, but call into one of they nice tea rooms in Union Street for afternoon tea on the way? My treat as a thank you fer taking me out.'

'Oh, no, we couldn't let you—' Mrs Barron protested.

'Of course you can!' Zeek beamed back. 'I'll brook no argument. Come along, Maisie. Wagons roll!' he cried, waving his arm forward in a circle.

Laughing at his antics, they set off back through the city streets, still reverberating with celebration. When they at last reached Union Street, Maisie suggested they gave their custom to the tea rooms she and Kitty had visited the previous Christmas Eve, the lady there had been so kind and welcoming. Everyone agreed, so when they reached it, Maisie popped inside to make sure there was a table free. In just the same way as it had been decorated for Christmas, the walls were today festooned with bunting, each table sported a little posy of red, white and blue flowers, and in lieu of the white, starched tablecloths, Maisie noticed there were Union Jack flags.

There was the same homely woman taking an order at one of the tables. When she'd finished, Maisie went up to her and didn't feel the least bit awkward asking if she'd mind them bringing in a wheelchair.

'Not at all,' was the beaming reply, and soon they were all seated around a table, Zeek ordering a full afternoon tea for them all.

'Don't know what he's missing, that miserable aud father of yourn,' he said to Maisie under his breath, giving her a surreptitious wink. Then he raised his voice so that they could all hear him clearly. 'Well, what a proper lovely way to end an amazing day!' he declared, grinning round at them all.

And Maisie couldn't have agreed more.

* * *

'Well, here we are again,' Kitty said as she and Maisie followed her parents and young Alan across the Hoe. 'Where did the summer go? Only seems yesterday we were watching the jubilee celebrations, and now here we are, the beginning of October.'

Yes, what had happened to the summer, Maisie agreed. The time had flown. At the start of the previous term, Miss Mitchell had taken her and Philippa aside for some extra tuition that required daily homework. Then, as the lighter evenings had lengthened and Maisie wasn't closeted with her father so much, she'd spent a lot of her time with Zeek, learning to take cuttings, and to grow flowers and produce from seed. Her own back yard was now festooned with sweet peas growing up canes, bright geraniums and softer begonias, while tomatoes, radishes and carrots grew in whatever makeshift containers she could devise, including orange boxes from the greengrocers lined with old sacking. Francis hadn't objected, as long as she kept it tidy and he enjoyed his share of the fresh produce.

Once the laundry was dancing on the line, Saturdays were spent with Kitty, and sometimes they were joined by Beryl and Philippa. On the odd occasion, they splashed out on a train ride, perhaps to the beautiful riverside village of Bere Ferrers, or on to the quaint old mining village of Gunnislake. Maisie's favourite destination, though, remained Dartmoor, where the sense of timelessness and spectacular scenery seemed to set her heart free.

Much of the time, though, they ambled about the Hoe or the old streets and alleyways of the Barbican. Occasionally, they'd taken the ferry over to Kingsands to sit on the beach and dip their feet in the water. They hadn't been able to paddle from the man-made terraces at the bottom of the cliffs on the Hoe because of the construction of the bathing pool, the grand opening of which they were on their way to now.

'Seems a funny time of year to be opening an open-air swimming pool,' Maisie frowned.

'*Lido*, if you please,' Kitty giggled back. 'You've been able to clamber into the sea from the terraces for years, but this is the first time we've had a proper swimming pool. We'll have to learn to swim proper like, won't we?'

Maisie responded with a wan smile. She wasn't too sure about learning to swim. You wouldn't find her wearing one of those revealing swimming costumes! Wouldn't the Reverend Mother be horrified. The girls had been allowed to hold up their skirts to paddle on the shore of Cork Harbour, but those swimming costumes were little more than vest and knickers combined. Maisie would never parade about in such a thing, even if the new pool was meant to be for ladies only. There would be absolutely no privacy from the mixed sunbathing terraces, and anyone could look down on the lido from the road above.

It would be even worse than when Kitty's parents had left Alan at a friend's house and taken them to an afternoon tea dance on the pier back in June as a joint celebration for her and Kitty's birthdays.

'You need to learn to dance now you're thirteen,' Mrs Barron had announced primly. 'That's how Cecil and I met, dancing. We'll teach you a few simple steps afore we go so you won't feel left out of things.'

In fact, learning to dance in the weeks before the event had turned out to be quite fun. Maisie had got used to the idea of dancing as a couple, and had picked it up easily. She and Kitty had practised in the playground, taking it in turns to be the man. Philippa and Beryl had joined in, and so, to everyone's amusement, had Miss Mitchell!

When it came to the big day, Maisie had put on the new floral dress with the fitted waist and flared skirt that Zeek had made as her birthday present. Her thick, chestnut hair now touched her shoulders, and she fixed it back with a couple of pretty hairclips. Kitty's parents had bought her some white sandals, and Kitty had given her some new white ankle socks with a pink trim. When she'd set off to meet the Barron family for the outing, she'd felt the bee's knees — and said a quick Hail Mary as penance for the sin of vanity.

At first, she'd enjoyed the experience as they sat at one of many tables round the edge of the ballroom, nibbling politely at afternoon tea while a palm court orchestra played on a slightly raised platform. When the dancing started, she and Kitty had partnered each other, and Mr Barron had also given them both a couple of turns around the dance floor. It was while Maisie and Kitty were taking a rest and Maisie was concentrating on watching Kitty's parents dance a quickstep with lots of fancy turns, that she suddenly felt Kitty digging her in the ribs.

She turned, utterly horrified to see two boys who must be a few years older than them, edging round the dance floor. Please, please, don't let them be coming here to us. But they were. Oh, heck.

'Want to dance?' one of them asked.

Kitty glanced at Maisie with an excited lift of her shoulders. 'I'm sure we would,' she answered.

She stood up, beaming, and stepped up to one of the boys. The other held out his hand. Trembling, Maisie dragged herself to her feet. It was the last thing she wanted, but for Kitty's sake, she felt she couldn't refuse. She placed her right hand gingerly in the boy's left, her other hand shaking as she rested it on his right shoulder. She shuddered when she felt his right hand on her back, pulling her closer.

She tried to lose herself in concentrating on the steps as they moved around the dance floor, but her mind went blank and she found herself treading on his toes. 'I'm sorry, so I am,' she mumbled, feeling the heat in her cheeks. 'I'm only just learning.'

'That's all right, I'm no Fred Astaire mesel.' The boy gave a smile Maisie wasn't sure about as they tried again. 'Us thought you two pretty girls was sisters, you'm so alike. But you'm not from round yere, is you?'

Maisie really didn't feel comfortable, but neither did she want to be impolite and walk away. But maybe she could put him off. 'Sure, no, I'm a convent girl from Ireland, over here on holiday. I'll be taking holy vows in a couple of years to become a nun, so don't be getting any ideas.'

She'd said it with conviction, deliberately strengthening her accent. Hopefully the boy knew nothing of her faith and didn't realise she was too young for that, even given the couple of years. But it did the trick. She saw him step back in surprise. He spoke not a word after that, and the instant the music stopped, he yanked his friend's arm and pulled him away. Maisie saw him whisper in his mate's ear, and the two of them glanced back at her and Kitty with a laugh before hurrying away.

'What on earth did you say to him?' Kitty pouted as they sat back down.

'Only the truth,' Maisie lied, relieved that her ruse had worked, though she still felt unsettled. 'That we're celebrating our thirteenth birthdays. They must be at least seventeen, I'd have thought. Far too old for us.'

She watched as Kitty took a deep breath and let it out with a heavy sigh. 'Yes, I suppose so,' she agreed, but she looked pretty disappointed.

'But guess what? They thought we were sisters!' Maisie deliberately chortled back, wanting to lighten the mood. 'What d'you think of that?'

The smile returned to Kitty's face. 'Really? Well, I've always reckoned we look quite alike, even more so now your hair's growing and I've lost a bit of puppy fat, as Mother calls it. It'd be nice to think we were sisters, wouldn't it?'

The incident with the boys had faded from memory as the summer passed, but as time went by, Maisie did feel she and Kitty had indeed become more like sisters. Now, as they crossed the Hoe in the October dusk, their arms were linked as they wandered towards Smeaton's Tower, which stood on the Hoe behind where the bathing facilities were situated. Getting caught up in the crowds, they followed Kitty's parents down the steps, paying a penny for the souvenir programme, and finding a suitable spot on one of the terraces so that Alan could see.

Fed by sea water, the huge circular pool looked clean and even inviting, Maisie had to agree. It was apparently shallow enough to paddle as you went in, getting deep enough to swim as you went further out. On a hot summer's day, it might be nice to cool off by putting just your feet in the water, she supposed.

As the evening light faded further, the lamp posts on the walkways around the perimeter were lit up, reflecting on the little ripples in the pool. A hush descended on the crowd as the loudspeaker system made a noise, and then the Lord Mayor, one Lieutenant Commander Rogers according to Mrs Barron, began a speech. By the time he finished and declared the pool open, darkness had fallen, and someone else switched on the lighting and the water pumps. With a gurgle and a splash, water spurted out of the three cascades in the pool. The whole site was floodlit, but the lights in the fountains went through three colour changes, making it all quite magical.

It all looked so pretty and Maisie was glad that Kitty had insisted she came. But there was still that doubt niggling at the back of her mind. Kitty was so adventurous, and Maisie was sure that, come the next summer, she'd want her to put on one of those indecent garments and come here to learn to swim. What if they bumped into those two boys again, or somebody worse? She couldn't imagine herself ever wanting a boyfriend or getting married. It was quite unthinkable. But how could she ever have a family of her own if she didn't?

As the celebration continued, she forced a smile to her lips as Kitty's face lit up with happiness. She couldn't even begin to imagine what the future held for her. If only she was still back home in Ireland, where everything had been mapped out for her: school until she was eighteen, college, a good job. But here the future just seemed so uncertain. Who knew how her life would turn out?

CHAPTER SIXTEEN

1936

'Your turn now, Maisie.'

'Yes, Miss Butterworth.'

As Philippa came back into the classroom, looking like the cat who'd got the cream, Maisie rose from the desk and going to the door, stepped out into the corridor. Miss Butterworth, the teacher they'd had for their final year at school, was really nice. And so was Miss Howard, the headmistress. Overall, Maisie considered her time here had been a happy one, and she'd be sorry to leave, so she would.

She was reminded of being back at the convent and going to face the Reverend Mother over some misdemeanour she'd committed. And yet it wasn't like that at all, really. She didn't know why, but since coming to England, she'd never been in trouble at school or got into any scrapes. Had she grown up, become more sensible, or was it that her father had sucked the spirit from her? Drained away her sense of mischief and adventure? Well, he'd jolly well see the old rebellious side of her again soon. She was determined to take the first steps on her way to independence, come what may!

And this was part of it. After the Whitsun break, Miss Howard was interviewing each girl in turn to see if there was any way she could help them out into the big wide world. There were seven weeks of term left, and then Maisie's school days would be over. And though her longing to be back in Cobh was fading, she still wished she'd had those two extra years at least at the pension school ahead of her, rather than having to take a humble position in the workplace, to start with, anyway. Mind you, she had ideas about that, too, as Miss Howard was about to find out.

Maisie knocked politely on the door to the headmistress's office, her heart fluttering with anticipation.

'Come in,' she heard Miss Howard's voice call, and when she opened the door, the head teacher beckoned her to take the seat facing her across the desk.

Warm June sunshine flooded in through the window, and as Maisie sat down, she could see dust motes dancing in the shafts of light. For an instant, she was back in the convent chapel with the musty smell of polish and candlewax. Her heart lurched. For it was in a skill she'd begun to learn in those far away days where she felt her future would lie.

'Now, then,' Miss Howard smiled, her face moving into deep lines as she looked up from the papers on her desk. 'I have an exemplary report about you from both Miss Butterworth and Miss Mitchell from last year. And I understand that in Ireland you were on a scholarship place for what I see was called a pension school. Such a pity your father refused to let me try and get you into the grammar school when you first came here. I'm sure you'd have made it. I asked him again recently and he still said no. But I can't make him give his consent, I'm afraid. However, as you know, both your teachers have given you extra tuition along with your friend, Philippa. They felt the least they could do was to give you the best education they could while you were here.'

She paused, steepling her fingers and frowning at Maisie before she went on, 'As a result, I can tell you that you are two of the brightest girls we've ever had in the school, and in my opinion, you should stand an excellent chance of getting any job you apply for. Probably have to start as an office junior, but with your quick mind, I'm sure you'd soon be in line for promotion. I'd also suggest that you go to evening classes to learn shorthand and typing and other secretarial skills. You'll go far, Maisie. So, what do you think?'

Maisie stared at her through a flaming mist. Miss Howard had wanted her to try for the grammar school, but her father had forbidden it? Everything the headmistress had said after that was a blur. Office junior. A boring, run-of-the-mill office job. That wasn't what she was thinking of at all!

'Is there any particular field you'd be interested in?' Miss Howard persisted, frowning slightly when she didn't answer. 'I have a list of firms looking for bright girls to train as office juniors, if you'd care to take a look.'

Maisie strained to keep her emotions in check. How could he! But it wasn't Miss Howard's fault, and Maisie fought to tamp down the black anger that had flared inside her.

'Thank you, Miss Howard, that's very kind,' she answered, amazed at how her words sounded so steady when her lips felt like rubber. 'But it's a tailoress I'm wanting to be. I want to design and make clothes. Work hard and build up my own business. Have my own shop. Sell good quality wear at reasonable prices for office staff, and then expand into leisure wear. I've always been good at the sewing since I was small. They taught us at the convent from when we were five. But my next-door neighbour's a retired master tailor, and I've been learning from him during the winter. But now I'd like a proper apprenticeship.'

Miss Howard's eyebrows crept skywards. 'Well, you certainly have ambition,' she said in a surprised voice. 'But have you thought it through properly? It'd be a long, hard road. With an office job, you'd have set hours, security, increasing pay. But an apprenticeship would mean very long hours and little if no pay. Indeed, until recently, you had to pay to take an apprenticeship. But if you're absolutely sure that's what you want to do with your life, leave it with me. I'll see what I can do.'

'Thank you, Miss Howard,' Maisie managed to mumble, still reeling at the revelation and trying not to stagger as she made her way back to the classroom. Her legs felt wobbly and she was grateful to sit back down at the desk.

How she made it through to dinner time, she didn't know, and she felt sick as they went through to the hall. To top it all, Philippa was full of her own news. She'd missed out on going to the grammar school before because she's been unwell during the exams and hadn't performed to her usual standard. But Miss Howard had managed to secure her a place for next term. Her parents had already been informed and had given their consent.

'I just can't understand why you're not coming with me,' Philippa frowned quizzically at Maisie. 'You're just as clever as me. Those tests we did last term. Miss Butterworth didn't tell us at the time, but they were the entrance exams. And when we went through them afterwards, you'd done just as well as me.'

A fist tightened inside Maisie's chest. She knew Philippa meant well, but her words were twisting the knife in her side nonetheless. She simply couldn't hold back, and blurted out, 'My father wouldn't give his consent, that's why, so,' before she could stop herself.

Her friends stared at her, slack-jawed. But she didn't want their sympathy. It might weaken her. And this evening, she'd need every ounce of her strength to face what she knew was coming.

So she shrugged and told them, 'Anyway, it's a tailoress I want to be. Have my own business one day, and you can all come and buy your clothes from me!' she concluded with a grin. But she knew in her heart that it would be second best to finishing her education at grammar school and then going on to study for whatever profession she decided upon. But there was no point considering such matters now. Her father had put paid to any ambitions in that direction. It was going to be hard enough persuading him to let her take up an apprenticeship. She gritted her teeth. She was going to have to prepare to do battle.

* * *

She wasn't going to wait. Wasn't going to give him the chance to belittle or humiliate her before she began. She'd cooked his meal as usual, while her own bread and dripping was already set out in her place. That was something else that was going to change, too.

Just as normal when he got home from work, he acknowledged her with nothing more than a grunt as he went out to use the privy. He came back inside, washing his hands at the scullery sink. When he turned back into the kitchen, she was waiting for him, blocking his path. Hands on her hips, back straight, eyes glinting like steel.

She saw the frown flicker across his face. 'What's all this, then?' he asked in a mocking tone.

'You mean Mr High and Mighty O'Sullivan can't guess?' she replied steadily, her voice like gravel. 'Well, I'll tell you. I want to know why you wouldn't let me go to the grammar school.'

His face took on its habitual sneer. 'You? Go to the grammar school?'

He went to push past her, but she stepped across in front of him, her lips compressed with determination. 'Yes,' she hissed back. 'Miss Howard told me I could have passed the entrance exam, but you wouldn't give your consent for me to take it and I want to know—'

Francis jerked his head. 'Well, she had no right to tell you that.'

'So you're admitting it, then? And sure, she had every right. It's my life. My future. You had no right to interfere.'

'Oh, I think you'll find that as your father, I have every right. Now where's my—'

He tried again to get to the table, but she barred his way determinedly. 'Well, I'm thinking you gave up your rights as a father the day you abandoned me at the convent. But the least you could be doing to make up for it was to let me go to the grammar. I could've become a teacher, a doctor, a lawyer, even. Well paid, respected—'

'And who'd have had to support you while you were studying, might I ask?' The derision had returned to his voice as he poked his nose forward into her face. 'Me, of course! Me! As for the grammar school, the tuition might be free, but where was I supposed to find the money for everything else, the uniform, the sports equipment, the pencils and compasses and what have you, eh? Did you expect me to scrimp and scrape while you sit in a cosy little classroom?'

But Maisie was ready for him. Goodness knows, she'd had long enough to think about that one!

'Don't be giving me that! You earn a decent wage. Other men bring up whole families on less than you earn.' That was what Kitty's father had said, anyway. 'I don't know what you spend your money on. For all I know, you've got gold bars hidden in that front room you keep locked all the time.'

She gasped in horror as Francis suddenly reached out and twisted her arm.

'That's none of your business,' he snarled. 'And you can forget any fancy ideas right now. It's all been settled. You're starting in my department in the accounts office at Dingles the Monday after you leave school. And there's an end to it.'

Maisie reeled backwards as he let go of her and pushed his way past. What? Oh, no! She wasn't having that! The resentment that had been fermenting inside her all those months burst out in a squall of rage, and grabbing his arm this time, she yanked him round to face her.

'Sure, if you think I'm going to spend all day in an office with you, as well as being cooped up here with you at home, you'd better think again!' She saw him open his mouth as if to throw a retort at her, but she wasn't going to give him the chance. 'All this time, I've just been your unpaid skivvy,' she seethed, eyes narrowed into slits. 'Washing, ironing, cleaning, shopping, cooking, and all for what? Never a word of thanks or a penny's pocket money, and bread and dripping for tea when I cook you a proper meal because you consider a few pennies each day for my school dinners is enough. Well, all that stops now!'

She paused, catching her breath. Sweet Mary, she was in for it now. Had she gone too far? But she wasn't going to stop. Her father's face had turned from astonishment at her outburst to rage, the veins in his neck standing out like cords.

'You little—'

'And before you try to say anything else,' she interrupted, raising her voice, 'I'm going to do an apprenticeship as a tailoress. I discussed it with Miss Howard at school today, and she's going to make enquiries. But I've spoken to Zeek as well this afternoon. He's been teaching me, and he still knows some people from when he had his own shop in Union Street. He reckons he can get me a paid apprenticeship, I'm already so good.'

She stopped, lips drawn into a mutinous knot. Her father's eyes were bulging from their sockets, and the next thing Maisie knew, his hand flew out and cracked against her jaw. She staggered backwards, clutching her cheek.

'That interfering old crone!' Francis spat, looming over her with spittle spraying from his cruel mouth. 'Well, I'll teach him not to mind his own business.'

He took a purposeful step forward as if to push past her and fly round next door there and then. Well, Maisie wouldn't let him. She straightened up and gave him such a hefty shove that he fell against the wall behind him.

'Oh, no, you won't! Zeek's been more of a father to me than you ever have! You're a monster, so you are, and I hate you!'

His face became a vicious mask. 'Hate me, do you? Well, I'll give you something to hate me for!'

He went to step forward again, but Maisie was ready for him. She sprang at him with all her might, driving him back against the wall. She heard him gasp and she stood back. Serve him right if she'd winded him. Teach him to threaten her. And for a few seconds, she watched him trying to catch his breath as hatred froze solid somewhere inside her.

She was dancing on the spot, ready if he came at her again. But he bent over further, breathless and wheezing. And then his right hand went across his chest, clutching at his left arm. When he lifted his head to look at her, his face was a strange colour, a bit like putty, and she saw dewdrops of sweat on his forehead.

He drew in a rasping breath, his mean lips bloodless. 'My tab-lets,' he croaked in a jagged whisper. 'Pock-et.'

For a moment, Maisie remained rooted to the spot. What did he mean? She'd never seen him take any medicine. But who knew what he did when he locked himself in the front room? Did he have something to take because of the strokes he'd talked about? Some tablets he kept in his pocket for emergencies?

She watched as he slithered to the floor, his face twisted in pain while his eyes gazed up at her beseechingly. Was he going to die? If he didn't, he'd surely blame her later for not doing anything. And wasn't it her Christian duty to help him?

Trembling, she dropped onto her knees and though it filled her with distaste, she fumbled in his jacket pockets. His eyes continued to follow her, though could she still detect contempt in them? There was a sort of rumbling sound as he fought to draw each breath, and it seemed he couldn't speak.

A dirty handkerchief. Some coins. As she threw them onto the floor, she noticed that among them was a key. She caught her breath. The key to the front room. Ignore it. She delved her hand in his pocket again. It was empty.

She leaned across him. Try the other one. Lo and behold, a little glass bottle rattled as she lifted it out.

She stood up, holding it in her shaking palm to read the label. Then she glanced down at her father as he lifted his right hand from his chest as if to reach out to her.

The thought flashed through her mind that she could stand there, watching him suffer. Letting him see how she hated him. Payback time for all his cruelty towards her. Then she shoved the thought aside. There was no way she could let him die. She twisted the lid of the bottle and spilling two small white tablets into her palm, held them out towards him.

He stretched up his arm, making a strange, squealing, gurgling noise in his throat. But as she tipped the tablets into his hand, his fist closed, his body went rigid, convulsing in a heaving jerk. His arm flopped down, his head lolled to one side, and he remained staring up at her with sightless eyes.

Maisie's body froze with shock. She couldn't move. The room filled with shattering silence. Her heart felt scoured of all emotion as she stared at him. He wasn't breathing, his face white. He was dead, she was sure of it.

Thoughts began to tumble around inside her head. Was it her fault? Had she killed him? Would she be blamed? She'd confronted him about her future. Could he have been so mean that his own outrage had caused him to have a heart attack or a stroke? Surely that meant he'd brought it on himself. Giving him a push would hardly have killed him.

The clock ticked on the mantelpiece. A lump of coal shifted in the range firebox.

At last feeling began to trickle back into her stunned senses. She couldn't stand there for ever. She stumbled uncertainly towards the door. Zeek would know what to do.

Her father's body blocked her path. She would have to step over it. Already it, not him. As she went to do so, her eye was drawn to the pile of coins and the key on the floor beside him. She bent down, retrieved the key, and hid it behind the clock.

* * *

'He be dead all right,' Zeek said, kneeling over the body. Maisie bent over to help him get back up.

'H-he wanted his tablets,' she stammered. 'I got them out of his pocket, put them in his hand, but he . . . he went before he could swallow them.'

'Ah.' Zeek nodded thoughtfully. 'Best put the bottle back in his pocket, I'd say. You didn't know ort about no pills, if you gets my drift. Just in case it gets out what a mean aud bugger he was, and anyone thinks . . .' He dipped his head meaningfully before continuing, 'I'll get mesel down to the phone box and call the doctor. Take me a while on these legs. You'm all right yere, or d'you want to go into mine?'

'No, I'll be fine here, thank you.'

Instinct told her she needed to think, though she didn't know what about. And she didn't have long. Despite what Zeek had said about his legs, the phone box was only at the end of the next street. If she needed to do anything, she needed to act quickly.

Zeek was right. She must put the pills back in her father's pocket. She wouldn't want anyone to think she'd snatched them from him. The two pills she'd tipped into his hand had fallen onto the floor, so she popped them back into the bottle before sliding it back into his pocket. As for the coins, surely a man would normally carry some change in his pocket and it might look odd if some lay on the floor next to him. There were two half crowns and a two-shilling bit. Those she stored behind the clock with the key, together with a few smaller coins that would be useful for the public telephone. The rest she returned to his pocket, and stuffed the handkerchief in afterwards.

Was there anything else she should do? What if Francis had anything else on him she might need, and the doctor took the body away before she had a chance to look? It filled her with revulsion to touch him again, but there would be a grim sense of revenge if she discovered anything of note. All she found was his wallet. Three pound and two ten-shilling notes. She left a ten-bob one, and took the rest. It seemed a fortune, but who knew what money she might need in the next few days? And everything of his was hers now, anyway, wasn't it, by law? Unless he'd left everything to a cats' home or something, though she couldn't imagine he'd be so generous.

She glanced around the room. Anything else? Her bread and dripping, while her father's place had been set for a proper dinner. It was evidence of how badly he'd treated her. Again, it could be misinterpreted, so she quickly removed it and put out another knife and fork instead.

None too soon, since Zeek came back into the room a moment later. He found her sitting innocently on one of the kitchen chairs. Jesus, Mary and Joseph, she couldn't believe all she'd just done. That she'd had the wit to think of all that when her father had just dropped dead in front of her. But really, she'd done nothing wrong. She merely felt as if she had. It was only her Catholic upbringing making her feel guilty.

'You'm shaking, cheel,' Zeek's kind voice observed. 'You sure you don't want to go into mine?'

'N-no, thank you,' she stuttered, her jaw beginning to judder now. 'I want to hear what the doctor says.'

She looked up at Zeek, amazed to find her eyes filling with moisture. Not for her father, but as a reaction, she realised, to what had happened. But Zeek gave her his warm smile.

'I sees there be a pot of tea on the table and it still feels hot. I thinks we could both do with a cuppa. It'll be a bit afore the doctor gets yere.'

Maisie replied with a watery grimace, and soon was warming her hands around a mug of tea. Ridiculous when it was such a sunny, June evening. Must be the shock, she thought.

'Got hissel in a twist, did he, when you telt him about wanting the apprenticeship?' Zeek suggested gently.

Maisie nodded. 'He wasn't best pleased,' she managed to croak. 'Wants . . . wanted me to work in the office at Dingles with him.'

'Ah, well.' Zeek sighed weightily. 'Won't have to now, will you? But I'd keep quiet about arguing with him, mind.' Then he cocked his ear as a firm knock came on the front door. 'Must be the doc. You keep sitting there, maid. I'll let him in.'

Maisie wrung her hands as she waited. She was feeling calmer, but other thoughts were starting to crowd in on her. What would happen to her now?

The doctor was younger than she'd imagined, perhaps in his forties, but he had a sympathetic smile. He swiftly examined the body, asking Maisie how it had happened. She explained how her father had suddenly clutched at his chest, fallen back against the wall and collapsed. Then she added that he'd had a stroke years ago that had robbed him of the use of his left arm.

The doctor nodded, felt in Francis's pockets, found the bottle of tablets and read the label. 'Ah, makes sense. Not my patient, you see. Right, well.' He took a small form from his medical bag, scribbled on it, and put it on the table. 'You'll need that to register the death. Now, you're his daughter, I understand from your neighbour here, and your mother died years ago. So have you any other family you can stay with?'

'No. Sure, it was just my father and me,' she whispered, her throat suddenly refusing to work properly.

'Is there no one else you can go to, then?'

'The poor cheel can bide with me, if she's a mind.'

The doctor frowned slightly as he caught Maisie's gaze. 'Would you be happy with that?'

'Yes, I would, so.' Maisie bobbed her head. 'Zeek's like a grandfather to me.'

'Righty-ho,' the doctor agreed. 'I'll have to send someone round from the Welfare in the morning. But in the meantime, d'you know if your father had made any plans in advance? With an undertaker, I mean. Some people do.'

'Not that us knows of,' Zeek answered for her. 'And he always said he had no money.'

'Ah. Then if you're happy, when I get home, my wife will call someone for you. Part of her job as a doctor's wife, I'm afraid,' he added grimly. 'They'll be round to collect Mr O'Sullivan quite promptly, so I suggest you say your goodbyes. My condolences to you both. Don't worry. I'll see myself out.'

And within a few moments, he was gone.

Maisie stared after him. Was that it? She'd been so worried he might have found a reason to blame her. So tense, she felt she might break. But it was all over. Very soon, Francis O'Sullivan would be out of her life for ever.

Something inside her suddenly snapped, and she burst into floods of tears.

CHAPTER SEVENTEEN

'You'm sure you want to do it alone, cheel?'

'Yes, I do, thank you, Zeek,' Maisie answered firmly.

'Well, you knows where I am if you needs me.'

Maisie could see the concern on the old man's face, and overspilling with love for him, kissed him on his stubbly cheek. What would she have done without him ever since she'd arrived here? But this was something she really felt she needed to face on her own.

Setting her chin determinedly, she let herself into her father's house. She was used to being there alone for part of nearly every day, of course, but now it felt filled with deathly silence. But she wasn't going to let anything deter her.

She went straight upstairs to her room to fetch her bag. She hesitated by the door to the front bedroom. She didn't imagine her father would have kept anything important in there. After all, he'd allowed her free access to make his bed every day, clean, and put away all his laundered clothes. No, it was the locked room downstairs that would hold any secrets.

Back in the kitchen, she took the money she'd put behind the clock and stuffed it into her purse. Her fingertips tingled as they brushed against the key, but that would have to wait. First she had to go along to the telephone box and dial the operator to put her through to Dingles. She had the pennies all set out, ready to press button A when she was connected.

Asking calmly to speak to someone in personnel, she informed them of her father's death with no more emotion than if she'd been telling them he wouldn't be coming in because he had a heavy cold. The woman on the other end sounded shocked, but Maisie told her that she'd be in in a day or so to sort out whatever needed sorting. The pips went and she didn't feed in any more coins. That was done, then.

Should she telephone her school? But they were used to pupils not turning up for a day or two, and then returning with a sick note from a parent. So no, she wouldn't bother with that just now. It was bad enough knowing someone would be coming from the Welfare. She didn't want someone from school as well.

As she covered the short distance back home, the morning sunshine warmed her back, making her feel more relaxed. Zeek's spare bedroom was empty of plants, it being summer, but what it also lacked was a bed. So she'd spent the night huddled in one of the armchairs in his parlour. Comfortable though it was, it wasn't ideal for sleeping, and with the traumatic events of the previous evening, hadn't she tossed and turned all night. But now the bright, clear day filled her with renewed strength.

Back home, she refused to let herself falter as she turned the key in the door to the front room. She had no idea what to expect. She knew the fabric of the building would mirror Zeek's next door, but the room felt totally different, cold and soulless, as she stepped inside.

A large, worn rug covered much of the floorboards, and on it stood a leather-upholstered armchair which had also seen better days. The grate in the attractive fireplace, similar to Zeek's, was empty and didn't look as if it had been lit in years. But then her father would have found it difficult to manage with his one hand, and doubtless hadn't allowed his cleaner in here any more than he had her. The only other furniture was a bureau in one of the alcoves next to the chimney breast, and a table by the window.

Maisie stepped over to this first. The only things on it were a pen, a bottle of ink and a pile of exercise books. She picked one up. On the cover was written in large capital letters and in a hand she recognised as her father's, the word *HAYDOCK*. What the devil did that mean? She opened it up. Inside were dates, times, other figures and odd words that sounded like names of some sort.

She chose another book. This one said *AINTREE*. Tree? Sure, her father had never shown any interest in the plants she grew under Zeek's guidance, let alone in trees. And she'd never heard of an Aintree. Inside, the pages were filled with the same sort of details. Whatever was it? Other books were labelled *CHESTER*, *BANGOR*, *UTTOXETER*, and then *EXETER* and *NEWTON ABBOT*, which she recognised as places that weren't that far away. Ah, so was Aintree actually a place? Then she found a book called *ACCOUNTS*. Again, it was full of dates and figures, all meticulously recorded in her father's neat hand. Down the side of each page were two columns marked *In* and *Out*. Now that she did understand. And the figures in the *Out* column outweighed those in the *In* column by vast amounts.

Maisie's frown deepened. Whatever this was, was it where all her father's money went? She would have to show everything to Zeek. Maybe he'd know what it was all about.

There was no point investigating further. So with a sigh, she went over to the bureau and steeled herself to open it. She almost wished it was locked, and found herself shaking as she pulled things out of the pigeonholes inside.

Opening a large envelope, she discovered various certificates, her parents' marriage, both their births and her mother's death. Puerperal fever. That meant something to do with babies, didn't it? And the date of death was little more than a fortnight after she herself had been born. So what her father had told her about that was true. Then she unfolded another paper and out fell a small photograph of a woman holding a tiny baby. It was grey and blurred, so she couldn't make out the features on either face. She turned it over. On the back was written in faded ink, *Me with my dearest little Maisie.*

She stifled a gasp, turning the photograph over again. If she remembered rightly, her father had still been working at the mill when she'd been born. As manager, he would have been well paid and must have been able to afford for the photographer to come to the house and then develop the photograph the same day. Had he known her mother was dying at that point? Had it been her mother's idea? Something for her husband and new-born child to remember her by in future years?

Maisie gently rubbed her thumb over the picture. So this was her mother. If only the image were clearer. If only she'd known her. But why had her father kept the photograph locked away? Out of grief? Would he have behaved any differently towards her, his daughter — loved her even — if his wife were still alive?

Maisie's gaze rested on the image a little while longer. She'd always imagined that if she ever saw a photograph of her mother, she'd instantly feel an emotional connection to her. But this woman felt like a complete stranger, even if she'd loved her enough to write such an endearment on the back of the photograph. Maisie vowed that when she had children, she'd be really close to them, but at the same time, would let them be their own people. She pulled herself up short. She still hadn't come to terms with the idea of how babies were made. Kitty, it seemed, couldn't wait to have a boyfriend, but for Maisie, well, she didn't think she'd ever want one, let alone a husband. So the question of children would never arise.

She placed the picture on the top of the bureau and inspected the last piece of paper. It was her own birth certificate. Her father's occupation was entered as master miller, just as it was as the informant on her mother's death certificate. So that part of the story he'd told her was indeed true. And she was sure that the Father Michael from Buttevant wouldn't have supported her father's application to send her to the convent if he hadn't come down in the world and found himself living in the ex-army accommodation he'd described, with no income after suffering the stroke. But none of it was any reason for him to have treated her as he had, and if she had any sympathy for him, it was driven away in moments.

So, what else was there in the bureau? She found the rent book. That would need sorting out. Then she discovered a half-used cheque book. All the stubs were neatly filled in, mainly cash withdrawals, rent, one for rates. But there were regular payments of reasonable sums to someone called Fraser. Who on earth was he? But there were also paying-in stubs marked Fraser mainly of lesser amounts, although one substantial one. So had her father been lending money to someone who was slowly paying it back? But why the continued payments out?

Maisie shook her head. It was a mystery, but one that would need solving. And then her fingers pulled out a couple of envelopes, each one addressed to an S. Fraser in Liverpool. So that could be a clue.

She was about to turn away, to go and fetch Zeek to show him what she'd found, when she spied a bunch of envelopes stuffed into another pigeonhole. More ready to send to Mr Fraser? But they somehow looked familiar. And as she withdrew them, her heart gave a great thud. No! They were all the letters she'd written to Noreen and Sister Agnes.

She stared at them, her thoughts spinning in a tortured dance. What a fool she'd been to have trusted him. He'd never posted them! If he were still alive, she could cheerfully have wrung his neck. No wonder her friends had never written back. But . . . they could have got her address from the Reverend Mother, and perhaps they had. She could understand them getting fed up, though, if she'd never replied, but surely they'd written in the early days? The post was delivered before she left for school, and the second round arrived during the afternoon, so she always saw it before her father got home from work. So there was no way he could have intercepted any post for her.

All she could think of was that he'd forbidden anyone to write to her, possibly claiming that she might have found it too upsetting. It was the only explanation. She balled her fists up so tightly that her fingernails dug into her palms. How dare he have cheated her like that! Well, she'd make sure she had letters in the post to Ireland before the day was out. But first, she wanted to know what Zeek would make of her other finds, and suppressing her fury over her final discovery, she went next door to fetch him.

* * *

'Well, I reckons as your father liked the gee-gees,' Zeek nodded wisely, looking up from everything spread on the table and removing his spectacles. 'They'm all race courses,' he explained, waving at the exercise books. 'Two near yere, but the others in easy reach of Liverpool, where this Fraser chap be. Now, officially like, you has to go to a race course yersel to place bets. But I reckons your father were paying this fella to put bets on fer him, and then to send him his winnings by cheque. Only he lost a mortal amount more than he won.'

Maisie was staring at him, wide-eyed. 'So he was gambling? Good Lord, I can't imagine it.'

'Well, they do say addicted gamblers often hide it well.' Zeek shook his head, sucking in his old, wrinkled lips. 'I mind you said he spent some time around Liverpool looking fer work when he fust arrived in England. Perhaps he met up with this fella who persuaded him he might make some quick money on the horses, and he got hooked. He'd just lost his wife, and grief can do strange things to a body's mind. And when he ended up yere, he continued this arrangement with our Mr Fraser. These touts can be pretty persuasive. And it wouldn't surprise me if, deep down, your father were ashamed of what he were doing, but couldn't stop hissel, which is why he were at such pains to keep it secret, like.'

Maisie took a deep, incredulous breath. 'But surely this Fraser devil could've been cheating my father left, right and centre.'

'No, cheel. They books. Your father studied form in great detail. He'd have known exactly which horses he wanted to back. He'd have known the exact odds, and seen the results in the papers. So he'd have known precisely what any winnings would be, less any fees he'd agreed to pay our Mr Fraser, of course.'

'So that's what he was doing,' Maisie mumbled. 'Wasn't he always engrossed in the sports pages of the newspapers, making notes on scraps of paper.'

'And then transferring them into his books. And I guess he sometimes went off to Exeter or Newton Abbot to place his bets in person.'

'I don't think so. He only had Sundays. And Wednesday afternoons.'

Zeek raised a knowing eyebrow. 'Well, it doesn't matter now. But us can write to our friend Fraser if you wants, to confirm it. And tell him to sling his hook.'

That sounded like a good idea, but before Maisie had a chance to think any more about it, there came a knock on the door. Their eyes met. The Welfare. Maisie went out into the hallway, grateful that behind her, Zeek went into the kitchen. She didn't want the official going into the parlour and seeing evidence of her father's suspect habits.

When she opened the front door, a stout, smartly dressed older woman carrying a briefcase was standing on the doorstep. She gave Maisie a tight smile.

'Maisie O'Sullivan?' she asked. And when Maisie nodded, her throat too dry to speak, the woman continued, 'I'm Mrs Oldridge from the Welfare. May I come in?'

'Of course.' Maisie forced a croak. 'This way.'

She led the woman into the kitchen, where Zeek held out his gnarled hand. 'Ezekiel Doidge, next-door neighbour and friend to this poor cheel.'

Mrs Oldridge shook his hand briefly and sat down at the table, opening her briefcase. 'Now, I understand your father died of a heart attack yesterday evening. May I express my condolences, dear. It must have been a great shock for you. And according to my notes,' she said, shuffling some papers, 'your mother died when you were a baby and you have no other relatives.'

'None that I know of, no.'

'And you spent the night with Mr Doidge, I believe. Well, we'll have to find some more suitable accommodation for you from now on. At least, until you're sixteen.'

'No need, missus. I wish to be appointed the maid's guardian.'

Maisie's eyes stretched wide with joy. But she noticed the woman frowning, and jumped in quickly before she had a chance to object.

'Oh, yes, please! Isn't Zeek like a grandfather to me. I can't think of anything I'd like better!' Wouldn't that be marvellous, Maisie thought. She couldn't have been happier! But the official's next words dashed her hopes to smithereens.

'I'm sorry, but I don't think it would be appropriate for Mr Doidge to be appointed as your guardian. I doubt the court would grant it. Besides, I don't wish to be rude, but you're of a good age, Mr Doidge. Maisie could end up as your carer which wouldn't be appropriate either.'

Maisie opened her mouth to protest. Hadn't she been her horrible father's carer, housemaid and skivvy for the past twenty months or more, and nobody had objected to that! If only Zeek had been her real grandfather! But he must have read her thoughts and gave her a warning glance. Best to keep quiet about her father's treatment of her.

'So,' Mrs Oldridge announced, consulting her papers again, 'I believe there's a vacancy at the Royal Dockyard Orphanage in Milehouse. You can stay there for the time being, at least. There'll be financial matters to sort out, of course. And the funeral. But for now, if you pack some of your things, I'll take you to the home and see you settled in. You can come back here at the weekend to sort everything out, but I expect that after that, the landlord will want to find a new tenant.'

The woman's words were like shards of glass in Maisie's heart. Live in an institution again, when she'd been used to the freedom of gallivanting all over the place with Kitty? Not on your nelly!

Bowing her head, she dutifully went upstairs, deliberately clomping on each step. Her pulse was flying as she then tiptoed back down, carefully avoiding the tread she knew always creaked, and slipped silently out onto the street. Then she ran, driving her anger and frustration into the ground beneath her feet.

By the time she reached Union Street, her chest was burning and she slowed to a walk. She had no idea where she was going or what she was going to do. She felt broken, her thoughts fragmented. Wanting to break out of the invisible bubble that enveloped her, but not knowing how.

Her feet took her to the Hoe. It felt so wrong that other people were sauntering about in the sunshine while she was floundering in despair. She found herself staring out across the Sound, the salty, tangy sea air wafting about her face and playing with her hair. She'd come from across the ocean, or at least the Irish Sea. Would they let her go back to the convent? But the truth was that she didn't want that, either.

She found an empty bench and slumped down onto it, letting tears stream down her cheeks. She would have to go back, of course. They might even send the police to search for her once they realised she was gone. Dearest Zeek would be frantic, thinking she'd run away, when all she needed was to clear her head.

'There, there, my lover, whatever's the matter?'

The soft, gentle voice sang through her misery, and she turned her head to see a kindly-looking woman with greying hair fixed loosely in a bun, seated next to her. The face seemed oddly familiar, and then Maisie recognised her as the pleasant lady from the tea rooms in Union Street she'd visited a few times. Remembering how friendly and welcoming she'd always been, Maisie's resolve crumbled and she burst out in fresh tears. At once, she felt the woman's arms about her, and she wept against her well-padded shoulder.

'There, there, you have a good cry,' she heard the lilting voice again as a hand patted her back. 'Always helps to let it out.'

Maisie sobbed away, but tears always eventually subside and she was grateful when the woman pushed a freshly laundered handkerchief into her hand.

'Now you can tell me to mind my own business, but talking about things can help, too. Whatever you tell Janet Mudge stays with Janet Mudge.'

Maisie sat back, dabbing at her eyes and sniffing back the remnants of her tears. She twisted the handkerchief in her hands. Yes, it would be good to talk, and she instinctively trusted the stranger. So she told her everything from the beginning, only omitting how cruel her father had been to her. She didn't mention his gambling addiction, either.

Janet Mudge was a good listener, nodding sympathetically and not interrupting. 'My poor lover,' she crooned when Maisie had finished. 'Now, it strikes me we could both do with a nice cuppa, and I'm sure a nice cake wouldn't come amiss. So let's go back to the tea rooms? It's on your way home anyways.'

Maisie nodded, already feeling better having unburdened herself to this understanding stranger. As they made their way back through the city, an easy conversation developed between them. Maisie learned that Janet Mudge had been widowed during the war. Her husband had been a chef and the premises had been a restaurant. When she found herself alone, Janet had felt she'd be better able to manage it as a tea shop, and had done so ever since. They'd not been blessed with any children before her husband was killed, so the tea rooms had become her life.

Arriving at the premises, it felt strange to be let into an empty building when Maisie had only ever known it as a bustling business. Janet locked the door behind them and then showed Maisie through to a garden at the rear with a terrace set out with wrought iron tables and chairs.

'Now you sit here and I'll make us a pot of tea,' Janet said. 'And I think there might be a slice of fruit cake going spare.'

Feeling more settled, Maisie realised her stomach was rumbling with hunger, and tea and cake would go down very well. It wouldn't stop what was going to happen to her, but she began to resign herself to that as she took in the bright geraniums, yellow marigolds and blue lobelia that filled the pots and flowerbeds around her.

'Here we are, then.'

Janet appeared, bearing a tray which she set down on one of the tables. She poured the tea into exquisite bone china cups, and waved at Maisie to help herself to cake while she herself sat back, holding the cup and saucer above her rounded bosom and sipping pensively at her tea.

'I've been thinking,' she began mysteriously. 'I might be able to help. But first of all, tell me, can you cook?'

Maisie raised her eyebrows in curiosity. 'A little,' she answered. But what did that have to do with going into an orphanage? 'My friend's mammy's been teaching us both, and isn't she a good cook. At least, I think she is. And of course, haven't I been cooking for my father all this time.'

Janet nodded thoughtfully. 'Well, I've a proposition for you. You seem a mortal personable cheel, just the sort I like working in the shop. Now, young Susie's leaving me soon to get married, so I need someone to replace her and I reckon you'd be ideal. In fact, if your friend's interested, I could do with two young maids, I'm so busy sometimes. I can only afford to pay you a small wage, but you'd have free board and lodging, and all you can eat. Now I reckon the Welfare might be happy with that arrangement, don't you?'

Maisie gazed at her, hoping and praying she'd heard right. Live and work with this lovely, homely woman, serve in the pretty tea rooms and cook and bake in the kitchen.

Tend the garden, even. Something like this had never crossed her mind. But . . .

'As for the apprenticeship you mentioned,' Janet continued, 'I'm closed Mondays and Tuesdays, so if that's summat you still want to do, you can do it then. Or wait until you're older to do it full time, though I believe I'd be sorry to lose you. Or you could use those days to go and see this Zeek of yourn, and let him go on teaching you. So, what d'you think of that, then?'

Maisie realised her jaw was dangling open, and she snapped it shut. Her face stilled in astonishment at this bolt from the blue. Could this possibly be real? She couldn't believe her luck!

'W-well, yes!' she stammered, hardly able to speak. 'Thank you so much!'

'No need for thanks,' Janet said, blushing with embarrassment. 'You'll be doing us a favour. And I hope your friend will be interested, too. Obviously, if you're unhappy at any time, you'd be entirely free to leave. So, are we agreed? Now, finish up your cake, and we'll go and find this woman from the Welfare, shall we?'

Bubbling with relief and excitement, Maisie nodded vigorously in reply.

CHAPTER EIGHTEEN

Six months later

'Hark the herald angels sing, Mrs Simpson's pinched our king,' Maisie and Kitty chorused as they cleared the table after the last customers. The only other person there was Nick Chantry, a pleasant young fisherman who, together with his father, also a fisherman, often came in for an early lunch of soup and crusty bread when they'd been out at sea all night. They always went home to bathe and change first, though, knowing of old that Janet would chase them out if they came in smelling of fish or engine oil. Today, though, Nick had come on his own.

'Better not let Janet hear you singing that,' he laughed, his generous mouth spreading into a cheeky grin. 'She's a bit of a royalist, and it's not quite the done thing for her genteel establishment.'

'Well, you are the only customer. Or at least I'm not seeing anyone else,' Maisie teased back, gazing around the tea rooms with a jovial frown.

But her heart filled with not a little pride. Janet had left her and Kitty to put up all the Christmas decorations as they saw fit, and the café now looked fantastic. They'd draped glittering tinsel and red ribbons across the pictures on the walls, made tiny arrangements of holly for each table with a red candle in the middle, and a small Christmas tree stood in the corner by the counter with shiny baubles and even tiny electric lights.

'And I'm glad of that.' Nick's voice cut into her thoughts as he suddenly took Maisie's hand. 'Because I want to ask you summat. Would you like to come to the pictures with me on Monday night? They'm showing a new short cartoon called *Christmas Comes But Once a Year*, and then the main film's the new Bing Crosby, *Pennies from Heaven*. You'd like that, wouldn't you? I'm sure Janet would approve of you coming with us. She's known Dad and me for years. Of course,' he faltered, seeing her hesitation, 'Kitty's welcome to come, too, if she wants.'

Kitty chuckled. 'You don't need me anymore than I want to play gooseberry!'

Maisie's eyes darted from one to the other. But she did need Kitty to come! Oh, crikey, what should she do? She liked Nick and always felt a surge of happiness whenever he walked through the door. He'd been her first real encounter with a youth of the opposite sex. He was so friendly and easy-going that he'd unknowingly helped her overcome her nervousness in the company of young men. But she only saw him as a friendly customer. She wasn't sure she wanted to go on a date with him! She knew he was seventeen because he'd recently celebrated his birthday. Was that too old for her? Could she trust him? The old uncertainty that persisted at the back of her mind suddenly flared up again.

But wasn't it time she began to think about boys? Kitty did all the time. And even Noreen had given up the idea of taking holy vows . . .

Maisie had written to her and Sister Agnes immediately after her father had died. She'd had a reply from Noreen almost by return post. Apparently Francis had written to the Reverend Mother saying that they'd moved to Liverpool and giving an address that Maisie recognised at once as the mysterious Mr Fraser's. So no wonder she'd never received Noreen's letters! Like herself, both Noreen and Sister Agnes had given up writing when they'd not received a reply after so many months. Her father had evidently wanted to cut her off completely from her old life. Maisie could only think that he didn't want her telling them how badly he was treating her, but she'd never know for sure.

Noreen had told her that Sister Agnes had left to do some missionary work in Africa just as she'd said to Maisie on their parting. Remembering that Sister Agnes had once said she'd never leave Cobh, Maisie wondered guiltily if this change of heart had something to do with the discovery of how she herself had been deceived for all those years. As for Noreen, she'd been doing some charity work with the poor in Cork when she'd met a young law student who was helping out at the centre during the summer break from university. They'd hit it off straightaway, and had become more than good friends. In fact, with Noreen coming up to nineteen, they were hoping to get her father's permission to become engaged. Not that they could marry for a few years, until Bartie was fully qualified and had joined a practice.

The thought of Noreen set Maisie's mind racing. Yes, she did like Nick very much. He was always great fun, and it was only an evening at the cinema. If Noreen was going as far as wanting to become engaged when previously she'd been planning to take holy orders, surely going to see a film was entirely innocent by comparison?

'We-ell,' she began hesitantly, since she had to give Nick some sort of answer, though she still didn't know what.

But Kitty jumped in with both feet. 'There you go, Nick,' she grinned. 'But no canoodling in the back row! I'm not having that!'

'The thought hadn't crossed my mind!' Nick retorted, though Maisie detected a teasing note to his voice. 'I don't know, just like sisters, you two, the way you stick together. Mind you, at first, I thought you were sisters, you'm so alike.'

'Well, we'm as good as, so any truck from you with Maisie, and you'll have me to deal with. She just wants to see the film. Pity it's not a Fred Astaire. She loves dancing, does Maisie. But I expect there'll be some dancing in it. So you let her watch it, all right?' she grinned.

'I promise,' Nick answered solemnly. 'Cross my heart and all that. So, if you like dancing,' he went on, turning to Maisie with sincerity in his dark eyes, 'maybe I could find a friend and we could make up a foursome to go to a dance on the pier? They must be doing summat there over Christmas. Would you like me to find out?'

His youthful, eager face was alight with expectation, and Maisie felt her heart give a little leap. He was so pleasant and gentle, maybe there was something inside her beginning to take seed. Perhaps she was starting to understand those grown-up feelings Kitty was always talking about. She was sure her cheeks were turning pink as she answered him with a shy smile.

'Well, we'll have to ask Janet's permission, of course. But, yes, I'm thinking a dance would be rather nice, too,' she dared to reply, and beside her, Kitty clapped her hands.

'And make sure you find me some handsome fellow to go with,' her friend demanded. 'Now I reckon it's time you paid your bill,' she announced with such feigned authority that both Maisie and Nick burst out laughing.

* * *

Maisie was laying a table with a fresh cloth covered in pretty little red hearts for Valentine's Day when the bell over the shop door sounded its merry tinkle. They'd spent the morning putting up red paper hearts in the window and pinning them to the walls, making the place look cheerful and inviting to customers with amorous intent.

'Hello, my flower. How are . . . ?'

She glanced up as Janet's welcoming voice faltered, and her own stomach instantly started to churn. Nick was standing in the doorway, not his usual spruced-up self, but still sporting his rough fisherman's jacket and thick Guernsey sweater beneath. Instead of coming forward with his usual cheery smile he appeared to waver on the spot. Maisie sensed at once that something was wrong. She hurried towards him in Janet's wake.

'Whatever's the matter?'

Coming up beside her, Maisie noticed dark stains on Nick's jacket. His youthful face was grey and smeared with something dark. Even as a frown began to crease her forehead, he staggered forward, looking as if he was about to collapse. She pulled a chair out behind him, and between them she and Janet guided him down onto it before he fell to the floor. Maisie dropped onto her knees in front of him and took his hands. They were filthy, the fingernails stained with something dark red. When she looked up, his head was bowed, his skin so ashen he seemed about to faint.

'Kitty, fetch a glass of water!' Janet called to the back of the shop, ignoring her other customers who were staring at them in curiosity. Turning back to Nick, she added, 'And I'll get you a cup of strong, sweet tea. That's what you need, whatever's happened.'

She bustled towards the counter, passing Kitty who held out the glass of water with shocked bewilderment on her face. Maisie took the glass from her and pressed it into Nick's hands, but he was shaking so much that she had to help him hold it.

'Here, have a sip,' she encouraged him, moving the glass towards his lips. He took a few gulps, almost choking, before she took the glass from him and placed it on the nearest table. 'Now, can you be telling us what's happened?' she asked, her voice soft with compassion.

Nick lifted his head, his eyes red-rimmed and dark in his haggard face as his gaze sought hers.

'It's my dad,' he finally managed in a croaked whisper. 'There were an accident at sea. He . . . he must've been tired or summat. Not concentrating. His . . . his arm got caught in the winding gear. It were ripped almost . . . We tried to stop the bleeding but . . . he died afore we could get back to shore.'

Maisie tried to stifle her gasp of horror. Cold spread through her body. Poor Nick! No wonder he was in such a state. She'd watched her own father, who she loathed, drop dead in front of her, and that had been bad enough. But to witness your father — who you loved, who loved you — bleed to death while you tried to staunch the flow . . . well, it was unimaginable. And poor Mr Chantry, such a lovely man. She gripped Nick's hand, realising now that it was blood that stained his hands and clothes.

'Oh, Nick, that's appalling.' She shook her head as she searched for the right words. 'I'm so sorry. Truly I am. I don't know what to say. So . . . where . . . ?'

'At the hospital,' Nick muttered, his head drooping forward again.

Maisie was at a loss in the face of so much sorrow. She glanced up at Janet who was approaching with the promised cup of tea. From the look on her face, she'd evidently caught the end of what Nick had said. She placed the cup and saucer on the nearest table and bent to squeeze his shoulder. What could any of them say to ease his pain? There were no words.

Maisie turned back to Nick as he stifled a sob. His chin quivered as he finally broke down. But it wasn't good, solid, kind Janet that he reached out to, but to Maisie. She held him tightly as he wept, and she rocked him gently, smoothing his ruffled hair while biting back her own tears. She really couldn't believe it. How could God let this happen to dear, thoughtful Nick and his lovely father? It simply wasn't fair, or right, or believable. But it had happened, and now she would have to support Nick through his grief while her own heart ached.

* * *

'Thanks so much for this, Janet.'

'It were the least I could do. He were a grand fellow, your dad. He'll be missed by so many.'

Standing beside Nick, Maisie could see tears misting Janet's eyes. The funeral had been very hard, and if Janet started weeping again, it would be tough on Nick. It had been so kind of Janet to shut the tea rooms so that the wake could be held there, but now it was over.

'Everyone's gone now, so we can be clearing away,' Maisie suggested, thinking perhaps it would be better for Nick to be distracted by more practical matters.

'Of course. But would you mind if I leave you to it?' Nick asked. 'I feel I need some air.'

'That's fine, my lover. I understand.'

'Actually, could Maisie come along of me, if you can spare her?'

Maisie hesitated. She and Nick had become quite close and she felt honoured that it was her company he wanted in his hour of need, but it was also a responsibility. She glanced at Janet, but the older woman nodded back sagely.

'I'm not opening until tomorrow, so I'm sure Kitty and I can manage when she gets back from taking Zeek home. So off you go.'

A few minutes later, Maisie was walking down the street with Nick, both wrapped up against the biting February wind. They instinctively made their way towards the Hoe, always a place to let one's thoughts escape. It was almost deserted on such a bitter, blustery day, just a couple of hardy souls walking their dogs. It was too cold to sit on one of the benches, so they kept walking, side by side. Nick seemed lost in his own thoughts and Maisie wasn't sure it was a good thing, so decided to break the silence.

'What'll you do now, then?' she asked gently, wrapping her arms across her chest to keep warm.

Nick let out a deep sigh. 'Well, I'm giving up the flat at the top of the house. Seems silly to have two bedrooms and a separate sitting room for just me, like. And it'd be a stretch money-wise on just my earnings now. But there's a bed-sit come free on the middle floor and Mrs Rawlins has said I can have that.'

'Sure, she's a nice lady,' Maisie commented. She'd met Mrs Rawlins, Nick's landlady, before, but had spoken to her at more length at the wake. She'd seemed very pleasant. Some of the other residents from the boarding house had been there, too, together with the captain and the other mate on Nick's trawler, the *Calypso*, and the crews of some of the other vessels in the harbour.

'So, I suppose you'll be needing to take on someone else on the *Calypso*, then?' Maisie enquired.

'Yes, the captain's got someone in mind. Needs to be someone who doesn't mind not being able to buy into her, you see. Dad's shares are being held in trust for me until I'm twenty-one, but I won't be selling them then, either.'

Maisie nodded. She'd learned about how shares in vessels were very often held by its crew members. Often they invested their life savings and it didn't mean they were at all rich. It was going to be heart-breaking for Nick, sailing on the vessel that had taken his father's life and seeing the spot where he'd died day after day. So she was surprised that Nick was planning on holding onto the shares even after he came of age. She didn't know what to say to this news, nor what to say in general to the morose Nick, who was usually so chatty and full of fun. She walked beside him for a while without saying a word until he suddenly stopped and put a hand on her arm. She halted and turned to him, relieved that he was about to resume their conversation.

'I . . . I just wanted to say what a good friend you've been to me, Maisie,' he said, his eyes boring meaningfully into hers. 'Not just now, with Dad. But ever since I met you. You know how to enjoy yourself, but you'm sensible with it. Not like Kitty, who can go a bit beyond sometimes.'

'Yes, she can be a bit of a flibberty-gibbet, can't she?' Maisie agreed fondly.

Nick gave a wry chuckle, and Maisie smiled to herself. It was the first time she'd seen Nick give a hint of a laugh since his father's death. Now they remained smiling at each other for some moments before Nick took her hand.

'Come on, let's get you home. I can see you'm cold.'

'No, it's all right.'

'I need to start sorting some of Dad's things, anyway, if I'm moving out of the flat, and we sail in the early hours. We've already lost a few days' fishing and none of us can afford that.'

Maisie could understand that. And she could also see that she meant something special to Nick. It was flattering and gave her a warm feeling inside that she was in some way helping him through his grief, but she wasn't sure if she was ready for anything more. Even if his father's death had brought them closer, for now at least, she just wanted to remain good friends.

CHAPTER NINETEEN

August 1939

Tears trembled on her lashes, distorting her vision.

'No, it has to be faced, cheel.' Zeek's voice was calm and resolute. 'I be eighty-eight, and none of us can live for ever, like. These last five year, you've given my life some purpose. Even when you went to live with Janet, you've come to me every Monday and Tuesday almost, done my shopping—'

'But you've been teaching me, too,' Maisie insisted.

'And a pleasure it's been, maid,' he smiled. 'You'm almost as skilled as me now. Better, I shouldn't wonder, with your young eyes. And it'll always stand you in good stead. As will this.'

He pushed an envelope across the table with a sharp nod. Maisie frowned as she picked it up and turned it over. It was sealed, and all that was on the front was her name.

'No need to open it yet,' Zeek explained. 'It's a copy of my will. For when the time comes. You'll find the address of my solicitors inside. And they've got your address at Janet's, too. Basically, I'm leaving everything to you, this house and all that's in it. And all my money which be a reasonable sum.'

Maisie stared at him, choked with emotion. 'Oh, Zeek,' she breathed, scarcely able to speak.

'Well, who else am I supposed to leave it to?' he teased, trying to make light of it. Then his face became more serious. 'But, with times being so uncertain, like, I've added an extra clause. I hate to think about it, but if ort were to happen to you afore you'm old enough to make a will of your own, young Kitty would inherit everything instead. That's what you'd want, wouldn't you, you two being so close as sisters?'

Maisie blinked, totally overwhelmed. It was all so much to take in. 'Yes, I would,' she answered in a small voice.

'But that's not going to happen.' Zeek gave a reassuring smile. 'So when the time comes for you to settle down, it'll be a nice little nest egg for you and that young man of yourn.'

Maisie felt herself colour. 'Nick's not my young man. We're just good friends.'

'Really?' Zeek arched an eyebrow. 'Well, you spends a mortal lot of time together. And it's always been Nick for you. Not like young Kitty. A string of boyfriends she's had, and not one of them the right one. Whereas you and Nick seem made for each other. Love doesn't always need to be a mad passion, you knows. Sometimes it's better to be built on friendship and trust. And best take your happiness while you can, with this war coming on.'

So many emotions swirled through Maisie's breast at his words, but at the mention of war, a shiver of fear ran through her. 'It really is coming, isn't it?' she murmured.

'I believe so, yes. And soon.' Zeek's tone was grave. 'That Hitler's not going to stop at Austria and Czechoslovakia. He wants the whole of Europe for hissel.'

Maisie nodded grimly. 'And his chum Mussolini's already taken Albania on his behalf, more or less.'

'Quite so, cheel. Who knows when he'll have Britain in his sights? And civilians'll get caught up in it this time. That's why we've been given they gas masks, and they've got everything ready for taking all the kiddies away from the big cities.'

'Not from Plymouth, though. They're even bringing some of them here, so they must think we're safe enough.'

'Then why've they been giving out Anderson shelters for those who've got gardens?' Zeek snorted. 'Doesn't make no sense to me. But let's hope aud Zeek is wrong.' He paused. 'And isn't it time you were going back, maid? But afore you does, I've got summat else to give you.'

He hauled himself to his feet and shuffled round to open a drawer. Pulling out a small wooden box, he handed it to Maisie with a wistful smile.

'I'd like you to have this now. Then maybe I'll have the pleasure of seeing you wearing some of it afore I go.'

Maisie could see his pale eyes were watering, and her heart squeezed. She'd guessed what was in the box before she opened it. Nonetheless, she couldn't help but draw in a gasp when she lifted the lid.

'They'm all proper gems, not just paste,' Zeek said quietly. 'I'd like you to keep them for ever, but if you'm ever stuck for money, I'd rather you sold the odd piece than starve. Make sure you go to a proper jeweller, mind, and get a good price.'

Maisie scarcely heard his words as she gazed at the twinkling jewels set in the couple of necklaces, a pretty bracelet, several brooches and an exquisite diamond ring that the box contained. 'Oh, Zeek, I could never, ever part with any of these,' she croaked, staring up at him. 'I'll treasure them for ever.'

'Well, keep them somewhere safe, cheel. I think the box'll fit in your bag. I'll just wrap it in some newspaper so it isn't obvious to anyone what it is.'

'Yes, good idea.' Maisie just managed to speak through the lump in her throat. 'Thank you, Zeek. For everything. But mainly for being my friend when I needed one most.'

'It were the same fer me, maid. Now off you go, afore Janet starts to worry.'

Maisie slid the package into her bag, then planting a kiss on Zeek's stubbly jaw, wrapped him in a tight hug. She was sure no one else in the world could ever mean as much to her as this lovely old man who was so full of surprises. She could feel tears welling in her eyes again and had to smother them by turning the conversation to practical matters.

'Are you sure you don't mind if I don't come tomorrow?' she asked guiltily.

'No, of course not. I's quite capable of finishing they blackout curtains on my own. You go and enjoy yersel. I know how you love going up on the moor. You make the most of it while you can. When this war starts, you mightn't be able to anymore. Didn't you say Janet's going to visit this mysterious cousin of hers while you'm out walking?'

'That's right. She'll be getting off the train at Dousland and walking down to Walkhampton where he lives. But Kitty and I'll be staying on the train up to Princetown and walking all the way back down, following the railway line. It's a lovely walk. Then we'll be meeting Janet back at Dousland.'

'And you've never met this cousin of hers?'

'No, never,' Maisie chuckled. 'But apparently he runs a bicycle repair shop in the village.'

'Still a bit of a mystery, though,' Zeek winked. 'Now, off you go, and I'll see you next Monday, like.'

'If not before, if I can make it. Take care, Zeek. And thank you again,' she said, dipping her head towards her bag.

'You deserve it, maid.'

Zeek threw her a beaming smile, warming her heart as she turned to the door. Outside, the sun was still strong, even as it sank in the sky. As Maisie made her way home, she went over that last conversation with Zeek. She hoped he was wrong about the war, and that all the preparations the government had been making would prove unnecessary. Surely this Mr Hitler would be content with the countries he'd taken over already. After all, what did England have that he could possibly want?

She tried to force such thoughts from her head and instead turned her mind to the jewellery box and the envelope now in her possession. Dear, dear Zeek. Her father had left virtually nothing, barely enough to cover his own simple funeral, and yet quiet, unpretentious Zeek was bequeathing her, well, she wasn't sure exactly how much, but a substantial sum by the sounds of things. She just prayed it was a long, long time before she inherited it.

For now, she was utterly content with her life as it was. She and Kitty each had a room of their own in the house above the shop. She loved her work, both cooking light meals and baking in the kitchen, and serving customers, many of whom were regulars. She knew and was fond of all their neighbours in the adjoining shops, and had soon learned that Union Street wasn't such an infamous place after all, though there were areas closer to the Devonport end that were best avoided at night. As for Janet, she really was like the mother Maisie had never known. For now, it was as close to having a family as she was likely to get.

But what was it Zeek had hinted at? That she and Nick had a future together? Nick would turn twenty come December. Many would be married or at least promised by that age. At only twenty-one, Noreen had a husband and a three-month-old daughter. She wrote of little else in her letters. And Kitty, well, from what her friend had inferred, she'd experienced more than just a peck on the cheek from some of her numerous boyfriends.

So how patient would Nick be? Would he wait for her? Maisie wasn't sure she'd ever feel able to give herself to him in the way you had to as a wife. Her whole being still reared away from the idea. Did she love him enough? She wanted to. And deep down, she still wanted that family of her own. She knew that was true from the pangs of envy that engulfed her when she read Noreen's letters. But would she ever be ready for everything else that it meant?

A couple of times recently, Nick had taken her in his strong arms. The sensation of his body pressed against hers had been warm and comforting. Had made her feel safe. And then he'd bent his head, softly tilting her face upwards, his eyes meeting her gaze tentatively before his lips brushed delicately against hers. The first time, she'd been stunned, not sure how she felt. But each time he'd kissed her since, she'd been amazed how the touch of his warm, moist lips had sent ripples down her spine despite herself. Could it possibly be that she was beginning to develop those desires Kitty was always on about?

She wondered if Sister Agnes could have given her some guidance, but she was thousands of miles away in Africa, still dedicated to her missionary work. She'd told Maisie in the most recent of her occasional letters that she had no intention of returning home just because of the threat of war.

Maisie wished she could feel so sure of things for herself. Maybe she should just let her relationship with Nick take its course. She was only seventeen, after all. And surely there were greater things to worry about, with war on the horizon? She prayed that Zeek was wrong about it being inevitable now. But really and truly, like everyone else, she knew it was a vain hope.

* * *

'Leave that now, Maisie,' Janet instructed as Maisie was setting out trays with a matching teapot, sugar bowl and milk jug each, ready for opening up at noon. 'It's nearly time, and after this, people mightn't feel like coming out anyways.'

As Maisie dutifully abandoned her task and went through to the kitchen, she was aware of the blood trundling through her veins. It was Sunday 3 September, and the prime minister was scheduled to make an announcement. In their heart of hearts, everyone knew this was going to be it, the news they were all dreading, no matter how hard they prayed that it wouldn't be. It would affect each and every one of them, and Maisie couldn't help but think of Zeek all alone in his house as he listened to his radio.

The wireless crackled as Janet tuned it in, and for once, Kitty fell silent, causing an unearthly hush to settle on the room. Maisie could feel the tension sizzling in the air as Janet got a good signal and sat down weightily in her chair. Maisie couldn't bear to look at either of her friends, and instead locked her gaze on her joined hands.

It was short and to the point. Neville Chamberlain, with his clipped, solemn tone, confirmed in the first two sentences what they were all expecting. Britain was now at war with Germany.

Maisie tried to quell her dread by concentrating on the remainder of the speech, but the prime minister's words were a blur to her. Beside her, both Janet and Kitty sat in stunned silence, waiting for the voice to stop. When it did, none of them moved. They'd known it was coming, but to have it confirmed was still a devastating shock.

Maisie waited for the news to sink in. Eventually it was Janet who stood up first.

'Well, we've got standards to keep up,' she announced, bustling now towards the hot-water urn. 'That Hitler needs showing the British Bulldog spirit. Now you finish laying up, and I'll put the cakes on display on the counter. Then we've time to make the sandwiches afore we open up. Though what we'll be putting in them if there's food shortages like in the last war, I don't know.'

'I thought we could register for special supplies based on last year's turnover?' Maisie frowned.

'That's right enough,' Janet agreed, padding past her with a chocolate sponge dusted with icing sugar. 'But that's no good if there's no supplies to be had! But at least they're saying we won't have to take ration coupons from our customers, or however they'll do it. We'll have rules to abide by, no doubt. But the most important thing is to give everyone a warm welcome. So you two get out there and open up, and put on your best cheerful faces. Not that I see anyone waiting outside like we'd normally have at this time. Still reeling after the news, I expect. And young Nick's at sea, isn't he?'

'Yes.'

Maisie's heart landed heavily in her boots. She hated it when she knew Nick was at sea, braving the elements, especially when the weather unexpectedly turned stormy. She could imagine his fishing vessel being tossed about like a toy by huge waves and towering swells, water crashing over the deck and washing him overboard. Now he'd be in danger from German ships and submarines, too. Even aircraft. A heavy constriction crushed her chest like an iron band. That must mean she loved him, mustn't it?

It was some time before anyone wandered into the shop. Usually they had a steady stream of customers wanting a cuppa with a slice of cake before going home to a late Sunday dinner. But today many of the regulars were absent, and those that did turn up were subdued.

'Have you heard the news?' several asked, grim-faced.

'Don't seem right on such a beautiful day, do it?'

Maisie tried to put on a brave face and smile, but it wasn't easy. What was it going to be like, being at war? Giant, inflatable bags called barrage balloons had been installed at various points surrounding the city to stop enemy aircraft, together with massive anti-aircraft guns at other locations. Just as in the rest of the country, an army of both men and women had been training as air-raid precaution wardens, and each civilian had been supplied with a gas mask to carry with them at all times. Hundreds of Anderson shelters had been distributed, and public shelters were being built. And yet the government didn't consider Plymouth would be a target for attack and refused to evacuate the children and other vulnerable citizens from the city, despite requests from the local authorities. It was all so confusing, and Maisie's stomach was tied up in knots of uncertainty.

But she mustn't let it show to the customers, and with a shake of her head, she dragged herself back to the present. Only half the tables were occupied, and as she cast her eye over them, ready to leap in if she suspected she might be able to persuade someone to another slice of cake or pot of tea, she spied Kitty almost falling over her own feet as she rushed towards the door.

Two young men in naval uniform, not ratings but officers of some sort, had just come in. Maisie didn't recognise either of them, and both appeared a little hesitant. But she needn't worry. Kitty had evidently taken them under her wing and was ushering them forward.

'I were just showing these gentlemen through to the garden,' Kitty said brightly as she led them past where Maisie was standing. She'd evidently taken to heart Janet's words about being hospitable! 'They've not been here afore, so they didn't know we have one. It's shaded, you see,' she went on, smiling sweetly at both men, 'and a lot cooler, so I thought it'd be more comfortable for you in they heavy uniforms.'

'Thank you, miss,' one of them nodded, and as they passed, Kitty shot Maisie a saucy wink.

Maisie was grateful for Kitty's exuberance, and the ghost of a smile hovered on her lips. Trust Kitty! One of the officers in particular was handsome in the extreme. When he removed his cap, a lock of blond hair fell onto his broad forehead. His eyes, Maisie noticed, were a pale, piercing blue and his mouth was set in a pleasing curve. He had faint crow's feet, though, and deeper lines about his mouth put him in his late twenties possibly, so Kitty really shouldn't be flirting with him.

But that was Kitty for you. She didn't know a thing about the fellow, but Maisie could see that her friend was taken by him. He was an officer, though of what rank, Maisie had no idea. She'd never got to grips with the different uniform insignia. But that probably meant he'd been in the navy for some time, and being that much older, likely had a sweetheart or wife at home — or a girl in every port, with his good looks.

'Kitty, can you make a fresh pot of tea for table five, please?' Maisie heard Janet's voice, and smiled to herself. Had Janet seen the starry-eyed way Kitty was looking at the strangers, and deliberately called her away? Maisie knew that Janet had promised Mrs Barron to keep an eye on Kitty. It was part of the deal the two older women had struck when Kitty's parents had agreed she could come to live over the shop. Janet took her role most seriously, and it wouldn't be the first time she'd had words with Kitty over her love life.

So it fell to Maisie to show the two naval officers to one of the few tables out on the terrace at the back.

'This is very pleasant,' the extra handsome one said as he sat down. 'A mighty nice little oasis. They say you Brits love your gardens.'

Maisie's pulse gave a little jump. So he wasn't British, then. A twang lilted in his voice, a little akin to the actors in many of the American films she'd seen over the years. And yet it didn't sound exactly the same. His attitude was light and friendly, just what she needed after the awful news on the wireless. He was one of the few customers who hadn't immediately started talking about the war. For that she was grateful, and she found herself answering him with a smile.

'It was better without the chicken coop, but Mrs Mudge reckoned we ought to produce at least some of our own eggs with the war coming,' she explained. 'But at least we didn't need an Anderson shelter. We've got a cellar, you see. But all these flowers and the lawn, they'll probably have to go so we can grow a lot of our own vegetables. Might be hard for you Americans to keep us supplied with all we need.'

'Oh, I'm not American, miss,' the officer grinned back. 'Common mistake. I'm Canadian. A volunteer at the Royal Naval Hospital. My old friend here, he's British. His father's something high up in the Navy and managed to pull some strings to get me a posting when I needed to get away for a while. And, of course,' he concluded, when his friend tossed him a warning look Maisie guessed she wasn't meant to see, 'I really did want to volunteer when I saw the writing on the wall.'

Well, Maisie now knew a bit more about him than Kitty did. She'd have to enlighten her friend if she asked. The chap seemed nice enough, but she suspected he was hiding something. Nevertheless, she had to admit she admired someone who'd volunteered to come to another country in its hour of need.

Given the circumstances, mind, she felt she'd rather not think about it. Instead, she handed the two men a menu each.

'I'll leave you to have a look and come back in a few minutes to take your order. If it's something savoury you're after, we have homemade soup and sandwiches. Or if you'd prefer cake, I can recommend the Dundee.'

Giving them a smile, she left them to it and returned to her own thoughts. What would this war bring? Fear gripped her stomach, and for the first time in years, she wished she could be back in Ireland where the war must seem far, far away.

CHAPTER TWENTY

'You all registered, then?' Nick greeted her as they met on the Hoe as arranged.

It was Friday 29 September and a pleasant enough afternoon. People were out on the green expanses, seemingly enjoying the last embers of summer, and yet there was a sombre feeling in the air. All over the country, enumerators had been collecting registration forms from every household, issuing identity cards as they went, and it had made the war feel horribly close.

'Yes,' Maisie answered grimly. 'Got our identity cards to carry with us at all times as well as our gas masks. You?'

'Yup.' Nick patted his jacket breast pocket. 'And the woman confirmed that fishing'll be a reserved occupation for any age. I'd liked to have done my bit, mind.'

'Would you?' Maisie's brow wrinkled into a painful frown. 'And be like all those poor souls who were lost when the *Courageous* was sunk? It was dreadful seeing the relatives scouring the lists outside the Royal Naval Barracks. I wouldn't have liked to have been among them. Over five hundred dead, many of them reservists and pensioners. And so early in the war.'

Nick sighed. 'Just a taste of what's to come.'

Maisie drew in her bottom lip. Sadly, she knew he was probably right, but it didn't bear thinking about. 'I just pray a fishing boat like yours won't be a target.'

'Don't worry. The *Courageous* were way out off the west coast of Ireland, and she was an aircraft carrier. Our trawler doesn't usually fish that far out, so we should be all right. The Germans have bigger fish to fry than us, no pun intended. Still, I'd have liked to do summat more for the war effort. Wouldn't you?'

'Well, yes,' Maisie admitted. 'It's annoying that Kitty and I are too young to do anything more than fire watch on our own roof. We're going to be trained next week in how to put out an incendiary bomb with a stirrup pump, but it can't be that difficult.'

'Better to have done a few dummy runs, mind, afore you face the real thing. If you ever have to, of course.'

'Yes. But I can't wait until we're eighteen and can start our training for the Auxiliary Fire Service proper. We're not allowed to go on official duty until we're nineteen, but that could change if things get really bad. Sounds ominous, doesn't it? As if they're expecting the war to go on for ages.'

'The last one went on for four years. I don't suppose this one will be ort less.'

Maisie gave a glum sigh. He was right, but the prospect was both alarming and depressing. 'No, probably not. But the thought of all this going on for years is horrendous — barrage balloons, anti-aircraft guns, searchlights, barbed wire all along the coast—'

'We won't be doing any swimming in the lido for a while, that's for sure.'

Nick was trying to make a joke of it, Maisie knew, but she only managed to reply with a grimace. The first time Kitty had persuaded her to visit the bathing pool three years ago now, she'd been reluctant to expose herself in a swimsuit and had made sure hers was of the most modest style possible. But once she'd got used to being in the water, she'd enjoyed herself tremendously, her old adventurous spirit returning. That was shortly before she'd met Nick, but since then, the three of them, with whichever boyfriend Kitty had in tow at the time, had spent many a happy hour at the lido, listening to the band playing on the terraces while sunbathing or playing in the water. But all that had come to an abrupt end now they were at war.

Now, she and Nick came to a stop, looking out across the Sound. It was no surprise to see a warship heading out from Devonport, and across the water at the RAF base at Mount Batten several Sunderland flying boats were moored up. Already, one had launched the first attack on a German U-boat in the Channel, and another had rescued every crew member from the cargo ship SS *Kensington Court* which had been torpedoed seventy miles off the Isles of Scilly.

Maisie shivered involuntarily. The war was creeping ever closer and this, Registration Day, had made it seem so much more real.

'You'm cold,' Nick observed, slipping off the strap of his gas-mask box and shrugging out of his jacket. 'Here, have this. Bit of a breeze up here.'

'Thanks,' Maisie answered. 'Just for a minute or so. I'm not really cold. It's just the thought of everything. You know.' Nevertheless, she was grateful for Nick's jacket about her shoulders. It smelled of wool and sea air, of him, and that in itself brought her some comfort.

'Yes, I do.' Nick's voice was grave. 'But I'm afraid I'll have to make a move in a minute. We're sailing on the tide.'

Maisie nodded. 'I've got to get back, too. It was good of Janet to let me pop out to meet you, knowing I won't see you for a few days. But Friday evenings are one of our busiest times. She's just got Kitty to help, and, well . . .'

'She's not as efficient as you. No need to tell me,' Nick said with a chuckle as they started to wander back towards the city. 'Kitty's great, but she's not like my Irish colleen, even if her lovely accent has faded.'

Maisie glanced at him in surprise. 'D'you think so?'

'Most definitely. Must be falling in love with a Devonshire man that's done it.'

He pulled her round to him, his tone teasing, and enclosed her in his arms. They'd reached the point where they had to part company, Nick heading towards the Barbican and the moorings of the *Calypso*, while Maisie would make her way home to Union Street. Nick lowered his head to give her a farewell kiss. As their lips met softly, a sudden overwhelming force swept through her. What if something happened to him, his boat sank or was attacked like the *Courageous* and the *Kensington Court* had been? The thought of losing him, of never seeing him again, pierced her heart. She realised she did love him, and a passion that astounded her rose inside her like a fountain. She raised herself on tiptoe, entwining her arms around his neck, her lips parting to kiss him long and deep. It was something she'd never felt before, and she gloried in the sensation, even though it was born of fear.

It was only a wolf whistle that made her draw away, flushed and embarrassed. She realised then that Nick's jacket had slid from her shoulders. They both went to retrieve it at the same time, and their eyes met, bright yet confused.

'I'll have to go away more often if I get that sort of goodbye,' Nick murmured with surprised amusement.

Maisie knew her cheeks were pink, but as she tried to shrug away her awkwardness, the anxiety rushed back. 'You just take care now,' she gulped.

Nick's dark eyes became serious. 'Of course. And you. I'll see you in a few days.'

With that, he turned and walked away, pausing to give one last wave before he disappeared from view. Maisie watched him go, letting the strange light flare deep inside her before she set off down the street. She felt bewildered by her own emotions, her head spinning. Had it taken this war to make her realise how much she loved Nick? Just as at the tea rooms, all the shops and other commercial buildings she passed had their windows blacked out and criss-crossed with tape to help prevent flying glass in the event of a blast, and many others were banked high with sandbags. The whole idea was horrific, and yet it had made something happen to her heart.

She felt a flicker of excitement in her stomach. That moment in Nick's arms had lit a flame inside her. Perhaps that fear of what you did with the man you loved was finally lessening. She felt safe with Nick, cradled. Trusting. She knew he would never do anything to hurt her. Love could grow out of friendship and trust, Zeek had said. She and Nick had been together in one way or another for nearly three years, long enough for those feelings to strengthen. She could never imagine giving herself to anyone else but him, but suddenly the thought of his lean body against hers was both delicious and intriguing. She'd never let him do it properly — unless they were married, of course. But the thought of a bit of canoodling as Kitty called it, was sending an entrancing thrill down to her belly.

* * *

'So what can I be getting you, sir?' Maisie asked pleasantly.

The customer glanced up and gave her a tentative smile. She recognised him at once as the Canadian volunteer who had patronised the tea rooms with his fellow officer several times now. This afternoon, though, he was alone.

'I'd like a black coffee and a slice of your delicious walnut cake, if you please, miss.'

'Of course. Coming right up.'

But as she turned away, his hesitant voice drew her back. 'Actually, miss, I was hoping to see your sister if she's around.'

'My sister?'

He seemed confused. 'Yeah. I've heard you call her Kitty?'

'Oh,' Maisie chuckled. 'She's not my sister.'

'Really? But you look so alike, I thought . . .'

'Don't worry, you're not the first person to be thinking that. But most people twig it when we start speaking. Kitty's from here. Plymothian. But I'm from the Emerald Isle. Can you not hear the difference?'

He shook his head with a baffled smile. 'Both just sound quaint to me.'

'Well, everyone tells me my accent's pretty well gone. I've been living here five years now, surrounded by local people, so I suppose it's rubbed off on me a bit. But why, may I ask, are you wanting to see Kitty?'

She saw the fellow's cheeks colour slightly. 'I was hoping she might agree to come to the movies with me,' he almost gulped. 'Or maybe we could make up a foursome if she'd feel happier. I've seen you've got a young man.'

Maisie's eyebrows lifted. Well, she supposed Nick was a regular visitor and would think nothing of giving her a peck on the cheek in public, so it wasn't surprising this customer had noticed. But you couldn't be too cautious, especially with so many strangers about. Although this one did appear to be an officer, of course, so you'd think he'd be respectable.

'We-ell, I'll go and tell her,' Maisie answered warily, though she knew precisely what Kitty would say. 'Who shall I say wishes to speak to her?'

'Oh, er, Mackenzie. Cameron. Doctor.'

He seemed genuinely nervous, and Maisie couldn't help but hide a smile at his awkwardness. Nevertheless, he was a stranger, a foreigner even, and a fair bit older than they were. And could you trust anyone, even if he was really a doctor? And what sort of name was that?

'Is that Mackenzie Cameron, or—'

'No, Doctor Cameron Mackenzie. I reckon my ancestors were Scotch immigrants way back.'

'Scottish,' Maisie corrected. 'We say Scottish. Scotch is what you drink. Scotch whisky.'

'Oh, I stand corrected.' He grinned easily now, and Maisie had to admit that his face lit up quite boyishly, making him look much younger.

'All right. I'll get Kitty to bring your order. But if she agrees to go out with you, she'll have to get Mrs Mudge's permission. She's the owner here. We're both only seventeen and she acts as our guardian. Well, actually she's my legal guardian, but she keeps an eye on Kitty on her parents' behalf, too.'

'In loco parentis.'

'That's right. Anyway, I'll go and see if Kitty wants to speak to you.'

She threaded her way through the tables towards the kitchen. Doctor Mackenzie, or whoever he was, must be well educated. She knew a certain amount of Latin from the convent, but it wasn't everyone who'd use a Latin phrase in general conversation. And most medical terminology came from Latin, didn't it? So she truly hoped he was genuine, for Kitty's sake.

A thousand stars shone in her friend's eyes when Maisie told her.

'Well, I know you fancy the socks off him, but don't get too excited,' Maisie warned. 'We don't know that he is who he says he is, and he must be years older than us. Maybe he's only after one thing, doctor or no, so you need to be careful. And the other thing is, that first time he came in with his friend, I got the impression there was something they didn't want us to know.'

Kitty pulled a face. 'Spoil sport.' But then she was instantly grinning again like the cat who'd got the cream. 'Where's your sense of fun? Too long going out with dependable old Nick, that's your trouble. Oh, but do say you'll make a foursome so as we can go out together?' she begged, grasping Maisie's hands and jumping up and down. 'Probably the only way Janet'll give permission.'

She was such a picture of excitement that Maisie felt obliged to agree. 'Oh, go on, then,' she laughed. 'But it might be difficult to arrange with Nick's fishing trips and this chap's duties at the hospital, if he really is a doctor. And only if Janet agrees, of course.'

'Oh, thanks, Maisie. I'll love you forever.' And giving Maisie a hug that almost squeezed the breath from her, Kitty danced out of the kitchen.

* * *

'I understand your reservations, Mrs Mudge, ma'am,' Cameron was saying a few days later, as he stood before Janet, who sat with her arms folded sternly over her bosom. 'But my intentions are entirely honourable, I assure you. I know I'm ten years older, but when you've been surrounded by serious people all your life and your work is all about the sick and injured, or the dying even, I can't tell you what a tonic someone as bright and lively as Kitty is for me. I promise to look after her.'

'Hmm,' Janet answered, making a sucking noise through her lips. 'And how do I know you are who you claim to be?'

'Oh, sorry, ma'am, I forgot.' Cameron pulled out some documents from the inside breast pocket of his uniform. 'ID card, passport, the letter confirming my appointment here. Of course, you could come to the hospital, but being a naval establishment, they probably wouldn't let you in.'

Janet wiggled her nose as she put on her spectacles to inspect the documents, and then lifted her head to meet Cameron's anxious gaze. 'You'll understand, young man, that I must be careful, acting on behalf of Kitty's parents. And what's this I hear about your being married?' she demanded.

Maisie saw Cameron's face blanch. 'Separated, ma'am, and filing for divorce. Another reason for volunteering. I needed to get away from it all. My wife decided that being floozy to some devil in the film industry was a more exciting prospect than being married to a provincial doctor. Divorce can be a lengthy process, mind. And having the Atlantic between us means correspondence will be even slower. And then there's the war of course. Anyway, here's the most recent letter from my lawyer back home to prove that what I'm saying is true.'

He handed over another piece of paper that Janet took her time to scrutinise. Beside her, Maisie could see that Kitty was holding her breath. No wonder. It had been a shock when Cameron had revealed his marital status, but he'd been perfectly open about it which in itself seemed to prove his honesty. No secrets, he'd said. And it was true that they'd all found him likeable in the extreme.

Even to Maisie it felt like an age before Janet removed her spectacles and carefully put them away in their case. Then she joined her hands together on the table in front of her, keeping everyone waiting on tenterhooks while she drew in a long, pensive breath.

'Well, this all seems to bear out what you say,' she pronounced, the usual homely smile creeping back onto her face. 'So you all get yourselves off to the pictures and enjoy your evening. Where you going?'

'The Savoy, ma'am.'

'Just down the road, then. So I'll expect you back here proper early, and we can all enjoy a nice cuppa together. But you're only to go out in a group until we get to know you better, like, Dr Mackenzie.'

'Oh, please, call me Cameron, ma'am.'

'As you wish. But I'll need to tell Kitty's parents about you, and if they forbid you to see her, then I'm afraid you'll have to obey their wishes.'

'Of course, ma'am. I wouldn't expect otherwise.'

'In the meantime, you may call me Janet.'

'Now you've really been approved,' Maisie joked. 'Come on. Don't want to miss the B film, do we?'

Beaming at Nick, she took his hand and made for the door. The other couple followed, Kitty hopping around Cameron like an excited puppy while he watched her, Maisie observed, with eyes sparkling with delight.

CHAPTER TWENTY-ONE

'That was truly delicious, Janet,' Cameron declared, politely wiping his lips on a starched napkin.

'Well, Lord knows what we'll be eating next Christmas Eve,' Janet moaned, 'what with rationing starting in a couple of weeks.'

'We'll always have eggs, mind, with our ladies out the back,' Kitty chipped in, referring to the hens in the coop in the garden.

'Provided they keep laying,' Maisie warned, and the conversation moved to a discussion on poultry care before Kitty suggested a game of Monopoly that kept them all entertained for a couple of hours.

'It's about time I got back to my digs,' Nick said a while later when they'd decided that Janet was the winner and nobody could hope to catch her up. 'Thanks so much for a super meal, Janet. I'll look forward to seeing you again tomorrow.'

'Don't forget to collect Zeek, will you?' Maisie reminded him.

'As if I would. I'm as fond of the old fellow as you are.'

'Make sure you tuck the rug around him properly in the wheelchair. It's absolutely freezing outside, and I don't suppose it'll be any better tomorrow.'

'Aye, aye, captain,' Nick joked back.

'Well, I wish I were going to be here instead of spending the day at Mum and Dad's,' Kitty sighed. 'It'd be far more fun here.'

'Never mind, honey,' Cameron replied. 'We'll all be back here on Boxing Day. My shift should finish at eight o'clock and I'll come straight over.'

'Well, I think it's rotten you're on duty Boxing Day when you're on duty all day tomorrow as well,' Kitty pouted.

'Someone has to be. One of the drawbacks of being a doctor, I guess. But I do have an early start, so I'll be getting along, too. Thanks again, Janet, for a lovely meal.'

'You're welcome, my lover. I do like to see people enjoy my cooking.'

The four younger people made their way through the tea rooms to the front door, the two men pulling on their coats as they went. There followed a chorus of goodnights. Maisie knew that she'd only get a peck on the cheek from Nick in front of the others. But the tall Canadian was less reserved and wrapped Kitty in a bearhug, before placing a juicy kiss on her eager lips, making Maisie and Nick laugh.

'Right, are we all done?' Maisie asked, serious now as she slid the bolts on the door and turned the key. 'Got your gas masks? Yes? Turn off the lights then, would you, Nick?'

They were at once plunged into darkness. As Maisie opened the door, a blast of arctic air stormed its way inside, and the two men groped their way out into the biting night air as quickly as they could. Outside was a thick fog as black as treacle, and they both stood for a moment, waiting for their eyes to adjust as much as possible. Even so, they'd be virtually walking blind.

'Go carefully, won't you?' she called out to them. 'We don't want any accidents.'

'Do our best.'

And then the two dark forms were absorbed into the night. Maisie locked and bolted the door again, then checking the blackout curtain with her fingertips, turned the lights back on. The bulbs were only a low wattage and painted blue, but it was enough to see their way back to the kitchen and up the stairs.

'I'll never get used to this,' Kitty grumbled. 'I like the bright lights, not having to think like this all the time.'

'Well, you'd better get used to it. It's going to go on for a long, long time. Talking of which, we're on duty soon. Time to get changed and get ourselves out on the roof.'

'Surely Hitler's not going to start bombing us on Christmas Eve?'

'Who knows? That's maybe what he's hoping we'll think, and we'll not be prepared. So you and I need to get plenty of warm layers on under our boiler suits and get ourselves out there. It's only till two o'clock when Mr and Mrs Nettlehayes take over.'

'You cheels nearly ready?' Janet called out as they reached the bedrooms on the second floor. 'Not that I hold with you being out on the roof half the night at your ages. I cas'n sleep with you out there. What if either of you fell off in the dark?'

'Oh, Janet, there's a balustrade all the way round. The only way we'd go over the edge would be if we jumped.'

'Well, you're still too young in my opinion.'

'Maybe, but better to be up on our own roof,' Kitty put in. 'Someone's got to do it, and sharing the shifts with our neighbours on either side were ideal.'

'I still don't like it.'

'Don't you worry, Janet. We'll be perfectly safe. I'm sure it's far too foggy for flying, so we're unlikely to get our very first raid tonight. You get a good night's sleep, but let us have a lie in tomorrow morning, eh?'

So saying, Maisie gave the older woman a hug. Then, draping the strap of her gas-mask box over her shoulder, she switched off the landing light. Carrying the flask of hot tea Janet had made them, Kitty followed her up the short flight of stairs to the door that opened onto the flat roof. As they stepped outside, a fug of freezing moisture wreathed itself about them, seeping into their nostrils and making them shiver.

'How do?' Mr Huggins, who had the hardware store next door, called from the adjoining roof. 'You maids all right?'

'Yes, thanks. And you?'

'Proper clever, thanks, but us is glad our shift's over and us can get into our beds. Don't think there'll be ort tonight with this snipey weather,' he added as with his son's help, he passed the stirrup pump they shared over the railing that separated the roofs. 'Still got your buckets of water and sand?'

'Certainly do.'

'Then us'll leave you to it.'

The shadows of father and son mingled into the darkness and disappeared. It was virtually the same conversation every night depending on how they'd arranged the rota, with Mr Huggins's son — only sixteen but as big and strong as a horse — never uttering a word. Mr Nettlehayes and his wife from the butcher's on the other side never said much either, so the handover was always quick and efficient. No one wanted to stay out on the roof on a cold winter's night longer than they had to.

'Right, drill practice,' Maisie announced.

'Oh, do we need to?' Kitty whined.

'Well, we've got four hours to fill. Now what have we got? Has the incendiary just landed or has it set fire to anything yet?'

'Just landed, I suppose.'

'Right, you pretend to pump, and I'll do the hose. So am I using the spray or the jet?'

'The spray.'

'And how many strokes per minute for the pump?'

'Thirty-five. And if it had caught fire, you'd be using the jet which needs sixty-five, if your arms don't drop off first. Oh, this is silly. We know what to do. Or we can just dump the sand on it.'

'Only if it's somewhere accessible. Anyway, it's good to keep practising so it'd be like second nature if anything did happen. And moving helps to keep us warm. So let's do our first round, shall we?'

Carefully, they edged their way around the roof's perimeter, peering across at their neighbours' properties on either side. With each minute, their eyes became a little more used to the dark, but the freezing fog formed an almost impenetrable wall about them, and clung to their eyelashes in tiny crystals. Patches of ice slithered beneath their feet and they could do no more than inch forward.

'Not my idea of Christmas Eve,' Kitty complained as they felt their way to the front of the building and paused to gaze down onto the street below. Not that they could make out a thing as it was like looking down into a swirling, inky chasm. 'The street should be swarming with people having fun, and we should be with them. Oh, Maisie, d'you really think we need to be up here? Surely no aircraft could fly in this.'

'What if it suddenly cleared? No,' Maisie said firmly. 'It's what we've agreed, and we've got to stick to it, no matter what.'

'I suppose so. But let's finish this round and then go and stand by the chimneys for a bit. At least you can warm your back up against them.'

'Yes, okay,' Maisie agreed, and they shuffled back towards the stacks that could at least offer them a little shelter from the perishingly cold night. 'I can't see my watch,' she said as they got themselves comfortable leaning back against the warm bricks. 'And there'll be no church bells chiming, of course, but I reckon it must be midnight by now, so Happy Christmas, my lover!'

She heard Kitty give a mere grunt of amusement at her impression of their dear Janet. 'Well, I'm not even going to see Cam tomorrow,' her friend grumbled. 'I'll just get it in the ear from Mum cuz she disapproves of him, being married, and all.'

'Well, at least she hasn't forbidden you to see him. And maybe she'll be changing her mind once his divorce comes through.'

'Perhaps. But that could take a couple of years.' Maisie was aware of Kitty releasing an exasperated sigh. 'In the meantime, she refuses even to meet him. And Dad backs her up. I bet they're hoping it'll fizzle out like all the others. But it won't, I'm sure. Not from my side, anyway. I really think Cam's the one. I know it's sudden, but you sort of know, don't you?'

Maisie caught the adoration in Kitty's voice and the corners of her mouth curved upwards. 'Yes, I suppose you do. I mean, I know Nick and I have sort of grown together, I'm guessing you'd say. But I can't imagine loving anyone else.'

'So, d'you think you'll marry when you're a bit older?'

Despite the frost congealing on her cheeks, Maisie could feel heat blooming on her skin. 'Maybe. If he asks me. But we've got to get through this war first, and it hasn't even started properly yet.'

'If we don't die of hypo-what's-it up here first,' Kitty groaned. 'Let's see if we can find that thermos and have ourselves a hot drink to warm us up.'

'Only a sip, mind. It's got to last us until three, remember.'

'Trust you to be the sensible one.'

Maisie gave a small laugh. Just for a split second, an image of her and Noreen back at the convent flashed across her mind. She was always the scatter-brained one, and now with her and Kitty, the roles were reversed. Strange how things could change. But just now, she agreed with Kitty that a mouthful of hot tea would be just the ticket to keep them going through the bitter night.

CHAPTER TWENTY-TWO

1940

'You sure you don't mind us going?'

'Course not, my lovers. This is history in the making. We missed the *Ajax* coming home, so you mustn't miss the *Exeter* and all. And she be a Devonport ship.'

'Thanks, Janet, you're a brick.'

'And are you sure you won't come with us?'

Maisie saw the wistful expression come over Janet's face. 'No, cheel. The *Exeter* lost a lot of men, too. And it, well, it reminds us too much of my Herbert.'

Maisie gave her a sympathetic half-smile and squeezed her arm before following Kitty into the shop. It was first thing in the morning and they had yet to take down the black-out blinds, so when a knock came on the front door, they couldn't see who it was before they opened it.

'Nick!'

'Morning!' he grinned. 'Oh, I see you've got your coats on. Heard the news, then? You coming down to the Hoe? They say the *Exeter*'s going to be anchored in the Sound for a while afore she goes up harbour. There'll be crowds all the way up to Devonport, but I reckon you'll still get the best view of her from the Hoe.'

'Sounds good to me,' Maisie smiled back happily as Nick took her hand. She was always so relieved when he got back safely from a fishing trip, and any snatched time with him was so precious to her.

The three of them stepped outside into the bitter half-light of the February morning. The cold, grey dawn wrapped its tentacles about them as they hurried through the streets, not wanting to miss the spectacle of the ship that, together with the *Ajax* which had limped home two weeks earlier, had played a part in the eventual scuttling of the great German battleship *Graf Spee* near Argentina, during what was being called the Battle of the River Plate. It was a strange sort of victory, but a victory it was nonetheless. However, the *Exeter* had been so badly damaged that she'd had to put into the Falkland Islands for temporary repairs to allow her to make it back across the Atlantic.

Now it seemed that most of Plymouth had come out to welcome her home, despite the early hour and the drizzle-saturated air. But then, the first thing people did when they got up in the morning was to turn on the wireless and tune into the local Rediffusion service. Like the *Ajax* before her, the *Exeter* had secretly sailed into the safety of the Sound under cover of darkness, so it was only in the early morning news bulletin that the announcement of her arrival had been made.

The mist was even thicker as they came out onto the Hoe, passing where the Corporation had turned a substantial area of lawn over to vegetable production. Crowds were swarming from every direction and the atmosphere was electric.

'I cas'n see a flipping thing,' Kitty complained as they peered out over the Sound. 'I'd have stayed in bed if I'd known.'

'Have a bit of patience,' Nick chided gently. 'This is the sort of sea fog that'll soon lift. Look, there's a band setting up. We'll be having music to keep us entertained in a minute.'

'And lift our spirits even more!' Maisie added, snuggling more closely against Nick for warmth. 'Come on, let's get as near as we can.'

As they made their way forward, they were almost propelled along by the surging mass of Plymothians wanting to show their appreciation of the *Exeter's* triumph. Mingled among the civilians were many men and women in uniform, from ARP wardens, military and naval personnel, to nurses and members of the WVS. It was certainly a morale-boosting occasion, and when the band struck up, the excitement grew.

'Kitty! Maisie!'

Maisie turned her head. She recognised the voice, but couldn't place it until Philippa had forced her way through the throng and appeared next to them.

'Pippa!' Maisie and Kitty cried as one, and took it in turns to hug their old friend. 'Haven't see you for ages.'

'Sorry. Been too busy studying. Got big exams in June, and then I've been accepted at the City Hospital to start my training in September. You two still at the café?'

'Don't let Janet — that's the owner — hear you call it a café!' Maisie laughed. 'It's a tea room. But yes, we're still there, and living over the shop.'

'I really must call in and see you.'

'Bring Beryl with you,' Kitty said enthusiastically. 'Haven't seen her since, well, I cas'n remember when.'

'Nor have I, I'm afraid. Not since she started work at the telegram office a couple of years back now.'

'That's a pity. Oh, you remember Nick, don't you?'

'Yes, of course,' she smiled. 'You two serious, then?'

Maisie felt herself blush. Philippa had always been a bit blunt. But Maisie didn't have to think up a reply as Nick answered for her.

'I hope so,' he said with a grin. 'We've been together long enough.'

'And you're a fisherman, if I remember rightly. So no active service for you. And what about you two? Enrolled for anything yet?'

'Yes. The Auxiliary Fire Service. Officially we're too young yet, but we'll be starting our training in June.' They'd been having to shout to make themselves heard over the clamour, but one of a group of Wrens behind them had yelled out so loudly that their conversation was at once cut short.

'Oh, look!'

Now all eyes turned out to sea. Though the bleak winter morning had chilled everyone to the bone, euphoric cheering rent the air as the sea mist suddenly lifted. There she was, the *Exeter*, her hull battle-scarred and riddled with pockmarks, but triumphant, as tugs and other small craft went out to greet her and accompany her up to Devonport.

The Wrens behind them let out a deafening roar and the cheers of the multitudes around them echoed across the waters of the Sound. Maisie couldn't hear herself think, let alone speak. The band was playing 'Rule, Britannia!' and loud, ear-splitting voices joined in the chorus. Everyone was whooping and cheering and waving their hats in the air as the *Exeter* slowly began to move away to the right, in the direction of her home berth in the dockyard, ready for repairs.

'They say the First Lord of the Admiralty has come down from London to give them an official welcome,' Maisie heard one of the Wrens announce as the noise died down.

'What, Winston Churchill, you mean?' said another.

'Apparently so. And Lord and Lady Astor'll be going aboard, as well.'

'Sure, they are the mayor and mayoress, and she's the MP for Plymouth, so you'd expect it, wouldn't you?'

'Oh, trust know-it-all Driscoll,' someone else said, provoking a chorus of laughter.

'Well, I must be going,' Philippa's voice drew Maisie's attention. 'I'm going to be late for school as it is, but I wasn't going to miss this. But I promise I'll call into the tea rooms,' she grinned, with cheeky emphasis on the words tea rooms. 'Must be off. Toodle pip, and all that.' With that, she disappeared into the crowd.

'Well, I suppose we ought to be getting back, too,' Kitty said. 'Any road, I'm frozed, and Janet might want to open up early. Might get a lot of custom with all this going on.'

'Yes, you're probably right. What about you, Nick?'

'Need to get back to the boat. Might see you later, mind.'

Nick wrapped his arms around Maisie and drew her in for a kiss. She knew the general elation had driven away his usual reserve. She felt the same and melted against him for a moment before he released her again, and with a cheery wave, made off towards the Barbican and Sutton Harbour.

'Come on, then.'

Kitty linked her arm through Maisie's and they turned away, coming face to face with the Wrens who were still chatting at the tops of their voices.

Then Maisie froze rigid.

She knew those eyes staring directly into hers. It couldn't be. But she'd detected a slight Irish lilt in one of the girl's voices. A sense of panic darted down to her stomach. It was older, of course, but she'd recognise the face beneath the Wren's cap anywhere. And now she thought about it, hadn't one of the others said that loathsome name? There was no doubt. It was Helen Driscoll.

A hot surge of the old animosity scorched through Maisie's veins. Had Helen recognised her? She had her answer as Helen gave that supercilious smile Maisie knew so well.

'Nice,' she said, dipping her head towards where Nick had become lost in the throng. Then she turned and joined her noisy, laughing comrades as they wandered away.

Maisie was still rooted to the spot as all the memories came crashing back. It wasn't until Kitty tugged hard on her arm that she was dragged back to reality.

'You all right, Maisie? You look as if you've seen a ghost.'

'Oh,' Maisie murmured, shaking her head. 'I thought for a moment I saw someone I knew a long time ago, back at the convent. But it can't have been.'

But as they set off, arm in arm, back towards Union Street, she knew jolly well it was. How the devil had Helen

Driscoll ended up in Plymouth? Well, obviously she'd joined the WRNS and been posted here. But even so, the chances of bumping into her must have been a million to one. Plymouth was a big city, and with any luck, they'd never meet again.

But what if that old enmity still lingered in Helen's nasty mind? Maisie's blood ran cold as she realised Helen must have heard every word of their conversation with Philippa, they'd been talking so loudly. She'd know Maisie worked in a tea rooms, had enrolled for the Fire Service and that her boyfriend was a fisherman. If not everything had registered with her, she'd evidently latched onto Nick, at least. Surely she wouldn't be so despicable as to try and get back at Maisie after all these years?

She tried to brush the feeling away as they walked back through the city, but it sat there, persisting like a clenched fist in her chest.

* * *

Maisie pushed hard on the front door, but it didn't open. Zeek must have forgotten to unlock it. He'd done so a couple of times recently. Maisie had noticed he was becoming a bit forgetful, and she wondered how long he could continue living alone. When she'd mentioned her concerns to Janet, the good woman had suggested Zeek came to live with them as she had a spare bedroom, after all. However, when Maisie had put the idea to Zeek, he'd merely replied that he would bear the kind offer in mind but would stay put for now.

Now Maisie took her own key from her handbag and let herself in. Thank goodness Zeek had seen fit to have one cut for her. Just in case, he'd said. As it was, this wasn't the first time Maisie had needed to use it.

'Morning, Zeek!' she called cheerily as she took off her coat. 'Only me!'

As she stepped down the hallway to the backhouse, she noticed the place seemed unusually quiet. Normally, Zeek would be up by now, sitting at the table with a cup of tea and some toast, the range stoked up and the wireless on. But when Maisie opened the door, the room was empty. Perhaps he'd only just come down, she told herself, and gone straight out to the privy. So she tried the back door. That, too, was locked.

She wondered if he had gone back to bed. He hadn't been sleeping well lately. She'd best just creep up the stairs to check on him without waking him.

She threw open the door and breathed a sigh of relief. There he was, propped up on the pillows, fast asleep and clutching the photograph of himself and his dear Ruth to his chest. He looked so peaceful, and Maisie paused at the foot of the bed to smile down on him.

And then she realised something wasn't right. Oh, God. She sprang forward in panic, a sudden dread tumbling down inside her. Reached out, praying, terrified. Placed her hand on his wrinkled forehead. It was stone cold.

Oh no. A brutal howl escaped her lungs. For several moments she couldn't move. Then her legs gave way beneath her and she sank down on the bed beside him.

'Oh, Zeek,' she whispered.

She sat, staring down at his beloved face. Her hand moved across, closed about his as it held the photograph against his breast. Had he known? Felt something wasn't right? Was that why he'd taken the picture to bed with him? At least it looked like he'd died peacefully in his sleep, and for that, at least, Maisie was grateful.

'Hail Mary, full of grace, the Lord is with thee. Blessed art though among women, and blessed is the fruit of thy womb, Jesus. Holy Mary, Mother of God, pray for us sinners, now and at the hour of our death. And may Almighty God, whose nature it is always to have mercy, grant eternal rest to this thy servant who has this day departed from this world.'

The words came out muddled from somewhere deep inside her, her lips twitching as she spoke them softly into the stillness of the room. She hadn't been to church since her father had drummed her religion out of her, or even looked at her missal. Through the veil of her shock, she wasn't sure she'd got any of it right, but she felt she had to say something to send this dear old man on his way.

She leaned over and placed a reverent kiss on his marble brow, then rested her head on his shoulder. Her chest heaved in and out as sorrow welled up inside her. Sobs racked her body as she wept against him. The person who meant more to her than anyone else in the world was gone.

She didn't know how long it was before she ran out of tears. She sat up, her throat aching, and gazed at him. Wanting to imprint him on her memory for ever.

She sniffed. The cold steel of acceptance came then. There were things to be done. She knew that from when her father had died. But this was different. This time, her soul was drenched in grief.

She stood up. Kissed her fingers. Lay them on his forehead one last time.

'Goodbye, Zeek,' she croaked as tears threatened once again. 'Thank you for everything. Be at peace now, with Ruth.'

She turned slowly from the room.

* * *

'May I offer you my most sincere condolences, Miss O'Sullivan,' Mr Jacobs the solicitor said kindly, as she and Janet took their seats opposite his desk. 'Mr Doidge was a remarkable and canny gentleman, and I'm sure will be greatly missed.'

'Thank you,' Maisie gulped, sadness tearing at her again. 'He was like a grandfather to me.'

'And you were like a granddaughter to him, he told me more than once. Which is why, as I believe he had told you, he left every penny he owned to you.'

Maisie nodded. Yes, Zeek had told her, but it all felt so unreal. And she'd have given every last farthing to have him back.

'Now, then.' Mr Jacobs withdrew a sheet of paper from a folder on his desk. 'This is the amount he had in the bank, minus the cost of the funeral which will be taken from his estate, of course. I hope the service brought you some comfort.'

Maisie nodded again, too choked at the recent memory to speak. It had been a small congregation, herself, Kitty, Janet, Nick and Cameron, plus a few neighbours. But it had been emotional and sincere. Unlike when her father had died and, apart from one work colleague who'd come out of duty, Maisie and Zeek had been the only mourners. Not that they had done much mourning. The ceremony then had been cold and meaningless.

'Perhaps you'd like to take a look,' Mr Jacobs prompted, pushing the paper across the desk. 'Together with the house, he's left you a substantial sum. Have you thought what you'd like to do with the house? Sell it, rent it out, or maybe live in it yourself when you're a little older, perhaps?'

Maisie didn't need to think. She'd already started to sort through Zeek's possessions and the process was painful. She knew she couldn't possibly keep the house which held so many memories for her.

'I've already made up my mind to sell it,' she answered. 'If I kept it, I'd just keep seeing him there.'

'Yes, I understand,' Mr Jacobs said gravely. 'Though as trustee to the estate, I'm not sure I'd recommend selling. With the uncertainty of the war, you might not get the best price.'

'Trustee?'

'Yes, my dear. You cannot inherit until you come of age. In the meantime, Mr Doidge appointed myself as trustee. However, I'm retiring at the end of next month, so my partner, Mr George, will be taking my place as trustee after that.'

'Oh, I see. Well, I still want to sell the house.'

'Yes, she'd already decided,' Janet put in.

'Fair enough,' Mr Jacobs agreed. 'I'll arrange to have the house put up for sale for you. Now, let me explain how the trust will work. All the funds will be kept safely in an interest-bearing account for you. If you need any living expenses in the meantime, just come to me — or Mr George after next month — for approval, and you can be granted a reasonable sum. On reaching your twenty-first birthday, that account will automatically transfer into your name. There will be some forms for you to sign, but that can be done by post if, say, you're living elsewhere by then. The money will then be there for you to do with as you please. So, all fairly simple from your end. You just need to keep us informed of any change of address.'

'Well, I hope she'll still be living with me, as her legal guardian.' Janet beamed proudly.

'Quite so. But it's possible that she could have married in that time. In which case, Miss O'Sullivan, I would need sight of your marriage certificate to make the necessary alterations. Mr Doidge did, indeed, mention a young man in your life.'

'Yes, that's right. But we're not engaged or anything.'

'Well, that's irrelevant at the moment. Now, I don't know if Mr Doidge mentioned it, but in this uncertain world and with this being a substantial sum, he wanted everything to be watertight. So he added a clause in his will whereby, should anything happen to you before you're old enough to inherit and make a will of your own, the inheritance will pass to your friend, Christine Barron.'

'Yes, he did tell me, and I'd be in full agreement,' Maisie replied. 'Not that I'm planning on meeting my maker just yet.'

Mr Jacobs gave a wry smile. 'None of us do, my dear. But in my job, you see so much of the unexpected. So, leave it all with me for now. If you can make an appointment to see me again in a week's time, I will prepare all the paperwork. And if you'd be so kind as to bring your birth certificate with you, everything can be verified. Does that all make sense?'

'Yes, I think so.'

'Well, any questions, just get in touch. I know it's a lot to take in, on top of your bereavement and with you being so young, but it was Mr Doidge's wish that everything be tied up securely.'

'Yes, I understand.'

'Well.' Mr Jacobs came round the desk and opened the door for them. 'I look forward to seeing you again next week. And once again, my sincere condolences.'

He shook both their hands as they passed into the outer office, where his secretary made another appointment for them before showing them back downstairs and out onto the street. It was a large, prestigious practice, and Maisie felt she could have every confidence in the kindly Mr Jacobs.

'Well, he certainly seems to know what he's doing,' Janet declared as they set off home. 'Makes me think perhaps I ought to make a will myself. I imagined everything would go to Cousin Wilfred as my only living relative, but perhaps I should make it official, like. Anyways, I don't know about you, my lover, but I could do with a nice cuppa after all that.'

'Yes, so could I,' Maisie nodded back. Zeek, bless him, had done everything he could to simplify matters. But she'd have given anything to have him back.

* * *

'So, how you'm getting on?' Nick asked as he followed her down the hallway and into the backhouse. 'Can I do ort to help?'

Maisie gestured to where she'd been packing up Zeek's best china, carefully wrapping each item in newspaper.

'There's not a lot I want to keep, to be honest,' she answered with a deep sigh. 'This china, the silver cutlery, the best of the ornaments and the paintings. The best pots from the back yard, some plants and seeds. Oh, and the sewing machine, of course.'

'Sounds a reasonable amount to me.'

'Well, not really. Most of it will be going in these boxes. Mr Huggins can get a bit of petrol for his van and has kindly said he'll come and pick everything up when I'm ready. The most precious things, though, are the photographs. There's just a few, but I need to keep a physical image of Zeek in front of me. I sort of feel connected to him when I look at his photo. Without it, I feel as if he's fading in my head. As if I'm losing him. And that makes me feel guilty.'

There was a catch in her voice, and she had to look away to hide the tears that were welling in her eyes. But she couldn't fool Nick and he put his arms around her in a loving embrace. She gave in at once, sobbing into his chest.

'I know how that feels,' he soothed, stroking her hair. 'I were quite young when my mother walked out so I don't really remember her. But when Dad died, I felt like that. Photos do help, but you never really lose them. They stay inside you. Here.'

Nick tapped his chest, and Maisie pulled back, sniffing and nodding at the same time. She felt Nick's finger beneath her chin, gently tilting her head up towards him. She met his eyes, deep pools of love, as his mouth curved into a smile. His lips came down on hers, so sweet and tender, kissing away her anguish. She was suddenly taken over by some powerful force, intrigued by the emotion that heaved inside her. Her arms went around his neck, her lips responding to his, her body aching. When his hand reached beneath her jumper and softly cupped her breast, she knew she flinched. But then it began to feel right, and she wondered if perhaps she could get used to it.

The breath became trapped in her throat, wonder, fear and grief mingling as one. When Nick's hold on her lessened and he ended the kiss with an understanding smile and a tiny tap on the end of her nose, she felt as if something inside her had changed. Yes, she thought, maybe, she could love Nick. Love him properly. And maybe her dream of having a husband and children of her own could come true, after all. But only with Nick. No one else. Ever. Just as Zeek had said, her love had grown out of trust and friendship. She wasn't ready yet. And she knew Nick wouldn't rush her, which made her love him even more. But that moment had sent something unknown spiralling up inside. One day, she felt sure now, she could be willing to yield to it.

CHAPTER TWENTY-THREE

'Come on, keep up, slow coach,' Maisie teased as she thrust the spade into Janet's lawn again.

'All right for you,' Kitty grumbled. 'You seem to have got the hang of it. It's mortal hard work and I just don't seem to have the strength.'

Poor Kitty. She really hadn't taken to gardening in the same way Maisie had. They were in the garden at the rear of the shop. The buildings had originally been constructed as desirable residences and had modest outdoor space behind them. Janet had been proud of her terrace, where customers could enjoy the grassed area and flowerbeds that Maisie had enhanced with the knowledge of plants she'd gathered from Zeek. But with Nick and Cameron's help, most of it had been dug up and planted with vegetables Maisie had grown from seed, and now they were turning over the last patch.

Maisie paused to wipe her brow. It was jolly warm work in the June sunshine. What a strange time it had been in the last few months, she couldn't help but reflect, and Plymouth was in the thick of it. Following the evacuation of Dunkirk, tens of thousands of French troops had been re-embarked from Millbay Docks for France to try and fight back against the advancing Nazi army. While Janet and Kitty had soldiered on at the tea rooms, Maisie had helped out at the Lord Mayor's Welfare Fund emergency canteens to feed and comfort the weary troops. Following their departure came streams of French and Belgian refugees, plus some British citizens who'd been trapped in France, such a terrible, pathetic sight. Once more, the canteens had been put into service and Maisie had taken up her post again until the refugees had passed through.

'Hi, you two!' a familiar voice called, and Cameron appeared from the shadows at the back of the building.

Maisie chuckled as Kitty dropped her spade and ran into his arms. He hugged her, kissing the top of her head, and then glancing at the row of turned turf she'd been digging, he frowned almost angrily and spoke sharply. Kitty pouted, shaking her head and looking quite stricken.

That was odd. Was something wrong? Maisie had never seen them exchange a cross word. It would break Kitty's heart if they broke up. Her instinct was to support her friend and she stepped forward.

'You mean you haven't told them yet?' she heard Cameron say as she came up to them.

Her gaze shifted from one to the other. Cameron was obviously cross about something, and catching her eye, Kitty was looking distinctly sheepish and flustered at the same time.

'Told us?' Maisie demanded. 'Told us what?'

There was a pause, during which the couple both seemed decidedly awkward. Then Cameron appeared to regain his composure and straightened his shoulders.

'You'd better fetch Janet,' he said gravely.

Maisie looked at them in surprise. That sounded ominous . . . She went inside. Janet only closed on Mondays now and was in the kitchen, baking cakes for the next few days. She was as surprised as Maisie, and dusting flour from her hands, followed her outside.

Kitty and Cameron were standing side by side, holding hands. Well, at least they looked like they weren't about to split up, so that was a relief. So . . . An idea flitted across Maisie's thoughts . . . Oh, dear, surely not?

'Kitty and I love each other very much,' Cameron said, drawing himself up to his considerable height while Kitty had her eyes trained on the ground. 'And we . . . well, we couldn't stop ourselves, and, well, we're having a baby.'

Maisie couldn't prevent her sharp intake of breath. Oh, heavens. Her guess had been right.

'Lordy love,' she heard Janet mutter. The older woman then put out a trembling hand, fumbling for a chair. Maisie sprang forward to help her, worried that in her shock, she might misjudge the distance and fall onto the ground instead. She got Janet safely seated, but before either of them could utter a word, Cameron stepped forward and kneeled at Janet's feet.

'I know you'll think badly of me,' he said levelly, 'but we really do love each other, and if it weren't for . . . well . . .'

'The small matter of your wife?' Maisie finished for him.

'Well, yes,' Cameron muttered, shamefaced. 'But as soon as the divorce comes through, we'll be married.'

'But that could be ages.'

'Yes, but I give you my solemn word. I'll sign any legal promise you want.'

'And in the meantime?'

'In the meantime, we've opened a post office account in Kitty's name and I'm putting virtually all my pay into it. Kitty and our child will be well provided for. And, well, I know it wasn't what we'd planned, but I'm delighted. When I realised what was happening with my wife and that she'd never give me a child, it was a huge blow. But now . . .'

He stood up, pulling Kitty to him and looking down on her with a boyish grin that made his eyes sparkle. Kitty somehow fitted against him like a glove, and though the news was a bombshell, to put it mildly, Maisie couldn't help but feel happy for them. Even a little envious. Kitty was going to have a baby. A family of her own. Just as Maisie had always wanted herself.

'And, oh, my, what do your parents say about it?' Janet finally spoke. Maisie could hear the tremor in her voice.

'They . . . they don't know yet,' Kitty mumbled.

'What?' Janet's face was pink as she looked up. 'They're going to blame me, aren't they? I'm supposed to be keeping an eye on you.'

'But, Janet, I'm eighteen—'

'Only just. And seventeen when it happened, obviously.'

'Yes.' Kitty brushed her words aside. 'But you cas'n have been expected to watch over me all the time.'

'And nobody's to blame but ourselves,' Cameron put in bravely. 'And myself in particular. I'll take full responsibility for Kitty and our child, and I'll put a ring on her finger the minute I'm able to. She'll be Mrs Kitty Mackenzie.' A proud smile blossomed on his face. 'How does that sound?'

'Wonderful.' The light was coming back into Kitty's eyes. 'In the meantime, cas'n you be happy for us? Please?'

Janet looked from one to the other, and she blew out a sigh through her nostrils. 'Well, there's that old saying. You're not the first and you won't be the last. I reckon there'll be lots of irregularities with this war, and so many strangers passing through Plymouth. But I'll hold you to your promise, Cameron Mackenzie. You'll have Janet Mudge to answer to if you break it.'

'Oh, Janet, thank you.'

Kitty broke away from Cameron and threw her arms round Janet's neck. A smile at last flowered on the older woman's face, and she patted Kitty's back.

'So, I suppose we should start looking after you, then. When's it due? You're not showing at all yet.'

'Christmas,' Kitty answered, relief clear on her face. 'I'm just three months.'

'The danger period, which is why she shouldn't be digging,' Cameron said sternly. 'I'd finish doing it for you, only I'm due back at the hospital. I only called in to tell you not to worry if you don't see me for a few days. With the Germans pushing west, they're evacuating all British troops trapped in western France before it gets to be another Dunkirk. They'll all be coming here, through Plymouth, and we could get an influx of wounded at the hospital. Your canteen'll be in operation again, too, Maisie, and wanting your help.'

'If I can.' Maisie chewed on her lip. 'I start my Fire Service training next week. It's a first-aid course in the evenings. On my own, I suppose. No point Kitty doing it now.'

'No, I suppose not.'

'Well, you take care of her for me,' Cameron smiled, pride glowing from his face as he glanced at Kitty. 'And I'll see you as soon as I can, honey.'

He gave Kitty a brief kiss before disappearing back into the shop, leaving the three of them alone.

'Well, this is a fine to-do.' Janet was the first to speak. 'We'll have to make some plans. I suppose the first thing will be for you to tell your parents, and see what they have to say about it.'

'Yes, I reckon so,' Kitty mumbled back, almost in tears. 'But please don't be cross with me, Janet. I couldn't bear that.'

'Well, it takes two,' Janet sighed. 'But Cameron should've known better, and him a doctor and all. But . . . you young people, and these be strange times. And Herbert and me, well, you know we were never blessed with chiller, so it'll be nice to have a babby in the place, since I cas'n imagine your parents wanting you back.'

'Oh, Janet, thank you!'

'I'm not sure how we're going to manage in the shop, mind. And we'll need to get you a cheap ring to wear. There's some as don't hold with unmarried mothers, and I don't want to be losing customers over it once you start showing. But,' she said, pulling herself to her feet, 'I'd best get back to work. They cakes won't bake themselves.'

They watched her go, and then Kitty turned to Maisie, her face taut and anxious.

'You haven't said much, Maisie,' she said, the tiny muscles in her forehead bunching together. 'You won't turn against us, will you?'

Maisie drew in a deep breath, then shook her head with an exasperated smile. 'Of course not. I think you've been stupid, but I'd never turn against you. You're like a sister to me, you know that.'

'Then . . . you're happy for me? Isn't it what we both really want in the end, a home and family of our own?'

'Yes, of course. Oh, come here! Congratulations!'

Maisie felt a tide of warmth ripple through her as she hugged Kitty tightly. It was what they both wanted, only Kitty couldn't know just how much Maisie also wanted it. For Kitty, it was just a natural progression, but for her, it had been a desire that had burned in her heart since she was a small child at the convent. Just to have what all the other girls had. Just to be normal.

As they waltzed round in a circle, Kitty beaming from ear to ear, Maisie had to hide the pangs of jealousy that rumbled inside her. Perhaps she should allow Nick a few more liberties. Not that she wanted to end up in the same position as Kitty. No. She wanted to do things in the right order. Still, it really wasn't fair on Nick to keep him so very much at arm's length. He'd been so patient with her. Maybe it was time to let him go a bit further. Encourage him, even.

But was she ready yet? Did she have the courage?

* * *

Maisie walked briskly down the street, wishing she felt a bit more confident. It would have been far better going to her first training session with Kitty at her side. As it was, not only was she going alone, but she was going to have to explain that Miss Barron was having to withdraw as she was in the family way.

This was, though, only an introduction. Every evening for the next few weeks, she'd be attending a first-aid course as the initial step to her training. It wouldn't be until September that she'd be going on a full-time course to learn the nitty-gritty of firefighting, as one jolly fireman had put it when they'd originally enrolled.

Back then, it had seemed the right thing to do. It had even felt like a bit of an adventure. But the hours spent out on the roof in the bitter cold had taught them otherwise. Sometimes, it felt like a waste of time, with nothing happening. The Phoney War, many were calling it. But recent events were making it suddenly seem more real.

As Cameron had said on the day Kitty's pregnancy had been revealed, all British troops had been withdrawn from western France as the German forces advanced. The new prime minister, Winston Churchill, had ordered the evacuation before it got to the same stage as Dunkirk. Better to have the army regroup to fight another day than be slaughtered on the beaches. Just as when the French troops had re-embarked, Plymouth Sound had been crammed with ships and would have been a prime target for the Luftwaffe. Once again, Plymouth had held its breath, but no attack had come. But it had brought the war even closer to Maisie for another reason.

'Jesus, Mary and Joseph,' she'd gasped when Nick had more or less staggered into the tea rooms one morning. Except for the day his father had died, he'd never come in after a fishing trip without washing and changing first, but here he was in his old sailing gear, his face grimy, unshaven, and his eyes red-rimmed with tiredness. He looked dreadful, bone-weary, as he slumped down into a chair.

'You look terrible,' Maisie said with shocked sympathy. 'I've not seen you for a few days, so whatever's happened?'

'We went to Brest,' he answered, leaning his elbow on the table and rubbing a filthy hand over his face. 'To help bring the troops home.'

Something like ice trickled through Maisie's veins. 'B-but you're a fishing vessel.'

'It were the skipper's decision. We're big enough to go that far, and we were needed. So I'm glad we did. It were hardly Dunkirk, but we did come under fire and their bloody planes followed us half way across the Channel. But we'm back safely, and I . . . I just wanted to see my girl afore I went home to bed.'

'Oh, Nick.' Maisie wrapped her arms around him. Jesus, he could have been wounded, the trawler sunk, or . . . or . . . She scarcely dared think it. 'You sit there and I'll get you a hot cup of tea and something to eat.'

'Thanks, love. Summat quick and easy afore I fall asleep. I've not had a wink for three days.'

The memory of that morning bit into Maisie's thoughts as she made her way through the Plymouth streets to the hall where the course was being held. The situation was even worse now. The news had come the previous day that France had capitulated. The grey foreboding of the past few weeks had come to an end. It would be Britain's turn to come under attack next. And there was no mistaking it: the war would be coming to Plymouth's door.

Maisie shuddered and tried to put out of her mind the reason why she was attending this course. As she came in through double doors into a small foyer, a woman in the red and green WVS uniform was sitting at a table with some sheets of paper on a clipboard. She looked up with a welcoming smile.

'Name, please?' she asked pleasantly. 'And which service?'

'Maisie O'Sullivan. And it's the Fire Service.'

'Ah, yes, got you,' the woman declared, consulting her papers and ticking off Maisie's name. 'I see there's someone else from the same address also listed here.'

'Yes. Christine Barron. But I'm afraid she's had to withdraw. She's, erm, she's expecting.'

The WVS woman looked up. 'Oh. Well, I'll have to delete her, I suppose. Now, then, I don't know if you've been told, but this is a joint course. The Fire Service comes under the umbrella of the Police, so we've got Auxiliary Police, WVS and ARP trainees, so it's mixed men and women. We've got, let me see, a Miss Robbins and a Miss Templeton for the Fire Service who've arrived already, with three more to come. Today's session is being run by some WRNS, but there'll be more highly qualified medical staff as we progress. So, if you'd like to go through, you'll find assembly points for each service on the walls.'

'Thank you,' Maisie nodded as she went through another set of doors and into a vast hall. The buzz of voices she'd heard from the foyer erupted in a bubbling cacophony of sound. She couldn't help thinking that it would have been so much better with Kitty, but she was going to have to do this on her own. She glanced around, and sure enough, hand-made cardboard signs had been propped on a dado rail along the walls. Dodging between all the strangers, she found the one for the Fire Service and gathering her courage, made towards the two young women chatting in front of it.

'Hello,' she said, marching up to them. 'I believe you're Fire Service, too?'

'Yes, hello. You come for the course? Well, of course, you have. Silly me. Yes, I'm Gladys, and this is Marjorie.'

Gladys, who must have been five foot ten tall with the broadest shoulders Maisie had ever seen in a woman, held out her hand.

'And I'm Maisie,' she answered, almost wincing as Gladys pumped her hand. Goodness, she was strong, but that would be good for the physical duties they would need to undertake. Marjorie had a firm handshake, too, though she was not as tall and was of a slighter build. Both had wide smiles, making Maisie feel easier almost at once.

'D'you two know each other already?' she asked. She was surprised by the reply.

'No, just met, don't you know. You going to be full time?'

'No. I work in a tea rooms in Union Street. What about you?'

'Given up my boring office job to go full time. Jolly looking forward to it, too.'

'And you, Marjorie?'

'Don't laugh, but I'm actually a car mechanic.'

'Crikey. That'd be useful in the Fire Service, I'm sure. So are you going full time, as well?'

'Not sure yet, but probably, if they want me. With pet-rol rationing and people taking their cars off the road, there won't be so much work at the garage. Oh, hello, come to join us?' Marjorie said as another slightly older woman came hesitantly towards them.

There wasn't much more time for introductions before someone blew a whistle and all the chit chat died down. There must have been fifty people in the room, some of them already kitted out in uniform. All eyes turned on the Wren standing in the middle of the floor.

'Good evening, ladies and gentlemen,' she boomed. Maisie frowned to herself. Hadn't she heard that voice somewhere before? 'If you can all grab a chair, I'd like you sitting in a big circle around the hall so that you can all see.'

The hubbub broke out again as everyone dutifully obeyed. The sounds of people moving about and chair legs scraping on the floor echoed around the walls until everyone was seated and hush descended once again. The loud-voiced Wren took up her position in the centre, glancing round at her pupils.

'Right. Today you're going to be learning about simple bandaging for minor injuries to different parts of the body. Later on, you'll be learning about more serious injuries, how to apply pressure pads to stop bleeding and so forth, but you'll be beginning with the basics. I will be explaining while my fellow Wrens demonstrate, and then I want you to divide into teams of three to practise on each other. We'll be walking among you to assist and answer any questions you might have. I'm Leading Wren Fairclough, and these are my colleagues, Ordinary Wrens Hansen, Liphook and Driscoll. Right, let's get started.'

Maisie had to stifle a gasp. Good Lord above, now she remembered where she'd heard that voice before. It was on the Hoe, the morning she'd gone with Nick and Kitty to welcome home the *Exeter*. And there, standing in front of her again, was Helen Driscoll. Back ramrod straight, chin raised proudly as her eyes travelled with that supercilious expression over the expectant trainees. And then stopped dead as they met Maisie's horrified gaze.

Jesus. Maisie thought she'd seen the last of her. But she wasn't going to be cowed by her old enemy. They were grown women now. Helen was a few years older than her, of course, though she'd still been at the convent when Maisie had left. Had she come over to England soon after Maisie, and maybe joined the WRNS when war had been declared the previous year? She'd probably liked the uniform, Maisie scoffed inside her head. But she'd evidently got a reasonable amount of experience under her belt if she was helping to train others.

Maisie gulped. She must focus her mind on what she was there for. She somehow managed to concentrate on what Leading Wren Fairclough was saying, but it rankled to have to watch Helen demonstrating with her two other colleagues. Later, Maisie palled up with Gladys and Marjorie to practise bandaging heads, wrists, ankles and knees, and putting arms in slings, taking it in turns to be the patient. The Wrens moved among them. Maisie dreaded Helen coming up to them, but felt ready to face her if she did.

When she did appear, just as Maisie was concentrating on applying a sling to Marjorie's arm, Maisie's heart jumped. Well, she wasn't going to get flustered. Even when Helen gave her that superior smile.

'So, what sort of sling are you applying?' Helen asked, her voice like sugary acid.

'Elevation,' Maisie answered steadily. 'She's got a bad cut on her wrist and it's bleeding a lot. I'll check the circulation in her fingers when I've finished to make sure the sling's not too tight. And I'll check it every ten minutes.'

'Ooh, someone's been paying attention, then,' Helen's mocking whisper came into her ear. And then she said more loudly — obviously for the benefit of the others, Maisie knew, 'Well done. Now you be the patient and let the others have a go,' before moving off.

Maisie was enjoying the company of her new friends, but the evening had turned sour. She couldn't wait for it to end so that she could escape the nasty atmosphere Helen had created. She just hoped she wasn't going to be there for the entire course. For now Maisie was determined to show her by being the best pupil there.

Nevertheless she breathed a huge sigh of relief when the session was over. Dusk was falling as she said goodbye to Gladys and Marjorie on the steps outside the hall. As she turned to go off in the direction of home, her spirits danced as there was Nick waiting for her.

'Oh, what a lovely surprise!' she cried, running over to him. 'And don't you look so much better!'

'Done nort but sleep the last few days,' he grinned back. 'We're sailing on the morning tide, but fishing for fish this time, not troops, but I thought I'd walk you home.' He pulled her towards him for a brief kiss before they entwined arms and began walking down the street. 'How did you get on?'

'It was good,' she answered, dismissing all thoughts of Helen Driscoll. She certainly wasn't going to waste her breath telling Nick about her. 'And I've made two new friends who are training for the AFS as well.'

She glanced over her shoulder with the intention of waving to Gladys and Marjorie if they were still chatting outside the hall. She couldn't see them. Instead, Helen was standing at the top of the steps — staring after Maisie with a fox-like smile.

CHAPTER TWENTY-FOUR

'There we are. A pot of tea for two and a coffee, three rounds of egg and cress sandwiches and three scones with jam and cream.'

Maisie smiled at the customers as she unloaded the tray. It was a good feeling, serving such fresh produce, eggs from their own hens, cress that she'd grown from seed on the windowsill, and scones fresh from the oven. The shop was really busy, but these particular customers were three elderly ladies who called in for an early lunch most Saturdays. They were always prompt. Today, it wasn't quite yet midday.

The bell over the door clanged and Maisie glanced up. If possible, they always liked to welcome customers with kind words and a wide smile before showing them to a table. But it was Kitty coming through the door. From the expression on her face, the visit to her parents to tell them about the baby hadn't gone well.

'Enjoy your lunch, ladies,' Maisie beamed at the customers, and then hurried to follow Kitty through to the back.

'I take it things didn't go too well,' Janet was saying, her mouth knotted fiercely. 'And why are you carrying they bags?'

'Last of my stuff,' Kitty answered, almost matter-of-fact. 'They don't want to see me ever again.'

Maisie managed to hide a sharp intake of breath. 'That's awful,' she murmured.

'Oh, no, cheel,' Janet chimed in. 'They'll come round, I'm sure.'

Kitty shrugged, but Maisie could see she was putting on a brave face. 'Dad might in time, but he were leaving for work. And he'll likely do as Mother tells him, and she won't change her mind. You should've seen her face. Anyways, I'll just take these bags upstairs and then I'll be down. Cas'n keep the customers waiting.'

They watched her make for the stairs. Poor Kitty. Maisie's heart overflowed with sympathy. You'd think her parents would be more understanding. It wasn't as if Cameron wasn't standing by her.

'Poor lamb,' Janet tutted, shaking her head. 'Some folk can be proper odd, like. It's their grandchild we're talking about. Must've been a dreadful shock to hear the news, mind. But they'll have a change of heart once they've got used to the idea.'

Maisie released a heartfelt sigh. 'I wouldn't count on it. I know you've met her mother a few times, but I know her a lot better than you. She can be really tetchy. Always made me feel uncomfortable. Her dad's not as bad, but he is a bit under his wife's thumb.'

'Oh, well, I suppose it were to be expected. But let's hope for the best, eh? Right now, we've got customers to serve. We can talk about it after we shut up shop tonight.'

Janet picked up the tray of sandwiches she'd just prepared, and Maisie hurried back out into the café. A young couple she didn't recognise, the man in the uniform of a naval rating, had just come in and were about to sit down at the only table left unoccupied.

'We have a terrace in the garden, if you'd rather,' Maisie suggested pleasantly.

'Oh, yes, thanks. That'd be nice,' the woman said, returning her smile.

As Maisie led them towards the back of the shop, Kitty reappeared, her face tight as she tied on her newly starched apron. And then they each stopped in their tracks and silence spilled over the tea rooms like a slick of oil.

An unearthly, spine-chilling wail like a howling banshee reverberated over the city. Rising to a ghoulish crescendo before tumbling down into the depths of hell. Wave after wave, the next one screaming out before the last had died away.

Maisie was astounded at herself. Something inside her took over. Had the little first-aid training she'd had given her confidence? She felt utterly calm, instantly knowing what she had to do.

'All right, everyone!' she called at the top of her voice. 'Don't forget your gas masks and come this way down to the cellar. Keep calm. You'll be perfectly safe.'

She didn't need to repeat herself. Every customer was on his or her feet in a trice, and she ushered them to the back of the shop, propping open the door to the cellar and turning on the light.

'Be careful on the steps and hold onto the handrail,' she instructed. 'Don't push. There's room for all.'

'Thank you, dear,' one of the old ladies said as she passed. 'I expect it'll be a false alarm like last week. At least this one's not in the middle of the night and getting us out of bed.'

Maisie replied with a fleeting smile. At least you expected a raid in the night. It was harder for the planes to be spotted and shot at by the anti-aircraft guns. On that previous occasion, she'd been out on the roof within a minute, expecting incendiaries to be dropped by the first wave of raiders in order to start fires to light the way for following bombers. But it was possible that incendiaries could be dropped by daylight, too.

'Kitty, you go down and make sure everyone's comfortable. Remember, there's a torch on the table by the door. If the electrics get cut, turn it on and then light the oil lamps.'

Kitty nodded, her face ashen and clearly relieved to have someone remind her what to do, even though they'd

rehearsed it a dozen times. Janet was herding in the customers from the garden, and met Maisie's eyes with a stern gaze.

'Now you come down off that roof if they start dropping explosives,' she growled. 'I'd sooner this place burned
to the ground than you got killed.'

Oh, Janet. Maisie's heart reeled. A moment of pure love
among the terror and chaos.

She pulled on her boiler suit in seconds and, grabbing
her gas mask and the tin hat she'd now been issued with,
raced up the stairs and out onto the roof. The warmth of the
perfect July day hit her like a wall, and her eyes searched the
azure canopy of the sky. Perhaps it would indeed be another
false alarm. But then she caught the sound of an aircraft.

'There 'tis!' Huggins Junior called excitedly from the
adjacent roof.

No time for pleasantries now. Tick, tick, tick, went
Maisie's heart. She heard the distant thud of ack-ack guns.
Then the puffs of white smoke as their shells exploded in
the air, pinpointing the direction of the attacker. Just one, its
wings occasionally catching the sunlight.

Jesus, Mary and Joseph. It passed overhead, way, way up
above, heading west. Must be aiming for Devonport. Would
be there in seconds.

It was hard to tell, but the plane appeared to have
dipped. An instant later, a booming explosion cracked across
the city, followed by another, and another. From up on the
roof, Maisie saw a column of dust and smoke spiralling into
the air.

Holy Mother. Hadn't she promised Janet that she'd run
down to the shelter of the cellar the moment any bombs
started falling. But the whole incident had happened so
quickly. The raider had turned and was heading back to
France, pursued only by a few shells from the ack-ack guns.
Maisie stood and watched, too shocked to move.

Pull yourself together, girl, she told herself. You'll
have to do better than that if you're going to be part of
the Fire Service. It was the sense of helplessness that had

overwhelmed her. She knew if an incendiary had fallen on the roof, it would have given her some purpose. She'd have been on it in a trice with her bucket of sand until Mr Huggins and his son had arrived with the stirrup pump in case the sand hadn't worked well enough.

Was that it now, or were there more planes to come? Somewhere had been hit, but she couldn't tell exactly where. She prayed to God no one had been hurt. And then it came again, that haunting, sepulchral wail echoing over the roof-tops. Only this time it was blaring out in one continuous drone rather than the repeated waves. Thank God. The all-clear.

Maisie's legs turned to jelly and she walked towards the door in a daze. She'd have to get used to it. They all would. This was just the beginning.

* * *

'Oh, Lordy love, not again,' Janet moaned, emerging from her bedroom in her dressing gown. 'And in the middle of the night and all.'

'It's what we were expecting.' Maisie was yanking on her boiler suit. 'It was a surprise the other raids were in daylight.'

'But this makes, what, five raids in a week,' Kitty grumbled.

'Well, stop talking and get down into the cellar,' Maisie ordered, making towards the roof door. 'I'll be down when I can.'

The last few days had steeled her courage. It was rumoured that the first raid had killed three people including a young boy on a housing estate near Devonport. The second, on the Sunday afternoon, had sent fear skittering across Maisie's chest. From her vantage point on the roof, she'd seen the German bomber come in so low over the eastern end of the city that she actually saw the lethal cargo drop from its belly. Dear God. The bombs would have fallen in the vicinity of Sutton Harbour where Nick, she knew, was working on the trawler. She'd felt sick and shaky, running through the streets like a mad woman after the all-clear, until she'd found Nick safe and well at the harbour, the bombs having exploded somewhere across the far side.

'Reckon he were aiming for the gas works,' Nick had said with unbelievable calm as he'd gazed across the water. 'Missed his target, but some poor sods must've copped it.'

As it was, five people were killed, Maisie learned later. Many more would have died if they hadn't rushed to their shelters on hearing the siren. But they'd lost their homes and all they possessed, poor souls, their houses reduced to rubble. But somehow the terror Maisie had experienced that day had made her feel stronger, more determined than ever to do her bit.

Since then, there'd been two early morning raids, one in the Devonport area and the other near the Hoe. Despite the high level of destruction, it was said only six more people had been added to the death toll. Only six? May God forgive her for thinking like that. Was the war already making her hard? No, of course not.

What was even worse was that in the most recent raid, people were machine-gunned from above as they ran for shelter. By some miracle, nobody was hit, but the incident filled Maisie with rage. It was just so cold-blooded. Even worse than the bombing in a way.

So now, as she opened the door to the roof, she was fired with the desire to fight back in whatever way she could. Her mouth was set with grim determination as she stepped out into the summer's night. Just a glimmer of light from the sky showed her that Mr and Mrs Nettlehayes, who'd been on fire-watch duty already, were waiting with the stirrup pump at the ready, while Mr Huggins and his son were emerging into the darkness on the other side.

'How do?' Mr Huggins greeted them all.

How do, indeed, Maisie scoffed silently, though she knew that was unfair. But how did he think they were as they watched bombs being dropped seemingly at random, though mainly towards the west of the city. It was a relatively minor raid, but there were three alerts that night. By the time morning dawned, everyone was shattered.

But there was still the day to face. The hens had to be fed, their run swept and cleaned. Maisie was to mince up and steam the kitchen leftovers, then dry them in the oven until she could crumble them up to mix in with the balancer meal to make the chicken feed go further. The tea rooms must be cleaned, spotless tablecloths spread out, soup, sandwiches and cakes prepared, and everything ready to open up at ten o'clock. There'd be plenty for customers to talk about, with the alerts having kept everyone up most of the night. And Maisie, Kitty and Janet would have to nail smiles on their faces the whole time. It was their job to cheer up their customers, no matter how they felt themselves.

When the bell over the door clanged and the first customers came in, Maisie tied on her apron and marched out into the shop.

'Good morning,' she beamed. 'How nice to see you. Where would you like to sit?'

* * *

'See you at the station in September, then,' Gladys grinned as they stood at the bottom of the steps after the final evening of the first-aid course.

'Unless you'd like to call into the tea rooms beforehand,' Maisie replied. 'You'd be very welcome. We do lunches as well as teas. And all good value for money.'

'You should be in advertising!' Marjorie laughed. 'You never know. But if we don't see each other before, take care of yourselves, and see you there.'

Maisie's smile broadened as she waved her new friends goodbye. Of the six in their group, she'd hit it off with Gladys and Marjorie best, although she didn't think she'd ever be as close to either of them as she was to Kitty. She was pleased, though, that she'd be going on the full-time course with people she knew.

She watched them disappear in the opposite direction before glancing round to see if Nick had come to meet her as he sometimes did. But no. Given there was no Nick tonight, Maisie stepped out alone onto the pavement.

'Sure, I hope you enjoyed the course,' Helen Driscoll's voice trilled in her ear. 'Wasn't it such a surprise meeting up again like this. Chance in a million, wouldn't you say?'

Maisie spun round, stumped for words. Was Helen actually trying to be nice? Maisie had pretty well ignored her during the sessions. She was there to learn, and not to reignite old animosities. Helen had appeared to do the same. So what did she want now?

'Yes, a bit of a coincidence, I suppose,' Maisie replied cautiously.

'Goodness, you don't sound Irish at all anymore,' Helen went on. 'So did you come straight to England when you disappeared from the convent? Maybe that's why you've lost your accent. You were so young and it must be . . . how many years?'

Well, Maisie had to answer really, didn't she? She couldn't believe Helen was making conversation with her. Surely she had some scheme up her sleeve, was hiding some ulterior motive?

'Six,' she said flatly.

'Ah, well, there you go. You were so lucky being rescued from the convent by a caring relative. At least that's what we were told. Didn't I have to stay on until the bitter end, when I was eighteen. And I hated it.'

Maisie's eyes widened. *Lucky*? If only Helen knew.

'Really?' she answered warily. 'I loved it there.'

'Well, weren't you always treated like someone special,' Helen scoffed. 'Sister Agnes's pet. I envied you staying on during the holidays when I had to go home to my parents. All they wanted was for me to act the dutiful daughter in front of all their business acquaintances. Sure, they were stricter with me than the Reverend Mother.' She paused, pulling a wry face. 'So I reckoned that during the holidays, it'd be more relaxed and even fun at the convent. And you and Noreen had something special between you, and I'd have loved to be part of that, so I would.'

'But you had Siobhan as your friend.'

'Siobhan?' she scoffed. 'Oh, wasn't she only out for what she could get. Never bothered with me once we left school,' she spat bitterly. 'So there was I, almost treated like a prisoner by my parents. They even tried to get me to marry a man nearly twice my age because it suited their business plans. Fortunately I managed to get away from them, but only last year. I joined up as soon as I got over here thinking it'd give me some freedom and a new life. Had no idea I'd be posted to Plymouth. Or that you were here, of course. Been quite fun so far, bar the odd air raid. Lots of handsome young officers. And your fellow's not a bit bad, either. Lucky you, being able to choose for yourself. Fisherman, isn't he?'

Maisie's eyes narrowed suspiciously. Had Helen latched onto that when they'd first bumped into her on the Hoe, or had she been spying on them each time Nick came to meet her? Maisie really didn't trust her. She wasn't even sure she could believe the yarn she'd just spun.

'I'm sorry, but I have to get back,' she said sharply. 'Things to do.'

She turned and hurried off down the street. She really didn't want to stay talking to Helen a moment longer. What was the older girl up to? Maisie hadn't wanted to rake up the past, so had never thought to mention bumping into her old acquaintance to anyone, not even Nick or Kitty. The only person she'd told was Noreen in her most recent letter — devoting all of a whole line to it. She really didn't want to waste her energy talking about part of her past she'd rather forget.

Well, now the course was finished she wouldn't need to bother even thinking about Helen ever again. So dismissing her old adversary from her mind, she made her way back to Union Street. It had made her think, though. Six years. So much had happened in that time. Her father, dearest Zeek,

Kitty, Janet, Nick. Her life had changed so much. Even the trams had gone from Union Street, she mused, though the overhead wires were still there.

What a silly thought. She had far more important matters to think about. She prayed there wouldn't be another raid tonight. There'd only been three major ones in the last few weeks, a teatime attack on the RAF Station at Mount Batten, and a night-time one over Cattedown. The third had been a prolonged attack of five raids spread over twenty-four hours from midnight. That one had been exhausting, up and down like yo-yos, and also the most worrying. The target, though completely missed, was clearly North Road Station. What if the Luftwaffe's next target was Mill Bay Station? The tea room was only a stone's throw further down Union Street. What if it was reduced to rubble like so many other buildings had been? Would they be safe down in the cellar?

Maisie shuddered as she let herself into the now closed shop. She found Kitty and Janet in the kitchen, baking for the following day. It seemed to her that baking was Janet's way of directing her mind from her fears of the war.

'Ah, good, you're home safe,' Janet said with a relieved smile, looking up as Maisie came in. 'Have a cuppa and then, if you're not too worn out, could you help Kitty ice they buns? Seems proper daft we've got to use up all our icing sugar by the end of the month. Could've eked it out for much longer, or even saved it for Christmas. But no. It's no more icing on the outside of a cake, and we've got to do as we're told. And here's me using grated carrot in this here chocolate pudding to save on the granulated in case that runs short. Don't make sense to me.'

As if to emphasise her words, Janet beat the pudding with extra gusto. Maisie had to smile and met Kitty's cheeky look. It was hard not to laugh, but neither of them would want to offend this homely woman they'd come to love as one of their own.

'I suppose it's easier to regulate if they say there's to be no more icing across the board,' Maisie attempted to soothe her, lighting the gas under the kettle. 'So how many more buns are there to ice?'

'They two dozen, and then there's another batch cooling.'

'Right. Only don't forget we're on fire watch from eleven.'

'No, I haven't forgotten, cheel.' Janet pursed her lips. 'Though what good I'd be, I don't know. But we cas'n have Kitty risking herself with the babby and all.'

'No. But you know what we've practised. If an incendiary fell on our roof, or near on either side, we could still use the stirrup pump. And if it were further away, I could jump over the barrier onto either of the other roofs and put it out with sand.'

'Aw, if only I were twenty year younger,' Janet sighed.

'Well, no use wishing for the impossible.' Maisie plonked a kiss on her cheek. 'And it's not for long. When I'm away training, the Hugginses and the Nettlehayeses are going to do longer shifts to cover, aren't they? And the Fire Service are going to send someone to help out, too, if they can. But let's not worry about that now, and let's have that cuppa. Then we can finish up here.'

'That'd be perfect, my lover. Well, this here pudding's ready to steam for a few hours. It'll be cooked by the time we finish our shift. I reckon we'll be able to spare a slice each as our reward, don't you?' she finished, forcing a mischievous tone into her voice.

'And save a bit for me!' Kitty protested.

'Oh, I don't know about that,' Janet retorted. 'What would the customers say if we ran out of my famous chocolate pudding?'

She said it so seriously that Maisie could see the shocked disappointment on Kitty's face. Then Janet laughed her big, happy laugh that made her ample chest wobble. In an instant, the girls were giggling helplessly, too. Maisie shook her head. Anyone watching would think they were all crazy, laughing so much over such a small thing as a chocolate pudding. But that was what the tensions of war did to you.

For who knew what was around the corner?

CHAPTER TWENTY-FIVE

'Well, ladies and gentlemen,' the steady, mature voice came over the public address system, 'thank you all for coming and I do hope you've enjoyed the evening. At least we've been blessed with fine weather. Please join your hands to give a big round of applause to the band!'

Lady Astor stepped to the side as she stood in front of the microphone on Plymouth Hoe's bandstand and gestured towards the small band. Maisie grinned up at Nick, her face aglow, and joined in the enthusiastic clapping. It had been a wonderful couple of hours, a relief from the constant tension of wondering when and where the next bombs might fall.

'The band will now play the National Anthem,' Lady Astor announced as the cheering subsided, 'after which, please take your partners for the last waltz. Goodnight, stay safe, and may God bless you all.'

A strange hush sank over the revellers as the band struck up again. Everyone stood silently, one or two in uniform giving a salute, Maisie noticed, as she attempted to quell the uneasiness that at once fluttered in her stomach. There'd been several small raids that month, but only a few days ago, Plymouth had endured its longest alert yet when relays of German bombers had droned overhead on their way to attack up north, as it turned out. The city, though, hadn't escaped completely, as several bombs were dropped, including some that fell on Ford House, the Public Assistance Institution, killing a dozen or so female inmates. Millbay had also been hit, making the glass rattle in the tea shop's window. The bomb-blast tape had done its job and stopped it from shattering. But it had been too close for comfort and Maisie was finding it impossible to drive the fears from her mind.

Now, she glanced up at Nick for reassurance and comfort. It had been just the two of them at the public dance on the Hoe. Cameron had been on duty and Kitty had declared that she didn't want to play gooseberry. Maisie was disappointed that her friend had missed the happy interlude — there was something special about dancing to live music in the open air, watching a spectacular sunset that had set the rippling waves of the Sound aflame. Maisie had snuggled against Nick as they'd watched the burnished disc of the sun sink below the horizon in a blaze of glory, allowing the grey light of dusk to descend over the sea.

Now, with the National Anthem over, the gentle tones of 'Apple Blossom Time' wafted out over the Hoe. Maisie turned back to Nick, and saw his eyes, soft and smiling, as the evening gathered in.

'Remarkable woman, like, Lady Astor,' he said, drawing Maisie into his arms once more. 'Been dancing among the crowds all evening.'

'She's certainly a person of the people,' Maisie agreed. 'It's no wonder everyone votes for her. And a jolly good thing it is, if you ask me, having a woman in your Parliament for the first time.'

'Says my little Irish colleen,' Nick teased.

'I can still have an opinion,' Maisie grinned back with a mock frown. 'And it's my opinion that I don't want to waste a second of the last waltz.'

'Exactly so. Especially with you going off on your training tomorrow. So come here, my lover.'

He crushed her even more tightly to him, tucking her head under his chin. Oh, that felt so good. A warmth flooded Maisie's veins, making her feel safe — for the time being, anyway. But it was more than that as she allowed her cheek to sink against his chest, breathing in the masculine scent of him, listening to his heart beating strong and steady while her own suddenly began to pound with excitement. All the other couples around them melted away. For a moment, it was as if she and Nick were the only people in the world, and she became lost under some mysterious spell.

Nick tilted her chin and kissed her softly, and when the tip of his tongue brushed along her lips, she felt a tingling sensation shoot down inside her. She'd felt it before when he'd kissed her, something magnificent and overwhelming but at the same time, a little bit scary. Tonight, though, it seemed extra special. When Nick eventually pulled back and she found herself staring up at him in a daze, she suddenly realised that the music had ended and the crowds were quickly dispersing.

She blinked up at Nick and saw his face break out in that familiar, gentle smile.

'Better get you home afore it gets dark,' he said in a light, almost teasing tone. 'You seemed in another world just then.'

'Perhaps I was,' Maisie agreed with a deep sigh. She didn't mind one jot admitting it to Nick. 'A world in which I could forget all about the war and think only of us.'

Nick raised his eyebrows. 'That sounds encouraging. But Janet'll have my guts for garters if I don't get you home.'

Maisie linked her arm through his elbow as they hurried through the darkening streets. It had been a magical evening, and now a waning moon was appearing out of the fading sky. Would there be a raid tonight? It was always at the back of your mind, wasn't it? She'd be up on the roof with Janet from three o'clock the next morning, but it would be her last shift for a while. Tomorrow afternoon, she was meeting Gladys and Marjorie and some others at North Road Station and heading off to the Fire Service training camp for a few weeks. She was trying not to think that she wouldn't see Nick again until her return.

She let them into the tea rooms, observing the blackout procedure, and led Nick through to the kitchen.

'Kitty and Janet must have gone to bed early,' she said as she filled the kettle from the tap. 'Janet likes to get a few hours' sleep in beforehand if we're on the late shift. She's looking forward to having the chaps from the Fire Service volunteers take over. They're both a bit long in the tooth, but fitter and more agile than she is. I think she'll be relieved to have a break from it for a while.'

'So we'm all alone down here?'

'It would seem so.'

As she turned from the sink, Nick took the kettle from her and placed it on the drainer. She giggled as he folded her in his embrace, pulling her against him, and his mouth came down, suddenly hot and urgent, on hers. His tongue sought hers and she felt her lips part as she was overtaken by a feeling that astounded her. Oh, Nick, she suddenly thought, I won't see you for weeks. What if something happens to you while I'm away?

The thought made her breathless and her mouth opened wide to return his passion. Her arms went around his neck, pulling him to her, feeling his body pressed hard against her. A need unfurled inside her, a desire she'd never felt before. He was undoing the buttons of her cardigan, her blouse. She'd let him stroke her breasts through her bra before, but now his fingers slid beneath and fondled her bare skin, and she stifled a gasp of wonderment and delight. It was amazing. She let her head drop back as he rained kisses on her throat and let his tongue trace down where his fingertips had gone before. Was this it? What Kitty had talked about? This overwhelming helplessness against what you felt for the man you loved?

Before she realised, Nick's hand was gathering up the hem of her skirt, and working its way up her leg. Her stomach was turning cartwheels, she felt strange and out of control. This was what it was to love, and she loved Nick so much. She must savour this moment for ever. For what if, while she was away, the *Calypso* was sunk by the Germans and she never saw him again?

Then an exquisite, almost burning sensation raced through her core as Nick touched that secret place between her legs. She gasped. All at once, it was too much. No, no! Seized with panic, she pulled away, pushing Nick hard, her eyes wide and horrified.

She watched as Nick stood back, dropping his arms to his sides. His mouth remained open as he drew in a breath, then shook his head slightly as his eyes closed for a moment.

'God, I'm that sorry,' he murmured. 'I were caught up in the moment, like.'

'I-I think I was, too.' Maisie was astounded that she could find her voice. 'It wasn't your fault.'

'Yes, yes, it was,' Nick gulped. 'I shouldn't have . . . I mean, I wouldn't have gone far. It's too soon for you. It won't happen again, I promise. Not until we're . . .' His face twisted with remorse. 'Can we forget it ever happened? I don't want us to part on bad terms.'

'No, no, of course not. I do love you, Nick,' she assured him, grasping his arm. No, he mustn't think she didn't! 'It's just that . . .'

'We need to take things slower,' he finished for her. 'I understand.'

'Yes. Oh, Nick, that makes me love you even more. And one day . . .'

She wanted so desperately for him to know how much she loved him, but it was so hard when there was something innate inside her holding her back. She couldn't bear to lose him, but neither did she want to end up like Kitty. Relief poured through her as Nick wrapped his arms about her and kissed the top of her head. She felt safe again as she leaned against him. She'd have to face it one day, but they were only young. They had plenty of time.

Didn't they?

* * *

'Penny for them!'

Maisie had been staring out of the carriage window as they chugged their way back to North Road Station the day after the Fire Service course had ended. There'd been delays on the journey, despite the fact that by some miracle, the railway line hadn't been hit. They'd been stopped between stations while a goods train rumbled past. Probably something to do with supplies for Devonport, which would have taken priority over a passenger train.

Maisie turned her head and answered Gladys with a smile. The compartment was crammed with girls from the course, all eagerly looking forward to being reunited with their loved ones after nearly three weeks of intensive training. Their first-aid knowledge had been extended and tested in mock-up situations. They'd been taught how to man telephones and operate a small switchboard, learning the different areas of Plymouth and familiarising themselves with maps of the area. As Maisie didn't know the city as well as some, she'd spent much of her free time — of which there wasn't a lot — poring over and memorising street maps.

Although that wasn't difficult, she'd preferred the more practical side of the training. They'd had lectures, teaching them to understand the nature of fire and how it behaved in different circumstances, and how to rescue someone from a smoke-filled room if required, though this was mainly a man's role. Holding the nozzle of a fire hose and directing the water into a fire was also considered men's work. Even so, it took at least two to control the power of one hose.

However, who knew what circumstances could arise, so the girls were taught how to do it, just in case, using three of them where possible. Their main role was to unroll and then roll up the hoses afterwards, and to be capable of attaching them to hydrants, as well as operating both trailer pumps and fire engines. Those who, like Marjorie, could drive, had been trained to take the wheel of one of the heavy cars that would be used to tow the trailer pumps, but they all needed to be proficient in hitching them together. Knowing all the procedures meant they could see where help was needed and lend a hand wherever they could.

So much information swirled in Maisie's head. When she'd be called upon to put it all into practice, she couldn't predict. Officially, her duties wouldn't start until her nineteenth birthday next year, but she'd be called upon for short training exercises in the meantime. And who knew if she might be needed before that if the situation became really bad? Gladys and Marjorie, who were joining the service as full-time paid workers, were old enough to start straightaway, as were most of the companions Maisie had shared a brick hut with, reminding her of the dormitories back at the convent, though possibly even more spartan. They'd formed a special bond between them, but all the excited chatter in the compartment had been lost to Maisie as they chuffed along.

She was thinking of Nick. She hoped desperately that what had happened on their last evening together wasn't going to spoil their future.

She dragged herself from her silent thoughts and joined in the chatter. They were arriving at North Road now, and gathering up their belongings. With a lurch and a bellow of steam, the train came to a standstill and the girls spilled out onto the platform. Once outside the station, there were hugs and cries of good luck as some went off in different directions, while Maisie, Gladys and Marjorie and several others took the bus into the city centre.

'Well, I guess this is TTFN, chaps,' Gladys announced as they alighted onto the pavement. 'I'm sure we'll meet again, but in the meantime, good luck and take care. So, right, tally-ho! Come along, Marge!'

Maisie watched them disappear into the crowds before picking up her little case and setting off towards Union Street. It felt as if she'd been away an age instead of three weeks, and she was glad to be back in familiar territory. The little bell above the door clanged in its merry way as she entered the tea rooms. Several tables were occupied, and Janet beamed across at her as she served a pot of tea and some biscuits to some customers. Maisie had hardly had time to put down her case when Kitty skipped up to her and enveloped her in a hug.

'Good to see you back!'

'You, too!' Maisie answered, extricating herself from the embrace. 'Goodness, your bump's grown so much!'

Kitty pulled a face. 'Look like a pudding, don't I? And I've got three months to go yet. But the babby seems healthy and that's all Cam and I worry about. Oh, you've got a visitor waiting out the back,' she winked, and gave Maisie a push towards the back of the shop.

Maisie's heart suddenly became tangled in itself. She must mean Nick. Oh, surely everything would still be all right between them? She left her case in the kitchen and then made her way out to the back garden, her pulse thudding.

Nick was sitting at one of the tables but sprang up the instant her saw her. A second later, he was holding her tightly, his lips meeting hers in a kiss as soft as gossamer. All at once, Maisie's fears emptied out of her. Everything was going to be all right.

'I've missed you so much,' Nick murmured against her lips.

'Oh, and I've missed you, too,' she answered, kissing him back.

'Here's a pot of tea and some iced buns,' Kitty chortled, appearing with a tray. 'Only without the icing, of course. Well, I'll leave you two love birds to it,' she sang, hopping away.

'Hasn't changed, has she?' Nick chuckled. 'Shall we?' he invited, gesturing towards the chairs. 'So how was it?' he asked once they were seated.

Maisie huffed out a breath. 'Interesting. A lot to learn. And jolly hard physical work. But we had a lot of fun, too.' And she went on to tell him some of the details as they munched through the iceless buns and sipped at the tea.

'This Gladys sounds a bit of a one,' Nick laughed as he poured more tea.

'Yes, but she's very bright and big and strong, too. I'd love to be on her team when I get called up to do my bit. If the war isn't over by the time it gets to my birthday next year.'

Her heart dropped as she saw a frown sink over Nick's face. 'I don't see that happening,' he said gravely. 'We're still battling the Luftwaffe in the skies up country. The Channel Islands have been occupied and we could be next. No. This is going to carry on for years if you ask me. And have you heard the latest? Probably not. The news is only just coming through, and that on the grapevine. Couple of nights ago, the Germans sank a ship evacuating children to Canada. God knows how many of them died.'

Maisie's blood ran cold. 'That's appalling,' she cried in horror. 'How could anyone attack a ship with children on board?'

'Don't suppose the Germans knew that. And even if they did, I don't suppose they'd have cared. Look how they've bombed London the last couple of weeks. Would've been children killed there. It's all going to make the British people so angry and determined to teach the Germans a lesson. And it's confirmed that my decision were right.'

'Your decision?' Maisie echoed. She'd detected an odd intonation in Nick's voice, and a dark shadow passed over her. What was he trying to tell her? Was it something to do with the way they'd parted, after all? Was he going to tell her they were over? But after the way he'd kissed her just now . . . 'What d'you mean?' she asked shakily.

Nick leaned forward, taking her hands in his. 'You'm going to be doing your bit. And I want to do mine, too. I'm joining the Royal Navy Reserve.'

'What!' Maisie's heart jolted with shock. 'B-but why? You're already doing a dangerous job. And it's helping to feed the nation. Surely that's enough?'

'I know. But I want to do more. Surely you can understand that?' Nick was gazing steadily at her, his eyes dark with anguish. 'The Reserve have been recruiting fishermen to lay mines. Even using converted trawlers. So in a way, it won't be much different. Only I'll be going to Lowestoft in East Anglia to train, and then I could be sent anywhere.'

Oh, no. Maisie couldn't believe what she was hearing. As it was, she lived in fear whenever Nick was away fishing, but this! Surely not . . .

'B-but you can't! I couldn't live without seeing you, always afraid—'

'I've already enlisted.' Nick's voice was steady. 'When the war's over, we'll be together then, I promise. But you'm not ready for marriage yet. I can see that. I'd been hoping, saving my wages, and my dad left me those shares in the trawler. But the other night, I realised . . . Besides, I'd been thinking about it for a while. And then I bumped into an old friend of yourn down on the quayside. She recognised us from when I met you from the first-aid course a few times. One of the Wrens helping to run it. She said you were at the convent in Ireland together. I were surprised you never mentioned her to us. Anyway, being in the Wrens, she happened to mention about the Reserve wanting fishermen. I told her I were thinking about volunteering, but talking to her helped make up my mind.'

Maisie's jaw fell open and all the old enmity rampaged through her body. What the blazes had Helen being doing down at the harbour? It was completely the opposite end of Plymouth from Devonport. Maisie's mind flashed back to her brief encounter with the girl.

All that jealousy she'd spoken about from their convent days must have been festering away ever since. And if what she'd said about her parents trying to force her to marry a man she didn't love was true, had she been so twisted by it that she considered if she wasn't free to marry whom she pleased, Maisie shouldn't be, either? She'd known about Nick. Known he was a fisherman. Had she deliberately sought him out? Tried to shame him into joining up and so break up their relationship? Maisie was more convinced than ever that Helen had her eye on Nick. She must have been delighted when he'd said he'd been considering joining the

Reserve anyway. All she needed was to direct a little persuasion his way.

Maisie was trembling with shock and hate. And fear and passion all rolled into one. Jesus, Mary and Joseph, she'd strangle Helen if she ever got her hands on her! It was all too much. Tears of frustration bit into the back of her eyes. She had to stop him!

'Nick, please!' she begged in utter desperation. 'Please don't do this! Please!'

But Nick shook his head. 'It's too late. It's summat I needed to do. I'd only have felt half a man if I hadn't.'

Maisie stared at him, yearning, terrified. Full of anger and hatred towards Helen. Why couldn't the past leave her alone? All she wanted was a family of her own, and she could never imagine creating a child with anyone but Nick. She could never love anyone like she loved him. And now because of that . . . that . . . witch, he was being taken away from her. Her future was being taken away from her.

And what if he was killed and never came back?

CHAPTER TWENTY-SIX

Not again. Not now. Please, not now.

Maisie lifted her head from the pillow as the all too familiar wailing penetrated the shroud of her misery. She'd been so brave all day, even holding her emotions in check as she'd said goodbye to Nick at the railway station. Tears had glistened in her eyes and something like a golf ball had caught in her throat, but for Nick's sake, she'd battled against the need to cry. If the worst happened, she wouldn't want him remembering her in his last moments as red eyed and blotchy faced. They said that, didn't they, that your life, your loved ones, flashed before you at the end. If you had the chance. You wouldn't if you were blown to smithereens.

She'd waved him off, running beside the window where he was leaning out, her footfall on the platform quickening as the train gathered speed and soon began to outpace her. She stopped then, waving frantically, as Nick's face, with those beautiful dark eyes, grew smaller and smaller. She couldn't see him anymore. The train disappeared from view until all she could see were the tell-tale puffs of grey smoke, and even they finally became lost in the distance.

She'd stood on the platform for some minutes, slowly lowering her arm, helpless now against the tears that meandered like sad pearls down her cheeks. Damn Helen Driscoll. But she knew she couldn't blame the girl entirely. It was partly her own fault. Would Nick have enlisted if she hadn't shrunk away from his advances? He'd been wanting to do his bit anyway. And he might not have been accepted if the skipper's son hadn't left school that summer and been training up on the trawler ever since. He didn't have Nick's years of experience but he'd been around boats all his life. It was enough of a reason for Nick to be allowed to leave his reserved occupation. And now Maisie felt as if her heart had been ripped from her chest.

She'd somehow managed to glue her usual welcoming smile on her face while serving customers all day, even though there was a constant ache inside her. Janet had chivvied her along with a sympathetic smile and a pat on the arm, and Kitty tried to distract her by chatting about the baby and could Maisie help her with a cot quilt she was making. Maisie had smiled indulgently, knowing Kitty was trying to cheer her up.

That evening after they'd shut up shop, Maisie had forced down the meal Janet had prepared while she and Kitty had mopped the shop floor, cleaned all the tables and the marble counter, and done all the washing up.

'Well, I'm off to bed for a few hours,' Janet announced when they'd finished eating. 'I'll just put the stirrup pump and the buckets outside the front door.'

'Don't worry, I'll do it,' Maisie offered. 'Then I'll try and get some sleep, too. See you just before two.'

She went through the shop, turning off the dimmed lights before opening the front door to place the equipment on the pavement. More and more apparatus was being distributed in towns and cities throughout the country, ready for the nearest person to put out any incendiaries before they could do any damage. That was the theory, at least.

Maisie sighed as she locked up and returned to the back of the shop. There'd been a few raids since she'd returned from her training course with remarkably few casualties, considering the damage that was caused. The Luftwaffe was concentrating on bombing London, but how long would it be before they turned their attention to Britain's Navy in Plymouth?

She caught Kitty mid-stretch as she re-entered the kitchen.

'Think as I'll turn in, too,' the other girl announced, tapping the growing mound of her stomach. 'This one's worn us out today.'

'We'll try not to wake you when we go up top.'

'I'm glad I don't have to do that anymore. Poor Jan finds it proper tough, doesn't she, being on fire watch?'

'Yes, but we can't have Harry and Len here every night,' Maisie answered, referring to the two elderly volunteers who guarded their roof and those of their immediate neighbours three nights a week. 'At least we share the rota with Mr and Mrs Nettlehayes and the Hugginses. Anyway, I'm going to get some shut-eye too before our shift.'

'Goodnight, then,' Kitty nodded, turning into her room. 'And,' she faltered, 'don't worry too much about Nick. He'll be all right, I'm sure.'

Maisie gave a wan smile and had to bite her bottom lip. Kitty, bless her, wanted to show her support but without making too much of it and upsetting her. Maisie appreciated it, but however kind people were, it couldn't really help how you felt, could it?

Alone in her room, she undressed to her underclothes and slid into bed. No point changing into her nightdress when she had to get up again in five hours and pull on an old jumper and her boiler suit. It was halfway through October and getting decidedly chilly at night up on the roof. She was dreading the bitterly cold hours of darkness that would come round again before too long, and she shivered as she remembered all the times she'd spent up there with Kitty the previous winter.

She snuggled down in the bed, her eyes trained on Nick's framed photograph on the bedside cabinet. What was he doing now? Had he managed to complete the long journey to Lowestoft? You couldn't tell with the trains nowadays. He'd promised to telephone as soon as he could. But when would he get the chance? And long-distance calls were often disrupted when lines were destroyed by bombings and so forth.

She reached out an arm and turned off the bedside lamp, plunging the room into darkness. The emptiness closed in on her, and the resolve to be strong that she'd clung to all day suddenly crumpled. Oh, Nick. If anything happens to you, it'll be my fault. I shouldn't have held you at arm's length when I love you so much.

An image of his face wavered behind her closed eyes, and a hollow pit opened up inside her. Holy Mother, she prayed, please keep him safe. She tried telling herself that Nick would be in no more danger than when the trawler was at sea, but it didn't help. The fear and frustration, the sorrow at their parting that morning, welled up inside her, making her eyes swim with unshed tears. Now she was alone, she could give into them, and her shoulders shook as she wept into the pillow.

And then it started, the blood-curdling shriek of the air-raid siren, rising and falling in wave after wave. If it weren't for Janet and Kitty who she knew would come in and insist she went down to the cellar with them, she'd have stayed where she was. But she dragged herself out of bed, pulled on some clothes and joined them on the landing.

'Aw, cas'n a body get some sleep?' Janet moaned as she led them down the stairs. 'I'd just dropped off.'

Kitty surreptitiously glanced across at Maisie and stifled a giggle. Janet in her curlers and hairnet, dressing gown and boots, was something to chuckle at, Maisie supposed, as they went through the kitchen, collecting the ready-filled thermos flasks and the tin containing the day's leftover sandwiches from the shop, before making their way down to the cellar. At least they were lucky that it was dry, and made quite cosy with three made-up camp beds and an electric light. Better than a wet, smelly, cramped Anderson shelter, anyway.

They got into bed. But Maisie couldn't settle, especially knowing she and Janet would be on duty themselves in a few hours. She could hear Kitty turning over, trying to get her bump comfortable. Maisie was staring at the ceiling, still thinking of Nick and blaming herself. And as for that harridan, Helen, she just prayed she'd never come across her again as she wouldn't be responsible for her actions.

Some dull thuds came then. Maisie held her breath. Bombs, not just a false alarm. But not close. Another part of the city. For now. About an hour later, the all-clear sounded and they crept upstairs, trembling as to what they might find.

But all was well. As it turned out, the north of the city had been on the receiving end of the attack. Water and gas mains had been fractured and buildings hit, including Farley's Biscuit Factory, where locals would normally have crowded to shelter. Luckily — as it happened — it was locked, and they'd dashed back to their homes. Only minutes later, a bomb shattered the factory shelter. There were other miraculous escapes that night. But how long would people's luck hold out?

* * *

'There's some post for you today,' Kitty grinned, waddling into the kitchen and holding out two envelopes to Maisie.

'Oh, you're popular, cheel,' Janet smiled encouragingly. 'I spy an Irish stamp, and the other one looks like young Nick's scrawl. You go and read them in private, like. We can finish up here.'

'Thanks, Janet. You're a dear.'

Maisie plonked a kiss on the older woman's cheek. She really was so kind and understanding. Hurrying up the stairs to her bedroom, Maisie's heart was bouncing with a mixture of excitement and worry. Of course, she was always thrilled to receive Nick's letters. Not that he was the greatest writer, so they weren't long, but it was just so good to hear from him. On the other hand, he could never give her the news she really wanted — that the Reserve didn't need him after all and he was coming home. It was a vain hope, she knew. The opposite was more likely. He'd been gone about five weeks, his training nearing its end, so he'd doubtless be going on active service any time now. And heaven knew when she'd see him again.

She tried to drive the thought from her mind as her trembling hands tore open the envelope. Nothing had been censored out, thank goodness. Not that Nick had ever written about anything he shouldn't. It was only personal messages he was sending. *My darling Maisie*, the letter read,

Hope you're well and Plymouth isn't getting too badly bombed. From what I've heard, it's not getting the sort of pasting London is. Take care, sweetheart. I don't like to think of you fighting huge fires like they've had there. I know you've trained in it, but I pray it'll be over by the time you reach nineteen next year. For my part, my training's about over and we're about to be sent off to different places. A group of us are going off soon. Don't know where and probably couldn't tell you if I did, but I reckon somewhere cold by the clothing they've given us. They'm good reliable fellows I'm with, certain to look out for each other. Maybies I'll get some leave and can see you afore I go. But if not, know that you'm in my thoughts always. I love you so much and hope things will still be good between us when the war's over and us can plan our future together. It's what I want and I hope you do, too. My letters might take longer to come through once I'm wherever I'm posted, so don't worry if you don't hear from me for a while. Give my love to Janet and Kitty, and wish her luck from me when the baby comes. Tell Cam to look after her, or else!
Love you and can't wait to hold you in my arms again
Nick XXX

PS, Keep writing to the same central address and they'll forward your letters to wherever I am, though it might take a while.

Maisie lowered the flimsy paper onto her lap and stared at the writing that swam before her eyes. Oh, Nick. What if that was the last letter she ever had from him? What if he was killed before he could write another? She was so stupid! She — and that minx, Helen — had driven him away. Would he really feel the same about her when — if — he came back?

She could feel the horrible pain scratching at the back of her throat again. Keep safe, my love, she whispered, retrieving Nick's photograph from the bedside table and bringing it to her lips. It would be grand if he was given a few days' leave. It would coincide with his twenty-first birthday. But then she'd have to endure the agony of saying goodbye to him all over again.

She sighed dejectedly. Either way would be unbearable. She reached out to replace the photograph and in doing so, her eye caught the other envelope. Perhaps Noreen's letter contained better news and her old friend would cheer her up with anecdotes of her little daughter. It was always like a breath of fresh air to hear what was happening back home in Ireland. Although Noreen and Bartie lived in Cork, Noreen sometimes took the train to Cobh to visit the convent and would relate any news from there, bringing back happy memories.

Maisie began reading, her heart feeling lighter with the thought of being pleasantly entertained. But as her eyes moved along the lines of writing, her stomach tightened. Noreen's tone was sombre. She was afraid she was the bearer of sad tidings. The Reverend Mother had been informed by the mission out in Africa that Sister Agnes had been taken ill with malaria. They'd done their best to nurse her through it, but sadly she had succumbed. In her dying hours, she'd asked in particular to be remembered to her dearest Maisie, her special girl.

Maisie's hand went over her mouth. Dear, dear Sister Agnes. This time Maisie couldn't stop the tears that welled up inside. No, no! It couldn't be true. Her Sister Agnes, who'd always been so kind to her. Been her rock when she'd felt so alone in the world. Had been like a mother to her. Had been so upset when she'd learned she'd been inadvertently lying to Maisie all those years that she'd gone to Africa as a sort of penance. At least, that was what Maisie believed. And now she was dead because of her.

All at once, she was choked by a sense of guilt. It was her fault Sister Agnes had died. Her fault Nick had joined the Reserve and might not return. Her fault her father had suffered the fatal heart attack. She slid off the bed and sank onto her knees in floods of racking sobs. Holy Mother, can you ever forgive me? First my father, then Nick and now Sister Agnes. Please show me how I can make amends. When I am called upon to do my duty, I will throw myself into my work, risk by own life to save others. Please, please show me the path to redeem myself.

Stifling a howl of misery, she reached up to the bedside cabinet, her hand fumbling for her rosary. Her fingertips closed about the first bead. She would say it right the way through as a start to her penance.

Hail, Mary, full of Grace, the Lord is with thee. Blessed art thou among women, and blessed is the fruit of thy womb, Jesus. Holy Mary, Mother of God, pray for us sinners, now and at the hour of our death. Amen.

* * *

'Oh, lordy love.' Janet put down her knife and fork and her eyes rolled towards the ceiling. 'Is three days all the respite that devil Hitler can give us? And you and I due on rooftop duty in an hour or so.'

Maisie's chair scraped the floor as she stood up, sighing as the air-raid siren howled through the late November evening. 'I think we should go up now and see what's going on, just in case. If it looks like heavy bombing, we'll join you down in the cellar, Kitty.'

'I wish Cam was here,' Kitty moaned, gathering up the necessary items. 'I hate being down there by myself.'

'It's probably a false alarm,' Maisie soothed. 'Now off you go.'

She gave Kitty an encouraging smile as she and Janet made towards the stairs, but her pulse was thrumming. It was a quivering you had to contain, every nerve on edge. They both dived into their rooms to get suitably attired. Getting changed with lightning speed at least gave something to channel that overwrought energy into. Hopefully it wouldn't be needed once they stepped out onto the roof.

The frosty night air closed about them, the mournful warbling of the sirens much louder now they were outside. Then it went quiet, a chilling silence filling them with dread as they waited.

'How do?' Mr Huggins's voice boomed out of nowhere.

'Ssh,' Maisie at once shushed him. 'Hear that?'

They all stopped to listen. There it was. Like the distant droning of bees. Getting louder. Steady. Menacing. The silver beams of searchlights pierced the sky, sweeping through the darkness, illuminating the barrage balloons like giant ghosts.

What came first, Maisie wasn't sure, the booming of ack-ack guns or the shape of an aircraft swooping over the city in the direction of Mount Batten in the Sound and the Air Force station there. Maisie held her breath as four shimmering flares fell through the sky, illuminating all below. As the plane banked away, a bomber streaked through the glow, sprinkling the air with explosives. Thunderous bangs cracked across the night, one so loud that Maisie and Janet instinctively dropped to their knees. The noise rang in their ears, and when Maisie recovered and gingerly got to her feet, a faint orange blush was already brightening the indigo sky.

Maisie had scarcely gasped when a third threatening shape screamed down towards the burning target and an instant later, an explosion ripped across the city. Maisie swore the building shook beneath her. She felt a tremor rock through her as Janet grabbed her arm in terror.

'Flaming heck,' Mr Huggins called from the next-door roof. 'Look! I reckons as they've hit one of the oil tanks on Mount Batten!'

Maisie turned her eyes from Janet's shaking form and glanced across the roof tops. She could see the tips of distant flames which must be leaping a hundred feet in the air. Soon the whole city was bathed in a lurid, flickering glare, illuminating a thick pall of black smoke that spiralled up into the darkness above.

Then they started coming, wave after wave of aircraft like buzzing gnats attracted by the gleaming inferno. Incendiaries showered down on where Maisie guessed would be Staddon Heights, so that the darkness above seemed lit by fairy lights. In the minutes that passed as she and Janet stood, frozen by fear and astonishment, more and more bombers plunged down over the east of the city and out across the water. The whirring of planes diving in low, the whine of incendiaries, the shriek and crash of high explosives, the shattering fire of ack-ack guns both on land and on warships, the gleam of searchlights, the sky on fire in a mantle of gold. It was macabre and unreal. Yet it was happening.

'Come on, cheel,' Janet's voice quivered. 'Time to get to the cellar.'

Maisie could feel the older woman trembling like a leaf beside her. She knew she was right. Kitty would be terrified down there alone. But a fierceness burned in Maisie's chest. She wanted to fight back. Didn't want to be defeated.

'Look out!'

The roar of an engine rumbled overhead. Both women threw themselves down as a plane came in low over the tops of the buildings. In seconds it was gone, leaving the pungent smell of burnt fuel fizzing sickeningly in their nostrils. Dragging herself from her shock, Maisie felt the adrenaline pumping through her limbs, and peered out from beneath her elbow.

Holy Mother! The plane had dropped a shower of incendiaries and two of them had fallen on their roof. Well, she wasn't going to lie there and watch. This was what she was trained for.

She sprang to her feet. 'Incendiaries!' she shouted, and glanced across at Mr Huggins and his son for help. But one had landed on their roof, too, and they'd gone to deal with it.

Maisie gathered her courage. She must save dear Janet's home, but the older woman was still on her knees, quaking in fear.

'Janet, quick! Get up! Help me!'

There was nothing for it. The first incendiary was still fizzling, so Maisie grabbed the bucket of sand and upturned it over the hissing stick. Pray God it would do the trick. But the second had burst into flame. Relieved to see Janet had recovered and was on her feet, Maisie spun round to grab two of the buckets of water, suddenly overcome by a calmness that astounded her as her training kicked in.

'You get the pump!' she cried to Janet as she strode across the roof to where a small fire was already burning. She must put it out before the lead melted and exposed the wooden beams below. Thank goodness each building had its own stirrup pump now and they weren't sharing, or it could well have been too late.

Janet appeared at her shoulder a second later.

'Right, you pump!' Maisie instructed. 'Remember, it's a fire now so as close to sixty-five strokes a minute as you can.'

She grasped the hose and, getting as close as was prudent, just as she'd been taught, she dropped onto her knees. Go in low, she reminded herself. As Janet pumped, the water spurted out of the nozzle into the seat of the flickering blaze. For what seemed an eternity, it had no effect, then the fire began to hiss and steam. Had they caught it in time? Like two guardian angels, Mr Huggins and his son appeared with their apparatus, tackling the sizzling flames from the opposite side as well. Almost at once, the dancing red tongues collapsed and smouldered, then were finally extinguished by the double jet of water.

Maisie drew her hand over her forehead. Looking up, she could see Janet's shoulders drooping. Poor, dear, kind

Janet could have seen her home burn down. Maisie was incensed.

'If you refill the buckets, Janet, then go down to the cellar,' she shouted above the cacophony of noise echoing across the city. 'I'll keep dousing this to make sure it's fully out, but then I'll stay up here for a bit, just in case. Mr Huggins will help, I'm sure.'

'Bless you, cheel. But you take care. And thank you, Mr Huggins.'

'Must help each other,' the fellow said, dipping his head.

Just for a moment, Maisie turned to watch Janet totter away on wobbly legs. Crikey. She wouldn't normally have been able to see her that far in the blackout, but the conflagration in the Sound was now lighting the sky almost like the sun. Maisie could see clearly where the two incendiaries had landed on their roof. Clearing away the debris with a small shovel, she found that the first had been fully extinguished by the sand, while underneath the second, the lead had been softened enough to cause a small dent, but didn't look as if it had cracked at all. Nevertheless, when Janet returned with the refilled buckets, she gave it a good dousing, and would keep an eye on it for a while, too.

Replenishing the buckets a second time, Maisie found herself alone on the roof, though in the glare from the distant blaze of light, she could still see Mr Huggins and his son creeping over their own rooftop. There were other silhouettes, too, moving about further along in this eerie, lofty world. She heard crazed cries and shouts as human forms were desperately fighting flames where an incendiary had caught fire several buildings down and was rapidly taking hold. Maisie felt sick as she watched the figures finally give up and disappear off the roof to save their own lives.

She was overtaken by horror and fury as she watched the blaze spread. She felt so helpless. And then she heard the clanging of a fire-engine bell. Steeling to the front of the roof, she looked down to see the Fire Service arrive along the street at a neighbouring shop. Was it the Sloanes and their boot and shoe business? Hoses were being run out, just as Maisie had trained in. Her legs itched. Should she go to help? But she needed to protect Janet's home and though their neighbours were possibly losing theirs, she didn't want Janet's to go the same way.

So she stayed put. The lull in the bombing didn't last. Before too long, wave upon wave of aircraft stormed and screamed through the skies, dropping their cargoes of death and destruction. Lit by the wall of fire Mr Huggins was sure was coming from Mount Batten, they were attacking the east end of the city. The night was rent with the growl of engines in the sky, the crash of explosives, blinding flashes, the deafening fire of the ack-ack guns. On and on it went, as if it would never end.

Maisie watched in horrified fascination. Was this blazing furnace what hell was like? How many innocent people would lose their lives that night? How many homes and businesses would be destroyed? Choking black smoke was drifting across the sky, heavy with the nauseating stench of burning aviation fuel. Maisie's stomach heaved and she forced herself to turn for the door. Time to give in and seek shelter in the cellar.

Sick with defeat, she made her way inside. Who knew if they'd survive the rest of the night? It was by far the worst attack the city had suffered so far. But was there worse to come?

CHAPTER TWENTY-SEVEN

'Oh, no, not again,' Janet groaned, pausing in her dishing out of the rabbit stew as the siren moaned over the city.

'At least they left us alone over Christmas,' Maisie sighed. 'And Harry and Len are on duty tonight so we can go and enjoy ourselves down in the cellar,' she went on with a sarcastic lift of her eyebrows. 'Come on, Kitty. Up you get.'

'I'll bring the pot and we can eat downstairs. We've got plates and whatnot down there.'

Maisie was already helping Kitty heave herself to her feet. Poor girl was a week overdue and as big as a house. The midwife had been that morning and declared her fit and healthy and not needing to be admitted to the maternity ward at the City Hospital. But getting Kitty down the stone steps into the cellar wasn't easy. Maisie was relieved when she finally got her friend down the stairs and settled in the armchair she and Cam had managed to manoeuvre down there for her.

'There, my lover,' Janet said, ladling out a good helping and passing it to Kitty. 'Get that down you.'

Kitty looked slightly guilty as she took the plate and balanced it on her bump. 'Actually, I'm not that hungered,' she almost whispered. 'I've been feeling a bit funny this afternoon.'

Maisie and Janet exchanged swift glances.

'Why didn't you say summat, then?'

Kitty's brow wrinkled. 'I thought as I was imagining it and it'd go away. But I really don't think as I can eat this, and—'

Suddenly she clutched at her stomach, her mouth opening wide. But what sound she made was muffled by a crashing boom. The ceiling shook, making the light bulb flicker. Maisie gasped. They had torches and oil lamps, but she didn't fancy the prospect too much, and what if the baby was on its way? She had a horrible vision of Kitty giving birth in the middle of an air raid, but she mustn't let her friends see her concern. They'd have had the same thought, she was sure, but it was up to her to keep calm. She was the one with the emergency training, so they'd be relying on her. At least, to her utter relief, the light bulb had come back on.

'Lordy, that were close.'

Maisie ignored Janet's fearful words. Removing Kitty's plate and placing it on the table, she squatted on her heels and took Kitty's hand. 'D'you think the babby's coming?' she asked, thankful that her voice sounded steadier than she felt.

Kitty drew in a painful breath and nodded. Then she exhaled heavily as the spasm passed, turning frightened eyes on her friend. 'Oh, Maisie, what am I to do?' she squealed.

Maisie gave her what she hoped was a reassuring smile. 'What nature intended. Now don't worry. It'll likely be hours before anything happens, and the raid'll be well over by then.'

'Not if it's ort like that last big one we had,' Kitty moaned, biting her knuckle. 'That went on almost all night.'

That was true. The attack when the Mount Batten oil tanks had been set ablaze had gone on a good eight hours. The inferno had lasted five days and could be seen for miles. A Sunderland flying boat and a fire boat had burnt out, too, and a dozen or more people had been killed when bombs had fallen mainly in the surrounding area but also further afield. For the next five days Plymouth had feared further attacks, what with the city being so brightly illuminated. But none had come, and the city had breathed a sigh of relief when the fire had finally died down after special foam appliances had been sent down from London. Two members of the Auxiliary Fire Service had perished in the battle to quench the flames, though, and four had been seriously injured — something Maisie tried not to think about. Her priority now was to keep Kitty — and Janet — as calm as possible.

'I'll go up and telephone the hospital, and then try and get a message to Cam,' she told them, trying to display as much confidence as she could.

'Be as quick as you can, cheel!' Janet called after her as she climbed the steps.

She didn't need telling, she considered grimly. But really, there was no knowing where was safe and where wasn't. It was all in the lap of the gods. Should she run up to the first floor and get some clean towels — just in case? But she'd make the telephone calls first before the raid brought down any wires.

With one ear cocked to the drone of aircraft and the occasional distant crash, she got through to the operator and eventually spoke to someone at the City Hospital. To her horror, she was told that the hospital had been hit. They'd send a midwife as soon as they could, but it was chaos there, and many fires had taken hold in the city, so what with the raid, they couldn't say when help would arrive.

Maisie replaced the receiver in its cradle. Well, she'd best be prepared. She tried the operator again in an attempt to reach the Royal Naval Hospital and leave a message for Cam, but without success. The switchboard must be busy with priority calls.

She knew only too well how haphazard the telephone system could be in a raid. When Nick had been given forty-eight hours embarkation leave, it had not been enough time for him to get home to Plymouth, so they'd arranged to meet in Reading. Maisie had been so nervous on the long train journey and had been relieved to arrive at the strange town and the hotel where Nick had reserved two rooms.

He'd never turned up. It wasn't until the following morning as she'd forced down a lonely breakfast that she'd been summoned to the telephone. Nick had been trying all of the previous evening to get through to the hotel. He'd got stuck on the other side of London because of a raid, and now he had no choice but to make his way back to Lowestoft without seeing her. It was the last time she'd heard his voice, and for a moment, she slipped back into that unbearable sense of sadness and frustration.

Another sudden crash brought her back to the present. She'd need towels, definitely. But how could she break it to Kitty that help might not be on its way?

'They'll be coming soon,' she lied to Kitty, thankful that the pregnant girl had her back to the cellar steps and wouldn't see her with the towels which would have been a giveaway.

'Thank goodness for that,' Janet sighed, bustling towards her. 'Her water's have broken.'

Oh, help. That could mean the baby was coming faster than Maisie had thought. On the course, they'd been taught some rudimentary facts about childbirth, but never in a million years had she expected . . . Now her mind raced through what she'd learned. A delivery with no complications she could probably manage, but what if something went wrong? And would Kitty mind her looking down there? Would she mind doing the looking? After all, back in the convent, it would have been considered unthinkable. But she must cast such thoughts aside. The most important thing was to do her very best for her friend. So she knelt beside Kitty, breathing with her through the contractions, praying she didn't have to put into practice what she'd been shown on paper diagrams.

'Listen!' Janet suddenly cried. 'I think it's the all-clear.'

Maisie held her breath as Janet hurried up the steps as quickly as her rounded form allowed and cautiously opened the door at the top. Sure enough, the long, continuous blare of the siren droned down into the cellar. Thank you, Lord, Maisie breathed silently. The raid had lasted little over an hour, but who knew what damage it had done? How many it had killed?

'Come on, Kitty, let's get you upstairs and get you more comfortable.' The words came out of Maisie's mouth without conscious thought.

But Kitty shook her head. 'No,' she groaned. 'I don't think as I can get up they steps. And what if there's another raid and we have to come down again?'

Maisie's brow puckered. Yes, there was that. If Kitty wanted to stay put, it could be for the best.

'Yes, all right. But Janet, could you bring down a few pans of boiled water so we know it's clean? We've got soap and a bowl and towels down here already.'

'Course, my lover,' Janet answered, disappearing from view.

Maisie turned her attention back to Kitty. 'You must be so excited,' she said, trying to chivvy her. 'I wonder if it'll be a boy or a girl. What did you say you were going to call him or her?' They'd discussed it before, but she thought it might take Kitty's mind off the pains if she asked.

'Don't you remember? As it's Christmas time, Mary for a girl and Joseph for a boy.'

'Well, I suppose you couldn't call him Jesus if it's a boy,' Maisie attempted to joke. She saw Kitty smile, but then her face screwed up as another contraction began and she squeezed Maisie's hand in a vice. 'Don't worry,' Maisie tried to comfort her. 'Now the raid's over, help'll be here soon.'

She couldn't wait for it to arrive herself! She really didn't fancy having to deliver Kitty's baby on her own. Once the contraction was over, she went to help Janet who'd returned with two saucepans of hot water.

'Heaven knows when they'll get through,' Janet whispered anxiously in her ear. 'I went up top. There are huge fires in the city centre and elsewhere. I wouldn't bank on getting any help. Could just be us.'

Maisie's heart sank like a lead weight. Closing her eyes, her lips moved in a silent prayer. Holy Mother of God, if I have ever needed to call upon you, it's now. Please let it be a straightforward birth. Please help me deliver my friend's baby and keep them both safe. You know what it is to bear a child, so please have mercy upon them now. Amen.

Maisie dipped her head and crossed herself. Please let her prayers be answered.

* * *

'Hello, Cam. Come and meet your son.'

Maisie glanced up as the tall Canadian came into the room on the first floor that they used as a parlour. A good fire blazed in the grate and Maisie was sitting in one of the armchairs, cuddling little Joseph in her arms.

If truth be told, she was annoyed that Cam had arrived. She was enraptured by the precious scrap of humanity snuggled against her, little button nose and tiny mouth wriggling even as he slept. Alone with him in the room, she'd been gazing down at him in enchanted wonderment, a miracle of new life. She'd unwrapped one of his little starfish hands from the shawl, enthralled at the way his minuscule fist curled around her little finger if she held it against his palm, as if telling her he loved her back. She'd bent to kiss his forehead so many times, drawing in the scent of him, lost in rapt fascination.

Kitty was so lucky! Maisie was going to be Joseph's auntie, a part of his life from the very moment of his birth. But just now, she'd been dreaming that he was hers, the child, the family she'd always craved, but without having to perform that act she was so afraid of. But she would do it with her dearest Nick, in order to hold her own child in her arms like this.

But what if Nick didn't come back? 'Here you are.' She forced a smile as she lifted the babe towards his father, whose face was glowing with pride and joy. 'Kitty's asleep so you can have him all to yourself.'

She reluctantly relinquished Joseph into Cam's arms. He looked so tiny against the broad, uniformed chest, and the pang of jealousy speared even deeper.

'I hear you delivered him,' Cam said without moving his eyes from his son. 'That was so brave of you.'

Maisie gave an awkward shrug. 'I didn't have much choice. And the midwife arrived just a few moments later so I didn't have to cut the cord or anything. And Kitty was doing so well, the midwife said there was no point in her going to hospital after the event.'

'Well, thank you, Maisie, from the bottom of my heart.'

Cam grinned at her, gratitude shining in his eyes, and then returned to marvelling over his new-born boy. Maisie looked on, unable to stop the smile that stretched her lips as she drove aside the thoughts she knew were so wrong. One day — one day — she would surely know that exquisite joy for herself.

* * *

'Might look like a little angel now, but he kept us up all night,' Kitty grumbled with a loud yawn. 'I'm that tired.'

'Well, at least we weren't dragged out of our beds by the siren, nor had we to go down the cellar, so be thankful for small mercies,' Janet chided her. 'And thank goodness I never had the old range taken out so we can still cook and have hot drinks. Which is more than most folk in Plymouth since the gas works was hit. They're saying it could be weeks afore we get the gas back on.'

'So are you still planning on doing hot meals for our customers as well as soup?' Maisie asked, glancing up from her study of Joseph now fast asleep in his pram. She couldn't believe how much he had changed in only three weeks.

'I am that. As soon as I can get supplies. Simple things like stews and baked potatoes. Just summat hot ordinary folk can afford.'

'It'll be a lot of extra work, and with us being a pair of hands down . . .'

'It will,' Janet agreed. 'But it'll make me feel like I'm doing my bit, and there'll be extra peelings and what have you for the pig bin. And Mrs Nettlehayes has offered to help.'

'Well, while I still have the chance, would you like me to take Joseph out in his pram while you catch up on some sleep, Kitty? I'll make sure we're back before we open up. And he'll be wanting his next feed by then, anyway.'

'Everything's in hand, so as far as I'm concerned you can, cheel.'

'And me,' Kitty said with a wide yawn. 'I'd love to go back to bed. But let me put some extra blankets on him. It's mortal snipey out. And don't forget his gas mask contraption thing.'

'Don't worry, I'll look after him,' Maisie grinned, cooing down at the sleeping infant. 'I'll just go and get my coat.'

Five minutes later, she was proudly pushing the pram down Union Street. It was a bitingly cold Sunday morning in mid-January, the streets only slightly quieter than on a weekday. Without gas over the whole of Plymouth, people were making their way towards Devonport — where the supply came from a different source — in search of a hot meal. Army stoves and boilers had been brought in, and some residents were on the pavement, handing out hot drinks heated on primus stoves. The sight of the contraptions made Maisie shudder as it reminded her of the miserable years spent living with her father. But at least they weren't being bombed then. And as she hadn't even met Nick at that point, her heart wasn't breaking with worry over him as it was now.

But she mustn't let herself think like that. She mightn't have many opportunities to take her darling godson-to-be out for a walk on her own. Her chest was overflowing with love for the little mite, and her besotted gaze kept being drawn down to his angelic face, framed in the warm bonnet she'd knitted for him. She had the pram hood up and the flap of the cover hooked up on it, so he was completely protected from the wind and was as snug as a bug. She cared for him as if he was hers. If only he was.

Mind you, there was nothing to stop her pretending he was. There was no harm in that. So, where would she take him if he had been? She thought of Zeek. The dear old man would have loved him. And who knew, if his spirit lived on in the little house that was his home for so many years even if someone else owned it now, might he not see the wondrous infant from above?

It was fanciful, she knew. But if she still believed in her Catholic faith, which to some extent she did even though she never went to church nowadays, maybe part of her still believed in the afterlife. Besides, it would give some purpose to her walk, so she proceeded in that direction. She ached with sorrow when she passed a burnt-out building or a mountain of rubble that had once been a home, tottering walls that had been shored up for safety, exposed staircases or rooms where people had lived. It seemed that nowhere had been left entirely untouched.

Hatred for the little man with the ridiculous moustache simmered inside, and she suddenly realised she'd covered most of the distance along the main road towards her old home. Memories of Kitty coming towards her brought a smile to her lips. Kitty, whose parents had disowned her because of the precious miracle slumbering peacefully before her.

The idea came to her in a flash. How could they resist the little cherub, their own grandson, if they saw him in the flesh? Kitty had written to them, telling them of his arrival, but had received no reply. Surely, if they actually met him, their hearts would melt as her own had the moment he'd come into the world?

'Sorry, Zeek,' she mumbled as she passed the end of her old street. 'Another time.' And she kept on walking.

Ten minutes later, she stopped outside Kitty's parents' house. Being Sunday, with luck they'd both be in. She negotiated the pram up the path to the front door and putting on the brake, rang the bell.

Her pulse pounded in her skull as she heard footsteps on the inside and the door opened. There stood Kitty's mother, her face prim as ever. When she looked down and saw Maisie standing on the lower step, her expression hardened to granite.

'You!' she spat viciously. 'How dare you come here after leading our Kitty astray!'

'Me?' Maisie recoiled in shock. But at once, indignation made her square her shoulders. 'Kitty got herself into trouble, if you want to call it that. It had nothing to do with me. But I thought you might like to meet your grandson.'

She stood aside then so that Mrs Barron could see the pram. She saw the woman's face blanch, and for a moment . . . But then her face suffused with rage, a white line forming around her lips.

'What would I want to see the little bastard for? I suppose she sent you, did she? Couldn't face us herself.'

Maisie felt anger spewing up inside her. 'No, she didn't,' she replied abruptly, turning to lift Joseph carefully into her arms. 'She doesn't know I'm here. But, look! This is your grandson. Isn't he beautiful?'

She felt the tug on her own heartstrings as she turned Joseph towards his grandmother. But when she glanced up, the woman's eyes were like ice.

'He's no grandson of mine!' she barked.

'What's going on here?'

Maisie sagged with relief. Mr Barron had appeared behind his wife. He was always the more understanding of the two.

'The Irish girl's brought Kitty's brat to show us, but I've told her to sling her hook. Thinks she can win us over.'

'Just look at him, Mr Barron, please,' Maisie came back. 'He's adorable.'

For just a second, she thought she saw a flicker of softness in the man's eyes. But then his mouth hardened.

'You heard what my wife said. Be off with you, and don't you or Kitty ever come here again!'

With that, he stepped back, pulling his wife with him and slamming the door in Maisie's face.

She stood, staring at the closed door, unable to absorb their hostility. How could they be so unfeeling? So cruel? Little Joseph, so sweet and innocent, was their own flesh and blood. How could they possibly reject him? Tears burned in her eyes as she tucked Joseph back in the pram and manoeuvred it back down the path. But as she began to walk back along the street the way she'd come, her desperation turned to disgust and anger. Well, they'd made their bed. They didn't deserve to have such a beautiful grandchild. If they wanted nothing to do with him, so be it. The little treasure had enough love to surround him. He didn't need them. And if they ever sought him out in the future, she'd give them the length of her tongue and send them away. As far as she was concerned, they'd burned their bridges. She never wanted to see them again and she was sure Kitty felt the same way.

CHAPTER TWENTY-EIGHT

'Well, I never thought as the day would come when I caught a glimpse of the king and queen,' Janet declared wistfully as they were clearing the table after their evening meal. 'Just a pity they only came here to see the bomb damage and boost morale. But thank you, my maids, for holding the fort here so as I could go.'

'Well, I couldn't really go with Joseph,' Kitty smiled.

'And you know I wasn't fussed,' Maisie added. 'The English king and queen aren't exactly favoured back in Ireland.'

'Wouldn't know you're Irish now, my flower,' Janet mused. 'You're accent's gone and you two look so much alike, you could be sisters.'

'So many people say that. But Irish or not, I want to do my bit against Hitler. So I'd best be off.'

'Well, I doesn't like you going to that there fire station,' Janet objected. 'You're too young in my opinion, and what if there's a raid? I wouldn't want you caught up in it.'

'I'm only going to help check over the equipment and keep my hand in,' Maisie tried to pacify her. 'It'd be a waste of my training not to when they haven't got nearly as many people as they need. Besides, it's not long till I'm nineteen, though it's rumoured they're about to drop the age to eighteen, just like they've done for ARP wardens. Anyway,' she concluded with a shrug, 'we've not had a really serious raid for a while.'

'All the more reason why we're due one,' Janet riposted, lips twitching in disapproval. 'I cas'n see as Hitler's finished with us yet, not with Devonport and all else on our doorstep. And any raid's serious enough if you're caught up in it.'

'And it's pot luck as to whether you get caught up in one or not.' Maisie paused, her face softening. 'Dear Janet,' she sighed. 'Try not to worry, eh? I'll be back by nine at the latest.'

She brushed a kiss on Janet's cheek and glanced across at Kitty with a meaningful lift of her eyebrows. Kitty replied with an almost imperceptible nod to indicate that she understood. Joseph was her first priority, of course, but she'd look out for Janet, too. Motherhood seemed to have matured Kitty, Maisie considered. She was far more sensible now, and both of them felt protective of the dear woman who'd given them both a home. But as Janet's fear of the war had deepened, it was their turn to care for her.

Just now, though, Maisie had other matters to think about as she zipped her boiler suit over her thickest old jumper and slacks, and collected her gas-mask box and tin hat. As if she didn't have enough to worry about, one particular concern was niggling at the back of her mind. Why hadn't she heard from Nick recently? Although she'd had one or two letters from him since Christmas, he hadn't written to her for a while. At least, she hadn't received anything from him, which wasn't necessarily the same thing with the war on. Or was it? They said absence made the heart grow fonder, but were his memories of her fading the longer he was away from her, his feelings lessening? His mind too occupied with his duties and the dangers he faced? For herself, her entire being longed for the moment when he'd return and make her his wife. She was utterly ready for that now, she was sure.

But perhaps that was no longer his intention. Or, and the thought drove horror through her body, perhaps he hadn't written because he couldn't. What if he was injured or missing, or — she scarcely dared to think it —dead, and the news hadn't reached her yet? Oh, please don't let it be that!

Her heart was in turmoil as she made her way through the darkening streets by the sliver of light peeping through the slit in the tissue paper covering her torch. She must concentrate on where she was going rather than on such horrendous thoughts about Nick if she wasn't to join the ranks of those who'd had a nasty fall in the blackout. But when she arrived at the fire substation, all thoughts of Nick at once slid away.

'Bally glad to see you!' Gladys boomed. 'We're two men down tonight, both part-time volunteers, and we were undermanned before that anyway, so we're well under strength.'

'Well, I'm only too glad to help,' Maisie grinned back, pleased to see her friend again. As a fully trained and now quite experienced full-timer, Gladys had been put in charge of the women on her shift. 'What would you like me to do?'

'Help the girls over there checking the hoses would be good.'

Maisie nodded, and went over to where a group of women were running out hoses, inspecting them for wear or fraying, particularly on the ends where they joined onto the nozzles, and then rolling them up again ready for action. Some of the women were volunteers, others full-timers like Gladys. Maisie knew most of them either from her training or from previous times helping out at the station. They acknowledged each other briefly. There'd be time to chat when all the work was done, and doubtless there'd be some banter with the men who were busy checking the trailer pumps and making sure the converted cars that pulled them were in good working order. The men were mainly younger, regular firefighters, and the sight of one mechanic wiping his oily hands on a rag made Maisie think of Marjorie, who she knew was stationed at the nerve centre at Greenbank. They hadn't seen each other for a while. Maisie had been too involved with Kitty and the baby as well as everything else that was going on in her life. She made a mental note to look Marjorie up as soon as she could.

When all the checks had been completed, enamel mugs of tea were handed out. Maisie glanced at her watch. She'd promised Janet she'd be home by nine. There was just time for a quick cuppa and a chat before she needed to leave. She was just about to begin her goodbyes when the all too familiar siren rolled out over the city. The usual feeling of dread settled in her stomach. What should she do? She doubted there was time to get home before the raid started — if there was one, of course. It might be a false alarm. And she'd only be going down to the cellar since Harry and Len were on the rooftop rota that night. So she'd be better off seeking safety in the nearest public shelter.

She was just about to say so and beat a hasty retreat when Gladys caught her arm.

'Jolly good luck you're here,' the older girl proclaimed with enthusiasm. 'If there's a bad raid, we could do with your help. If you're up for it, that is.'

Maisie's heart rammed against her ribs. It was what she'd trained for, but she hadn't expected this sudden opportunity. It would take her mind off missing Nick. Off the emptiness inside. For a while, at least. Time to do her bit. But . . .

'I-I'm not supposed to until June,' she began hesitantly.

'You can act as runner, at least,' Gladys told her. 'Anything else will be unofficial. We need good people like you. There's many a blind eye being turned when needs must, don't you know.'

Maisie drew in a shaky breath and found herself nodding, her head in a whirl. But she had no more time to think as the ominous thrum of aircraft swooped overhead. They kept on coming, and everyone was gazing up at the ceiling as the engines droned past. They could hear the dull thud of ack-ack guns, but no loud explosions.

'Dropping incendiaries, I reckon.' One of the regulars voiced all their thoughts. 'So us'll be needed.'

'We've got to know the different engine sounds,' Gladys explained in Maisie's ear. 'The bombers'll be next, once the fires take hold.'

Maisie nodded. She didn't say so, but she, too, had learned to tell the difference when on rooftop duty. There was also a certain shriek as a stick of incendiaries rocketed downwards, easy to hear when you were outside but fainter from inside the station. As the men grabbed their waterproofs, the auxiliary women cut the lights, then opened the doors, ready for action. At once the noise of the attack blasted in as Maisie went to assist in hitching up the trailer pumps to the cars: the ferocious rush of aircraft diving down to release their cargo of destruction, the whine of falling incendiaries, the rattle of ack-ack guns and the thump of their shells bursting over the city as they tried to repel the attackers.

Maisie held her breath, a coiled spring inside her ready to unwind and catapult her into action. Her nose twitched. Already she could detect a faint smell of burning in the air over and above the fumes from the aircraft. Janet's prediction had been right. Plymouth was for it that night.

Maisie could sense the tension in the black, barely discernible figures around her. The sudden shrill ring of the telephone made her jump, and her strung out nerves tightened further.

'The Royal Hotel!' the woman manning the phone shouted. 'All appliances!'

Within seconds, Maisie found herself swept along as they all piled into the waiting cars. Engines roared into life and swung out along the street. All was noise and pandemonium, and Maisie's pulse drummed as she prayed that Janet, Kitty and the baby had reached the safety of the cellar.

Incendiaries were falling all around them. Those that landed harmlessly in the middle of the tarmac were left to burn themselves out while the vehicles swerved around them. Peering out of the car window, Maisie saw ghostly forms emerging from a building that was emitting smoke.

The car behind drew to a halt. Maisie knew they would check everyone was safely out, but would then carry on to the hotel. Orders were there to be obeyed.

A grey mist was settling in the air, and the unmistakable stench of smoke was seeping into the vehicle, catching at the back of Maisie's throat. The Royal Hotel wasn't far, but already, instead of the intense darkness of the blackout, she could easily distinguish human shapes scuttling about, made visible by the lurid glow of fire.

The cars screeched to a halt and the team spilled out onto the pavement. The grand old hotel was already burning, flickering fingers of orange darting out of the upper windows, and smoke billowing from the lower storeys. Murky figures stumbled out of the opulent building, some milling around in shock, others gesticulating as they bellowed orders, yelling to make themselves heard above the clamour of the planes roaring overhead, the boom-boom of the ack-ack guns and now the crackle of flame as the fires took hold.

It was unreal, both appalling and fascinating, and for a second, Maisie stood frozen in awe. The fire officer in charge, she realised, was talking to a man with a clipboard who seemed to be ticking off people's names as they reported to him. The hotel manager, presumably. The fire officer beckoned to some of his regular men, and Maisie was pitched back to reality as they pulled on what seemed inadequate breathing masks and ran into the burning building.

'Right, chaps, we know what to do!' Gladys's voice thundered above the deafening noise.

Maisie scarcely had time to think as she helped uncouple the trailer pumps, link them up to water hydrants and run out hoses, connecting the nozzles to the jets. The men positioned themselves two to a hose, Gladys, with her unusual strength for a woman, among them, and the pumps were turned on. In the firelight, Maisie saw the flaccid hoses wriggle and take on a life of their own as they filled with water and stiffened. In seconds, streams of water were being poured into the upper floors of the building, battling against the licking, hungry flames. Thick smoke on ground level was spitting forth shadows as human forms were escaping the inferno, running, collapsing on their knees in a coughing fit, or carrying others.

Maisie could only pray everyone had got out. She dared not consider what would happen to anyone who hadn't, and ran forward to help anyone she could. Get them as far as possible from the danger. Tend to anyone who was hurt. Burns should be kept clean and dry. She hadn't been issued with her own first-aid kit, but the other AFS women had theirs. An old lady with a feather boa around her neck and dripping with jewellery tumbled into her arms. Maisie half carried her across the road. She heard bells, then. Ambulances. Maisie managed to sit the elderly woman down on the opposite kerb, since she appeared unhurt, and went to see what else she could do.

The heat seared her face. Despite the thousands of gallons of water spewing into the building, tongues of flame were leaping higher into the air, the blaze spreading along from the main part of the hotel to the palm court, long bar and assembly rooms. All the windows were lit up from inside in a curtain of fire, glass shattering and falling into the street in showers of glittering splinters. Maisie tried to ignore the danger but kept a wary eye as she continued to ferry people across the road, many of those who'd escaped the burning building either disorientated or paralysed by shock. The area was filling up with personnel, ARP wardens directing victims towards the nearest shelters, first aiders, police, civil defence, even WVS ladies passing round bottles of water.

A great whooshing roar reverberated above the crackle and hiss of the flames, followed by an ominous, cracking sound. The chief officer yelled as loudly as he could, and his men leaped back as the roof of the glorious hotel collapsed and crashed in on itself, causing millions of sparks to rain down over the area. At a petrified scream, Maisie turned to see that a spark had ignited the boa around the shoulders of the old lady she'd helped earlier. In an instant, Maisie had lifted it from her shoulders and was stamping it out on the ground.

'Well done, miss,' an older man with a red cross on his sleeve rasped, taking charge of the elderly woman.

Maisie nodded, words temporarily failing her. She glanced up, heart jolting further when she saw that even nearer to the city centre, the sky was alight with an incandescent glow wreathed in clouds of smoke. The whole business district must be ablaze. She staggered backwards as figures ran past her, and her numbed brain recognised naval, army and air force uniforms rushing through on their way to help other parts of the stricken city.

Maisie spun round to see that the entire inside of the hotel and all along the block as far as the new Royal Cinema was one huge wall of fire, flames shooting out sideways through what was left of its windows. Surely it was hopeless, despite all the efforts of the firefighting team.

'Maisie!' Gladys shouted, panting up to her, face so black and grimy that she was almost unrecognisable. 'We need you to run back to the station and ring through to HQ for help. But take care! Cripes, here come the bombers!'

Together they glanced up at the ochre-tinted sky as the throaty thrum of the heavier aircraft grew louder and the great demons from hell rumbled overhead. A few seconds later, the air blasted around them and the ground shook as high explosives were dropped onto the already burning city.

Maisie gulped. The conflagration was bad enough, but to pour explosives into it was hell itself. But she'd been instructed to do a job, and do it she would. Anything to fight back against this evil.

She set off, too frightened, too appalled, to think. Her legs moving mechanically, every nerve taut and ready to snap. The noise in her head was deafening, and yet she was scarcely aware of it as she ran back the way they'd come. To her horror, so many other buildings were either alight or smouldering, but she mustn't stop.

She was almost back at the station when a shrieking whirr lifted her gaze skyward. She froze. The distinctive shape of a small, high explosive was plunging down towards the opposite side of the street just where a Wren was hurrying along the pavement.

Maisie reacted in a split second. 'Look out!' she screamed across the street, then threw herself into a shop doorway that was banked on either side with sand bags.

The explosion resounded in her ears like a thunderclap. The air about her wobbled, and she held her breath, hand clasped tightly over her mouth. The backlash of a blast could tear your lungs out, kill you without leaving a mark. She waited. Somehow she was still alive. She kept still. Listening to the clatter of masonry and broken timbers and roof tiles, and waiting for it to stop. Then she peered out through the cloud of choking dust.

In the murky glimmer she could see that the building opposite was now a tumble of bricks and splintered wooden beams that resembled matchsticks. Had anyone been inside? Where was the Wren? Maisie went cold as she realised the young woman was nowhere to be seen.

She ran across to the broken building and called out. Had the occupants been in a shelter? The rooms at the back were still standing and open to view. No one. Hopefully they were safe. But what of the Wren?

'Hello!' she shouted again, then tried to listen through the ringing in her ears. Was she imagining it, or could she hear a faint moaning?

She began pulling frantically at the debris, a brick at a time, calling out as she worked. She was supposed to be getting a message through to HQ, but the hotel was surely a lost cause whereas she might be able to save the Wren's life. She dug, little by little, the echo of further bombs reaching her from the city centre all the while. She must be nearly there, the trapped girl's voice a little louder. Hair, then. A head. Pained eyes looking up at her from a face covered in dust.

'Jesus, isn't it you, Maisie O'Sullivan?' the weak voice whispered.

Maisie's heart jolted. Of all that was holy, wasn't it Helen Driscoll! What had she been doing here when so many of her comrades had been rushing to the defence of the city that was now one blazing furnace? Shirking her duty, hoping that in the chaos, she wouldn't be missed? Or, like herself, had she been sent on a mission?

Maisie hurled such thoughts aside. 'Are you hurt?' she asked through gritted teeth.

'My leg,' Helen groaned, her face twisting in pain. 'Isn't it agony.'

For a moment, Maisie hesitated as a wave of the old resentment from the convent days rushed over her. She could never forgive Helen for her part in sending Nick away. But neither could she leave her, possibly to die in agony.

She glanced round in frustration. She wasn't strong enough to free Helen on her own, but at that moment, the street was deserted.

'Hold on there. I'll get help,' she told Helen, and went to scramble from her knees.

'No! Please don't leave me!' Helen sobbed. 'Maisie, please!'

'But I can't move all this on my own,' Maisie protested. 'I'll get help, I promise.' And then, to her utter relief, she saw tin-hatted figures running along the street. 'Over here!' she yelled, waving her arms. 'There's a Wren trapped!'

'Right-ho! Coming, miss!'

'There, they're coming,' she told Helen. 'I must go. I've got to take a message to the fire station.'

She saw Helen give a tiny nod. 'Thanks, Maisie,' she croaked. 'Reverend Mother would be proud of you.'

Maisie frowned, totally confused. What was that supposed to mean? All she could think of was to wish Helen 'good luck' in return, and then she ran on down the street.

Ten minutes later, having reported to the station, she was hurrying back the same way. By then, the Royal Hotel wasn't the only building that had been brought down. In the semi-dark, Maisie was having to concentrate on clambering over the debris strewn across the road. The place was swarming with personnel now, and she was relieved to see a figure she assumed was Helen being carried on a stretcher to a waiting ambulance. She just prayed the vehicle would be able to find a way through back to the hospital. By the time she got back to the Royal Hotel, the place was just an unrecognisable mountain of blistering heat and looming, fluorescent flame. Where was Gladys? Or the fire officer? Maisie gazed about her in bewilderment. With the stench of fire all around, the confusion and jumble of fallen, burning timbers and people come to help with the rescue, it took her some precious moments to locate the chief fireman. She stumbled up to him, wheezing from the smoke and from the physical battle of hurrying through the streets.

'There's two appliances coming from HQ!' she shouted at him to make herself heard, her voice hoarse and rasping. 'Should be here soon. But that's it. All the others are out somewhere. The whole of Spooners is ablaze, and there's fires all over the city. But there's help coming from elsewhere. Saltash, Tavistock, Exeter and further afield, but it'll take them a while to get here,' she spluttered, ending in a harsh cough.

'Blooming heck,' the man uttered, his smeared face crestfallen beneath his hat. 'At least everyone's out as far as we know. We'm just trying to stop it spreading to the cinema. Just hope the water mains don't get hit or we'm done for. Thanks for your efforts, Miss O'Sullivan.'

At that moment, they both instinctively ducked as another crashing explosion slammed through the night from another bomb not far away. But it didn't have their name on it. So, in an instant, everyone carried on with their work. Maisie caught the clang of bells above the cacophony of towering, crackling flames, splitting wood, and the hiss of streaming water, as the regular fire engines trundled into the area in front of what was left of the hotel. More uniformed men sprang into action, but they were powerless against the ferocity of the fireball in front of them. Maisie did what she could to help, but she knew it was hopeless.

It must have been gone midnight before the all-clear bellowed out across the city and the bombers ceased to pour their destruction into the already blazing buildings. No one breathed a sigh of relief. Fires still raged everywhere. The sky shimmered an incandescent orange-grey glow, the air a thick smog of choking smoke and dust. The terrifying drone of aircraft, booming explosions, ack-ack guns and bursting shells might have ceased, but the crackle and spit of fire was even louder. In grim desperation, beyond fear, everyone toiled on. Maisie and two other auxiliary women even took over one of the hoses to give the exhausted men some respite. Her heart was pumping furiously, every muscle strained and aching. She felt as if her arms were being dragged from their sockets, but she must carry on.

Hours passed, and yet time stood still. When a cold, grey dawn finally broke, Maisie sat down with her comrades on the kerb opposite. The entire hotel block was a gaunt, burnt-out shell, nothing more than a massive ruin of smouldering rubble, blackened walls and twisted steelwork. All their hard work, for nothing. And they knew it would be the same in so many locations throughout the city, smoke hanging in the air like fog.

The road was awash with water, empty hoses twisted across the tarmac like a nest of vipers. Sodden. Grimy. At least the water supply had held up, and they hadn't needed to use the open reservoirs that had been set up at various points in the city.

Maisie glanced along at Gladys and all the other fire-fighters, grimly silent as they took a break before clearing up the unholy mess and taking all the appliances and trailer pumps back to their relevant bases. To be cleaned and checked and prepared — for another night of terror? Maisie sincerely hoped not, for how many people had already lost their homes, their livelihoods — or their lives — that night?

It didn't bear thinking about. She hoped — yes, she hoped and prayed — that Helen was all right. With all the horror she'd seen that night, she couldn't wish anyone ill, not even her.

'You working today?' Gladys's croak beside her drew her back to reality.

'At the tea shop, yes,' Maisie grated back, her throat parched and cracked. 'If it's still there.' Somewhere inside, she felt the judder of fear, but quite honestly, she was too exhausted to recognise it for what it was. 'I'll just help wind up the hoses—'

'No. You get off home. We regulars can manage here. We'll be off duty for the rest of the day while you've got to work.'

She hesitated. 'Well, if you're sure.'

'Of course. Now, off you go. And thank you, Firefighter O'Sullivan.'

Gladys gave a beaming, weary smile. Despite everything, Maisie felt a twinge of pride. If she never did anything else in this war, she had done her bit that night.

CHAPTER TWENTY-NINE

Bone-weary, eyes bloodshot and blurry from the smoke that still lingered in the air in a bitter haze, Maisie tottered homeward, almost on her knees with fatigue. She felt so cold too, the legs of her boiler suit wet through from the water that had dripped from the hose jets, and her hands blue and stiff. She stumbled her way directly along Union Street, planning to have a quick wash down and fall into bed. But what had happened to Janet and Kitty and darling little Joseph during the night? They had to be all right!

As she neared home, Maisie's stomach was turning sickening somersaults. The street was as busy as ever, though the atmosphere was a strange mixture of quiet shock, raging anger and rigid determination. People who'd been up all night were gravely silent as they worked on to clear up the mess as best they could. Maisie passed a couple of gutted buildings whose familiar façades had been reduced to smouldering mountains of charred embers and broken rubble. Her mind went into overdrive. What if . . .

Relief washed over her. The next section of Union Street was still standing, Janet's tea rooms still intact. Well, almost.

Maisie staggered to a horrified halt. Despite the anti-blast tape, the plate glass front window had been blown in, great jagged shards jutting dangerously from the frame edges. The blackout blind had been ripped to pieces and was dangling in tatters. It was little damage compared to the destruction Maisie had witnessed during the night, but this was her home. She stared, on the verge of tears.

'Maisie! Oh, thank the dear Lord!'

So stunned was she that Janet had lurched up to her without her noticing and enveloped her in a crushing hug, almost knocking her off balance.

'Oh, cheel, we were so worried about you!' Janet's voice was shrill with emotion as she finally stood back, her eyes travelling swiftly over Maisie's soot-coated, dishevelled form. 'Oh, Lordy love, what happened to you?' she cried in dismay.

'I ended up helping out,' Maisie said simply, her mind too fragile to offer any greater explanation. But now the initial, stultifying terror was over, her thoughts were immediately with her friends again. 'And what about you?' she asked quickly. 'And Kitty and—'

'We're all fine. I hardly slept a wink, mind, once the raid were over, I were so worried about you. Kitty got a few hours' kip, though, I think.'

Maisie's sore eyes took in the concern etched on Janet's face, and felt overwhelmed with remorse. 'I'm sorry,' she mumbled. Was that her voice? Her lips felt numb and seemed to be working all on their own. 'The raid started so quickly after the siren went, I didn't have time to get home. And then I got roped into helping. It's what I've trained for, after all, and they needed every man they could get.'

She saw Janet's beloved face moving in a mix of resignation, pride and worry. 'Yes, I reckon they did,' the older woman groaned. 'Must be pretty bad out there. I dread to think . . . Oh, poor Plymouth.'

'Yes,' Maisie whispered brokenly. 'Half the city centre's gone. We were sent to the Royal Hotel.'

'The Royal?' Janet was aghast. 'But that's only a spit away.'

'I know. We tried to save it, but it was hopeless. The whole block's a burnt-out ruin. It was the same with Spooners.'

'Spooners!'

'Yes. I haven't seen it myself, but they're saying the magnificent department store's nothing but a blackened shell. That and the Royal were the biggest fires apparently. But the new post office, and so many others are all gone, too. And several of the civic buildings. Either bombed or burnt out. The whole place . . . It was just too much. The Fire Service was just overwhelmed. They brought in help from elsewhere, even from other counties. But by the time they got there, it was too late. And some of their equipment didn't fit with ours, so they were useless anyway.' She paused, shaking her head. For some reason, she wondered if Dingles was still standing, once her own father's and still Kitty's father's place of work. The thought left a resentful taste in her mouth, and then she gave a bitter laugh. 'Derry's Clock is still standing, if that's any consolation,' she told Janet.

She saw a wry cloud pass over her dear friend's face. 'That's something, I suppose,' Janet murmured. 'But what about all the people that must have been—'

'Don't think about it, Janet. Let's just put our minds to getting this place ready to open at ten, as normal. There'll be more people than ever needing something to eat and drink after last night. I'll just go and get cleaned up.'

Minutes earlier, she'd been dropping with exhaustion, but somehow she'd gone beyond weariness and didn't think she could sleep. Now, seeing the state of the shop, she felt she couldn't rest until she'd helped restore it to some sort of working order.

'Bless you, cheel.' She could see that Janet's smile was forced. 'Kitty's just seeing to the babby and then she'll be down. And fortunately, Mr Huggins has some hardboard in stock and he's going to board up the window for us.'

'Oh, that was lucky.'

It certainly was. Maisie was wondering how on earth they'd deal with the window with half the city either burntout or blown to smithereens. But now they needn't worry. As she climbed the stairs, a wave of tiredness overcame her, but then she met Kitty on the landing. The other girl's eyes opened wide with shock and relief to see her friend standing there in a bit of a state, but alive.

'Oh, Maisie!'

She stepped forward to hug her, but Maisie jumped back with a grimace.

'No! I don't want to get you covered in grime,' she said with a laugh that didn't sound real. 'Janet gave me a hug before I could stop her, but I don't think she realises it rubbed soot all over her.'

'You thinks that matters? Oh, come here!'

They hugged anyway, swaying round in a circle before Kitty pulled away.

'I'm that happy to see you!' she cried. 'I daren't say so to Janet, but I were terrified summat had happened to you.'

'And me, you. And Joseph?'

'Sleeping like a babby,' Kitty joked back.

'Good. Well, I'll be down in a few minutes to help.'

Maisie went into her room and gasped when she caught sight of herself in the mirror. Her red-rimmed eyes stood out like saucers in her sweat and smut smeared face, her teeth a white slash in a filthy mask. Her hair, usually fixed in a victory roll so that she and Kitty looked almost identical, looked as if she'd been dragged through a hedge of brambles.

She pulled off her boiler suit and hung it over the chair to dry — ready for action again the very next night if need be. Then she went into the bathroom to have a wash. Thank goodness the water mains hadn't been hit and they still had water. Her hair would have to wait, and once she'd changed into some clean clothes, she tied it up in a scarf ready to go downstairs to grab a cup of tea to ease her parched throat and join Janet and Kitty in the shop.

But as she crossed the landing and passed Kitty's room, she hesitated by the slightly open door. Joseph was snuffling softly in his sleep, and she couldn't resist tiptoeing in to take a peek at him. He looked so pure and innocent after all the horror she'd witnessed that night. Her throat choked with emotion.

'I'll do everything I can to protect you, so I will,' she murmured, gazing down on him. 'As if you were mine. You shouldn't be here in such danger.'

Her heart contracted with dread. What if they came again that night? What if Union Street wasn't so lucky? Already some of its buildings were gone. The thought was terrifying.

She crept out of the room, not wanting to disturb the sleeping infant, taking with her the empty feeding bottle Kitty must have forgotten when she put Joseph down. Kitty had been upset that she hadn't been able to feed her son herself. The birth had taken a lot out of her, and Maisie had been concerned when Kitty lost so much weight. It was no surprise her milk had dried up after only a few weeks, but in all other ways, she was as fit as a fiddle and Joseph was thriving on the baby formula. But carrying the bottle downstairs had given Maisie an idea, and she was suddenly tingling with animation.

She placed the bottle by the sink in the kitchen, ready to be boiled in the giant saucepan they kept especially for that purpose, then went to help Janet and Kitty clear up the mess in the shop. But as she passed by the counter area, Janet was on the telephone, which by some miracle was still working.

'Hello, Wilfred, my lover,' she heard Janet say as she walked past, and gave a little smile to herself. Was it a case of great minds thinking alike? Had Janet just had the same brainwave as she had? Or was she simply letting her cousin know they were all right after the raid?

'Sounds like Janet's on the phone to her cousin Wilfred,' she observed as she came up to where Kitty was sweeping up the broken glass.

'Yes.' Kitty paused with the broom in her hands. 'She's going to see if he knows anywhere Joseph and me can go and stay safely for a while.'

'Really? That's exactly what I was going to suggest. Only I was going to discuss it with you first.'

Kitty pulled a face. 'Janet did. At least, she told me she'd be sending us away if she could find somewhere. Said she'd brook no argument. Seeing as my parents don't want to know, she says she's still acting in their place and I've got to do as she says.'

'Well, it defeats me as to why the government have refused to evacuate children and mothers from Plymouth all this time when the local authorities have been crying out for it. But maybe they'll change their minds after last night. So it'll be good if you can go somewhere. Joseph's safety must come first in everything.'

'Of course.' Kitty released a resigned sigh. 'I'll miss Cam so much, though.'

'But if you're just up on the moor somewhere, he'll be able to visit you quite often. Right, best get cracking if we're to be ready to open up at ten. We need to knock out the rest of the glass so that no one catches themselves on it. I'll go and get my thick gardening gloves and that hammer we bought when we were making the chicken run.'

Maisie went out the back into the garden and returned with the stated items. Each time she passed Janet, the older woman was still on the phone. Maisie caught snippets of the conversation, but couldn't tell what the outcome might be. It wasn't until she'd finished carefully tapping out the remaining broken glass that Janet put down the phone and bustled to the front of the shop.

'Well, that's settled,' she announced with a satisfied but firm nod of her head. 'You know Cousin Wilfred lives in a little cottage in the village separate from his shop, and he's already got two young London evacuees in his spare room. But he's said you can have the room over the shop if you've a mind to. There are some tools and bicycle bits up there, but he's going to clear those out straightaway, so you can go today.'

Maisie's eyes moved from Janet's obvious relieved satisfaction to Kitty's crestfallen expression.

'Today?' the young mother gulped. 'B-but what about the pram and the cot and everything else I'll need for Joseph?'

Janet replied with a thoughtful frown. 'I'm sure we can sort summat,' she pondered. 'But you'll be safe and cosy there. It were a cottage for many a year afore Wilfred turned it into a shop, and a stable or suchlike afore that. There's a small range downstairs you can use for cooking, and a fireplace upstairs to keep you warm. But while I think about how to get everything there, you should ring the hospital and leave a message for Cam. He'll want to come and say goodbye, though I'm sure he'll manage to get up to visit you afore too long.'

'Yes, I will. And don't think I'm not grateful Janet, cuz I truly am. But I'll miss you both as well as Cam.'

She glanced round and Maisie saw that Kitty wasn't the only one whose eyes were shining with unshed tears.

'Well, hopefully it won't be for long, and Walkhampton's hardly a million miles away and not hard to get to by train provided they're still running,' Maisie said. A voice inside her said it wouldn't be nearly so bad as when she'd been forced to leave Ireland. She'd miss her dear friend, too, and darling little Joseph, but it was the best thing to do. 'But come on. We'd best get on,' she said, neatly changing the subject.

'I'll just call the hospital, then I'll be back to help.'

They set to, sweeping up the rest of the glass that seemed to have gone everywhere. The ripped blackout blind was no use anymore, and wouldn't be needed once the window was boarded up, so they removed it completely and took it out the back to be disposed of. Dust and smut had blown in and covered everything in sight, so the tables and chairs had to be wiped down and the floor mopped. Fortunately they completely cleared the massive, solid marble counter each evening, storing all remaining produce in the kitchen overnight, and all the clean crockery was kept in closed cupboards. But it was still going to be a race against time to have everything shipshape by opening time. And although their bread was delivered from a bakery, there were still the day's cakes and soups and so forth to attend to.

Mr Huggins came round to board up the window. Kitty went upstairs to check on Joseph and Janet and Maisie went outside to see how the café looked with its new frontage.

'Doesn't look too inviting for a tea rooms, does it?' Janet moaned.

'Tell you what,' Maisie said perkily. 'You've got some old tins of paint down in the cellar. I could paint some flowers on it. Oh, and an *Open as Usual* sign, of course.'

'Excellent idea,' a voice behind them said. 'Grim, isn't it?'

Maisie turned to nod at Mr Nettlehayes whose shop next door was in an equally sorry state with its window boarded up, too. 'Got to make the best of it, mind.'

'Don't know about that, maid. But I've heard lots of folk are driving up onto the moor tonight, those what have some petrol left. The wife and me are going, too, and us wondered if you'd all like to come along of us, especially with the babby and all. If you don't mind going in the back of the van, that is.'

Maisie and Janet exchanged glances. Both knew at once what the other was thinking.

'That's proper kind of you,' Janet thanked him. 'But would you mind taking Kitty and the little one to Walkhampton? She's going to stay there in my cousin's shop, but she'll need the pram and the cot and what have you, and we were wondering how to get them there.'

'Be my pleasure. Near Dousland, isn't it? But what about you and the maid here?'

'I'm with the Fire Service now,' Maisie told him, and watched as he nodded gravely.

'But we should be able to squeeze you in, Mrs Mudge. As a butcher, I get a bit of extra petrol ration for my deliveries, so we'll be going up on the moor each night for as long as we can.'

'You're a treasure, Mr Nettlehayes. And maybe we can make ourselves comfortable in my cousin's downstairs room. Be better than sitting in a cold van all night.'

'That'd be mighty kind. All got to pull together, haven't we? But better get some work done now. Customers'll be here soon. So . . . see you this evening.'

They all nodded their heads at each other, and Mr Nettlehayes disappeared inside his shop.

'Well, that were a stroke of luck, and so kind of Mr Nettlehayes,' Janet declared. 'There's only a few trains up to Princetown each day, so I wouldn't be able to stay at Wilfred's each night and run the shop if I had to go by train. But by road, it won't take long. Now if we get that paint, you can get on with making us look a bit more inviting, and maybe do something for Mr Nettlehayes's window, too. And then you'd better get a bit of shut-eye if you're going to be fighting fires again all night.'

Maisie could tell Janet was trying to inject some forced humour into her voice, and gave a wry smile. Certainly by the time she'd jollied up the outside of the two shops as best she could, she was ready to fall into bed. By now, the exhaustion had returned and she tumbled into a deep sleep the instant her head hit the pillow.

She remained dead to the world for some hours. She awoke with a start, worry at once taking hold of her again. For Nick, of course, his face smiling at her from his photograph. Please keep safe, she prayed. At least Janet, Kitty and Joseph would be out of harm's way if the Luftwaffe returned that night.

She nipped across to the bathroom and, pulling the scarf from her head, gave her hair an ultra-quick wash with some of the shampoo they had left. How long before such a thing became unobtainable, she wondered grimly. Rubbing her hair as dry as she could with a towel, she went back out onto the landing. Sounds were coming from Kitty's room, and she put her head around the slightly open door. Joseph was awake, kicking his legs as he lay in his cot, gurgling happily. Kitty had a small case open on the bed and was packing a few clothes into it, together with a pile of napkins. She looked up as Maisie came into the room.

'Can't take as much as I really need,' she grumbled. 'Nappies take up so much room. But Janet says she'll bring up a whole lot more tomorrow night when there's more room in the van without the pram and the cot.'

'Can I help with anything before I go down to the shop?' Maisie offered.

'Help me check I've got everything? You're more organised than me. I'm taking that rucksack as well, with all the essentials in, so everything's handy.' Kitty paused, sighing as her eyes moved over all the items spread out on the bed. Then she looked up, her face taut. 'I so wish you were coming, too,' she cried, and Maisie saw that her eyes were suddenly glistening with tears. 'Keep safe, Firefighter O'Sullivan, won't you?'

'Of course. I have no intention of doing otherwise.'

They met each other's gaze, and in that moment, all the love Maisie felt for this happy-go-lucky, carefree girl who'd befriended her in those dark days when she'd first arrived from Ireland washed through her in a torrent. She opened her arms and Kitty stepped into them. They held each other tightly, Maisie almost choking on the emotion that rasped at the back of her throat.

'And you look after my godson,' she croaked in a tiny voice.

'Yes, but he's your nephew. You and me, we're sisters now, remember?'

Maisie gave a sad, wistful smile as she felt Kitty pull away. 'Yes, of course. Always.' She hesitated, feeling her tears threatening. She must think of something to stop them. 'And will you do something else for me, too?'

Kitty tipped her head in puzzlement, and Maisie stepped back.

'Just a minute.' She turned and hurried to her own room. In the top drawer of her bedside cabinet was the box Zeek had given her. If anything happened to Union Street, if the building . . . and then she thought of something else, too.

'I want you to have this,' she said as she went back into Kitty's room. Over her arm was draped the woollen dress in a distinctive plum-coloured pattern that Kitty had always admired. It was the last item of clothing Maisie had made for herself before the war. 'I promised I'd make you something similar, didn't I? I will when the war's over, but I want you to have this now.'

The surprise on Kitty's face was so comical that it made Maisie chuckle.

'Oh, Maisie, I cas'n—'

'Yes, you can. You can give it back to me after the war when I've made something for you, too. But with Nick away, I've no need to look too glam. But you'll still be seeing Cam sometimes, and you'll want to look nice for him, won't you?'

'Maisie, thanks so much!' Kitty took the dress from her and planted a kiss on her cheek. 'I'll wear it this evening. Cam's coming after his shift to say goodbye. But . . . that's Zeek's jewellery box, isn't it?' Maisie saw her expression change, and she shook her head. 'No. You'll not give me that as well.'

'Only for safekeeping!' Maisie laughed. 'I want you to look after it for me. It'll be safer with you. If this building was hit, it'd be lost. Besides, if anything did happen to me, they'd be yours anyway. And all the money in the trust, don't forget. But . . . the box'll be too bulky, so I'll put everything in this.'

Opening the box, she took out a small velvet pouch, dropped each item into it and tightened the drawstring. 'I'll put them at the bottom of the rucksack. They'll be safe there. Then what else d'you need in it?'

'Spare nappy and rompers. Just in case.' Kitty deliberately pulled a face, and Maisie grinned back. 'I'll make up a couple of bottles nearer the time, and pack some tins of Cow and Gate in the case. And I'll put my gas mask in the rucksack as well, and tie on that monstrous babby contraption thing as it's too big to go inside.'

'Don't forget your identity cards and ration books,' Maisie reminded her. 'And maybe both your birth certificates. Just in case anything happens here and they get lost. And that post office savings account book. You'll need that.'

'Yes. It's a good job Cam's been putting all that money into it, and I've been adding to it when I can. Cousin Wilfred's said we can stay for free, but I'll need to buy food and coal, and I don't reckon there'll be any work I can do, not with Joseph. It's why this has worked out so well, still being able to work in the tea rooms. Janet's been a brick.'

'Hmm, I wonder what this Cousin Wilfred's like. If he's as generous as Janet, you'll be as comfortable as anything. Talking of Janet, I ought to get down to help in the shop.'

'Me, too. I'll be down as soon as I've finished packing. If little trouble here has gone to sleep, leastways.'

Maisie gave a small laugh and turned out of the room, her heart uneasy. She was so relieved that, within hours, Janet, Kitty and Joseph would be heading for safety. But it was the end of an era, even if it was only a temporary measure. And it really didn't feel right at all.

CHAPTER THIRTY

Maisie took a deep breath to calm her jangling nerves. They were waiting at the front of the shop, the packed suitcase standing ready next to the door. The pram and cot, together with the bedding for both of them, had been loaded into Mr Nettlehayes's van which was parked outside the butcher's next door.

Maisie, Kitty and Janet were sitting at one of the tables, the rucksack at Kitty's feet. None of them knew what to say. Janet's attempts at conversation were just met with wan smiles. Maisie sensed that her friends were feeling as jittery as she was. Baby Joseph had fallen asleep in the drawer Janet had padded out for him to use in the time since his pram and cot had been spirited away. They'd placed it on the floor behind the counter, and had left him there so as not to disturb him until the last minute.

A knock on the door made them all jump, even though they were expecting it. It would be Cam come to say goodbye. Now was the moment.

Kitty leaped up to turn off the lights and open the door. But when she did so, the shadow looming in the darkness was much shorter than she'd been expecting.

'Me and the missus be all ready.' Mr Nettlehayes's anxious tone came through the blackness. 'We hope your young man won't be long. We'll be waiting in the van.'

'Oh, I'm sure Cam'll be here in just a minute,' Kitty told him.

'Well, we cas'n wait all night. We want to be away afore ort happens. I'll give you ten more minutes.'

'Yes, of course, Mr Nettlehayes.'

Maisie could hear the worry in Kitty's voice as she shut the door and turned the lights back on, and she could see the agitation on Kitty's face as she sat down again.

'You look lovely in that dress,' Janet commented — just for something to say, Maisie imagined. 'Everyone always said how nice Maisie looked in it. Proper generous it was of her to give it to you.'

Maisie was about to say something herself, but at that moment, there was another knock on the door and Kitty sprang up again. This time it was Cam, and Maisie watched as the big Canadian took her in his arms and kissed her thoroughly.

'Can't tell you how grateful I am for this, Janet,' he declared when he finally let Kitty go. 'And don't you worry, honey,' he continued, turning back to Kitty, 'I'll be up to visit as soon as I can. In the meantime, here's some more cash to start you off. And you just let Janet know if there's anything else you need.'

'Oh, thank you, Cam,' Kitty said, taking the handful of notes and stowing them in her purse in the rucksack. 'That'll keep us going for a while.'

'Well, let's hope it won't be for too long. And then . . .' He paused for effect, and even in the dimmed lights, Maisie saw his blue eyes twinkling. 'And then Janet can work her magic in the food department. I've just signed the final documents for the divorce. As soon as it's finalised, we can get ourselves hitched up. A summer wedding'll be great, don't you think? And we can get a proper ring on your finger!'

'That's fantastic news!' Maisie exclaimed as Kitty flew into Cam's arms again.

'Hey, don't knock us over, kid!' Cam laughed, pretending to lose his balance.

And then Maisie and Janet were hugging them, too. It was a merry note to lighten the moment of departure. But the fact that Mr Nettlehayes would be knocking on the door again at any moment snapped Maisie from her pleasant thoughts. Cam would obviously want to say goodbye to his son, so while the happy couple enjoyed their last few moments together, Maisie slipped away to the back of the shop to fetch little Joseph. She couldn't help feel a twinge of envy. Everything was going well for Cam and Kitty. If only she could have that same certainty with Nick. How she missed him, longed to feel his arms about her again. She was ready for marriage now. Ready for a family. But would he ever return? If only she'd heard from him, knew he was alive. Sometimes she felt as if she was being torn in two.

Pushing her worries aside, she reached the back of the shop and kneeled down behind the counter next to Joseph to say her own goodbyes to the beloved infant. He looked so peaceful in his makeshift cot. So tiny and helpless. She'd miss him terribly. Oh, little one, she silently whispered, I'd do anything in my power to keep you safe. But her place was at the fire station now, to act as runner if nothing else. As soon as everyone had left, she'd don her boiler suit, grab her helmet and gas-mask box from the hook by the door, and make her way down the street, all the while praying they weren't in for another night like the previous one.

She leaned over, about to lift the slumbering child into her arms. It was then that she heard it. The rumbled droning low overhead. God, it was so loud! A split second of shock. Of panic. Then the screech of something hurtling towards the earth.

And she knew.

She flung herself across Joseph just as the floor rocked beneath her. All in slow motion. Time held its breath. A thunderous blast ripped through her skull. She clamped her hands over her ears. The roar reverberated through her body, a strange, muffled deafness in her ears. Then the crack of crumbling masonry, the clatter of broken bricks raining downwards, the splintering of wood and plaster as beams and ceilings crashed and fell. The shattering of glass and china. Something hit her back. A second later, a sharp pain seared through her head. Her brain went fuzzy. Stars danced behind her closed eyelids. Turning red. Everything went blank. She was no longer there.

* * *

Nothingness.

A void.

A slow awakening. Consciousness dribbled back. An odd numbness. Where was she? Was she alive?

A wave of panic stung through her and she tried to peel herself from the floor. She felt a weight slip from her back, and then she was free. Her head hurt, it was all so dark. She realised her eyes were shut and had to force them open. She could see, she was alive. Disorientated, confused, but alive.

An uncanny, deadening silence boomed in her ears, and yet a high-pitched, squealing whine filled her head until she thought it would burst. Her brain was stumbling through nothingness, detached and living through this nightmare, staring as if through glass, real and yet unreal. Somehow she managed to sit up and rock back on her heels. She could feel fragments of plaster in her hair. Thick dust choked her throat. She could taste it, foul, on her lips. This couldn't be happening. And yet it was.

What now? Her eyes were beginning to adjust to the gloom. There was a peculiar, flickering glow, a bit like candlelight, but so, so dim. Her heart jerked.

Joseph!

Holy Mother, was he all right? She could feel the soreness in her ribs now from the sides of the drawer as she'd thrown herself over him. Pray God he was alive. She peered down at him. In the shadows she saw him give a little wriggle, and then he snuffled as he settled back to sleep, miraculously unaware of what had happened around him.

In that instant of relief, the floor shuddered again, focusing Maisie's mind, and a booming explosion broke through her temporary deafness. Then another. And another. The broken ceiling above her head groaned, and she quickly pulled the drawer right under the counter as a further shower of debris rained down on them. She had to get them out before the entire building collapsed.

Her training kicked in. Always assess the situation first. If she just grabbed Joseph and tried to clamber out, if the place was unstable, it could make matters worse. No. Think. She jammed the makeshift cot as far as it could go beneath the solid marble counter. Joseph would be safe there for a few minutes.

Slowly, cautiously, she lifted herself to a standing position and peered out over the counter. She froze in horror. The front of the shop was . . . gone. Like all those in that part of Union Street, the front of the building was only single-storey. Now, it wasn't even that. It was open to the sky. The wall separating it from the butcher's was gone, and that, too, was nothing but a roofless heap of rubble and broken beams. And on the other side, the wall between the tea rooms and Huggins's next door was only half standing.

Maisie stared, paralysed with shock. She could see that where Mr and Mrs Nettlehayes should have been waiting in their van, there was nothing. Just a wavering pillar of flame giving an unearthly amber luminescence that illuminated what was left in macabre, dancing twilight. And a familiar smell. The gas main must have been hit. The bomb must have landed directly outside.

Panic ripped at Maisie's throat. So where were . . . ? She turned round, praying her friends had got to the relative safety of the back of the shop before . . . But there'd been no warning, no air-raid siren. She could see broken tables and chairs and other debris had been flung against the back wall, blocking the entrance to the kitchen and the cellar. But no sign of any of her friends. She realised then that the heavy counter had shifted slightly — taking the impact and shielding her and Joseph from the worst of the blast.

She gulped, heart bucking in her chest. She must try and find her friends. She crawled forward, testing the debris beneath her all the time, so slow, frustrated, not hearing the whimpers that whispered from her lips. She noticed that, across the other side of the room, Kitty's suitcase was bizarrely still next to where the front door had stood until a few moments ago. Moments, minutes? Maisie had no idea. All she knew was that the case had merely been blown on its side and from where she was, appeared to be intact.

She scrambled forward, knees, elbows, hands leaning on hard objects as she moved, bits of furniture, broken bricks, twisted metal. At least the only glass would be over by the door seeing as the window had already gone, she considered bitterly. But where . . . ? Frantically, she called out their names. The muffled sensation in her ears was clearing and she was sure she'd be able to hear their replies. But nothing. Just the crack and hiss of that menacing flame outside.

She gasped as her hand touched something that felt like material with a solid yet soft form beneath. A limb? Had she found someone? Her fingers came into contact with something wet and sticky. Blood. Her pulse ratcheted up as she began to move debris aside. She pulled. A leg. A whole, heavy leg came away in her hold. A leg. In naval uniform. But it was just a leg, unconnected to a body.

She dropped it with a cry of anguish, and her stomach heaved. But you could live without a leg. If she could find him. Force down the bile. Keep searching. Feel, dig. Pray. Keep on, though her heart was crippled with fear. Further forward. The flickering light was brighter now. Bright enough to show . . . an arm, the wrist blown open, bone, unrecognisable flesh. A shoulder. Ripped apart. Jagged. Part of a torso. Nothing else.

Helpless against the nausea, she leaned aside to vomit up her recent meal. No one could survive that. She was shivering now, teeth chattering. But she had to press on. Cam was dead, blown apart. But there was still a chance for the others. She must save Kitty.

She began hurling aside . . . exactly what, she wasn't sure. Didn't care. If only she could find her dearest friend. Tears of desperation streamed unheeded down her cheeks. She must . . .

She found the straps of Kitty's rucksack. She must be so near. And then . . . a hand. The white cuff she recognised at once, against the distinctive material of the dress she'd given Kitty. She scrabbled feverishly in the rubble, her own fingers scratched and bleeding. Mother of God, she prayed, let there be a body attached to the hand. Not like . . . Despair, hope, terror circled her heart, then relief and joy surged through her as she uncovered Kitty's intact form. Dear, dearest Cam had protected his beloved girl with his own strong body. Given his life for hers.

For a moment, Maisie was too shocked to move. She crouched there, gazing down on Kitty. So strange. In her own dress. With Kitty's hair identical to her own, all in a mess now, hiding her face. It was like looking at herself.

She reached out and tenderly drew Kitty's tangled, dust-laden hair from her face. Then she reared away, emitting a horrified, strangled scream. Nothing more than mangled flesh and spongy matter, thick, congealed blood and splinters of white. Dear, darling Kitty. Maisie stared at the lovely, funny, devil-may-care girl who had rescued her from her own misery all those years ago and who had become like a sister to her. Maisie's heart was shattered with grief, beyond tears. Rest in peace, my dearest friend. And Maisie carefully rearranged Kitty's hair so that she still looked alive, just asleep and beautiful.

What would happen to poor little Joseph now? His grandparents wanted nothing to do with him. They'd made that patently clear. But Janet could bring him up as his foster mother, surely? The welfare people had been happy enough for Maisie herself to live with the homely woman when she'd been only fourteen, after all.

Janet. Oh, surely . . . ? Had she still been standing by Cam and Kitty when the bomb had fallen, or like herself, had she considered the pair should spend their last few moments together alone, and started towards the back of the shop? Maisie hadn't found her as she'd worked her way forward, but she could easily have been hidden beneath the mounds of debris.

'Janet!'

Maisie desperately shouted the woman's name, but her voice came out as a croak. She stopped. Strained her ears. Nothing. Janet must be here somewhere. She had to be alive.

Maisie searched, dug, squeezed her hand through gaps to feel where she couldn't see, scraping her knuckles, tearing her nails. Slowly inching her way back towards the counter. Tiny sobs wheezed from her throat, tight with dread and exhaustion. The gloom seemed less intense now. Were her eyes adjusting to it, or was the light source growing stronger? Was the gas main about to explode? Was that why help hadn't come yet? Were they waiting for the entire mains to be shut off? She must be quick! But could she leave, knowing Janet could still be alive?

And then something glinted just in front of her, buried beneath a twisted metal beam hidden under a jagged table top. Maisie caught her breath. Could it be . . . ? Hoping against reckless hope, she used every last vestige of strength to drag the table aside. Yes, she was sure . . . She'd found her! For a moment, all Maisie felt was relief. But . . . the dear woman's eyes were fixed wide open, staring, unmoving.

The bud of hope withered and died in Maisie's chest. She recoiled, yet couldn't drag her gaze from the beloved face. All her family, the family she'd finally discovered, were gone. Tearing grief closed her throat. She wanted to scream but the sound echoed silently inside her head. There was nothing left.

Then a calm, serene voice cut through her distraught mind. *That stubborn, determined little girl.* It was almost as if Sister Agnes was telling Maisie what to do. Maisie gulped. Shook her head. The decision was made.

Her brain couldn't work out the logic. Couldn't foresee the consequences. She just knew she had to do it. Instinct told her that she had no choice. She had no time to think. Had to act now, this instant. Another vibration could bring the upper storeys of the back part of the building crashing down, or that broken gas main could explode. No. Whether or not it was the right thing to do, in that moment, it seemed the only thing to do. Her duty.

She crawled back to where she knew Kitty's body lay, swallowing down bile from her rebellious, heaving stomach as she turned back to the sickening sight. The glow of fire was flooding in now, not just from the burning gas but a red, smoky mist she recognised from the previous night. Thousands more incendiaries must have been dropped and buildings must be alight all over the city. But thank God it was still murky enough inside to hide the worst of the horror. Of what Hitler's bomb had done.

She wouldn't look too closely. Didn't want to see Kitty's mutilated face again. But if she was going to do her duty, she must pull the pretend wedding ring from Kitty's finger and slide it onto her own. Her hand trembled as she touched Kitty's still warm flesh. *I'm so sorry, my flower. I'm doing this for Joseph. For your son. For my son now.*

Her mind reeled, but she must hurry. She grasped the straps of the rucksack. Yanking hard, it came free, together with the cumbersome baby's gas mask that was securely attached to it. She knew exactly what was in the rucksack, had helped pack it, making sure everything was there. The papers. Something clicked in her brain. She had to make sure . . . She glanced desperately towards the suitcase and where the door should have been. Her gas-mask box had been hanging from a hook on the wall. The wall that was now half demolished. If she could find it . . . and by some miracle, there it was. She reached out, stretching her arm from its socket. Fingertips touched. She had it. Pulled it towards her. Took her own identity card from her pocket and put it in the box. Wedged the box into the space left by the rucksack so that it was half buried in the ruins. Next to dear Kitty.

Now she looped the rucksack straps over her shoulders. Hurry now. She could hear voices in the street, the clanging of fire-engine bells. Must get away. Scramble back to the counter, scoop Joseph in her arms, cradling him against her chest. Step as carefully as she could over broken furniture, jagged metal and chunks of masonry. Reach where the shop front once stood. Shift Joseph into one arm, pick up the suitcase with the other.

She staggered out into the street. She could see now that the pillar of flame was coming from a deep crater just outside, exactly where her kind neighbours had been waiting in their van. A direct hit. They would have been blown to smithereens.

Just for a second, she lost time, disorientated. The street bore no resemblance to the familiar place she'd known for so long. Many of the buildings were ablaze, like black skulls with bright, gleaming eyes. Terror was dripping down from the sky as more bombs were falling. Pray God they hadn't survived one explosion only to be taken by another. That would be too cruel. She had a job to do. She must succeed. She must.

She must get to a shelter, dodge the danger. Get as safe as she could for the rest of the raid. And then she would have to see.

Towards the city centre, most of Union Street was on fire. She turned in the opposite direction, stumbling, lurching, battling to avoid the debris strewn across the road. That way was almost as bad. Buildings tottered, their insides ripped open like tin cans. But mainly they burned. She could feel the blistering heat as she hurried past, leaping out of the way of fire engines and trailer pumps as crews set up to pour thousands of gallons of water into the conflagrations. Their dark figures ghostly against the looming flames. Their efforts useless, she knew all too well. The noise was horrendous and deafening even though her hearing was still slightly muffled. Crackle and roar of fire, the very sky aflame. And above all, the drone of aircraft, thud of defending guns, echoing blasts when the ground shook beneath her feet.

She reached the octagon where Union Street opened up into the pleasant lozenge shaped area. Surely as she got further from the city centre, the destruction would be less? But no. She stood, slowly turned round. She was engulfed in a circle of fire, the fashionable shops, Jay's massive furnishing store, one huge, hellish inferno. The air was thick with acrid smoke and flying cinders. She coughed, spluttered. Held Joseph's face more tightly against her chest to try and protect him. But surely this was the end? There was nowhere to go.

'Come along, maid!' a voice sliced into her terror. 'Nearest shelter's this way. I'll take the case for you.'

Maisie's streaming eyes looked into the smoke-smudged face of an ARP warden. Not their own, who might have recognised her, but a stranger. He prised the case from her rigid hand, took her by the arm, and propelled her forward.

CHAPTER THIRTY-ONE

'Can I have your attention, please,' the voice of an ARP warden, a different one from the fellow who'd rescued Maisie, called across the half sleeping assembly in the early hours of the following day. 'If you couldn't hear it clearly from in here, that were indeed the all-clear. But it's proper grim out there. I wouldn't advise going out until morning.'

A reluctant murmur rumbled among those of the shelter's occupants who weren't fully asleep. Only one or two made their way towards the exit. What was the point in stepping out into the darkness where firefighters would still be battling to extinguish the flames engulfing so many buildings, if the previous night was anything to go by? Might as well wait until morning to find out if one's home or place of work was still standing, or reduced to a pile of rubble or burnt-out shell. And who knew if there wouldn't be another raid before the night was out and you'd want to return to the shelter anyway?

Maisie already knew she had nowhere to go. Staying put was the only option. The public shelter was of a reasonable size with certain facilities run by a team of WVS ladies. Seeing her with a baby, one of them had found her a space on a mattress on the floor in a secluded corner.

'And here's a coat for you, dear,' the good woman said, reappearing a few minutes later. 'About your size, I'd say. Got a store of donated clothing, we have. Got caught out by the raid, did you, and left yours behind? Looks as if you were off somewhere,' she added, jabbing her head towards the suitcase.

Maisie wanted to keep to herself, but felt obliged to answer the helpful woman. 'Yes. Some neighbours were taking me and the babby up onto the moor, but the raid started and I don't know what happened to them.'

She felt her heart jump, astonished at herself. It was a half-truth, but she did know what had happened. Mr and Mrs Nettlehayes had been blown to kingdom come, but she really didn't want to think about it. But putting on the Devonshire accent had come so naturally, and when she thought about it, what better way to disguise any lingering Irish lilt in her voice? Thankfully it must have sounded genuine enough as the WVS woman didn't bat an eyelid but just nodded sympathetically.

'I'll get you a nice cuppa,' she said, hurrying off.

Maisie breathed a silent sigh of relief. She was still shaking, the horrific images of her dear friends' broken bodies flashing across her mind. But she'd got Joseph to safety and right now that was all that mattered.

He began to grizzle as she tried to settle him on the mattress. It was a miracle that he'd slept through the explosion and the dash through the burning streets. But now, within minutes, it was clear he needed a feed.

Shortly before they'd been due to leave, Kitty had made up a bottle in case Joseph needed feeding during the journey. She'd wrapped it in a towel to keep it at the correct temperature. The drive would only have taken about forty-five minutes, so it would still have been safe for his little tummy. But the rucksack had been half buried in the blast. Maisie opened it, fully expecting to find the towel damp and the bottle broken. But by some miracle, it was still intact, and a few moments later, Joseph was in her arms and guzzling greedily, utterly unaware of the trauma going on around him.

'I'll bring you a bowl of warm water to wash his little face when he's finished,' the WVS lady said when she returned with the promised mug of tea. 'You're both of you covered in dust, and . . . Oh, there's blood in your hair. Something must have hit you. Let me look.'

She set down the mug and Maisie stiffened as the good woman inspected her head. Ouch, it was certainly tender. And then she remembered something crashing into her skull before she lost consciousness.

'Hmm, that's a nasty cut and you've got a swelling the size of an egg. One of our team's an ex-nurse. I'll get her to clean it up for you when you've finished seeing to the baby. And have you got another bottle made up for the little soul for later?'

Maisie blinked up at her. She hadn't thought that far ahead. Her mind was still in pieces, and she was so grateful for the woman's help.

'Er, no, I haven't,' she answered shakily. 'I weren't expecting to need one. We were going to someone's house, like. I've got some dried babby milk in the case, mind.'

'Well, I'll come back later when the little mite's finished. We've got a couple of primus stoves and a bowser of water, so I can boil up the bottle and sterilise it for you, and then make up a new feed later when baby needs it.'

'Thank you so much!' Maisie had to bite back tears of gratitude. 'I don't know what I'd have done without you.'

'My pleasure. It's what we volunteered for.'

Maisie watched her pad away towards the volunteers' station around the corner. It was a substantial shelter, one which Maisie remembered seeing on one of the plans she'd had to study during her training. She'd never imagined then that she'd be huddled down there with Kitty's baby rather than fighting fires above ground.

Her head was really starting to ache, thumping like a drum. She'd ask for some aspirin when the ex-nurse came to patch her up. For now, she'd try and relax while Joseph finished his feed, though heaven knew it was hard to let go when every nerve in her body was stretched to breaking point.

'Did you hear there were a stray bomber got in under the radar and dropped a cartload afore the siren went off?' she heard someone say. 'Some poor blighters will've copped it afore they got a chance to take shelter.'

Maisie caught her breath. If only she hadn't heard those words. She knew who some of those poor blighters were. She wanted to scream it out. Perhaps that release would ease her pain a little. But she had to remain anonymous, so she left the agony to simmer inside.

Someone started singing, and for a while, many joined in a general rendition of some popular tunes, interrupted now and then for a split second as the ground shook and the lights flickered. But once the children present were settling down to sleep, all became much quieter, those not wanting or not able to sleep themselves talking in low murmurs. Once Maisie's head wound had been tended and the aspirin had worked, she tried to blot out everything else and think. Joseph had finally nodded off again, having been cuddled and entertained by various willing neighbours, and now a strange hush blanketed the slumbering crowd.

Maisie's brow furrowed above her closed eyes as she tried to make sense of everything. What she'd heard explained what had happened. A stray bomber coming in under the radar had dropped its cargo before the alert could sound. She'd been knocked unconscious by the brick or whatever had hit her head, so wouldn't have heard the siren when it had finally gone off. So how long had she been unconscious? Not that long probably, since help was arriving as she'd escaped from the ruins.

Her stomach rolled with tension. She was here now, as safe as she could be in the shelter with Joseph. But with no home to go back to, and a future swathed in uncertainty. Her thoughts were darting around inside her head like piercing arrows. What on earth was she to do now?

She could still stick to the truth. Saving Joseph's life and taking the rucksack and case with his things in them when his parents had just been killed in an air raid, was the natural thing to have done. The fact that she'd put her identity card in her gas-mask box ready for when she was heading out on duty was also perfectly reasonable. If in the blast, it had landed near poor Kitty's body, well, that was by the by. The strangest things happened in explosions sometimes. A whole terrace of houses might be blown up, but full milk bottles might still stand unbroken on the doorsteps. So the only thing Maisie would need to do was lose Kitty's ring from her finger and there'd be no harm done. The authorities might be able to help her find some new accommodation, and since her place of work had been destroyed, she'd probably go into the Fire Service full time.

But what would happen to Joseph? They'd take him away from her, wouldn't they? She was still only eighteen, an unmarried woman and no relation of the poor mite. They'd hardly consider her a suitable candidate to adopt him. They might try and foist him on his grandparents, but they didn't want him. Wouldn't deserve him. He'd grow up on the sharp end of his grandmother's tongue, feeling miserable and unloved. Maisie couldn't bear to think of that.

But neither could she bear the idea of the alternative. It was more likely he'd be spirited away to a children's home, brought up as an orphan without a family of his own, just as she had been. She knew how that felt. Raised in an institution, however caring, made you feel alone and inferior. She'd been so lucky, eventually finding friends like Kitty and Janet who'd become like family to her. The future mightn't be so kind to Joseph.

No. She and Joseph had to stay together. It was what Kitty would have wanted. He was her son now. She had to take care of him. It was her duty. And there was only one way to make sure that happened.

They'd never met Cousin Wilfred. No one in Walkhampton would know she wasn't Kitty. The only people who knew they

335

were going to the village were all dead. Kitty would be identified as Maisie O'Sullivan. They'd always looked so similar, and with no . . . Then there was the dress, if anyone recognised it. And it would be assumed Kitty had taken her son to safety.

But what about Nick? Maisie's resolve stuttered as his face wavered before her closed eyes. She missed him so much, yearned to feel his arms around her. Feel his hand brush her cheek, his finger caress her throat. The more she longed for him, the more she could imagine those warm feelings Kitty had described rippling down and lighting a fire in her belly. She wanted him, needed him. Was ready for what should pass between a husband and wife. But when would it ever happen? Her stomach tightened as the worst fear took hold of her. Was he even alive, or was his body floating in the ocean somewhere?

No, she mustn't think like that! She must assume he was still safe and well. But . . . her heart fluttered and then gave an enormous jolt. She couldn't write to him, could she? It was hardly something she could put in a letter. She'd need to tell him face to face, make him understand. And who knew if her letter might be intercepted, read by someone who would immediately betray her? She couldn't take that risk. But neither could she write to Nick without telling him what had happened. She couldn't give him her new address as he'd write to her under her own name, and the postman would see. No. The whole world must believe that Maisie O'Sullivan was dead. She couldn't even write to Noreen anymore.

She felt as if the whole universe was pressing down on her throbbing head and she stifled a tearing groan. If she was to save Joseph from a life of being unloved and uncared for, she would have to make untold sacrifices. He would have to be her entire world from now on. If Nick didn't return or abandoned her when she was in a position to confess the truth, she could never trust anyone else. Never love anyone else.

Could she do it? Should she do it? Her brain kept going round in circles while those about her slept or dozed. But gazing down on Joseph's little face, compassion swelled inside her. She couldn't let him down. Couldn't let Kitty down. She had no choice.

* * *

She stepped onto the platform at the tiny Dartmoor station of Dousland and drew the pure, clean air into her lungs, driving out the smoke and dust from the hell that was Plymouth. Safety, peace, quiet. The kind WVS lady had made up another feed for Joseph when he'd woken at five in the morning, and another to take with her. Grim with determination, she'd made her way straight to North Street Station where to her utter relief, she'd found the trains still running. When she'd got to Yelverton, she'd had to wait some time for the connection to the Princetown branch line, and had fed and changed Joseph in the waiting room. He'd been awake and alert on the journey, gurgling happily at her when she tickled his tummy, sending joy rippling through her. She was convinced she'd made the right decision. She wouldn't look back.

She knew that Walkhampton was about a mile down the hill from the station and set off at a determined pace. At first, she could see up onto the moor, but soon high hedges on either side of the lane blotted out the view. Joseph was sitting happily on her hip in time-honoured fashion while she carried the case in her other hand and the rucksack with the baby's gas mask strapped to it bounced on her back. Her arms began to feel like lead and she had to keep stopping, her optimism waning and her head starting to spin again. She'd had so little sleep in the past couple of days and that awful throbbing had returned. Thank goodness it was downhill, but she was beginning to think she'd never get there, and Joseph was starting to get restless and was wriggling in her arms.

At length the hill began to level out and she passed a couple of buildings on her left and opposite, a house with what looked like a garage or forge attached to it. Soon afterwards, the lane opened up at a T-junction into a sort of triangle with a war memorial in the middle. There was a small shop opposite, and to one side, a brook gushed its way under a tiny stone bridge beside a cluster of houses and what looked like a pub up to the right. So this must be the centre of the village.

But Maisie needed a rest before she went in search of the bicycle repair shop. She stopped at the memorial and put down the case. Joseph felt like a ton weight, and she sat down on one of the steps around the stone cross. Both her shoulders felt on fire now and her head was thumping, making her feel dizzy. Joseph, please don't, she begged silently as he began to wriggle in her hold. She was utterly exhausted, fighting against the fatigue that racked her body, head drooping . . .

'Are you all right?' a concerned voice asked, and she looked up into the kindly face of a tall woman in her forties who'd suddenly materialised before her.

She stood up. And swayed.

'Larry!' she heard the woman shout. And then the last thing she remembered was thrusting Joseph into the woman's arms before her vision went black and she felt someone catch her.

* * *

When she came to, she felt warm and comfortable, wrapped in a blanket in an armchair beside a roaring fire in a stone-built fireplace. There on a rug, the woman was on her knees, laughing as she played with Joseph who looked as happy as a sandboy and none the worse for all his adventures. Maisie sank back into the chair, wrapped in a sense of peace.

The woman glanced up and a serene smile spread over her face. 'Hello, my dear. How are you feeling?'

'Better, thank you. My head's a bit muzzy, mind.'

'You've had a nasty blow. I've sent for the doctor. So . . . how did it happen? You'm not from hereabouts.'

Alarm bells rang in Maisie's head. She must be on her guard. 'No. We'm from Plymouth. I'm looking for a Wilfred Easterbrook. D'you know him? He runs a—'

'Oh.' The woman's eyes opened wide. 'Are you the cheel his Cousin Janet was sending to live over the shop? He's been that worried. He were expecting you all last night.'

Maisie's mouth was suddenly dry. She couldn't speak, the words she wanted to say sticking in her throat. She managed a nod instead.

She saw the woman's mouth close in a sympathetic line. 'Just a moment. I'll send my husband to fetch him. You'll be all right for a second?'

Maisie nodded again as the woman got to her feet and disappeared out of the door. Maisie gazed down on Joseph. Last chance to tell the truth.

The woman was back in a trice. 'Larry's gone to find him. He won't be long. I'm Grace by the way. Grace Vencombe. This is the wheelwright's house. And you must be Kitty.'

It was a statement rather than a question. Maisie's pulse thundered against her temples. She was too weak. And she nodded. Oh, Lord. It was done. No going back.

An instant later, the door opened and in came two men. Both were dressed in working men's clothes, but the elder one, who was shorter and more rotund, sank down onto the armchair opposite Maisie and wrung his cap in his hands, his face tortured.

'W-what's happened?' he blurted out. 'What's happened to my Janet? There were another terrible raid in Plymouth last night. We could hear it. Oh, God, don't tell me . . .'

Maisie stared at him. Her heart shattered and twisted with anguish. She didn't want to think about it. Didn't want to remember. Wanted to lock all the horror in a box and throw away the key. But she had to tell them.

She dropped her head into her hands. Couldn't look at them as she spoke. Fighting against the savage grief that ripped at her throat.

'They'm all dead,' she rasped. 'Direct hit, right outside. Killed the people who were bringing us here, like. Dear Janet, my . . . my friend Maisie and . . . and my darling Cam. He were . . . blown to pieces . . .'

The vile, horrific images flashed through her mind again. Her voice closed up. No, no, please don't let me see them again. There were arms around her, rocking her close, gently shushing her. Her tear-blurred vision peered out over Grace Vencombe's shoulder. The other man who must be her husband Larry had his hand on Cousin Wilfred's shoulder, and quietly led him from the room.

'There, there, my lamb,' Grace crooned softly. 'We'll look after you now. You can stay with us for a few days until you feel better and then we'll help you settle in over the shop.' She pulled back, still supporting Maisie by the shoulders. 'You get some more rest now. Are you feeding the baby yourself?'

Maisie found herself shaking her head. She must be careful what she said. 'No. I didn't have enough milk for him. If you bring my rucksack, there's an empty bottle in there. And there's babby milk powder in the case.'

'It's here, by your side,' Grace said, lifting the rucksack onto Maisie's lap.

Thank goodness for that. Maisie didn't want anyone rummaging inside it. There was the money, and Zeek's jewellery hidden at the bottom. But she also felt she could trust this woman implicitly.

'Well, I'll look after the little fellow while you relax and try to get some more sleep.'

Maisie watched as Grace hoisted Joseph onto her hip and taking the empty bottle and a tin of Cow and Gate with her, left the room and quietly shut the door behind her. Maisie sank back in the chair and closed her eyes, letting herself float beneath the comforting waves where it was warm and safe.

* * *

'Mild concussion,' the elderly doctor pronounced later that morning. 'Just plenty of rest for a few days until you feel better, and some aspirin for the headache. But please don't hesitate to call me if you start feeling worse.'

'Of course, doctor. And thank you.'

'I'll see myself out,' the physician smiled, and turned out of the room.

'There. Now you just stay there and I'll bring you some lunch,' Grace told her. 'Unless there's anything else I can do for you?'

'You'm so terribly kind,' Maisie answered, relieved that she was thinking straighter now and managing to keep up the accent. 'I just can't help thinking . . . it were just so awful . . . what might be happening . . .'

'Ah.' Grace nodded slowly, her face creased with compassion. 'Larry and Wilfred are going into Plymouth tomorrow to sort everything out. They're talking about mass graves for the victims, but we'll arrange for all three bodies to be brought back here. We're the village undertakers as well, you see. It'd be nice to have them buried up at the church here. Larry's going to have a word with the vicar this afternoon. They weren't from this parish, but under the circumstances, I'm sure he'll allow it. That . . . would be good, don't you think?'

Maisie drew in a breath. 'Yes. Janet always liked coming here, and Maisie loved the moor, too. We used to come up here and walk for miles. She were from Ireland originally, an orphan, like. And Cam . . .' She paused as misery overcame her once again. 'He were Canadian, but he loved the countryside so I'm sure he'd rather have been buried here than in the city.'

Grace nodded again, and patted her hand. 'They'll go to Janet's shop, too, and see if there's ort they can rescue. And get death certificates if they can. It . . . helps you to accept it if you see it in writing.'

Maisie felt her soul cave in. She didn't want to see her own name on any death certificate. See the lie. But she would

341

have to. And, it suddenly hit her between the eyes, if she were to keep her inheritance from Zeek, she would have to prove that Maisie O'Sullivan was dead. In Zeek's will, if anything happened to her, Kitty was to inherit instead, wasn't she? It was crazy, but it would have to be done. For Joseph's sake. To secure his future. Everything she was doing she was doing for him, even if it was literally breaking her heart.

If only she could turn back the clock! Less than twenty-four hours ago, the world had seemed so straightforward. Horrible with the war, but uncomplicated. But now it seemed that her world had been shattered into a million tiny fragments, and she would have to battle to piece it back together.

A new, fragile life of lies and deceit was beginning, but there was no way out of it now. The die was cast.

CHAPTER THIRTY-TWO

April 1946

Maisie glanced around the room that had been her and Joseph's home for the past five years. When they'd first arrived, whoever would have thought that they'd have found such contentment there? After the horrors of the Plymouth Blitz, it was a haven of peace. Maisie cast her mind back to the very early days when they'd heard in the distance the continuing air raids on the city, and later the planes heading in and out of the Harrowbeer Airfield over the other side of the railway at Yelverton. But generally speaking, it was so quiet and peaceful in the little village nestling at the base of the hill that it was hard to imagine that there was a war on.

Back along . . . now that was a Devonshire expression that would slip so easily into Maisie's vocabulary now that she wouldn't even notice. Back along, before Cousin Wilfred had turned it into the bicycle repair shop, the small building had been a cottage, and before that, an agricultural storage area or stables tacked onto the humble farmhouse next door. But Grace had told her that this one-up, one-down cottage had once been her own family home. Maisie could hardly imagine it. Grace's parents had raised five children within its thick stone walls. It was bigger than it looked from the outside, but it must still have been a terrible squash. They'd had the downstairs room as well, of course, whereas Maisie and Joseph only had the upstairs, with use of the sink with its running water and the range in the shop to cook on in the evenings. But it felt as if the whole village was their home. The village and the moor surrounding it.

Everyone had been so kind and generous, donating anything they could when she'd arrived with virtually nothing, a plate here, a saucepan there. Maisie was known as Widow Mackenzie to stop any wagging tongues. Only Cousin Wilfred, Grace and Larry knew that she was unmarried, and Grace had sworn to secrecy the owners of the village shop she had to register with because, of course, she and Joseph had different surnames on their ration books.

On that morning after the raid when they'd gone into Plymouth, Larry and Cousin Wilfred had been denied entry to the ruins of the tea rooms. It was deemed too unstable. So all Maisie had was literally what was in the case and the rucksack. How glad she was of the sewing skills Zeek had taught her. Grace had advised her to buy material from Tavistock market and fortunately she'd managed to make herself and Joseph some new outfits before clothing coupons had been introduced a few months later. In fact, over the years, Maisie had built up a nice little business altering and mending clothes for the villagers and local residents, her reputation spreading to neighbouring villages, too. It all helped to supplement her small income.

Not that she'd hidden from Grace the fact that Maisie had inherited a legacy from an old man who'd been like a grandfather to her, and that were that to fail — as was the legal expression — everything was to come to her, Kitty, instead. She couldn't help thinking how ironic that was. But she had kept hidden what a substantial amount it was. Claiming it had been quite straightforward. The solicitors' office had been bombed out and, like many businesses, had moved out to Mutley Plain. But Maisie hadn't needed to attend in person, the war making everything so chaotic. Not that it would have mattered if she had. As he'd said, Mr Jacobs had retired and his clients had been taken over by Mr George whom she'd not met before. As it was, she'd merely had to send in Maisie's — her own — death certificate and her own — Kitty's — birth certificate, and sign some papers sent through the post.

So, for five years, life had been one of calm and contentment. They'd been made welcome by the whole village and especially Cousin Wilfred, Grace and Larry. Maisie had hated lying to everyone, but she had no choice. The important thing was that Joseph had a happy home, and he certainly had that. With most of the younger men away at war, there were few babies in the village and Joseph was spoiled rotten by one and all.

But now the war had been over for nearly a year. At least the conflict in Europe had been, with the hostilities in Japan ending a few months later. Could Maisie imagine herself living in Walkhampton for the rest of her life? She wasn't sure. Even if one of the cottages with two bedrooms became available for her to rent, would it be right? Joseph would start at the village primary school in September, but even if he eventually won a place at Tavistock Grammar, would it give him the best start possible for his adult life?

And what about herself? A few sewing jobs a week had been enough when she had her hands full with Joseph, but would she be content with that as he grew up and she had more time on her hands? What about her ambition to have her own shop, making good quality, fashionable clothes for her customers as material became more widely available again, as she was sure it would in time? But would a shop expose her to discovery?

And there was something else, too, that gnawed at her heart every day. Nick. Had he survived the war? She had to know. She'd been telling herself there was no point going to Plymouth to try and find out as minesweepers were still being deployed in the clean-up operation which could go on for years. But the truth was that she'd been putting it off regardless, scared of what she'd discover, and not knowing if she should take the risk. But it was eating away at her like a cancer and she felt she'd break if she didn't find out.

What she truly wanted was for Nick to be alive, and to understand what she'd done. To love her with the same passion he had before, and to still want to marry her. To keep her secret, and to move away with her to start a new life. She wanted him so much. Sometimes she lay awake at night, imagining him making love to her. Her body hungering for his touch. If only she'd felt ready for him when she'd had the chance.

She thought she'd lose her mind if she didn't at least find out if he was still alive. A trip to Plymouth and the Barbican was risky. What if she bumped into anyone who knew her? But was she likely to? It was a big city, after all. It was madness, but she had to go.

'Joseph, would you like to see the sea today?' she asked. The little boy stopped playing with the wooden train Larry had made him, and beamed up at her.

* * *

Her pulse was beating hell for leather as they walked across the wide cobbled street at the waterfront at Sutton Harbour. Joseph had been enthralled by the sight of the sea from the Hoe and hadn't wanted to come away. It was only by promising to take him to see the boats close-up at the harbour that she'd managed to drag him away. And it was only by holding his little hand in hers that her heart didn't fly out of her chest.

Fishing boats lined the quayside. She felt weak with anticipation and dread, and knelt down beside Joseph to point out their little flags fluttering in the breeze to stop herself keeling over. For there in front of her was Nick's trawler, the *Calypso*.

She gulped. Took a hold on herself. Stood up. Her eyes moved over the deck. A couple of older men were scrubbing out some wooden boxes but though she waited a minute or so, there was no sign of Nick. Did that mean . . . ?

She took a deep breath, girding up her courage. 'Excuse me, I'm looking for Nick Chantry,' she called as casually as she could. 'I think he used to work on this boat afore the war.'

Both men glanced up, but only one of them straightened up from his work and peered across at her. A shiver of fear slid down Maisie's spine. Had this fellow been at Nick's father's funeral and if so, would he recognise her? But surely, with her and Kitty looking so alike, he wouldn't remember who was who, and with it being so long ago? To her relief, the expression on his face showed no signs of recognition.

'Still does,' he called back at her. 'We'm just back in from a few days out and he's hurried off to see his wife. Only been spliced a few weeks so he were eager to see her, like!' he finished with a knowing grin.

Maisie stared. She heard a voice, her own perhaps, mumble a thank you, and then watched as the fisherman went back to work. All her hopes crashed down inside her. Nick. Married. And only a few weeks ago. She'd left it too late.

Joseph pulling on her hand scarcely dragged her from her misery. The golden future she'd yearned for had been snatched away. If only she'd plucked up the courage sooner. But for Nick to have returned from the war and found someone else to love, to marry, felt like a betrayal.

'Come along, Joseph,' she muttered, arranging her face into a smile when all she wanted was to cry out. 'Let's see if we can get some fish and chips.' Though how she'd force them down her throat, she didn't know.

She squeezed Joseph's hand. He would be her life now. She should be so happy that Nick was alive. Had survived the war. And she was. But now the years seemed to stretch ahead of her, empty but for the little boy, her son, who was hopping along beside her.

They turned back to the maze of narrow, cobbled streets that made up the Barbican. Maisie wondered if the fish and chip shop she and Kitty used to frequent was still there. It would somehow bring her some comfort if it was. They turned down the familiar passageway and almost collided with a young woman being pushed in a wheelchair. One of the poor soul's legs appeared to end below the knee. Maisie mumbled an apology and drew Joseph aside to let them pass. And then her eyes locked on those of the man pushing the wheelchair.

Her heart stopped. The world fell away. They stared at each other. In silence. Unbelieving. Stunned. Maisie wanted to turn and run, but her legs had turned to jelly and she couldn't move.

'Maisie,' Nick croaked, just when she thought the silence was going to last until eternity. 'I . . . I thought you were dead.'

Maisie's voice stuck in her throat but she must force some words from her lips. 'No. As you see,' she barely whispered.

Nick gave a small shake of his head. 'I don't understand. When I came back, I went straight to Union Street,' he faltered, his voice trembling. 'The tea rooms had been demolished. I were told everyone'd been killed.'

'Not quite everyone,' she rasped.

'But . . . you hadn't written. And when they said you were dead, I thought . . . And Helen believed you were dead, too.'

'Helen?'

A cold sweat oozed from Maisie's skin as her eyes swivelled to the woman in the wheelchair. The invalid turned her head, her face ashen as she met Maisie's horrified, broken gaze. Was . . . was Helen Nick's new bride? No!

But Helen appeared to recover herself at once. 'Aren't you going to congratulate us?' she asked with a shaky smile.

Maisie felt a knife of pain twist in her side, but she mustn't let it show. 'Yes, of course,' she managed to articulate. 'I hope you'll be very happy. But how . . . ?' she said, her questioning gaze moving from Helen to Nick and back again. She felt she would die.

'As soon as I was able, didn't I go to the tea rooms to thank you for saving my life if not my leg,' Helen told her in a small voice that seemed to grow in confidence as she continued. 'If it hadn't been for you, sure, I'd have died, and I'll always be grateful to you for that. I knew where the tea shop was, but when I got there it was in ruins and, like Nick, I was told everyone had been killed. I stayed in Plymouth because my Wren friends were here, but when the war was over, didn't I keep a lookout for Nick down at the harbour. I wanted to break it to him gently. Make it less of a shock. Be of some comfort to him.'

Oh, yes, I'm sure you did! Maisie had always been convinced that Helen fancied Nick, from the first time they'd met on the Hoe to when he used to meet her after the first-aid classes. She hoped for Nick's sake that Helen really loved him, and that it wasn't just some twisted sense of triumph that had made her wheedle her way into his affections. But it didn't stop Maisie steaming with anger and hurt. Although she knew it had ultimately been Nick's choice to join the Reserve, if it hadn't been for Helen putting her oar in, he might not have done, and she and Nick could have been together all along. But now, with him being married to Helen, there was no chance.

'As it happened, I'd beaten her to it,' he put in quietly, and Maisie heard a tremor in his voice. 'The vessel I were serving on were such an old rust bucket, she were decommissioned early. So as reservists from reserved occupations, we were demobbed pronto. Unlike others who are still clearing the mines. And then after I found out you were dead, I went to pieces. But then I met Helen and one thing led to another, and . . . But I see now why you stopped writing.' There was a hint of bitterness in his tone as he jabbed his head towards Joseph. 'You must've found someone else pretty quickly after I left to have this little chap.' He bobbed down on his heels to be on the same level as Joseph, and asked, 'Hello, little fellow. What's your name?'

Maisie froze. And before she had a chance to say anything, Joseph piped up with his name.

'And how old are you, Joseph?'

'Five,' Joseph answered with his most endearing smile.

Maisie saw the muscles in Nick's brow twitch. His eyes remained on Joseph's face for a few seconds, then he held Maisie's gaze as he straightened up. Shock and regret and something else Maisie couldn't fathom were clear on his face. But he knew.

She had to say something. Had to sound natural. 'Cam was there that night,' she faltered as the horrific memories seized her again. 'He was killed, too. So I've been bringing Joseph up.' Well, that was true, at least. And she remembered telling Nick about Joseph's birth in one of her last letters and giving him his name, so she couldn't lie on that score. But he mustn't know — not now — that she'd stolen Kitty's identity in order to have Joseph as her son. Would it cross Nick's mind that the Welfare wouldn't allow a single young woman to adopt a baby? And if Helen found out the whole truth, Maisie wouldn't put it past her to report her to the authorities. Not only would she lose Joseph, but she'd be sent to prison to boot.

She glued a tight smile on her face, while her heart was both screaming in agony and beating a crazy tattoo at the same time. 'Well, it was nice meeting you, but I won't keep you any longer,' she said as breezily as she could.

She saw a frantic look come over Nick's face. 'But . . . we must meet up again—'

'No, I don't think so. Come along, Joseph,' she ordered, grabbing the child's hand. 'This way.'

But she felt Nick's hand on her arm as she turned. For one split second, she felt his love pulsing into her, setting her blood on fire. But it was too late. She must hold herself together, and she glanced back over her shoulder. 'I'm so pleased you survived the war,' she whispered, and then hurried away down the alley, ducking into a narrow street, weaving in and out so that he couldn't follow with the wheelchair.

'Fish and chips, Mummy,' Joseph reminded her as she half dragged him along.

'I'm sorry, sweetheart. I haven't got enough money. Another day. We need to go home now.'

She felt terrible at disappointing him but she had no choice. She hurried him along, wending their way back to the railway station. As luck would have it, there was a train just leaving and she breathed a sigh of relief as they chugged away from the platform.

But what if Nick tried to trace her? Thought to enquire at Plymouth's stations? A young woman accompanied by a striking looking boy of about five with blond hair and eyes like pale cornflowers could be quite memorable. If they were seen getting off at Yelverton and changing onto the Princetown line, might Nick put two and two together, knowing about Janet's cousin in Walkhampton? There was only one thing for it. All the vague plans she'd tinkered with came rushing together in her head. No one must ever know.

They didn't get off at Yelverton. Instead they stayed on until Tavistock, paying the excess fare on arrival. Then Maisie went to the bank where her nest egg was stored, told them of her plan and was provided with some documents. With Joseph complaining about his empty stomach, she bought him the promised fish and chips, and they sat on a bench by the churchyard to eat them while they waited for the bus up to Princetown. By her reckoning, they'd easily catch the afternoon train back down to Dousland. With luck, no one would think of that obscure route.

Her mind was racing. They had to get away, somewhere they could never be found. Nick, please, she thought, don't come looking for me. If you love me, stay away. Please just stay devoted to your wife.

'Did you have a nice day?' Grace asked as she crossed the village square.

'Yes, we did,' Maisie somehow beamed back. 'Bumped into someone I were friends with when we was tackers. She's going to bide with her sister over in Cornwall for a few weeks, and asked if we'd like to go with her. Only she's going tomorrow, so I need to pack a few things tonight.'

'How exciting for you!' Grace returned her wide smile. 'And we've just heard our Alison's coming home! You know she were doing some war work up country, but it's all over now so she's coming home for good!'

'Oh, you must be proper happy, like!'

Maisie was genuinely pleased for her, but inside, her heart dragged with guilt. Grace and Larry and Cousin Wilfred had been so good to her. Could she possibly deceive them again?

Cousin Wilfred was more than happy to keep Joseph with him down in the shop while she packed. The older man was always delighted to have his little helper while he mended punctured tyres and replaced worn brake pads. Meanwhile Maisie packed the suitcase with as many of her and Joseph's clothes as she could squeeze in. There was so much she'd have to leave behind, but it couldn't be helped. She retrieved Zeek's jewellery from its hiding place beneath the floorboards under the bed. Hopefully, she wouldn't need to sell any of it, but she might have to. The rucksack was once again stuffed with essentials, papers, money, but thankfully there were no gas masks to worry about this time. She'd already made Joseph a little satchel out of some strong material ready for when he started school, and she filled it with tightly rolled up socks and underwear. His few books and the toys Larry had fashioned for him, she crammed into a bulging string bag, and he could carry his own teddy bear.

There. She cooked them some dinner, gave him a good wash and read him a bedtime story. All his usual routine.

'And tomorrow, we're going on an adventure,' she told him as she kissed him goodnight.

She sat in the chair next to his little bed, watching his beloved face as he settled down and gradually drifted off to sleep. Their last night in this home that had been their salvation and their haven. Where would they lay their heads the following night? A boarding house, perhaps. Thanks to dear, dearest Zeek, she had money. Money to start a new life. She'd often wondered about the place names you saw on the railway maps on station platforms. Removed during the war, of course, but now being replaced. When they got down to Yelverton in the morning, she'd run her finger along them and pick one she fancied. Somewhere towards London, maybe. And if she didn't like the first place they stopped, they'd move on until she found somewhere that felt right. A small country town where she could open her shop. Find her dream at last.

But could she really leave, disappear, without saying a proper farewell to her friends in the village? After all they'd done for her? And when she didn't return, wouldn't they be worried sick? Might even call in the police? She couldn't have that. If the police were involved and the truth came out, everything would be ruined. No. In all conscience, she must explain. In part, at least. A note, left somewhere not too obvious so that it wouldn't be found too quickly. Not that anyone would come upstairs for a few weeks until they began to worry. The door at the top of the stairs had a key, and she would leave it locked. Cousin Wilfred had a spare, but he wouldn't use it until it was thought necessary.

And having made the decision, she reached for pen and paper.

My dear Grace,

You've been so kind to me that I couldn't leave without an explanation and a big thank you for all you've done for me. I've been so happy here and without your help and understanding, I'd never have got over the loss of my darling Cam and my dear friends. The thing is, though, my visit to Plymouth, seeing the city centre flattened, brought back such memories that I suddenly feel stifled and that I need to get away. It's a woman thing so I'm sure you'll understand and explain to Larry and Cousin Wilfred. I can't thank them enough for all their kindness, too. But I really need to leave. Start afresh. I'm not sure where yet. One day, in the future, I might let you know, but for now, I want to be on my own with Joseph. Please don't worry about us. This is my choice. I have money and we'll be proper grand.

Thank you so much for all you've done,

I'll never forget you.

Kitty XXX

There. It was enough, Maisie hoped, to put Grace's mind at rest when she found it. To put her off the scent, even, with the mention of Cam. Maisie shut her eyes against the guilt. And against the tears. But it was the only way.

That stubborn, determined little girl.

She'd made a new life for herself once before, and she could do it again.

CHAPTER THIRTY-THREE

Old Basing, Hampshire
July 1965

'Mu-um!'

When I hear Joseph let himself in the front door, I look up from making a cup of tea. He has developed a lovely mellifluous voice just like his father. Even though he's grown up and married, he still pops in to see me a couple of times a week after work, and we often go to each other's houses at the weekends. He's been a wonderful son, my rock when I was going through the treatment. I pray that isn't about to change. But the time has come.

'In the kitchen!' I call back.

He fills the doorway, tall, broad-shouldered but slender of waist, eyes that incredible blue, his hair a darker blond than it was when he was a child, but he probably gets that from Kitty. Ah, dear Kitty.

'Want a cuppa?' I ask.

'Please. Everything all right? Fiona said you haven't been into the shop the last few days.'

There's concern in his tone, and I give him a reassuring smile as I grab another mug and pour a second tea from the pot. I feel amazingly calm.

'Let's have this on the terrace,' I say brightly. 'Shame to waste a beautiful summer evening.'

He follows me outside and I put the mugs down on the bistro table. Beside the envelope. But first things first. We both sit down and I blow on my tea before taking a sip. I have to tell him gently.

'Actually,' I begin tentatively, but he has to know. 'I had an appointment with the oncologist last week.'

I see his eyes widen. 'Just a check-up?' His eyebrows twitch. He's trying not to look worried.

I hesitate. This isn't going to be easy. 'I'm . . . no longer in remission.'

His hand judders and he nearly spills his tea. He replaces the mug on the table. 'You don't mean it's come back?' His words tremble, as I knew they would.

I nod. Slowly. Watching his expression as he tries to stifle his horror. But I can see it.

'It's spreading,' I tell him with a resigned sigh. 'There's nothing more they can do. They've exhausted all the treatments. It's just a matter of time now. But I might still be bothering you this time next year!' I attempt to tease, and he forces a shocked smile. 'I actually feel fine.'

'Then why haven't you been into the shop?' he says, his face taut.

'Ah.' I breathe out in a slow, steady stream. 'I wanted time to get used to the idea. It's funny, but I feel quite relaxed about it. I'm not afraid. I've had an amazing life. You, the shop. But mainly you.' I pause. Look at him. I have to engrave the image of his loving face on my heart. Just in case . . . 'But . . . there's something else, too. Something you should know. That's the other reason I haven't been into the shop. I couldn't just tell you. I thought if I did, it might come out wrong. So I've written it down instead.' I incline my head towards the envelope. 'It's taken me a few days, but it needed to be right.'

He lowers his gaze to the table, his frown deepening.

'You might hate me once you've read it,' I dare to say. 'I thought about leaving it for you to read after I've gone, but I'm hoping you'll understand and forgive me.'

'Forgive you?' He sounds stunned. 'But . . .'

He looks so confused, my darling son. So I indicate the envelope again. 'Just read it,' I instruct. Gently. I feel calm about dying, but not about this. The truth.

He picks up the envelope, shoots me a questioning glance, then draws out the sheets of foolscap. There's thirteen of them. I hope that's not going to be an unlucky number. It's going to take him a while to read them. But I had to explain it all. Right from the beginning.

I see him stifle a little gasp as his eyes travel along the first few lines. It will come as a shock, but I couldn't think of any other way to begin other than telling the bare truth. About not being his real mother. About not being Kitty Barron. His gaze flicks up at me for a moment, but then I see his head tipping to one side as it always does when something catches his interest. I relax back in the chair, my own eyes closed. And wait.

At length, I hear him lay down the papers and I dare to look across at him. He shakes his head.

'That's . . . amazing,' he finally murmurs. And I finally breathe again. He hasn't gone for me. Yet. And then, 'Is that why you called the shop Calypso?' he asks.

I blink. That wasn't a reaction I'd anticipated. I give a small chuckle of relief. 'Yes,' I answer. 'It's made me feel as if Nick was always by my side.'

His eyebrows move almost imperceptibly. 'You loved him very much,' he says. 'And you sacrificed that love for my sake.'

I'm so relieved that he's asking questions rather than rejecting me. 'I loved Nick with all my heart,' I tell him. 'It wasn't a raging, passionate love. My upbringing held me back from that. It was more a gradual, trusting love that grew over time. But when I was ready, it was too late. He was already married. If he hadn't been, I'd have told him the whole truth. I'm sure he'd have understood. We might have married. Brought you up jointly as our son. But what I did was never a sacrifice. I did it because I loved you. Because I knew it was what your parents would have wanted. They wouldn't have wanted you growing up in an institution like I did. And I also did it quite selfishly because I knew you might be the only chance I'd ever have for a family of my own. I didn't know then if Nick would survive the war and I could never imagine loving anyone else. So you see, I didn't feel I had any choice. I didn't want any other choice.'

I watch as he steeples his fingers over his nose and his eyes lock on mine, steady as rocks. It's a lot to take in. I can tell he's mulling it all over.

There's just the sound of birdsong, and bees buzzing around the lavender. 'There's another piece of paper in there,' I say to break the silence. 'It's the address of where your grandparents lived. That part of Plymouth wasn't hit so badly in the Blitz. They might still be alive and living there. Only don't tell them about me. Let them still believe that I'm Kitty and that I never want to see them.'

'Because if they knew the truth, you could go to prison.'

I feel a stab of fear in my chest but I manage to shrug. 'Under the circumstances, I expect I'd get a suspended sentence. And the war brought about so many strange situations.'

'Well, don't worry.' He's smiling now, with a sort of fierceness. 'If they rejected me as a baby, I don't want anything to do with them. They'd be nothing to me.'

I consider the determination on his face, and I see Kitty in him so strongly. 'But you have an uncle. Alan. You might want to trace him and that would be a good starting point.'

'No.' His voice is strong, so adamant. He leans forward and takes my hands in his. 'I've lived this long without any other family, and I don't want any strangers coming into my life now. You're my family, Mum, the only family I want or need.'

'And Sam.'

'And Sam, of course.' His smile broadens. They've only been married a year and are devoted to each other. 'Talking of whom, I'd better get home. She'll be wondering where I am. But . . .' he hesitates, 'I'll have to show her this, Mum. We have no secrets between us.'

I nod as he lets go of my hands and stands up. 'Yes. But she'll understand.'

'Yes, she will. And, Mum, you're the best mum I could ever have had.'

My heart swells. 'But can you forgive me?' I mutter.

'I don't see that there's anything to forgive. I can only thank you for what you did.' He bends to drop a kiss on my head. 'I'll see you in a few days. But you know where I am if you need me. You know, about the hospital.'

We give a mutual, understanding nod, and with that, he strides in through the back door. I watch him go. So strong and kind, just like Cam. I take a deep breath. What now? The roses need deadheading. I'll go and fetch the secateurs.

* * *

He comes back a few days later, bringing the lovely Sam with him. The first thing she does is hug me.

'Your secret's safe with me,' she whispers in my ear.

Joseph's brought a bottle of Babycham each for Sam and me, and a beer for himself. We sit in the garden again. It's another warm evening, peaceful in the little village. We talk. Joseph asks so many questions. I've always told him about Cam, and how his parents, that is Cam and me — Kitty — were never married. I suffered some disapproving looks in the past when I had to explain why my son and I had different surnames, but it never upset me. I knew how desperately in love Cam and Kitty were, and that was all that mattered. But now I tell Joseph all about Kitty. How she was funny and devil-may-care. How she haggled with the stallholders in the market on my behalf when I'd never have had the confidence to do so. How she was so kind and loving, and the best friend

I could ever have had. How we were more like sisters than friends. How I felt as if half of me was missing after she died. But I don't tell him exactly how she died. What I saw. I must spare him that.

'Well, we'd better be off,' he announces after a couple of hours. 'Work in the morning, and I expect you're going into the shop, too. But I'm afraid we won't be able to see you at the weekend. We're going to Swanage for a few days.'

'You love it there, don't you?' I smile back. 'Have a lovely time. A last-minute thing?'

'Well, we're a bit slack at work, and Sam was able to get the time off, too, to make a long weekend of it. So we thought while the weather holds . . . But . . . you'll be all right?' he questions, his forehead furrowed.

'Yes, of course,' I assure him. 'You enjoy yourselves and don't worry about me.'

I see them out and wave as they drive off. A late dusk is falling and I feel a little chill in the air. I lock up. I decide I'll go into the shop every day from now on. Until I start feeling bad. And on Sunday, it'll be good to be alone with my thoughts. I must tell Joseph that when the time comes, I'd like to confess to a Catholic priest.

* * *

It's Wednesday afternoon, and half-day closing. I've been at the shop every day. It's made me feel normal. I haven't told Fiona the bad news yet. She's so reliable as a manager. I'm lucky to have her.

The weather's still glorious. I'm sitting under the shade of the old apple tree in the garden, doing some sketches of new designs for the autumn. I'm not sure I like these new fashions, but I have to keep up. The New Look was my favourite.

I hear a familiar voice call, and glance up. My heart gives a little skip of happiness. Joseph is striding out of the back door, looking so handsome.

'Hi, Mum!' he calls, coming across the lawn.

'Hello, love,' I beam back, laying down my pencil. 'I wasn't sure when you were coming home. Did you have a lovely time?'

'Yes, we did,' he mumbles, bending down to kiss me. I catch uncertainty in his words. I hope nothing's wrong. 'We've brought a visitor,' he says, and I see him bite his lip.

I glance towards the cottage. Sam steps out onto the patio, then turns to beckon someone else out into the sunshine. A figure emerges. A man. Tall, but not as tall as Joseph. And dark as Joseph is fair.

Something stirs in my memory. Butterflies hover in my stomach. I straighten up in my chair. I must be seeing things. My mind is playing tricks. It must be the dappled shade that flickers above my head.

He stops for a moment, then comes towards me. So familiar. That same gait. Shoulders broader than I remember, fuller, more mature. But then he'd be into his mid-forties now. Hair slightly threaded with grey at the temples. But still a handsome man. And those eyes, deep and questioning. I stare into them as he comes to a halt not six foot away.

I'm hardly aware that I rise to my feet. I want so much for it to be him. Can it possibly be? And then he smiles. And I know.

I stumble forward, aware, as my pulse jumps wildly, that Joseph is right behind me, ready to support me if need be. It isn't necessary. In a trice, I'm in Nick's arms, holding him, breathing him into me. Feeling his love pulse into my being. If only it weren't too late.

He's muttering something into my hair, but I don't know what. All I know is that my soul is flying. He mustn't know how I've hungered over the years to feel him against me.

I pull back, tears of joy and sadness in my eyes. 'Oh, Nick, what a wonderful surprise!' I exclaim, trying to hold back the maelstrom of emotion circling my heart. 'But how . . . ?' I ask bewilderedly, glancing at Joseph and Sam, who's joined us now.

'We actually went to Plymouth,' Joseph admits, looking shamefaced, though he needn't be. 'I said we were going to Swanage in case things didn't work out, and I didn't want to get your hopes up. I hope we did the right thing.'

'Oh, yes, of course!' I cry. After all, now that I'm dying, it'd hardly matter if Helen were to betray me.

I realise I'm holding Nick's hand. I let go. I'm overjoyed but he mustn't know how much. 'Nick, sit down,' I invite him, indicating the other chair.

'Sam and I'll put the kettle on,' Joseph says, and leads Sam inside.

I look across at Nick, unable to stop the smile on my face. 'It was so good of you to come all this way,' I grin as we sit down. Nick's here, sitting opposite me. I can't believe it.

'I'd have come to the ends of the earth to find you.' His voice is low, sincere.

I frown, confused. 'B-but what about . . . ?'

'Helen?' he almost scoffs. 'We're divorced. I mean, when we got married, we both honestly believed we were in love. Whatever we think about Helen now, she were as shocked as I were to learn you were dead. It sort of drew us together. We comforted each other. But when we found you were alive and kicking, things started to go wrong, and we'd only been married a few weeks. She realised I still loved you. We tried to make a go of it, but a couple of years later, she got a really good prosthetic leg, and didn't need me anymore. She got a job in a camera shop and met a photographer down from London. It was all society parties, that sort of thing. A humble fisherman weren't a very exciting prospect compared with that.'

Something inside me gives a little jump. 'And are you still a fisherman?'

'Not now. But that's how Joseph found me. Through the *Calypso*. It's *Calypso Two* now, though. But I'm not still fishing. I did. For a long time. But when Helen left me, I did other jobs as well to fill my spare time. In the end, I'd saved up enough, together with selling my shares in the *Calypso*, to buy my own boat. A small one. So now I take folk on fishing trips or up the river when the tide's right. Other days I run a ferry over to Cawsands.'

'Yes, I remember I used to love doing that! Kitty and me . . .' I break off, realising it's the first time in twenty-five years I've said that out loud. Kitty and me. I am Kitty now.

I see Nick's eyelashes swoop down. Does he know?

'It were clear that day we met that you didn't want me to, but after Helen left, I searched all over for you,' he tells me, his eyes meeting mine now. I feel a cold sweat slick my back. 'Of course, I were looking for Maisie O'Sullivan not Kitty Barron, which didn't help. I couldn't find any trace of you in Plymouth, and then I thought about Janet's cousin in Walkhampton. But when I went there, I were told you were buried in the churchyard with Janet and Cam. I were just so confused, like. But then a nice lady, a Mrs Vencombe, if I remember, told me a Kitty Barron came to live in the village during the war with her babby son and stayed for about five year afore mysteriously disappearing.'

My heart suddenly beats harder. 'Yes. I've always felt guilty about that. She was such a lovely lady, and so good to me.'

'She certainly seemed very kind,' Nick goes on. 'But it were what she said made the penny drop that you were using Kitty's name. That it must be Kitty buried at Walkhampton and not you. You were always so alike.'

I feel the colour drain from my face. What if he'd unwittingly let on to Grace? But it was so long ago . . .

He must have seen my terrified expression and gives a reassuring smile. 'Oh, don't worry. I've never let the cat out of the bag. But I began my search again, this time in Kitty's name. But in the end, I gave up. There were no trace of you anywhere. But now Joseph's told me everything. And you were right. I would've understood. If I hadn't already married Helen when we both believed you were dead, I'd have found a way for us to be together. There's never been anyone else for me.'

'For me neither,' I whisper, choked. All those wasted years. 'If it hadn't been for the war,' I sigh.

There's a silence we both share, a deep silence, full of regret. I'm grateful when Nick breaks it, giving that winsome smile I always loved.

'But I understand you got the shop you always dreamt of.'

I nod, relieved to have something else to talk about. 'Yes. I don't know why, but I liked the name of Basingstoke. When we got off the train, it felt right straight away. A small market town, but a busy one. When I found the shop to rent, it was perfect. I made all the clothes myself at first, working all hours God sent. I had some wealthier customers and used to design and make bespoke garments for them. That's where the real money was. Nowadays, I mainly buy in. We lived over the shop for many years, but a few years ago, I was able to take out a mortgage on this little place. Only ten minutes' drive to the shop. I didn't know then I was going to get ill.'

I think we both feel the cloud descend on us. I guess Joseph has told him.

'Then we must make the most of things.' I don't think I've ever heard Nick's voice more serious. 'I'd still like you to be Mrs Maisie Chantry. Then you can lay Kitty Barron to rest. And if anyone asks why I call you Maisie, we can say it was a misunderstanding when we met, and I still call you that. So, what d'you say?'

I stare at him, amazed. Unable to say a word. When I don't reply, he goes on, 'It'd be a bit odd. I could spend a lot of time here during the winter, but I make most of my living in the summer season. But Joseph says you've a good woman looking after the shop, so you could come to mine. I've a little old place in the Barbican. That area weren't hit too much in the war. Not like the city centre. You wouldn't recognise it now. They've completely rebuilt it along modern lines. All square and like a grid. Not a scrap of character.'

'A bit like here,' I answer, all the time thinking he wants to marry me. 'They're modernising the centre of Basingstoke.

I'm expecting a compulsory purchase order on the shop. But I probably won't be around to see it all.'

'Don't say that.' His tone is soft. 'But say you'll marry me.'

His face swims before my tear-blurred vision. 'Yes, I will.' I can't believe how firm the words sound when I'm shaking inside. I don't know what to say next, so I ask, 'How long can you stay? And where are you staying?'

'Oh, I . . . er . . . Joseph and Sam have kindly asked me to bide with them,' he answers awkwardly. 'Joseph's a grand fellow. You've brought him up proper well, like.'

'No, I mean, yes. I'm so proud of him. But you must stay here. With me.' And now I feel like a skittish child again as a flush of excitement tingles through me. If only I'd felt like this all those years ago. But now I'm more than ready. I don't want to die a forty-three-year-old virgin.

'Here we go, then.' We're interrupted by Joseph and Sam coming back out into the garden, carrying a tray with mugs of tea and a plate piled high with scones. 'We brought back some Devon clotted cream,' Joseph announces.

'How wonderful! A celebration tea!' I crow, looking up at my darling boy. 'We have something to tell you!' But maybe he's already guessed.

* * *

Nick has stayed a week, a week in which we've talked and talked about the past — about Janet and Zeek and Kitty and Cam — and about our future, such as it might be. We've taken walks in the countryside, walks along the disused canal. And at night . . . Nick is so gentle with me. I wonder why I was scared of it before. When I look back, I think it was those years in the convent, the bathing shroud, being told we should hide our bodies. Now I know that when it's with someone you love, it's something to be gloried in. And we're making up for lost time.

It's Nick's last day, but I'm not sad. I've a wedding to arrange in his absence. It'll just be a small affair, but it'll be the most wonderful day of my life. The weather has been fine most days. We're sitting on the patio again, enjoying mid-morning coffee, drenched in sunshine and happiness, when the phone rings.

When I come back out, I almost stagger to my chair, and Nick reaches out in concern. I feel muzzy-headed.

'You all right, my lover?' he asks, making me smile and clearing my vision. A common term of endearment in Devon. But now I really am Nick's lover in the full sense of the word.

'I'm . . . not sure,' I reply quite truthfully, since I am feeling a bit shocked. In a pleasant sort of way. I think. Well, to be honest, I'm not quite sure how I feel. 'That was my oncologist,' I answer now, somewhat dazed. 'He's said he's got me a place on a drugs trial, if I want it. He says he couldn't promise anything, but the results so far have been very encouraging. It's all a bit unknown, of course, but his advice is for me to accept.'

Nick leans forward towards me, his eyes so wide he looks almost comical. 'Then you should. It's taken all this time for me to find you, and if there's a chance we can be together longer, then you must take it. I'll be with you every step of the way. But whatever happens, however short or long a time we have, we'll be together. Together, as a family, with Joseph as our son. And that's the most important thing.'

His hand reaches across the table and closes around mine. The diamond in the engagement ring we chose together in the town flashes in the sunlight. No matter what the future holds, however long God allows me on this earth, I'll have Nick, and I'll have Joseph and Sam. A real, proper family at last. It was all I ever wanted.

That stubborn, determined little girl.

Yet again, I can hear that beloved voice. Thank you, Sister Agnes, I think to myself. You've given me the strength to face the future.

'I'll ring back and tell him yes, then,' I say, and my eyes meet Nick's loving smile.

THE END

AUTHOR'S NOTE

Dear Reader

I do hope you enjoyed Maisie's story. The first part of the book is based on my mother's childhood in Ireland, and many of the anecdotes in the story such as the incidents with the prunes and the boot blacking, are real. Although my grandmother died when my mother was two and not in childbirth, everything else that happened in Buttevant is a true part of my family history. Unlike Maisie, my mother wasn't an only child, but the first time she met her father was when he came to collect her and an older sister from the convent to take them to England.

It was, however, to Mitcham in southwest London that my mother and her sister were taken, not to Plymouth. But my mother did have a very close school friend in England, Paula. If my mother was always getting herself into scrapes in the convent, Paula was the one who led her into mischief in England. When remembering some of my mother's tales about Paula, I immediately thought of my good friend, Christine Barron, a dear lady I was privileged to know for the last twelve years of her life. She was such a lovely, warm, caring lady, a nursing sister all her life. She was nearing eighty when I first met her, and always had such a twinkle in her eye. From the start I saw her as Kitty. Though she married into the Barron family, using her name in the book was my way of honouring her memory and our treasured friendship.

Returning to my mother's life, she didn't face the same moral dilemmas from her childhood that Maisie does, although she remained in the Catholic Church for many years and had to obtain dispensation from the Pope to marry my father, who was not of the faith — not an easy thing to achieve in wartime with the disruption to international postal services. Theirs was also a fascinating, romantic love story — inspiration for another novel, perhaps? Though my father sadly passed away many years before, my mother survived into her nineties. Let us hope fate was kind to Maisie, and that she, too, lived a long and happy life with Nick. I think she did. Don't you?

I must thank my agent and my publisher for their faith in my work, but also my dear friend, Lady Amanda Willats, for lending me all her books on the history of Plymouth. Also another good friend, Jill Male, who gave me such support, hosting so many signings when she owned her bookshop. She also took time to introduce me to local historian Chris Robinson. Thank you so much, Chris, for your time. It was Chris's revised version of H.P. Twyford's history of the Plymouth Blitz, *It Came to Our Door*, which was my 'bible' when writing this story, and I also used his DVD of the Plymouth Blitz and his book on the history of Union Street for reference and inspiration.

If you have enjoyed this book, a review, however short, on Amazon, Goodreads or your own preferred platform, would be greatly appreciated. And if you haven't already read them, why not try all my other Devonshire sagas? You might even spot a link with a previous story! There are also my four twentieth-century tales set in London and the South East, including award-winning *The Street of Broken Dreams*. You can find details of all my books on my website at www.tania-crosse.co.uk and can follow me on Twitter @ TaniaCrosse and on Facebook under Tania Crosse Author.

Thank you for your support and for your interest in the background to this story.

Happy reading and warmest wishes,

Tania Crosse

Thank you for reading this book.

If you enjoyed it please leave feedback on Amazon or Goodreads, and if there is anything we missed or you have a question about, then please get in touch. We appreciate you choosing our book.

Founded in 2014 in Shoreditch, London, we at Joffe Books pride ourselves on our history of innovative publishing. We were thrilled to be shortlisted for Independent Publisher of the Year at the British Book Awards.

www.joffebooks.com

We're very grateful to eagle-eyed readers who take the time to contact us. Please send any errors you find to corrections@joffebooks.com. We'll get them fixed ASAP.